Detour Man

Charles Puccia

Detour Man
Copyright © 2019 Charles Puccia
www.charlespuccia.com
Published by Carduna Publications

Paperback ISBN: 978-0-9963234-8-2
Audiobook ISBN: 978-0-9963234-7-5

Edited by Ben Way (benjaminway.co.uk)
Copy edit and proofreading by Ian Howe
eBook formatting and cover design by FormattingExperts.com

* * *

If you enjoyed reading *Detour Man*, please rate this book or leave a review for other readers. It means a lot to me—and to Vinnie, who is busy investigating crimes at BIG with Blanca, and complicating his relationship with Ben.

1

Crossing the room was tough going for the galaxy-sized man. At least five seconds to transit the Briggs Investigative Group threshold. Vinnie Briggs's finger drummed impatiently. He had thirty minutes, forty-five tops, for this unscheduled meeting. It was likely that half that time would be spent waiting for Gunter Hoffman to reach the guest chair.

Gunter swayed, legs spread to avoid chafing his massive inner thighs. The exaggerated bodybuilder's walk was usually a ruse to impress gawkers, but in Gunter's case the spread was genuine. And if he didn't do pretense for run-of-the-mill anthropoids, then he either had something to say or something to hide.

Three hundred and forty pounds of muscle and bone was incongruous in the modern office. But so too was Vinnie's tasteful male prints alongside his official New York State private detective license—but not as much if he had mounted the homoerotic graphics that adorned his home office walls.

With bulwark jaw and bunched brow, Gunter delivered a draggy dirge of death while Vinnie scribbled on a notepad. Nothing made sense, at least not what he gleaned from his notes. In the entire twenty minutes not a single word suggested Gunter required investigative services. If the gargantuan man with more muscles than seemed possible to fit onto one body didn't reveal a serious crime soon, Vinnie was prepared to commit one just to end the interview.

Gunter took a prolonged inhale. His fifty-gallon chest wrapped the room, making a Christo installation an under-achievement. "I should have called the cops, but I didn't."

"What for?" asked Vinnie, who regurgitated Gunter's main point or rather his non-point. "You saw two guys carrying someone to a car. So? Was he drunk?"

Gunter's lips twisted.

Either his balls are bunching up or he's straining to think, thought Vinnie, who himself was straining to avoid throwing his pen into Gunter's face. He chose to hurl it onto his desk.

"A mugging? Murder?"

Gunter jolted upright.

"Or just friends helping their drunk buddy? If that's a crime then a significant proportion of New Yorkers should be behind bars." Vinnie's flailing hands matched his rapid speech.

Gunter twitched. "They were carrying him. It didn't look right."

Vinnie groaned. "Then why didn't you call the cops?"

"Dunno."

Spread lips camouflaged Vinnie's disgust. He'd heard too often the disingenuous "dunno" excuse, which he labeled "The Dunno Defense." Pure bullshit. Clients, especially the guilty ones, knew the truth but put the onus on the PI to ferret out the answers.

2

Gunter's gut-spilling amounted to nothing more than around midnight he'd seen two men pick another off the sidewalk and shove him into a black town car.

"And where was this again?"

"Sakura Park. You know it?"

"The one near your place?"

"Yeah, Upper West Side with Grant's Tomb."

Vinnie nodded. Most New Yorkers knew that President Grant was buried somewhere near the Hudson River but most didn't know the name of the park. And Vinnie was certain almost no one knew it was near Gunter's home.

"So how much did you see?"

"Not much. I was about forty or fifty yards from the street, and with the shrubs and iron fence my view was blocked. I didn't even see the whole car, not until it drove by."

Vinnie Briggs did as he did with all the Briggs Investigative Group (BIG) clients—he made circles with smiley faces on his pad, sometimes adding a mop of curly hair. When really bored, he drew triangles. As founder and chief private investigator of BIG, scribbling impressed corporate clients, luring them to believe he thought everything they said mattered. It really didn't, but it stroked the egos of self-important blowhards with noses stuck so high they rubbed snot on his ceiling.

Gunter wasn't a real client either—he was in the cracks between freebie and paying customer since Ben Hausen, Vinnie's husband, covered expenses. The reason was simple—Ben trained Gunter. And the real reason Vinnie didn't like this freebie, if he was honest with himself, was jealousy. Not that he thought Ben and Gunter were doing it behind his back, but they were doing it metaphorically or something like that. Ben spent more time with Gunter than with Vinnie. Fuckin' bodybuilder stuff and contests. Bullshit, like this story.

Gunter paused, and Vinnie pushed his notepad aside. Among interview rules Vinnie gleaned from studying a PI handbook, the best thing to do during pauses is to wait. Let the client fill the silence. After all, nature abhors a vacuum.

Vinnie waited, checking the rise and fall of Gunter's brow lines for signs of outright lying or spinning a tall tale. Gunter's eyes seemed divorced from his thick black eyebrows.

"Did they see you?"

"Uh, yeah, I think so."

"What?"

"I mean they didn't look me in the eye."

"And they say something? Ask for help or threaten you?"

"Nah. I mean one guy waved a knife at me."

Vinnie groaned. "That's a threat. And it means he saw you. You sure he didn't say anything?"

"No, just waved the knife."

Vinnie bowed his head and touched his brow. Most people would run seeing a knife bandied about, but when you're Gunter's size running is not an option and is pretty much unnecessary. Who charges a bear with only a knife? Gunter was leaving out too much.

"Let's go back to the start, to the first moment you saw something."

"Like I told you, a guy on the ground was being picked up."

"No, you didn't tell me."

"Meant to."

"And then?"

"Nothing. The second guy drove up in the car and the first guy whistled. The two lifted the one on the ground and carried him to the car."

"Wait. That means only one picked the guy up in the park. Is that right?"

"Uh, yeah. I guess. But he whistled and the other came out of the car to help."

Vinnie's eyes closed to picture the scene. Midnight darkness, the August tree leaves blocking streetlamps, no one around, and empty streets. Why didn't the men go after Gunter, the sole witness to the crime? If it was a crime then Gunter was the only witness, and it sounded like a crime to Vinnie. Did Gunter's size frighten them? Didn't they have guns? Who commits a crime these days without a gun? Kids in school carry guns. Every criminal has an arsenal.

Vinnie hummed while thinking about what he'd have done, or any sensible person for that matter. It was obvious but before he asked Gunter said, "I didn't have my cell with me."

Vinnie rested an elbow on his desk, rubbed his chin, then stood with his head against the window to look out on lower Central Park. The bright blue sky proclaimed a glorious August morning. Gunter rocked. The chair legs creaked. Vinnie made a mental note to ask Blanca, his assistant, to order a new chair because this one would soon break at this rate. Something sturdier too, if Gunter was going to continue as a client.

Vinnie's next question was a follow-up to Gunter's previous preemptive answer. "And when you got home did you call 911?"

Gunter folded his double-barrel, fully loaded arms, the bulging guns straining the shirt seams. Vinnie waited, the silent pause longer than the last. Even Gunter's chair legs stopped creaking.

"Why not?"

"Dunno."

"They'll find you and ask. You know that, right?"

"Who?"

"The cops. Once they find the body."

Vinnie stared at Gunter's frozen, inanimate block-head processing the last comment.

"They'll check cameras at the scene and around the neighborhood. Columbia has their own campus security cameras too."

Even Vinnie doubted what he said. Didn't matter as long as Gunter believed it.

Gunter's brutish face, shyness, stilted speech, and humongous size made him a credible suspect or accomplice, more so than the average-sized person. But the lame responses might actually work in Gunter's favor, might help the cops buy his story as so dumb as to be believable, take him off the person-of-interest list.

"And if they don't find the guy?" asked Gunter.

The astute question surprised Vinnie. There were several scenarios that Vinnie winged and revised as he explained. There weren't many possibilities, just small variations. Vinnie concluded that only one answer had merit, the original supposition—eventually the body would lie on a morgue slab because the people who committed this crime were not professionals so wouldn't know how to dispose of a body.

"You'll have to file a report," said Vinnie. "It gives you an alibi."

"Why do I need one? I didn't do nothing."

Vinnie moaned, revising his earlier "Dunno Defense" to the "I Did Nothing Defense."

"Look Gunter, I've been here myself. All sorts of things can happen. Even before the body gets discovered, a friend or family member will file a missing person's report, unless the guy's homeless or a mobster. But that seems unlikely. And if the guy's important, then the cops will look harder."

"Uh... and so?" asked Gunter.

"And when they find this murdered person, the friend or family will identify as many people associated with the murdered man as possible, including you."

"But I don't know the guy."

"You sure? Maybe you ran into him at UltraFit. Or on campus. Even if he didn't talk to you and you don't remember him, he probably told his friends about you."

"I never met him, I'm sure of it," said Gunter, his tone defensive.

Frustrated, Vinnie went into a longer explanation about murder investigations. The casting of wide nets so what seemed small or trivial became significant. He didn't want to argue but Gunter wasn't getting it. Was he hiding information or did he truly not know the guy or remember meeting him? "Maybe a photo of the dead man will jog your memory," Vinnie offered. Gunter insisted it wouldn't.

Vinnie held back his real belief that Gunter knew the man and the reason he wanted advice was to learn how to cover his tracks.

"Look, you saw a murder. Deal with it," said Vinnie angrily, "and—"

Gunter unfolded his arms, his hands cupped over his ears stopping Vinnie from completing his sentence. The hands appeared to force the head to nod in agreement.

Vinnie finished his sentence. "...and who did this will determine the dumping location. This is too sloppy to be a professional hit, so the body will be discovered sooner rather than later."

Gunter's fingers linked across his chest. "I screwed up, didn't I?"

Vinnie looked at the wall clock. This would not be a forty-five-minute favor, it looked like it would take a half-day. Gunter had just become a client. Doing this favor was proving a fuckin' mistake. Vinnie called Blanca on the intercom requesting she reschedule the next meeting—a corporate high-tech client paying above the standard BIG fee for premium service to take over the in-house espionage surveillance.

"Fuckin' mistake," Vinnie muttered looking over at Gunter, a typical bodybuilder who spent his entire day pumping iron. His drooping eyes and slack narrative reeked of complicity to a murder, not that he believed Gunter was the killer. He was trying out a cover story. Vinnie maintained a weak smile while surveying Gunter's bulging mass, and his oversized cranium mixing facts with fairytale crap.

"One more time," said Vinnie while thinking, *if I'm going*

to help him fabricate I might as well be sure of the details.

"How much longer? I'm missing my morning session."

Vinnie waited.

"I saw him as I turned the bend," said Gunter, spewing out his words.

"Hear anything?"

There was no answer.

"Words, a cry, sentences... you know, the kind of things people do to communicate."

"Uh... not that I remember. I'm not sure."

"So two guys carry a body out of Sakura Park late at night. One guy had a knife and waved it at you. Is that about right?"

"Yeah, I think so. Maybe the knife was sticking out of the man."

Nothing infuriated Vinnie more than having a story change as it was being told.

"I thought you said the men carrying the body waved it at you. Which is it?"

"He did. Maybe he pulled it out and waved it. Or from the car. I can't remember."

This isn't helping, thought Vinnie. "Are you sure two men put another man in the trunk of a private town limo? Is that still true?"

Gunter nodded.

"And the men didn't say anything? That's still true?"

"Hey, it's all true," said Gunter, his voice rising, "I don't lie."

Vinnie grinned, thinking, *Yeah, just like every other liar in the world. Without liars I'd be out of business.*

Gunter rubbed his nose and drip-fed details. "I think I heard the men yelling to each other... I mean their voices but not the words, I think they sounded foreign."

"And the man they were carrying, did he say anything?"

A rise of Gunter's chin made it seem he didn't understand the question.

"What about clothing? Any special kind of jeans, sneakers, a sweatshirt?"

"Yeah, the sweatshirt looked like the Columbia colors. And maybe blood."

Not good. His story's jumbled. Vinnie looked around the room.

"By the time I was on the path they were at the car."

"But you were close enough to see the vehicle and two men."

"Yeah, but... I don't know. I mean..." His blocky chin gave a slight shiver, a finger swiped at his eye.

A smile hung from Vinnie's lips. He should pity Ben for having to spend so much time with this babbling blockhead. And unattractive. A construction crew would have trouble fixing his cinderblock face. Ben definitely went for good-looking men. And while Ben was no fashionista, he didn't like sloppy dress. Zero intellectual curiosity was also a turn-off.

Vinnie knew Gunter wasn't stupid, but he didn't radiate brilliance either. He'd give him points for being polite, friendly, empathetic, and he had a dry sense of humor. Probably not gay, but Vinnie knew gaydar didn't exist so couldn't rule it out. Maybe Gunter was at the park for a tryst and came across the scene.

10

"Let me look into it, see what I can find out," said Vinnie, leaning over and tapping Gunter's shoulder.

As if stirred from sleep, Gunter rose, filling the three-dimensional space with his four-dimensional body. Momentum propelled him to the exit.

"Hey," called out Vinnie, "I don't think you should worry. We'll check hospitals and police reports."

Gunter stopped, ducking under the office doorway's lintel and missing it by inches as Vinnie called out.

"Wait for my call. Pump as much as you want. We'll know enough before you've added another five pounds of muscle to your body." A chalked grin smeared Vinnie's face.

"I'm no longer in the mood. I'll catch the subway on Fifty-ninth and Columbus Circle and go home," Gunter said.

Vinnie watched the man who was six feet three inches in all directions decide to miss a session. A first. Now to wrap this up and return to paying clients. *Shouldn't take long*, he thought.

2

Gunter carefully shut the main office door with the glass imprint displaying "The Briggs Investigative Group" and beneath, in bold, gold leaf, "B I G." Vinnie gingerly approached Blanca's desk knowing she would blast him, regurgitating her insipid maxim that important clients are difficult to reschedule. What annoyed Vinnie most was her being right.

He leaned across her desk and she sat back in her chair, fingers sliding off the computer keyboard. He saw her usually cool eyes blazing into him.

"Oh, it's that bad?" Blanca asked.

Vinnie nodded.

"Is he going to be okay?" Blanca questioned as if expecting to hear a secret.

"Yeah, pretty sure," said Vinnie with a pretend laugh, earning a scowl from Blanca.

For the next ten minutes Vinnie summarized Gunter's night with a dead body in Sakura Park.

"Let's make this your priority. I'll handle the cancelled meeting with the corporate client, and you learn about the dead guy using your inside police connections. Do not reveal we know about the murder."

Blanca gave Vinnie the middle finger. This was not her first time getting information from cops without showing her hand.

"But if they found the corpse, then they'll be seeking witnesses," said Vinnie, who looked down at his wristwatch, "giving Gunter twenty-four to forty-eight hours to prepare a statement."

Blanca nodded, her long fingernails rhythmically clicking on the desk. "Shouldn't he report it anyway, even if the cops don't find out he was in the park?"

Vinnie's non-committal shrug earned Blanca's clucking tongue.

"Okay, here's my best guess. The cops find and identify the body. If Gunter goes now, he'll be a prime suspect. The cops will leap to this conclusion by looking at his size and his face, plus his plodding speech, and use his delay against him. The more we know means we can provide him with a better excuse for his lack of action than his bullshit."

"And what am I looking for?" asked Blanca, examining her nail polish.

"Any connection between Gunter and the dead man? Sex? An affair?"

"But you said he's not gay."

"As far as I know. Or he's deep in the closet and it was a casual meet-up. Or maybe it was just for money."

"Wait, you mean Gunter is a gay prostitute?"

Vinnie took a deep breath. "I know he needs cash and feels guilty that his mother supports him. A bodybuilder attracts a certain type of gay man."

Blanca shook her head, telling Vinnie he was wrong.

He hoped so, which is why they needed to know about the body. He listed his concerns. Was the dead man gay? Did he hang out around other bodybuilders? Was he active on Grindr? Scruff? Other gay sites and apps? What was he doing in the park near midnight? Was the killer an ex-lover or pimp? Did he solicit gay men? Why two men?

"We'll tailor Gunter's excuse based on what you learn. We'll create a sop that the cops will accept wholesale. Gunter will be fine, I'm certain of it," said Vinnie.

Blanca retorted with a Puerto Rican curse about things that happened to people who were so sure they knew the future.

* * *

Vinnie watched the local TV channel's late-night news. He was surprised to see a reporter update her report of two days earlier, the same day he had talked to Gunter. She reminded listeners of a police request for witnesses for a body found on Sunday in a popular Harlem nightclub's parking lot. What surprised Vinnie was the release of a detail—it was unusual for the police to do this while next-of-kin had not been located. The police's new information was that the dead man wore a Columbia University sweatshirt. The reporter had no explanation for this detail but assured viewers of an update as soon as a name was released.

Vinnie called Blanca before the TV news ended.

"Do you know anything?" asked Vinnie, cell in one hand, TV remote in the other with thumb on the mute button.

"Yeah, I know how late it is, which you clearly don't. Couldn't this have waited until morning?" Blanca muttered

15

a few Spanish curses before continuing. "Yes, I learned something this evening and unlike some people I prioritize what constitutes an emergency and needs a late-night phone call."

She waited for Vinnie's exasperated sigh to peter out.

"My cop informant said the investigative team knows the body was not killed at the Harlem nightclub but dumped in its private parking lot."

Vinnie whistled. "And why Columbia? The news said nothing about him being a student, just that he might have been near the campus."

"His university sweatshirt."

"ID on him?" Vinnie asked, his voice impatient.

"No."

"So not a student?"

"The CSI contacted campus police with a photo of the dead man and one said he'd seen a man that looked like the guy."

Vinnie sighed before asking, "Did you get his name? And the other things we talked about?"

"No on the name—even my guy said asking more was too risky for him as the next of kin have not been notified. As for the other concerns, I only asked about bodybuilding, which freaked my friend out to say the least."

"And?"

"Nope—no connection or reason to believe the victim was connected to bodybuilding. In fact, the opposite. He was a thin guy and probably last saw the inside of a gym in high school. Lifting books was probably a strain for him."

"And the other thing?"

"Didn't ask."

"Why not?"

"Uh, besides being politically correct, what was I going to ask? Was he gay or raped? Like that wouldn't seem suspicious."

"You could have asked discreetly."

"And what, pray tell, is discreet for *métetelo por el culo?*" asked Blanca with Bronx gusto. Before Vinnie responded she explained she had checked popular gay dating sites. Vinnie pointed out no one used their real name, for which he received choice English curses. It was just her hoping to get lucky and she reminded Vinnie of her responsibility to three kids and a husband, then hung up.

* * *

At nine o'clock sharp, Vinnie opened the UltraFit X-room door to the symphonic clanging of metal plates that pricked his eardrums. He avoided this exclusive, below-ground X-members invitation-only room, a space filled with serious bodybuilders and weightlifters tossing steel girders. He eyed the room full of Jurassic creatures. *This is the kind of place people go to hang themselves.*

He could have called Gunter with the news, but cell phones were not permitted during training. The quickest way to reach him was to take the straight-line approach and use the UltraFit elevator from his penthouse to the subterranean X-room.

Vinnie threaded past men with a single leg bigger than his entire body to a squat rack barbell loaded with a container ship's cargo on both ends.

"Hey, Gunter. Got a second?"

Replacing the barbell, Gunter gave a chin wave.

Vinnie explained that the police believed the victim at the Harlem nightclub might have been near Columbia University on the night of his murder. Gunter wiped his nose with his forearm.

"Time for you to make your report. I'll come along. Tomorrow okay?"

"Can't."

"Oh?"

"The moving company called. They have work for me this Friday."

"No problem," said Vinnie, surveying Gunter's sweat-soaked shirt stuck to his torso that made the other body-builders look like a third-grade project. "A few days won't matter to the police investigation." The delay provided Blanca with extra time to investigate the dead man's sexual activity, thought Vinnie as Gunter moved to another barbell.

Grunts and expletives rang out around the room.

"One fucking more. Go, go, go!" yelled a man.

Metal clanked.

"Yeah man," a voice sang out from across the room, "that's the way." A man grunted incoherent profanities as he lifted impossible weights.

Walking to the exit, Vinnie gawked at a man squatting between another's legs helping him with sitting curls. *He's going to sniff his fuckin' crotch.* Vinnie hated the testosterone-soaked X-room. Looking around he spied in a far corner Rita Light, his co-investigator and one of the few female X-room members. She wasn't on this non-assignment—after all, Gunter wasn't a real case yet—but out of courtesy he gave her an update. She shrugged, agreeing that this was a nothing case, and resumed her workout.

Yeah, Vinnie thought, *Gunter's police report can wait.*

3

Across the Hudson River, about the same time Vinnie left the X-room, another man walked out of a different gym. Ten minutes later he was on a narrow path to the front door of a nondescript two-story, wood frame house with fifteen-year-old peeling beige paint faded to a diaper brown. The small structure lay midway along a Jersey City block, easily overlooked.

Dimitri Karimov heard the front door slam shut. He charged down the staircase, pink-cheeked, lips open while tying a knot in his sweatpants' string. He saw his cousin Vasily Karimov kicking his sneakers off as he stared at him.

"Hey, Vasi. You're home early. Something happen?" asked the younger Karimov cousin.

Perched on the last step, Dimitri stretched to emphasize his height advantage. The effort was wasted as Vasily's compact, rugged, sinewy body and pit bull attitude diminished Dimitri to the status of an inferior species.

Vasily's fist pumped up and down as he barked, "You finished? Best to enjoy as much porn as you can. There is no Internet for a long time after we complete the plan."

Vasily's pidgin English had a strong accent that sounded

Russian. A few told him so only to have Vasily's fist box their ears so they would listen better next time—he spoke Tajik, not fucking Russian.

Dimitri had the opposite language deficit—his poor, heavily American-accented Tajik came from hearing his immigrant parents chatter at the kitchen table. As a natural-born US citizen, he went to Tajikistan on travel visas, combining educational tourism with family visits to paternal and maternal grandparents, and other relatives including Vasily. The cousins compromised their linguistic limitations, each using their respective mother tongues when alone. Outside the house, they stuck with English to avoid xenophobic paranoia, even though that was not undeserved in their case.

"What! No, I was..." said Dimitri but his protest evaporated, too unbelievable even to himself.

Vasily's hand was held up in the universal stop signal, and he spoke in a lowered voice as he turned into the living room.

"Don't argue. I cut short my sparring session. Anyway, the guy was no good," said Vasily, puffing on a cigarette. "Tariq's notes showed detonator components." Vasily tapped a notepad.

"Big deal."

A plasticine smile didn't hide Vasily's smug self-satisfaction as he spoke. "Look, his notes say the big electronics store on Route 46 in Clifton has the parts." Vasily chuckled. "He was good. Too bad he turned traitor."

Vasily's cigarette glow reflected in the mirror over the fireplace.

"Why don't we order online? It's a lot easier and probably cheaper," said Dimitri, who took a last drag of his cigarette, tossing it into a glass with a quarter-inch of leftover milk.

"Are you fucking dog stupid? You go to college yet you're still so stupid. A delivery leaves a trail. The fucking CIA will easily find us... you. Then you become a fugitive. No more fucking American life."

"FBI."

"What?"

"Not the CIA."

"Shut the fuck up."

Dimitri gave a contained smile. He hated his cousin's constant berating. Being called stupid. He knew more than Vasily. He spoke better too, not Vasi's half-ass broken English mixed with Tajik. And he was in college, not Vasily. *So what that I'm in summer school for a failed course? Not my fault. The college should ban campus parties during the week, then I wouldn't go out every night.*

What did Vasi know? His education came from the boxing ring and MMA fights. Thinks he can lob vitriolic words at me. Look at him strutting, moving on the balls of his feet. His stupid light-footed toe-stepping like he does in the ring. I know why he does this. It's to surprise his opponent with an unexpected crushing blow. Well, I'm sick of his verbal punches.

"Get smart, stop being stupid," grunted Vasily.

Dimitri's smile vanished. *He's the stupid one. And I box too.* Even Dimitri knew this was a limited boast given his failure to make the Rutgers varsity boxing team.

Vasi's arm crossed Dimitri's shoulders.

"Okay, we'll fix this and make the bomb work too. You're better than me at understanding Tariq's notes." Vasily kissed Dimitri's cheek. "We work as a team, that's how we reach the goal."

As always, Dimitri succumbed to praise from his famous cousin, just like the rest of the family. A Tajikistan idol. A shoulder punch and Vasi's bark broke through Dimitri's thoughts. "Get to work. Read Tariq's notes. Make sure you know how to build the detonator."

Dimitri wanted to prove himself, even with his limited circuitry knowledge. He craved Vasi's approval. He reread Tariq's notes given to him at Sakura Park. The notes identified every electronic component and supplier. His schematics, unfortunately, were mere sketches. Dimitri searched online to compare detonator designs with Tariq's. He would learn how to build the device and make Vasi proud.

The study of electronic diagrams bored Dimitri. He switched his activity to log on to his pay-to-watch website, a live cam with his favorite babe, Candy. She leaned forward to expose the back of her thick thighs and bulbous ass.

"Fuck, yeah," he said out loud to encourage Candy to move closer to the camera. *I do this job for Vasi and he's gone forever. No more sharing my house. I'll bring girls here to get laid anytime I want. Maybe I'll drop out of college.*

It didn't take Dimitri long to ejaculate, his spunk spurting more than usual with Candy's bending backwards. He held his breath, hearing shouts that were not from Candy but from downstairs. With a mouse flick, the computer monitor went black. Dimitri quickly wiped himself and pulled up his jeans while scurrying to the living room.

He didn't see Vasi at first, but a glance at the fireplace mirror reflected his cousin's concealed form, flat on the couch with hands tucked behind his upward-tilted head and eyes roaming the ceiling. Vasi was straining to quell a rage.

Unfolding his arms, Vasi gave two powerhouse punches—one of the ingredients for an Olympic boxing champion and a winning MMA fighter. Fearlessness was another ingredient that Vasi had in abundance. He parked whatever humanity he had on the other side of the ropes, making him dangerous even for sparring partners, including family members. No one escaped his ring contempt, which Dimitri had learned in a practice lesson. A right jab followed by a rapid left power punch demolished Dimitri's nose and voided his college boxing hopes.

Vasily seethed, cursing the hooded man in Sakura Park. Each breath increased his rage at the thought of the man who could invalidate all his planning.

"I really don't think that guy will matter," Dimitri said, wiping hands on his jeans from behind the couch, eyes focused on the mirror. "Tariq's body was found in Harlem, like we planned. End of story. Clearly the guy never went to the police, so let's not create a problem."

"Hmm. We'll see," said Vasily, turning on the TV and drinking more of his third beer.

Dimitri withdrew to his bedroom, hoping by morning Vasily would be focused on his next fight and he could finish reading Tariq's notes.

He accepted Vasily's desire for vengeance as justified, yet he felt conflicted. Dimitri liked his American comforts, the gadgets, clothes, and women, either real or on the Internet.

Yet he was proud of his Tajikistan roots, the country loved by his parents, grandparents, and cousins. And he was very proud to be Vasily's cousin, one of Tajikistan's greatest world-class boxers. If he did this, he'd vicariously garner Vasily's glory.

But he also wanted him gone.

4

"Dimitri!" Vasily yelled, an hour after his last outburst. "This is a real fuck-up. We have no choice but to act."

Vasily entered Dimitri's room, head searching around until he spied the TV remote next to Dimi's computer. He grabbed it and tuned in to a local news channel.

Dimitri moved from his desk to his bed, sitting upright, arms crossed. He couldn't wait for this mission to be over and Vasily gone. He regretted that the bomb would kill so many people but if the detonator design worked correctly he would be far away and would not witness the carnage or hear the screams, just the boom. And then he would be rid of Vasily forever.

"Yeah, what now?" asked Dimitri, rubbing his sore eyes from an hour spent working on his essay that was due the next day. He had stopped admiring Candy's live gyration in her red-laced, crisscross forty-four double D brazier pushing up her twin peaks. He stared at his cousin's squirrel face. *More fucking complaining.*

Dimitri poured from a half-empty vodka bottle a thumb's width in a smudged glass sitting on a bedside table. He waved the bottle at Vasily, who sneered and dismissed him with the hand holding the remote at the TV screen.

"Yeah? Big cousin knows best. Well, fuck you," said Dimitri, swishing the liquor in his mouth before swallowing. He looked at Vasi's receding hairline. *Yes, Vasi will be like his dead father, bald before fifty.*

Vasily's open-palm hand tapped Dimitri's face short of a slap, and he snarled, "See the goddam news?" and he twice jabbed a finger at the TV with the reporter holding up a typical Columbia University sweatshirt to emphasize the police's new information. The shot panned the Harlem nightclub parking lot.

"Same old, same old. Robberies, bad weather, people bitching and moaning."

"No!" Vasily kicked the bed leg, adding in rapid Tajik, "The fucking cops are asking the public for witnesses to Tariq's murder. They say the man at the nightclub wore a Colombia sweatshirt."

"So? If they are seeking a witness it means they don't know who he is or what he saw. They still think Tariq was murdered at the nightclub."

"We should have chased him. It is bad to leave a witness."

"But he was too far away. We'd never have caught him, and if we'd chased him he would have hidden. And if he had a gun, then what?"

"If he had a gun, he would have come after us. Americans love to shoot people," said Vasily, pointing a finger pistol at Dimitri who rolled his eyes. Vasily continued with a diatribe against Americans and all things American.

Dimitri pulled at his ear, ignoring Vasily's whining tirade

as he retreated into his own petulant thoughts. *Not a fucking word about all the money he earns here with mixed martial arts matches arranged by my father, our uncle, and other ex-pat Tajiks. His prize money and illegal side bets bring him more than a two-year wage for most Tajiks, all on a six-month visa! Fucking more than me chauffeuring every weekend for the family limo business.*

Vasily's rant suddenly stopped with him biting a cigarette, blowing smoke at Dimitri. "He saw the limo insignia and car license plate."

"Who?"

"The guy we saw. Now we have to find him. Get rid of him before he tells the cops about us."

"I could hardly make out his face so he couldn't have seen ours."

"You're stupid. Of course he doesn't know us. But if he watches the news? And they'll offer a reward. Money will help him remember the limo," said Vasily, switching off the TV as an advertisement replaced the news reporter. "We have to find him first."

"How?"

"I have an idea," said Vasily, taking Dimitri's arm and tugging him off the bed and over to his desk. "Do a Google search."

"What?"

"You said you saw the man's sweatshirt had a patch. Yes?" Vasily's question was more like a statement.

"It was dark… I don't really remember," said Dimitri as he pushed the computer mouse to awaken his computer and quickly deleted a flashing porn site from the screen.

"Try."

The word *Ultra something* came to Dimitri because he had thought it strange. He didn't see all the words, given the long distance and small letters. He typed Ultra and *New York* into a Google search that returned over eight million hits. He thought about the sweatshirt, which made him think of words like gym, fitness, training, running. By substituting Manhattan for New York, Google spat out a long list but at the top was a link for the UltraFit Health Club.

Dimitri clicked the link and a website appeared in a new tab with the header containing a logo—a muscular man and shapely female posed sideways with, in larger letters, the word *UltraFit* supported by their shoulders. Wedged between their buttocks and legs were the smaller words "Health Club."

Vasily kissed Dimitri's neck, gave him a strong hug, and beamed a smile. "You did it. You're a fucking genius."

Dimitri's face soon darkened as Vasi said they would hunt the man down and kill him. Dimitri slumped, withdrawing his hands from the keyboard.

Committing violence, especially close-up, was not in Dimitri's constitution. He lacked a killer instinct as he had proved with Tariq. His nervous knife thrust had missed Tariq's heart by inches. He panicked, calling Vasi's cell, leaving Tariq on the path's edge while he ran to the curb to wave Vasily over to his location. He had no endurance for violence—it was another reason he failed to qualify for the Rutgers varsity boxing squad—that and his broken nose heightened his skittish demeanor. *How could killing this stranger salvage his first fuck-up? It might make it worse.* He would have protested if not for fear of provoking Vasily's outrage. In his hesitation, he heard Vasily uttering curses against the stranger. There was no deflecting him.

Violence permeated Vasi's blood, which Dimitri knew only too well. For each semi-annual US visit, Vasi took over Dimitri's home. The dominant alpha even though he was a guest. He made all the decisions, including that Dimitri should knife Tariq to atone for recruiting the traitor. Dimitri recalled the sting of Vasily's smacks for the botched job.

And now Vasily made another decision, one that Dimitri approved. Vasi would kill the stranger and take no chance that Dimitri would make another half-ass job of it. This appealed to Dimitri and he didn't think of it as a slight at all. If asked, he would bow out altogether.

Yet the hubris was typical of Vasily. Displaying superiority that fueled Dimitri's acrimony, which was based on jealousy. His father and uncle contributed to Dimitri's discontent. They showered accolades on Vasily for his growing collection of national boxing medallions. They lauded the honor brought to the homeland by the Tajikistan Olympic boxing team. And all the time they demeaned Dimitri. A spendthrift pretty boy who bought more than he earned. No honor to himself, family, or country.

Yet a mere hug or kind word from Vasily turned Dimitri's vitriol to admiration. He idolized him, proud of his Tajikistan roots. Proud of a national boxing team that ranked among the world's best despite the country's small size.

Dimitri sat on his bed. He fretted over the killing of a stranger, even if it were not to be committed by him. Nudged by Vasily, Dimitri created space on the bed for his cousin to sit beside him.

"We must find him. This man could jeopardize the whole plan," said Vasily, draping his arm over Dimitri's shoulders.

"Isn't this too risky? Can't we leave it alone?"

The hug tightened, moving Dimitri's ear closer to Vasily's mouth. "We must. I'll do it, no problem. With your help, we can act at the best time. This stranger will not defeat the Karimov cousins. We are great family."

Dimitri felt Vasily's body warmth, his strong arms pulling him, his fingers snaking beneath his shirt, fingertips swishing his chest as if smoothing away wrinkles and lingering doubt.

5

The black town car limo reached the tollbooths of the George Washington Bridge without delay.

"Fuck, Vasi, did we really have to leave at six in the morning?"

The car cruised at just below sixty, ensuring no overzealous state trooper delayed their journey. Dimitri was glad Vasi had an international license and that he loved to drive the luxury car, which was much better than the Tajikistan junker.

"Take a nap now, that's why I'm driving," said Vasi in Tajik.

"What?" said Dimitri, yawning.

"I said real athletes work out early, then eat and rest before an afternoon or evening session. They are not lazy college boys," Vasily said, removing one hand from the steering wheel and pointing at Dimitri.

"Fuck you," answered Dimitri, resting his head on the passenger window, eyes half shut. "Besides, who says he's an athlete? Maybe he works days and trains at night. That's more logical given we saw him at night. Ever think of that?"

"No gym bag," said Vasily, tapping his temple. "I think

of everything. You're a scared little college boy who wants to go home to bed."

"Just shut the fuck up, Vasi," said Dimitri, pulling the hood over his head and closing his eyes tight.

Vasily paid the sixty-five bucks parking at the UltraFit Health Club underground garage, missing by fifteen minutes the early entry discount of forty-five dollars before seven in the morning. The extra cost wasn't his concern.

The cousins set up on a bench just inside Central Park. They had a clear view of the UltraFit entrance and their powerful binoculars made identification easy. Every few minutes they swung their binoculars upward although they never spotted anything with feathers. At eight thirty Dimitri said, "Let's go. He's not coming. I'm not even sure I'd recognize him."

"Shut the fuck up, Dimitri and keep looking."

Dimitri peered at his cousin's crown. He wanted to spit into Vasi's thinning black hair. Exposed to the morning breeze, an overcast August sky threatened showers. The unseasonal cool punctured Dimitri's cheap windbreaker. He made a grand sweep of the tree branches to catch house sparrows and crows before lowering the binoculars to the sidewalk where a large, dirty pigeon filled the lens.

"Let's go," whined Dimitri. "He's not coming."

"No," said Vasily, pulling Dimitri's hood down.

"Well, I'm bored. I'm going to look around inside the gym. Better than sitting on my ass another hour."

Vasily nodded. "Yeah, that's a good idea. It might tell us something."

At the corner, Dimitri waited for the pedestrian crossing

signal. Before the light changed he pivoted and whistled to Vasi, then waited for him to stand next to him.

"Look there."

"Where?"

"The bus stop. See?"

Following Dimitri's outstretched finger, Vasily saw a man seizing most of the available sidewalk, swinging a gym bag like a teenage girl's lucky charm bracelet. Vasi said in Tajik, "Hurry, let's get ahead of him before he goes into the gym."

The cousins reached the UltraFit façade ahead of the big man. Dimitri turned with his back to the entry and faced Vasily standing curbside. Dimitri faked a pose while Vasi raised his cell phone. The large man moved behind Dimitri and Vasily shifted to the side, tilting his phone lens. With three snaps he captured all sides of the man's image.

Dimitri trailed the man but stopped as the center door opened and a woman in a business suit came out. The big man opened the glass door wide with a tug that might have ripped it off its steel hinge. Stepping closer, Dimitri overheard the conversation.

"Oh, thanks, Gunter. You just arriving?" asked the woman.

"Yeah. Legs day."

The woman looked down, her eyes widened, mouth forming an *O*. "Guess you'll be a while."

"Three hours."

"Well, enjoy." she said with a small, effortless smile.

Dimitri waited until Gunter went through the doors before he returned to Vasily.

"Three fucking hours."

"Like I said, he's a real athlete."

"And?"

"And we wait for him to come out."

Dimitri cursed in both English and Tajik. He fumed and pleaded and was worried someone would notice them loitering for three hours, find it suspicious, and report them. Vasi nodded, looking in both directions along the street.

Pedestrians filled the sidewalk, jostling the cousins with their brisk pace. Sprinkles fell and umbrellas opened that impeded their movement.

"For fuck's sake, I have an essay to write."

"Quit now and get a degree in computer porn. You'll earn more."

Dimitri spat, his phlegm expelled into the gutter. "Let's work on Tariq's design. That'll be more productive than standing around to follow a guy who looks dumb as shit. He looked right at us and didn't recognize us." He stared at Vasily, who didn't respond.

"Fuck this, I'm going," said Dimitri.

Vasily's arm draped around Dimitri's neck and dragged him to the street corner. His mouth brushed Dimitri's ear as he cursed in Tajik. "You do and I'll push you into the traffic." Vasily pinched Dimitri's neck with his index finger and thumb, and his other hand tugged Dimitri's shirt, pulling him to the curb's edge. A bus headed toward the stop. Dimitri tried to step away but Vasily held him curbside, pulling him back at the last minute as the bus streaked past.

"I wouldn't hurt you," he said, laughing. "We're family! Let's get out of the rain and eat."

Dimitri rubbed his neck. The entire idea had annoyed

him from the start. He had been sure they would not find the man, who he now knew was called Gunter. Now they had to wait three hours for the guy to finish his leg workout. He brooded over a coffee and muffin inside a luncheonette.

After two hours, Vasily motioned to leave, reigniting Dimitri's anger. "Fuck, Vasi, it's not been three hours yet." Vasily countered that workout times were estimates. "This Gunter guy might get injured or displeased with his workout performance or something else that could make him leave early. Or late."

Returning to their previous park bench position they resumed their bird-watcher postures. Gunter emerged three and a half hours after he first entered UltraFit. Vasi approved of the man's dedication.

They trailed him to a Broadway bus stop, and loitered in the background, waiting at the end of the line before boarding the northbound bus toward Harlem.

The cousins recognized the landscape from the night with Tariq. Gunter got off the bus at 120th Street, two blocks from Sakura Park. The cousins followed, their pace slow to avoid overtaking Gunter's lumbering canter. They waited on the sidewalk as he veered into a corner deli. Five minutes later he emerged eating a hero. The ensemble walked a half-block until Gunter opened the front door of a four-story, 1940s art deco apartment complex.

"We'll prepare tonight and return tomorrow."

"Vasi, didn't you see the size of him? He's a fucking giant. His arms are bigger than my entire body."

Vasily's reply was a vulgar sneer. They'd return tomorrow prepared to tackle the giant.

6

At seven in the morning Vinnie relayed Blanca's message to Gunter: "Nada." The word brought no response so Vinnie spelled it out. "There is no news about a murder anywhere near Columbia. Any deaths near a university, especially an Ivy League School, would make headline news."

Gunter grunted into his cell.

"It means your police report can wait until Monday. Just thought you'd like to be reassured."

"Yeah, thanks. But I wouldn't miss work anyway. Like I told you, I need the Bulldog job," said Gunter as if reciting lines. He gave Vinnie details on the good pay, guaranteed assignment, and the owners appreciating reliability and loyalty. "I take time off from lifting if he needs me."

Vinnie snorted. "It's carting furniture, so that's lifting, isn't it? I'll call you if anything comes up."

Gunter stopped at the corner deli for six scrambled eggs, two raisin bagels, a large coffee, and two extra large roast beef sandwiches on rye to go for his morning break. He'd grab lunch at a fast-food joint closest to the job.

The deli bustled with harried people rushing every which way. A handful of customers occupied the three booths with windows facing the street. The fourth was unoccupied and had no window. Most patrons either stood at one of the six chest-high round tables or a counter mounted against the front window with a panoramic view of the masses rushing by on the sidewalk and traffic flowing along Broadway. The deli was bright and airy, despite a tired interior with scuffed floorboard, bleached yellow walls, and fifties-style Formica countertops. Gunter once heard a non-local call the place the kind of diner Elvis would have frequented.

Most mornings the booths and tables were half-occupied. Today only one booth was free, the last and least desirable— windowless and tucked away at the rear. But it was Gunter's preferred location even when other booths were available. With his back to the wall, he had a good command of the deli's interior. The humid atmosphere forced him to remove his UltraFit light jacket and tug to stretch his work T-shirt across his chest. Reclining against the cheap wood paneling, Gunter was the load-bearing wall.

He didn't notice that the Karimov cousins had followed him from his apartment or entered the deli. Gunter glanced briefly at Vasily's straight stance, one leg crossed over the other at the ankle, chest puffed out, and sinewy forearms on the round tabletop. He barely registered Dimitri's frown and chewing at his lip. In under a second Gunter turned away from the men to the deli counter.

A line of customers formed at the cashier station to place orders. The cashier called out each meal to the short-order cooks in the kitchen. "Adam and Eve on a log." "Cow feed SOS." Most of the orders ended with "make it walk." Customers waited along the counter, reading and sending text messages.

"Gunter, your usual is ready," called the counterman. Gunter didn't have a number like the others. He politely excused himself as he gently nudged people aside to reach the counter. A few people smiled, but most bowed their heads and moved back. The tattooed arm of the counterman extended a tray with two large brown bags on it.

From his booth, Gunter watched two women standing at the counter who he had noticed because of their height difference. He saw them retrieve their order and struggle to pass waiting patrons. They walked in front of the man with feet crossed at his ankles and his scowling friend at the high counter table. The women jostled across to the first booth at the entry but it was occupied by four people. Gunter lowered his eyes to his plate to scoop up his food. He looked up to see the shorter woman in front of him. He thought her large breasts made it awkward for her to hold her tray in the confined space. The taller, thinner woman stood behind her.

"There's no place. The shower has stopped so let's go outside," said the tall woman.

"No, I want to stay in," replied the friend.

"Where?"

"Look, this is unoccupied." The short friend pointed to a small square table on the side of Gunter's booth.

As they lowered their trays two men arrived and pointed to their briefcases. Lifting their briefcases to the tabletop left no space for the women.

Gunter felt his table shudder as the shorter woman's rear end nudged his table, avoiding a collision with a man rushing into the narrow hallway leading to the men's room. She turned and spoke, startling Gunter. "Do you mind if we park here? Nothing else is available."

The woman's long blonde hair reminded Gunter of a lifter's girlfriend who everyone called a suicide blonde because after two dates you felt like committing suicide. The short woman's bosom projected over the table while she slid her tray across. She pointed to the unoccupied bench and sat down.

"Is this okay?" asked the taller, small-framed woman who remained standing. Gunter thought her nicer than the rude shorter woman already sipping her coffee.

He shook his head, giving the woman permission. He liked the tall, polite one. And despite the shorter woman's ample chest, the taller woman was prettier.

"So, Bulldog, you come here often?" asked the shorter woman, pointing to Gunter's work shirt emblem, *Bulldog Movers*.

Gunter's eyes moved left to right, then rested on the taller woman in front of him.

"Shy, are we? I'm Sue and this is Katia. Do your friends call you Bull or Dog for short?"

"Please excuse Sue's rudeness," interrupted Katia, "she can be a bit blunt. What's your name? I'm sure it's not the name over the logo on your shirt," continued Katia.

"Gunter."

"Really? So cool," said Sue. "Like, are you Irish or something? Do you speak with an accent?"

Gunter's jaw crunched half a bagel, then stopped chewing, remembering his mother telling him he sounded like a disposal unit stuffing too much food into his mouth.

"Sue, leave the man alone. We've already disturbed him enough." Katia flashed Gunter a smile and winked.

"S'okay. I'll be done in a minute. Can't be late for work," Gunter said, putting the rest of the bagel in his mouth.

"Please, don't hurry on our account," said Katia.

Resting his gammon hock forearms on the table, Gunter said, "Hurry is a little difficult for me." He flashed a brief smile.

"Oh, like, because of your work?" asked Sue.

"I think he means his size." Katia winked at Gunter.

"Yeah. I went for a run this morning. Worst two minutes ever." Gunter grinned, longer than before. Katia laughed out loud.

"I'm an easy catch, just hard to release."

Placing her hand over her mouth, Katia giggled.

"Why would anyone chase you?" asked Sue.

Katia shook her head, removing her hand to reveal a broad smile. He liked that Katia understood him, unlike rude Sue, as he had nicknamed her.

He swept the table top with a paper napkin, placing it next to the dirty dish on his tray. His fingers checked the seal on his takeout bags. He picked up his second bagel but stopped when Sue spoke.

"So is that why you work for a moving company? Your size? Do you, like, lift refrigerators and pianos all by yourself?" she asked, her coffee mug inches below her nose as if imbibing through inhalation.

Katia sighed.

Gunter finished the second bagel. With head tilted, he

held his mug near vertical to empty the remaining coffee. Taking his brown bags with his mid-morning snack in his left hand, his right gripped the table edge to guide his slide out. Katia placed her hand over his. Gunter stopped, looked down at Katia's hand, then to her face. He noticed her large eyes, their hazel green color, like his but not as deep green. Her teeth were TV commercial white. He also saw her surveying his body. He knew the look because he experienced it every day on the street, the bus, and the UltraFit lobby, from those that knew him as well as from first-time gawkers.

Moving his hand from under Katia's, he stood. But she held his fingers. "Look, we've bothered you," she said, releasing her hold to touch his forearm, then gripped his bicep.

Gunter looked at Katia's hand, than tensed his arm, igniting synapses to fire sinew that bunched. A bulge rose. Her vibrant eyes widened, the green iris with a yellow tinge expressed wonder. Her tongue tip extended across her partially open red lips.

"Oh my God." Her hand rubbed his bicep as if seeking proof that it was real. He relaxed and she pulled her hand away.

"That's incredible. I've never felt a muscle that hard."

He liked her. Her small nose and dimpled cheeks were a perfect size for her face. She radiated. He smiled but said nothing.

"Ooh. I mean, ooh, well, I'm sorry…"

"Why? I've heard others say it. Maybe more 'ahh' than 'ooh.'"

She laughed. "You're funny, has anyone told you that?"

"Sure. I tell good jokes but you have to *weight* for them."

Katia burst into laughter. Sue's mouth hung open. "What? Why's that funny?"

Gunter shook his head, smiling broadly and staring at Katia. She was tapping the tabletop as she spoke "I... well... this is crazy and last minute, but I'd like to invite you to a little party at my place tomorrow night. Will you come?"

"Uh, I guess."

"Please. You'll be a hit. Everyone will want to see you."

"Uh... you sure?" He stared into Katia's big green eyes. She was very pretty. And he liked her easy-going manner. And she was polite. He thought she was the kind of girl his mother would like.

"Great."

She recited her address and added, "It's the Stuyvesant Town area near the East Village. You'll know it since you're a mover." She paused with a short tinkly laugh that he began to recognize. "It's an easy number to remember because it rhymes with mighty fine. Get it? Number Ninety-nine is mighty fine."

Gunter's expression remained unchanged. He was fixed on her curled lips that formed an unrestrained smile. He wondered if she was always this nice or was she flattering him?

"No? Okay, what's your cell?" said Katia as she pulled out hers.

Gunter recited his number and Katia repeated her address out loud as she texted. Stepping back, he knocked a stranger to the floor, the scowling man he'd noticed at the counter table.

"Sorry. I didn't see you there. You okay?" asked Gunter as he bent over to take the man's wrist and hoist him to a standing position.

The stranger turned, retreating to the men's room.

Sue sang out, "Holy shit! You lifted him like he was a puppy. Like, do you carry stuff on your back and save the moving van gas? Ha ha ha."

Her chalk-scraping laugh irritated him. He walked away, no goodbye wave, upset that Katia's was not the last voice he had heard.

"Wait," called out Katia, holding up his jacket.

He took it from her, saying, "Thanks. Anything not wrapped for takeout is unimportant."

Katia repeated her now familiar laugh and caused Gunter to smile. "Look," she said, "I know it's forward of me, but I really would like you to come. And I'll be honest," she paused rubbing his arm, "your body fascinates me. I have your number. I'll call you tonight to talk about the party."

"Okay." Gunter walked out, unsure he had made a good decision. Katia was okay, but not Sue. Did he have to go? He wanted to. He'd been obsessed about finding a female friend. Could Katia be that person? Dr. Stein in therapy suggested parties were a good way to meet women. And Internet dating wouldn't suit him according to Dr. Stein, explaining that unless Gunter posted his bodybuilding photos—not a good idea—then he'd shock a woman on the first date. And only a Pulitzer winner had the writing skills to portray Gunter's size or personality in emails or texts.

Katia's party was his first invite that didn't come as a pity-date with a niece or daughter of his mother's colleagues, and even those could be counted on one hand.

Dimitri emerged from the hallway. Being knocked to the floor had upset him, but he was also pleased that he'd not been recognized.

"He's like a battleship," said Dimitri, rubbing his wrist, "and there's no way we could stab him or push him in front of a subway," referring to Vasi's two elimination methods.

"But that woman—" Dimitri's head tilted to indicate Gunter's booth, "the tall one. See her?"

Vasily nodded.

"She's invited him to a party tomorrow night."

Vasily's lips formed a crooked smile. "You know, this could be an easier way to rid us of this guy."

7

"Blanca found something new," said Vinnie, munching his Saturday morning cereal breakfast while on his cell to Gunter. He was treating him like a real client, meaning he'd give him weekend updates. He apologized for talking and eating but he was pressed for time. He and Ben were taking their godchild to a matinee show while his parents went to a fancy fund-raiser to help teenage girls with anorexia.

Vinnie had moved Gunter up the client priority scale after Blanca's inside informant said the victim in Harlem was Tariq Mamurov, a Columbia University graduate student. And he definitely was not killed in Harlem.

"Where?" asked Gunter.

"Don't know." Vinnie stopped chewing to connect the dots. He relayed that Blanca's informant said a check of the Harlem nightclub parking lot showed a town car limo with Jersey plates. Vinnie garbled, "Not..." crunch, crunch "...unusual because clients use limos..." crunch, crunch "...to arrive at fancy clubs, especially if they intend to drink and do drugs."

"So?" asked Gunter.

"Most limos street park, even if it's illegal." Vinnie swallowed. "Or return at a prearranged pickup time."

"Uh-huh. And this is important because?" asked Gunter.

"Limos in the parking lot are rare," said Vinnie, wiping his mouth before adding, "but not super rare. The cops won't take special notice but... uh, you say the town car you saw had Jersey plates. Are you sure about that?"

"I think so, but like I said it was dark, and I was in the park, not on the street."

"Yeah," snickered Vinnie, "and all these fuckin' vanity and specialty plates makes it hard to tell among states."

The doorbell rang and Vinnie said, "My guest is here. Can't keep a six-year-old waiting for his big date with the godparents."

"Same for twenty-six."

Vinnie coughed out, "What!"

"I've got a date myself. Okay, not exactly a date, but I've been invited to a party tonight."

Hanging up the phone, Vinnie muttered out loud, "Fuckin' unbelievable," unaware Ben had entered the room holding their godson Anthony's hand.

"Vinnie, language. Anthony's here," said Ben.

Vinnie thought the boy's smile was so big it almost didn't fit his face.

* * *

The pleasant August breeze and light drizzle cooled Gunter's neck as he mounted Katia's brownstone duplex stoop. A buzz unlatched the bolt. He imagined her finger pressed on the button.

He wore an Italian leather jacket gifted by his mother who claimed it would impress. He arrived prepared, leaving nothing to happenstance.

The dimly lit hallway had a pungent odor of cleaning fluid that trailed him up the staircase. On the second-floor landing his hand tightened around the wood railing waiting for the apartment door to open.

"Hey Gunter, come in. I'm so glad you made it," said Katia, in the style of an entertainment coordinator greeting passengers on the gangplank of a Caribbean cruise ship.

Gunter extended his hand.

"They're lovely," Katia said, burying her nose in the rose bouquet.

His head tilted as he recalled his mother's words that *girls like flowers*. It had been her second suggestion for the party.

Katia's hand swept the room, guiding his entrance.

"We've started on drinks and stuff," she said, pointing to the living area with identical beige divans facing each other and a single upright chair in front of three half-opened bay window panels. Gunter saw three people in the room and looked around.

"Two weeks it's been on the floor," said Katia, pointing to an air conditioner unit sitting below the sill, "and brutal during last week's heat wave. I'm glad for this unusual cool spell even if the beachgoers are sad about it. And at least my bedroom unit works," she said, continuing with a light tone. "I have a typical New York super. If the problem doesn't fix itself in six months he comes around. He'll fix my AC during a January blizzard. I'm sure you know what I mean."

Gunter nodded, but concentrated on what he thought were a lot of empty beer bottles for a party that had just started with only four people. A throwaway plastic ashtray and rolling paper strewn on a beat-up wooden coffee table caught his eye. Marijuana smoke perfumed the air with a sweet and distinctive odor in contrast to the hallway disinfectant.

He wondered about the thumping bass background music that he heard outside, and now understood it was from the open bay window. He didn't like it. It was not the kind of music he'd use in his on-stage bodybuilding contests, not that he had competed in many recently.

Katia touched his arm with one hand, the other held out an index finger pointing around the room. "You already met Sue." Her finger swung to a tall, thin man on the other divan. "That's Eric…" Moving around, Katia pointed at a lanky man about her height but not as tall as Eric. "…and that's Les."

She told everyone Gunter's name and Sue called out, "Hey, Bulldog. That's what I call you. Right, Bulldog?!" Sue cackled.

Gunter remembered Sue's crow laugh from the deli. She had been giggling from the moment he arrived.

Eric said with a carefree, unhurried manner, "Hey, dude. Want some weed? Good shit too. My man Les knows where to score."

Gunter looked around and turned to Katia.

"Anyone else?"

"This is it," she said and took a drag on the blunt.

He hadn't expected Katia to use weed, but why wouldn't she? Everyone at the gym did, even the hardcore bodybuilders—as well as other drugs but with different outcomes. He used drugs too, just not weed.

Les was grinning. "Take as much as you want, man."

Gunter shook his head to say no and Katia handed him a beer. He listened to the jumbled conversation and felt disconnected, unable to contribute. He made several glances to the front door as if anticipating a horde of new partygoers to arrive. Sue's clucking got his attention.

"Hey, Bulldog, let's see your muscles. That's why you're here, right?" Sue was grinning as she shifted in her seat.

"Yeah Bulldog, give us a show," called out Eric.

A smattering of applause followed.

Gunter looked to Katia and waited. She spoke with a timid chortle. "Is that okay? We talked about this during our chat last night and you agreed, remember? I sent a reminder text too. This will be so different for us. I'd like it, we all would."

"Yeah, I know. I just thought, well... I'd wait until everyone arrives."

Katia laughed. "This is it. I did ask a friend but she had a date and another guy I know from acting class didn't want to come. Anyway, I thought you'd prefer something smaller and more intimate." She stopped and put her hands together. "Please. But if you don't want to I totally understand. I just thought I'd like... we'd like to see your development, all the work you put into your body."

He had agreed on the phone and came prepared, wearing his poser suit and with his music playlist on his cell. He didn't tell his mother. He hadn't told anyone. He'd never done anything like this before.

"You sure you want me to?" asked Gunter, looking into Katia's eyes, which had more of a glaze then he remembered.

"Oh, yes! Sure, it'll be fun."

"Yeah, do it!" barked Sue.

He liked Katia's sweetness and her polite manner. He was finding Sue's cackle more annoying each time. Katia's voice also seemed a little strange, not exactly as he remembered. *Must be the pot*, he thought.

Moving behind the single chair, Gunter draped his leather jacket over the back. He removed his sneakers and kicked them aside. He dropped his pants and carefully folded them to place them on top of his jacket. From behind the chair, his bare legs were hidden to the group. With a rolling gait he moved to the front of the chair, his prance forward better than most Lipizzaner horses. He was on full display in a tight, shiny, gold poser brief that revealed most of his ass and nearly his privates.

Most people would be self-conscious, but Gunter's modesty had been numbed over the years by performing at contests, in photographic studios, and at the gym mirror. Ironically, his self-awareness came out only when fully clothed on the street when people ogled him open-mouthed.

Les yelled, "Shit, man, look at those fuckin' legs!"

"What an ass," cried Eric, "like he's stuffed them with, uh, you know, those things they knock down buildings with." Eric's eyelids drooped.

"Wrecking balls," blurted Les.

"Yeah, thanks, man! Wrecking balls."

With a gnomic grin, Sue babbled words of encouragement.

Gunter shook a leg, jiggling a gelatinous thick thigh until he tensed, solidifying the quadriceps into an inverted teardrop flanked by sinew rising to the surface. He made a half turn then bent on one leg, extending the other behind. The calf muscle resolved into high-tension wire cables.

Someone yelled, "Fucking unreal."

Resuming an upright stance, Gunter faced the window with his back to the group. He pulled his loose-fitting half-sleeve light summer jersey overhead to appear headless. His hands reached up, tugging the shirt off to reveal a continent-wide back. Only the poser briefs kept him from being naked, even though ninety-five percent of his skin was on display.

He turned on his phone, the cell music tinny. Katia reached to tune the phone to her Bluetooth stereo and amplified the music.

Gunter began his competition routine. With hands on hips, he spread his condor-size latissimus dorsi. The four friends sucked down the room's oxygen. He turned to face the group, ignoring their squeals. All noise stopped as he raised both arms and muscular lava flowed into peaking cones. He strained, contorting his face as he turned crimson with his hard tensing. Sweat trailed down his brow onto his eyelids.

"Holy fuck. FUCK!" screamed Les.

"Holy shit, that's ridiculous," said Sue.

"He looks like that... uh, what's he called, you know, the tire guy," said Eric, sputtering and smacking his forehead. "Michelin Man, that's it." Eric waved his arms around but his eyes were fixed on Gunter.

Shouts compared Gunter to bridges, buildings, mountain

ranges—each outburst followed by hooting laughter.

Gunter lowered his arms to shift sideways into a chest pose. Les described Gunter's pectorals as like the Verrazzano-Narrows Bridge entry ramp.

"Yeah, and look at those nips. Like fucking baby gorilla sucking size," said Les.

"Like, uh... like... Christmas... uh... uh tree bulbs," choked Eric as he inhaled his blunt.

"Look," said Les expelling spittle, "his fucking nipples point to his toes." He turned to Katia. "Those are real big tits. Bet you wish yours were like his."

Gunter knew he should stop as Eric pointed to his crotch, but continued with his practiced routine as the music played on.

"Hey, Bulldog, you got a sausage in there?" Eric's words were slurred. "Bet it's a big wiener."

"Is that right, Bulldog?" asked Les, doubled over.

Gunter turned sideways for another chest pose. He wanted to stop, but he saw Katia's eyes fixed on him, her mouth gaping. He could ignore the men if he concentrated on giving Katia the show she wanted.

"Fuck and fuck! Them are some tits, Bulldog," said Les as he unfolded and leaned back.

Gunter turned to the front, shooting another double-bicep flex.

Les sat up. "Do you have balls? I heard steroids shrinks them to Planters." His pitch elevated. "You want Katia to touch your little poodle wang and peanut balls?" His delight was obvious in his tone.

Gunter held his position. He knew the competition rule:

complete the routine, never quit.

Katia stepped up, touched his flexed arm, her hand barely covering one-third of his bicep.

"You're so strong. I just can't get over the way these feel."

Her hand moved to his shoulders, then to his pectorals.

"Like, what have you done to yourself? You're a balloon!" yelled Sue.

A chorus of chants began, words slurring.

"Ha ha. Balloon."

"Monster balloon," someone began to sing out. "Gunter, Gunter, bo bunter balloon galloon."

The giggling and howling escalated.

"Goon, goon, bo balloon-loon."

"Loon, bo balloon, loon, Gunter balloon."

"Gunter bo dumbo balloon," called out Katia, inches from his face, her hands on his chest.

With Katia's words, Gunter's vision blurred. He pushed her hand away hard and she stumbled back. She looked at him with contempt.

In under a minute Gunter had his pants and shirt back on. Katia had stunned him. A torrent of blood rushed through capillaries to flood his cranium. His cheeks flamed and his eyes misted. Katia's words felt like they had slapped him, unlike the childish singsong of Sue and her two male friends. With cringing humiliation, he scuttled to the front door and shrunk into insignificant smallness.

Gunter carried his socks, sneakers, and leather jacket out of the room to speed his exit. He slammed the door to avoid hearing Katia's jeers and the men's hoots of laughter that he knew were coming.

Leaning over the banister, Katia called out to Gunter, who was sitting on the bottom step putting his shoes on. On hearing her voice he stopped what he was doing and his hands covered his face. The first-floor apartment door opened and he lowered his fingers. The door shut as quickly as it had opened and his hands returned to cover his face again.

Katia sat behind him, unable to squeeze past.

"Gunter, I'm sorry," she said, speaking to his back. "We were just having some fun. Please come back. We'll behave, I promise."

He hunched, rounded into a fortified rampart as he tied one sneaker's laces.

She massaged his back. "Please. It was a fuck-up, I made a mistake."

He laced the other sneaker and stood up. Katia tried to take hold of his forearm but failed, her hand too small to encircle even his wrist as he pulled away.

"Please. I'm so sorry," her voice choked. "You're so big. We've never seen anything like you before in the flesh."

He turned, and with Katia perched on the second step he had direct eye contact. His anger flushed his face. "ANY... TH... ING," he said, dragging out the last syllable, then paused as his voice cracked trying to complete his sentence, "like me!"

Wiping his cheeks, he flung the front door wide open.

"Gunter, come back. I'm sorry!"

His fast pace, faster than he should move for his size, had him halfway down the block. Katia stood on the stoop.

She called out, "Gunter, stop. Wait… Gunter!"

He walked between two parked cars to cross the street.

Katia leapt down the steps, sprinting after him. She crossed the street at the same point, stretched her hand out for his jacket sleeve. Gunter did not halt, dragging her with him. She stumbled, falling to one knee. He stopped, her face wet with tears, as was his. Her knee was bleeding profusely.

"Gunter… I'm… so sorry. Please, can't you forgive me? Come back. We'll start over."

He choked as if something constricted his larynx. "I thought you were nice. A good person."

He rubbed his burning eyes and wiped snot from his nose. He saw her wipe blood off her knee while struggling to stand.

He bent over and put out his arm. She grabbed his sleeve and he pulled her upright. He looked into her eyes. "I… I wanted you to like me," he said in a barely audible, trembling voice.

He waited until she was steady, then withdrew his arm. His body shook. The only sound exchanged between them was mutual sobbing.

He walk away, hearing Katia's subdued voice call out, and he pretended not to hear her say, "Me too."

* * *

The first cell phone ping came as Gunter descended the subway stairs. The second ping arrived as he sat down in the subway car, hands over his face. He wasn't hiding from staring travelers but avoiding his reflected image in the subway car window. Another ping came one stop from his destination. He had tried to avoid reading the texts, but three times made them too compelling.

10:43 p.m. TEXT: Gunter, come back, pls. I didn't mean it.
10:52 p.m. TEXT: Gunter so sorry. Pls forgive. What we did was mean.
11:07 p.m. TEXT: Pls. I'm sorry. I'll stay up all night for you.

He switched the phone off, missing Katia's last message:

11:45 p.m. TEXT: Are you going to hurt me for wh#

8

Following the same surveillance protocol they'd used at UltraFit, Vasily insisted on arriving two hours before the party
started. Dimitri fumed because Vasily's decision proved
wise. The early arrival meant they had time to circle the
Stuyvesant Town neighborhood block seven times. On the
eighth lap, Vasi nabbed a spot vacated in front of Katia's
apartment for prime surveillance.

"See," said Vasi smugly in slow Tajik, "now we can sit
in the car, inconspicuous from spying Americans. And we
not get rain soaked."

Dimitri wanted to wipe away Vasi's smugness, pointing
out the rain had stopped and the dark clouds were dispers-
ing. A quarter moon shone from behind fluffy cumulus
clouds. They dropped their McDonald's takeout paper bags
on the floor, with cleanup allocated to Dimitri before his
next chauffeur assignment. He seethed, shut his eyes, and
stretched his legs in the luxury car's ample backseat space.

For two hours the Karimov cousins sat without speaking,
engine off and the radio muted. Tinted windows prevented
anyone passing by seeing inside except if they looked directly through the front windshield or through the small

crack in the driver's side window that prevented fogging.

Dimitri and Vasily reclined in the rear seats. But as they sprawled, their legs tangled, aggravating their dispute until Dimitri dozed off.

Vasi's nudge brought Dimitri out of his slumber. Two women came out of the apartment at nine o'clock. An umbrella held between them protected them from water droplets falling off drenched leaves. The cousins twisted in their seats to peer out the rear window as the women walked past to go to a corner liquor store.

After ten minutes they returned. "That one's called Sue," said Dimitri, pointing to the shorter woman holding a six-pack in each hand, "and she's Katia," he added, pointing to the taller woman.

"I know. Shut the fuck up," said Vasily.

They saw Katia held a brown satchel in one hand with a Frito bag poking out the top and juggled holding the umbrella high in the other.

"Bet the stronger stuff is underneath," said Dimitri.

Vasily chortled, "Hope it's good vodka."

For a half-hour there was no more activity except a woman walking a dog. After they passed by, Vasi touched Dimitri's shoulder and pointed to two men in light windbreakers climbing the front stoop of Katia's apartment. The dark evening sky seemed to turn coal-black with a passing cloudburst that lasted five minutes.

Dimitri didn't see a reason to leave the car but followed Vasi, who pulled his hood over his head with large droplets running off moist branches replenished by the recent shower.

"He's not coming," Dimitri said, and adjusted his New York Yankees ball cap as he moved closer to Vasily.

"We wait," said Vasily, blowing on his hands before inserting them in his hooded sweatshirt pocket.

Dimitri hated the damp, and like Vasi placed his hands into his hooded jacket. His fingers caressed a stun gun's rounded shaft, gifted by a Jersey City boxing club patron, no questions asked or permit required in New Jersey. Not true in New York but compared to murder a negligible violation.

"Vasi, he's not coming." Dimitri knew he sounded relieved and tried to cover up his tittering excuse. "She called the party off or he decided not to come."

"We wait," Vasily said, irritated but resolute.

Dimitri paced, his steps random. He pulled out a cigarette pack from his pocket. While fumbling to take out a single cigarette he said, "Fuck," and pointed with the pack.

Vasily drew close as Dimitri continued to point at a large figure a half-block away heading toward them. "Is Gunter," Vasily said.

"What's he carrying?" asked Dimitri.

A passing car slowed as Gunter did a short jog to cross the street. The car's headlights spotlighted a floral bouquet.

The cousins exited the car and crouched in the space between their limo's front bumper and the rear of the car in front. Gunter was within thirty yards of Katia's apartment and them.

Vasily pulled out his serrated fishing knife, the same one he used on Tariq. He stood back and watched Dimitri prepare his stun gun, ready to discharge 1.8 microcoulomb high-energy volts into Gunter's rib cage. The maximum level, enough to cause excessive, paralyzing pain in an average-size person, so would impact even Gunter's enormous mass.

Getting to his toes, Vasily tensed, ready to quickly leap and drive his knife into Gunter's left ventricle with an upward thrust. He didn't think one jab would be sufficient for someone of Gunter's size and it might require repeated thrusts. But he was not Dimitri, not weak physically and mentally. He would not be ineffectual as Dimitri had with Tariq. He was a true warrior and a champion.

He watched Dimitri move forward, his motion tentative as he approached Gunter. The stun gun was withdrawn from the pocket until Vasi called out in Tajik: "Stop."

A young couple had stepped out of a building adjacent to Katia's. Descending the stoop, they stared at Gunter. With the man draping one arm over the woman's shoulder, he guided her across the street toward Vasily. By the time they passed, Gunter was pressing the bell to number ninety-nine.

"Fuck, now we have to stay until he comes out. Fuck and fuck." Dimitri nearly zapped himself, his finger hovering over the stun gun's trigger as he reentered the limo's back seat.

"Stop complaining. Sit in the back by yourself and surf porn on your cell. I'll raise the window divide and not disturb you. Satisfied? First, get us more coffee." Vasily released the handle of the serrated knife wrapped in plastic and replaced it in his pocket. He took the stun gun from Dimitri, discharged it, set the safety catch, and put it in his pocket.

"This is fucking bullshit," said Dimitri.

A stern scowl plastered Vasi's face.

"Okay. I'll get pizza at the joint on the next block," said Dimitri. He returned fifteen minutes later with coffee and two pepperoni pizza slices. He ate stretched across the back seat with his head on the plush door armrest, a good angle to see Katia's apartment bay window.

"Anything?"

"Stupid party," grumbled Vasily. "I count only two women and three men."

Dimitri smiled. He'd seen that combo on the Internet. After a half-hour he said, "I'm fucking cold. Turn the engine on and heat us up. How long do we have to stay?"

Vasily didn't start the engine, but said, "Until we finish and fix your screw-up with Tariq."

"I can't see a fucking thing," said Dimitri. He paused, adjusting the binoculars' focus. "What the fuck?"

Gunter could be seen removing his jacket in the front window and bending over. Dimitri knew from the movement that he had removed his pants even though his lower body was not visible from street level.

Dimitri's voice rose. "A sex party?" He refocused his binoculars, wishing he had a better view. He caught glimpses of Gunter's flexing. "Why don't the women come to the window? I'll bet they have a special kind of flexing." Dimitri was smiling.

Vasily brought his front passenger seat to a full upright position and opened the driver's window another two inches. The music blasted and the shrill laughter was easily heard.

Gunter had disappeared.

"Fuck, why can't we see anything?" said Dimitri, pulling his binoculars away from his face and lowering the rear side window three inches after hearing faint squeals. "Hear that? Must be a good time."

The music stopped and fifteen minutes later the building's front door opened, light spilling into the street. Vasily told Dimitri to exit the car and not slam the door. The men took the same crouched position between cars. They saw Gunter descend the steps, hurried but not running. They recognized Katia's shouting although she was hidden behind the opened front door. She opened it wider and appeared to leap down the steps, reached the sidewalk, and shouted Gunter's name.

Vasily jogged behind Katia, careful but closing his distance. Dimitri hesitated but followed, whispering, "Leave them. We can't catch him." Dimitri's pace picked up, wheezing as he reached Vasily's side. They were on the opposite sidewalk, parallel to Gunter and Katia fifty yards behind him. Vasily reached into his pocket and withdrew the serrated knife then pulled the stun gun from the other pocket. He removed the safety and handed it to Dimitri, who tightened his grip on the handle. Sweat beaded his lips. "This is too exposed. We can't."

"Shut up."

Gunter crossed the street to the same side as Dimitri and Vasily, his sudden move surprising them. He paused for a second, looked in their direction but seemed oblivious to their presence. Dimitri tugged at Vasily's sweatshirt, pulling him down. With Gunter resuming his fast walk, the cousins followed with a quickened pace. As the distance narrowed, they saw the couple from earlier in the evening, walking on the sidewalk, unclasp their hands to allow Gunter to pass between them.

Vasily and Dimitri ducked between two parked cars, pretending to cross the street. They waited for the couple to walk by. Dimitri whispered that Katia was getting closer as she dashed across the road. Vasily waved, creeping behind Katia and Gunter. Dimitri opened and closed his eyes, hoping the scene would change. Katia sped up, which allowed her to reach Gunter. Vasily signaled to move onto the street, using the parked cars as shields.

The men edged forward. Gusting wind shook water-soaked leaves. Dimitri and Vasily returned to the sidewalk, moving behind a tree within thirty feet of Gunter and Katia. Dimitri peeled off pieces of bark. Vasily's finger went to his lips to silence him. Gunter and Katia's words drifted to the cousins.

They heard Katia's lament and repeated begging. Vasily sneered at Gunter's blubbering reply. The cousins moved within five feet. Dimitri was sure Katia would spot them but she limped past, head down.

The men trotted but arrived too late. Gunter had turned onto the main boulevard, strewn with restaurants and discos with long lines, bouncers, and a panoply of external security cameras.

Vasily cursed. "No good. Too many witnesses." He walked back to the limo followed by a gleeful Dimitri.

"Can we go? Forget him?"

Vasily grabbed Dimitri's lapel, his voice rasping as they retraced their steps. "We finish tonight," he said, shoving

Dimitri into the limo's rear seat. "We wait. I need to think," Vasily added as he joined Dimitri. Vasily lit a cigarette, cracked open his side window, allowing air flow but still hidden from passing pedestrians.

The cousins huddled, dozing briefly to be roused by raucous voices scurrying across the humid evening air. With a hand swipe, they cleared the steamed windows to see the two men and Sue exit Katia's apartment—the same trio who had entered at the start of the night.

Vasily smiled. "I have idea. Good, too."

A glazed expression passed over Dimitri's face. This was not part of their original agreement.

"Can't we just go? She's got nothing to do with us and he's obviously not said anything or we would have heard from the cops."

The hard slap stung Dimitri, who raised his hand to cover his nose as Vasily's fist hovered inches away.

Dimitri's mood darkened, while the interior car dome highlighted Vasily's jaw barking out orders.

"The bodybuilder's a loose end. We're fucked if he talks. I'm not taking that chance. Besides, she had a fight with him. We finish this tonight and go back to the real plan."

"Okay, fuck it. Let's get it done and get the hell out of here."

9

There was no sleep for Katia. She sat upright in her bed, miserable under a light sheet. She was shamed by her actions, her part in ridiculing that sensitive and tormented man. She had never caused someone to cry before. And no one had ever run from her. She nearly laughed, thinking how she, at barely one hundred forty pounds, had caused a man the size of Gibraltar to run from her. She wanted to apologize. Even a big, unattractive man did not deserve rude treatment. She willed her cell to ring.

She reread the same page of her novel three times. Her eyelids almost closed as the doorbell rang past one a.m. With a dancer's leap she tore down the hallway, her heart at marathon rate as she reached the dark intercom screen.

"Gunter, is that you? I can't see you. The camera's blocked."

"Yes."

Hearing the words brought her relief, not quite joy, but a chance to exonerate herself. The tinny voice didn't sound like Gunter, but it was typical of her cheap landlord to install an inferior intercom.

Katia stood on the threshold of her open door. A man

she didn't recognize came up the stairs. He smiled, his hand extended. She peered behind him, expecting Gunter to be in the hallway, but was surprised rather than shocked when another man stepped forward. Before she spoke, the second man shoved the first, pushing him into her, and they stumbled into her apartment.

The second man spoke a foreign language to the first, who bolted her door shut behind him.

"What do you want?" asked Katia in a steady tone, with no trace of anxiety or panic.

"Same as you planned to give your boyfriend Gunter," said Dimitri, glancing at Katia in her soft yellow nightgown, her breasts poking at the fabric. Despite the small boobs, her tall body and strong legs excited him. He liked her long eyelashes, full lips, high cheekbones, and button nose. He imagined her on a computer camera being fucked. Only this was real. He could be the one fucking her. His eye caught Vasily, moving around the apartment closing curtains and windows with businesslike efficiency. Nope, he wouldn't dare ask Vasi to allow him to have sex with Katia.

"Let's talk. Bring us some vodka," commanded Vasily, staring at Katia as he plopped onto the couch. "We need to know what Gunter told you. Did he tell you about his late-night park walks, for instance?"

"Especially around Columbia University," added Dimitri.

"Who are you? Did Sue send you? Well, tell her to go fuck herself. Is this to get back at me for pouring the bucket of water on her and her two roommates?"

"I said vodka!" screamed Vasily.

"What vodka? You need to leave," said Katia in a strident

voice, "and tell Sue this isn't funny. She and her two little boys should stay away."

Vasily's face soured, his lips bunched. "No vodka?" He stood and with a prison guard's hold dragged Katia into the kitchen. She protested but he slapped her face, startling her into silence. His strength and martial arts skills twisted her arm back, the grip unbreakable.

The flower vase with yellow roses sat on the kitchen table. "A pretty gift from your boyfriend Gunter?" said Dimitri, searching the kitchen cabinets for any kind of liquor.

"Fuck you and fuck Sue. Get the hell out of my apartment," Katia said as Vasily shoved her into a chair at the table.

Stepping from behind Vasily, Dimitri slapped Katia's face hard, saying, "You don't speak to this great man like that."

If Dimitri's slap stung, it was nothing compared to Vasily's sharp jab to her ribs or the stun gun's electrical discharge that buckled Katia's legs and stopped her screaming. He recognized the creases that came with Vasi's narrowing eyes. They appeared friendly, concealing his anticipated joy of the harm he was about to inflict. Dimitri knew this expression, the one Vasi wore when he had mercilessly pummeled him as his sparring partner. Katia went limp on the third punch, her cheeks bruised and mouth bleeding. She sobbed, brave stoicism abandoned, pleading ignorance about Sakura Park or Gunter's night strolls.

Dimitri tied a dishrag around Katia's mouth to prevent her screaming then searched the kitchen for household items that he found under the sink. Both men covered their shoes

71

in plastic and put on disposable latex gloves, and even tied baggies over their heads to cover their short-clipped hair.

Vasily removed his jacket. His rapid blows broke Katia's nose, cheekbones, and several teeth. Her eyes swelled closed. Blood covered her chin and stained her nightgown. Each punch was masterful, executed with precision. Dimitri admired Vasi's skill, but the outcome of the violence revolted him. Katia was rendered undesirable, deformed, her beauty gone. Only beautiful women excited him. If they screamed during sex he assumed it was because of the pleasure of his hard thrusting. He never disfigured them even in his zealous carnal release. In his mind the women's cries were caused by joy. Vasily ruined Katia for him and he felt sick. He couldn't care less about this ugly woman now.

Two more blows rendered Katia unconscious. Vasily stepped close, placed one arm under her neck and the other around her forehead. With raw power he twisted, snapping Katia's neck—a clean break.

"Give me the knife," ordered Vasily.

This is Vasily's perfect finish, thought Dimitri as he retrieved the knife from his cousin's jacket pocket.

Vasily angled the blade under Kati's ribcage, stabbing her twice.

"Wait," said Dimitri as Vasily returned the knife to the plastic carry bag. "Just leave it. It'll confuse the cops. They'll check and find Tariq's DNA. They'll be confused and make Gunter look even more suspicious."

A smile crossed Vasily's face and he kissed his cousin on both cheeks. "Sometimes you're not as stupid as you look.

That's a good idea." He placed the knife under the kitchen table, leaving Dimitri to lift Katia's corpse from the chair to the floor. He removed the dishrag from her mouth and wiped all surfaces with Katia's household disinfectant.

Dimitri turned out the lights as he left Katia's apartment. His heart pounded as he reached the foyer. He had become excited like nothing before. He heard Vasily signal from the door that the sidewalk was empty.

Soggy reddish-green leaves blocked the streetlamps, concealing Dimitri and Vasily's exit. With arms linked, the cousins looked like two companions on a predawn stroll should anyone drive past and notice them.

They climbed into their town car in silence. Vasily drove, using the longer route to Jersey City via the George Washington Bridge. Dimitri knew the reason was not extra precaution, but consistent with Vasi's routine after an MMA fight. He'd take long drives after winning, accompanied by one of his sparring partners or an ardent fan. He never took Dimitri, so this was special. Dimitri saw Vasi smiling and taking long inhales, then rubbing his thigh. He knew that, for Vasi, the attack on Katia was as if he'd won an MMA combat fight, and Dimitri was for the first time in the car for the victory drive, but Vasi never looked at him or said a word. Passing through the tollbooth, Dimitri asked, "How long before they find her?"

After a long pause and deep sigh, Vasi answered, "A week. Maybe sooner if she misses important meetings. Doesn't matter. The cops won't bother us, which is not true for Gunter..." Vasi took irregular breaths before continuing to say, "He'll enjoy the prison weights and strong men."

Vasily laughed out loud. "And find that fucking men is enjoyable if you know how to do it right."

Dimitri thought his cousin's comment strange, hearing in them an imagined pleasure between two men coupling. *A really weird comment.*

The first thing Vasily did on arriving home was to half-fill two highball glasses with vodka. He moved to the living room, unbuttoned his shirt, and removed his pants. Turning to Dimitri, he said, "Take off your clothes. Wash them now." He sat on the couch and switched on the TV.

Dimitri loaded the washing machine before he took his glass to his room. He sat quietly in his underwear, adjusting his desk chair. He did not turn on his computer. He took a long swig and imagined his fantasy—choking a woman during sex. He almost had done so. He'd seen how to do this on porn sites and read about asphyxiation increasing sexual pleasure. No disfigurement. No blood and bruises if you're careful. No screams. Was Katia excited when he smacked her? Would he have had heightened sexual pleasure if she choked him? He touched himself.

Dimitri finished his drink as he recalled the sound of Katia's snapping neck. Her suffering was unnecessary, but especially the gruesome disfigurement. His last image of her repulsed him, he could not fantasize about sex with her. Vasily had ruined it for him. His erection withered.

He turned on his computer, waiting for the website to flash up on the screen. He recognized the homepage by the sound of a cracking whip. He found the video he wanted, a masked woman and a naked, buff man. Dimitri swirled his chair to check his bedroom door was closed and latched.

The buxom woman knelt before the well-endowed man. He was in a green bandit's mask and cape, and had tattoos across his broad chest. The screen filled with the woman's enormous tits. The camera shifted to the man's engorged cock, then moved back to show his sequined black gloves and the marks they left on the woman's shoulders and arms with each strike. The man tied a rope around his neck then pulled it tight. As he did she put his cock in her mouth.

Dimitri's hands moved beneath his underwear to join the action. He took hold of his hard penis as the woman sucked the on-screen man's dick. He shared their excitement. And as the action increased, the man tightened the rope and his gloved hands struck the woman's arms and shoulders. The woman shuddered on climax and passed out. The man ejaculated but not Dimitri, his libido sublimated by thoughts of Katia's snapping neck.

The man untied the noose and the woman gasped, then smiled as if grateful. The satisfied man closed his eyes and moaned softly while touching his penis.

The final scene confused Dimitri. The woman showed no bruising because the man's punches were false, controlled. She bore no resemblance to the damage done to Katia. And he thought of Vasily, who found pleasure in Katia's neck snapping and his weirdo comment about Gunter learning to enjoy prison rape.

Dimitri looked at his limp dick. He needed Vasily gone and never to return. He never wanted to lock his bedroom door or lower the speaker volume again. He wanted to be excited by the simulated violence. He did not want to see beautiful woman made ugly. He did not want to hide in his own house or ask permission to watch porn. He had solved the Gunter problem and after the last act he deserved to be rid of Vasily.

10

Gunter didn't turn on the living room overhead light as he walked to the couch and tossed his leather jacket across the back. He removed his cell from his pocket and squeezed the casing. After a few seconds he hit the on button. The flashing blue screen alerted him to new messages from a now too familiar number. *Her fourth or fifth?* Ignoring them, he threw the cell on top of the leather jacket.

At the kitchen table he concocted a brownish-gray sludge by mixing milk with a powdered protein. His sweat-soaked T-shirt was glued to his skin and he felt humiliated. He peeled off his shirt but not his sense of disappointment. In three chugs he emptied the drink, retrieved his cell, and moved to his dark bedroom. His lips knotted into a snarl as Katia's texts scrolled. He flung his cell next to the floor pad, which was his bed.

He changed into loose workout shorts but kept his torso bare. He sat semi-naked on his floor-pad bed. With V-spread legs he leaned his bare back against the wall. Gunter turned his head to stare at a wall-to-ceiling mirror. The mirror image man had an outcropping of coalesced fibers all over his body. The mirror man looked like Gunter's bodybuilder poster idols stuck on the opposite wall. Men displaying their champion physiques and idolized by thousands.

Gunter dissociated from his reflection and the glory men. He was small and weak, incapable of lifting a ten-pound dumbbell. The mirror man curled a hundred-pound dumbbell in one hand. He would never be rebuked. Gunter the imposter had nothing in common with the monument-worthy poster men or the mirror man staring back at him.

Scanning the room, Gunter sought some hidden pit to hide his anger away but instead he saw the glowing cell phone. He felt remorse. But why? He had done nothing wrong. But he had ignored Katia. He pulled her down and her knee was bleeding. He didn't want that.

Should he have gone back? Should he have called Katia? Should he call her now? What for? More humiliation?

Gunter slid down to rest on his side, his face burrowed into his arm and knees pulled into his chest—a fetal position. He stayed that way for ten minutes that felt like an eternity, but sleep did not come. Eventually he got up, head lowered so there was no accidental look at the mirror. He traipsed barefoot into the hallway then stopped outside his mother's bedroom. He hesitated, his eyes half-closed, his mouth twisting. His hand rubbed his other arm, and unconsciously he flexed.

Staring into the room he saw his mother as she lay to one side of the queen mattress, *her side*. To him it looked as if she expected her dead husband of sixteen years to settle in the vacant space.

The hall light cast Gunter's elongated shadow in front as he walked into the bedroom. Tears swelled behind his closed eyes. He stood over the bed, his *father's side*; his thumb and index finger pinched the sheet. He pulled it back slow, silent, a methodical act.

* * *

The first time Gunter slept in his mother's bed was the night his father died and every night thereafter for three months. A ten-year-old Gunter had arrived home from school to find the building corralled by an ambulance and three squad cars. Yellow police tape blocked the sidewalk as if for a festive celebration. Gunter stood behind the tape but even from fifty feet away he recognized the clothing on the body. His father didn't move. Helene pushed past the policeman blocking the front door and ran toward a huge black cop holding her son.

"He's too young to see this," yelled the bulky policeman. "How old is the boy? Seven?"

"I'm ten," cried Gunter, wiping his tears. "Is my Dad okay? Mommy, what's happened?"

The big cop's hand swallowed Gunter's as he dragged him to Helene, attempting to shield his view. Helene cried out, imploring her son not to look. As Gunter ducked under the yellow tape, ignoring his mother's instructions and the cop's attempt to shield, he saw his father's crushed skull, and next to him lay a large carved stone split in two. The granite lintel above the portico entrance had dislodged at the moment Gunter's father stood beneath.

Gunter's pattern of sleeping with his mother abated but never completely stopped. He oscillated between Helene's bed and his own, depending on if he'd had a bad school day or nightmares or great disappointment, such as losing a contest.

Becoming big became Gunter's relentless pursuit. His bedroom was remodeled into a gymnasium. At first, his mother thought school bullying was the reason, which it was, but that wasn't the origin. She didn't learn until much later that her son's body dysmorphia started with someone Gunter called the Detour Man.

Therapy had revealed the defining moment. Detour Man was a Herculean homeless black veteran with mitts for hands and the devil's voice, and Batman's chest that intimidated people on the other side of the street. He stood at a subway entrance during the morning commute, holding a homemade *DETOUR* sign scrawled with dire predictions if people didn't take a detour in their lives. The vet collected spare change while exchanging banter with commuters. He'd been doing this for a long time. Most people ignored him but some dropped a few coins in his basket.

Detour Man's favorite subway entrance was Gunter's fastest route to school. One morning he took notice of the schoolboy. He wrapped his muscular fingers around Gunter's spaghetti arm. With his strong hands, he crushed the boy's muscle against his bone and admonished him for his puny size and weakness. That night Gunter lay in bed next to his mother.

From that point on, if Gunter spied Detour Man he took the bus instead of the subway and arrived at school late. On rare occasions Detour Man was at the station in the afternoon, shocking Gunter on his exit. The encounter resulted in Gunter being yelled at, grabbed or hoisted in the air. On one occasion Detour Man shook Gunter, sneering derogatory words as he rattled Gunter's small frame.

Depending on the severity of the interaction, Gunter retreated to his mother's bed when he arrived home. The day Detour Man shoved Gunter into the gutter as a bus passed within a foot of Gunter's head was the day he resolved to get big. And the day his nightmares began.

For sixteen years Gunter found refuge in his physical bulk and solace of sorts in his mother's bed. At the party, his muscle armament had failed him, and so he retreated to his safe asylum. He climbed in next to his mother, burrowing into the foam, finding his impression that had been molded into the mattress over the years. He curled, forcing his knees over the edge of the bed. He swiped at his eyes but his tears continued. His self-embrace reduced his quaking and a hand over his mouth stifled his sobs.

Helene snuggled into him, her warmth a tight fit on his spine. Her arm stretched across his shoulder but could not reach over. He dwarfed her. A fast rollover could crush her. He loved the comforting and familiar embrace like when he was a boy, except now she struggled to hold a fraction of his body. Yet it was effective. His breathing slowed. Would she say something? She never had. A single word and he would dissolve.

My fault, thought Gunter. *She knows I'm incapable of meeting a girl. I'm defective. A freak with a bodybuilding obsession—a disease. I'll never have a girlfriend.*

He could hear Katia's laugh, her non-stop chant reverberated in his head: *You're a balloon.* And her apology a nasty reminder he was a freak. Her words, *"Any...thing!"*

Foul words, yet true.

Rage replaced self-pity. He stopped crying. He was angry. He would not text her. *Things* couldn't text. He would not answer her voice messages.

Helene's hand poked him. He lifted his arm to let hers snake beneath his armpit and reach his chest. With a tug, she pulled herself closer.

I'm a friendless freak. His tears returned.

No one liked him. No one understood his need to be big.

His mother's head nudged him, and his breathing became less erratic. Not so his thoughts. He wanted a friend, a girlfriend, and wondered if that was too much to ask. Was Katia right? *He was a thing.*

Gunter's eyes closed. He'd return to the gym sanctuary in the morning. He'd pursue his goal of getting bigger— something he could achieve if he worked at it—and he'd forget about the girlfriend fantasy.

Forget companionship.

Forget Katia.

He'd not think about her again.

11

The local Channel 4 station announced "Breaking News" at seven Sunday night. Vinnie had switched on the TV after he and Ben returned from a meal in the East Village, Vinnie's old stomping ground before he met his husband.

"I'm going to change, listen to music, and read in bed," said Ben, who was not much of a TV fan.

"Oh! Well, I'll be in soon to quiz you on your book. A romance, right?"

Ben smiled and showed Vinnie his middle finger.

"Yup, just what I thought," said Vinnie, laughing. "My kind of book."

"Uh-huh. Don't take too long or I might be too engrossed to be distracted."

"You'll be distracted all right. And I'll in-gross you in ways you won't find in any book."

Ben smiled, which was returned by Vinnie, his grin happy and wide. Their relationship had definitely improved. Ben was never into sexual innuendo or banter so this demonstrated an easing of tension. Helping Gunter was turning out to be a good thing after all.

With Ben out of the room, Vinnie turned the TV volume up. At first he wasn't sure he heard correctly, but the backdrop was definitely the Columbia University campus.

"Police are asking," said the well-known local woman reporter with an inset next to her showing a young man, "that anyone who has information about this Columbia University student contact them. The victim was discovered murdered in Harlem a week ago, but his identity withheld until next of kin are notified."

"Fuckin' unbelievable," said Vinnie, walking into the bedroom. Ben was sitting nude in bed except for boxer briefs.

"Now what?"

Vinnie explained and Ben put down his book. They talked about what they knew of Gunter's stabbed man in Sakura Park.

"Might be the graduate student," said Ben tentatively.

"Might?! Of course it's him," said Vinnie sharply while undressing, "and no name but a picture. You know what that means, don't you?"

Ben shrugged.

"Foreign student. The cops and university haven't or can't contact his parents or relatives. And they can show the photo because the parents won't see the TV broadcast. Probably some kind of fuckin' foreign embassy protocol."

"What does it mean for Gunter?" asked Ben.

"It means he stops fuckin' procrastinating and he goes and makes his report tomorrow. I should have made him do it on Friday but he said he had to work and then Saturday he had a party. Fuckin' waited too long." Vinnie bleated further obscenities.

Ben moved under the bed sheet and held it high for Vinnie to slide in. "No anger allowed here, you got that?" said Ben.

"Yes sir," answered Vinnie, ready to enjoy Ben's strong arms crushing him and the ensuing contentment after vigorous sex.

* * *

The following morning, Vinnie and Gunter passed through the metal detectors at the 26th Precinct with no problems, except the officer on duty felt it necessary to wand Gunter as well. Vinnie thought this was because the man imagined the only way anyone could be as big as Gunter was by concealing a rocket launcher under his coat. While in the line waiting to speak to the desk receptionist they sipped coffee from Styrofoam cups.

"Now remember, just the basics, no details. Don't embellish but don't hold back either," said Vinnie.

"Yes, how can I help you?" said a rather cheerful policeman sitting in a cage behind bulletproof glass.

"It's about the request for information on the Columbia student. It was on TV last night," said Gunter in a barely audible voice.

Vinnie stepped around and nudged Gunter without budging him, so he spoke himself, loudly from the side. "I saw the news last night and my friend thinks he may have seen the man pictured on the screen, only he missed the news program."

"So how do you know he saw the same man? Did you?"

"Uh... no, but he told me about it."

The cop directed Vinnie and Gunter to seats and told them to wait for someone to take the report. They sat there for five minutes with Vinnie grumbling and Gunter bent over and head almost touching his knees.

"Are you the gentleman here to report information about the student?" An African-American cop an inch taller than Gunter glared with his chin protruding as he spoke.

Vinnie answered for Gunter and they followed the policeman to his metal desk, jammed against a windowless wall in a room full of similar desks regimented three across and in two rows. The tall cop looked like he was sitting at a kindergarten desk. Gunter took the single guest chair and Vinnie stood behind him.

The cop questioned Gunter. The interview focused more on Gunter than what he may have witnessed. At least eight or nine questions were about Gunter by Vinnie's count, but he had lost the exact tally around five.

Vinnie rubbed his thighs as the cop asked how long Gunter had been at his current address and details about any previous address.

"Just the one. I was born at the Presbyterian Hospital near us and lived all my life where I'm at now," said Gunter, turning to Vinnie.

"Should he tell you about what he saw," asked Vinnie, "or would you like to know about the night he was conceived?"

The cop gave Vinnie a mean look, his voice meaner still. "This is as much a pain in the ass for me as it is for you. It's called procedure. The sooner I tick off the boxes, the sooner you'll be out of here."

After asking a few more questions on Gunter's background from the interview sheet, the cop finally turned his attention to the incident.

Gunter relayed his story—the stroll in Sakura Park, the man on the ground, the two men carting him away. "That's all I know," he concluded.

"So you didn't actually see the guy on the ground or get a look at the men picking him up?"

"No."

"And you didn't call 911 or anyone when you saw this happening?"

"No."

"And you said nothing to the two men?"

"No."

The cop put down his pen. "Let me get this straight. You saw a guy on the path, two men picked him up, and one may or may not have had a knife. You didn't see any faces, and you said and did nothing. Is that about it?"

"Yes."

Vinnie leaned forward. "And the guy on the path was wearing a Columbia University sweatshirt."

The cop looked at Vinnie as if he were a talking toad.

"Okay. I've got your report and I'll pass it along to the investigating officers. We have your details should we need to follow up. Thank you, Mr. Hoffman, for coming down today and doing *your duty as a citizen*." The officer emphasized his last words as if teaching a civic class.

"Fuckin' waste of time," said Vinnie, walking out of the precinct to the waiting cab. "Unless you solve their case for them they don't give a fuckin' rat's ass."

During the ride back, Gunter wondered if he should have mentioned that the guys looked at him or the knife-waving. Vinnie assured him it was irrelevant and repeated his line, "Never volunteer." Gunter nodded then asked if he had time to work out before meeting with Rita at the BIG office.

"Yeah, why not? Nothing urgent going on. We'll get Rita up to speed on what's happening, which is fuckin' nothing. Should take all of two minutes. Go ahead, have fun getting a hernia." Vinnie continued to grumble about time-wasting cops for the entire cab ride until they entered the UltraFit building.

12

Blanca held out a small piece of paper across Vinnie's desk.

"What's this?" he asked.

"Notes from my talk with my cop informant," answered Blanca, her hand extending a little further over the desk.

Taking the Post-it note he turned it over. "That's it? The victim was a Columbia student. We already know this from the news."

"Grad student," corrected Blanca, pointing at the first word on the Post-it note, her head swiveling slightly side to side.

"And what am I supposed to do with this fuc... fudging information? You know how many grad students there are at Columbia?"

"A little over four thousand," said Blanca, holding up her middle finger. "You want me to break that down by major, *pendejo*?" She smacked her rear end to emphasize the meaning of her insult as she walked out of his office.

"Thanks. Thanks a lot! You're a big help," yelled Vinnie. He leaned back in his swivel chair, shook his head, and then walked out, passing Blanca's desk in the outer office, and muttered something sounding like *culo* followed with, "I'll be at Columbia interviewing four thousand grad students. Don't wait up." The slamming front door shook the glass, giving a shimmy to the gold-leaf BIG letters.

Vinnie rode the No. 1A subway to the Broadway stop at 116th Street. He knew Gunter and Helene's apartment was nearby on the university grounds. He walked briskly to the main campus but was stymied by what he should do next. He expected information about the murdered student would be plastered on boards around the campus but he saw nothing. If only the cops had released the student's name. He scanned a few placards around the courtyard and notices stapled to trees but saw nothing relevant. He thought of his student days and knew the real buzz was at the student union.

Luck was on Vinnie's side. Arriving at the building, he saw a small notice about a prayer vigil by the Campus Ministry for the deceased chemistry graduate student, Tariq Mamurov. The notice didn't mention murder. The service would be multi-denominational, led by the imam at a local mosque and a member of the Columbia chaplaincy.

The religious service didn't interest Vinnie, but learning Tariq was a chemistry student determined his next destination. Checking the campus map, Vinnie walked down the quad, flanked by Gothic buildings suggesting that Socrates lectured here. He entered Havemeyer Hall's imposing central portico.

Students flooded the hallway, some scurrying past him, others strolling. He instantly identified this cohort of yapping people as undergraduates and therefore of no interest. A gaggle stood before the elevator so Vinnie climbed the staircase to the second floor. He opened the large steel door and looked down the hallway to see students with laptops and notebooks enter classrooms. Nope. On the fourth floor he spotted a man in a white lab coat entering a room at the end of the hallway.

Vinnie walked along the corridor, peering into the door windows on his left and right. Each room was outfitted with lab benches and apparatus—wasn't that the word? That's all he could remember from high-school chemistry, as well as his B-plus grade, which wasn't bad for someone planning on a liberal arts degree.

He entered a room with three people in it. A man in a loose-fitting white lab coat stood at a bench with several pieces of glassware filled with liquids and didn't look up. Two women in white coats in the back of the room headed toward him. He assumed all were grad students by their youthful appearances. The man wore goggles, making him hard to identify. One of the woman appeared to be of Asian origin. The other woman's distinguishing characteristics were her height and cropped red hair. Goggle man was swirling liquid in a glass flask with gloved hands.

"Hey, you mind if I ask you a few questions?" said Vinnie cheerily and head slightly bowed.

"Uh, who are you? You shouldn't be in here," said the redhead, who was looking down on Vinnie's five-foot-eight-inches.

"I'm here about Tariq."

The Asian woman emitted a small squeal and put her hand to her mouth.

"What about Tariq?" asked the redhead.

"We're following up on the events leading to his murder. My name is Vinnie Briggs and I'm with a private investigating firm that's working on a police report."

"So why not send a cop?" asked goggle man, removing them and his gloves. He was Vinnie's height with brown eyes and a pleasant face.

"You know how it looks when uniforms show up on campus. And the university likes to keep things low-key. I'm sure you understand." Vinnie paused, not getting any response. "And frankly, city-wide budget cuts have resulted in understaffing within the NYPD." He liked this addition because it sounded like it might even be true. With the three grad students nodding, Vinnie felt satisfied with his excuse's plausibility and made a mental note to use it again.

"So," said Vinnie, closing the door and walking further into the room, "can you tell me a little about Tariq? What was he like? Who were his friends? Where did he hang out? That kind of thing."

The students looked at each other. The tall redhead continued in her role as group spokesperson.

"Tariq was a good-hearted person but stayed pretty much to himself. We're all devastated by his murder."

The other two nodded their heads.

"And his friends?" asked Vinnie.

"Like I said," the redhead continued, "he pretty much kept to himself. He had a group from mosque and one or two—"

The Asian woman interrupted, "Artur from Uzbekistan... er... what's his name?"

"Nuri," said the man, finishing the sentence, then added,

"you know, the guy defending his thesis at the end of this term. He's from Turkey."

"Oh yeah," she answered. "I don't know him, but you've been here a year longer than me."

The lab group seemed to forget Vinnie as they talked about who was defending their theses at the end of the semester.

Vinnie interrupted the banter. "Did he socialize, go to parties, hang out at a local club?"

The students gave a collective shrug.

"He'd stay for the socials after the weekly seminars on Thursday afternoons. The Department serves coffee, tea, water, juice, and snacks," said the Asian woman, who had a provincial accent, which Vinnie, as a born and bred New Yorker, placed in the Midwest somewhere but couldn't specify the state.

"And he always came to the department holiday party," added the man. "And he was smart, too. His questions during seminars and in class were not just to impress the professor, like some people around here. There are many show-offs, but not Tariq."

The two women also praised Tariq's intelligence.

Vinnie thought the group struggled to show they knew Tariq with impersonal praise like the kind given at a memorial service. And all were cautious not to speak ill of the dead. Would they have said the same if he were alive?

"One last thing. Did Tariq date anyone? A girlfriend?" Vinnie wanted to add boyfriend but didn't think this was the time to show gay solidarity. And it was quite likely that foreign students would be reluctant to broadcast their sexual orientation to all and sundry.

None thought Tariq dated, or at least not that they knew. Vinnie was leaning toward Tariq having a homosexual relationship. It explained Tariq's late-night Sakura Park stroll. Vinnie had his own experiences of evening strolls. Did Gunter ever see men in the park at night?

He asked about Artur and Nuri. Artur was an organic chemist, which placed his lab at the back of the building, whereas this was an inorganic lab. As for Nuri, he was writing his thesis and that meant he was in the library or his office two flights down, also in the back of the building.

Vinnie decided to stay on the same floor and look for Artur first. He found him in an identical white lab coat to the one worn by the three inorganic students. He repeated his introductory spiel and was unsurprised the brilliant chemistry students didn't see through his hand-waving, low-profile bullshit. In Vinnie's college experience with science majors, they thought people behaved like the laws of physics and obeyed Einstein's dictum that God doesn't play dice.

"So, Artur—may I call you Artur?" Vinnie waited and received the nod to go ahead. "Good. Now, Artur, I'm trying to understand more about Tariq." He repeated the questions he asked the other students, receiving the same reply. He added a question: was Tariq a devout Muslim?

Artur gave a bubbly laugh. "You don't get to be top of your class in chemistry hanging out at the mosque. But he prayed and observed Ramadan, sure."

"Sports?" asked Vinnie, another question omitted from the talk with the others.

After a few seconds, Artur answered. "Wrestling and

boxing. Any of the martial arts. Not the fake TV shows but the Olympic stuff—judo, karate, tae kwon do, that sort of thing."

Vinnie's eyebrows raised. *Did Tariq enjoy more than the matches? Maybe the tight suits? Bodybuilders wore skimpy thongs, posers. A turn-on for many gay men.*

Artur's voice broke into Vinnie's thoughts. "He once went to New Jersey to see a competition. He came back non-stop gloating over it. I think the guy had been on the Tajikistan Olympic team and won a medal or something."

"Do you remember when or who this was?"

"No, just that Tariq was excited. Eight or nine months ago or sometime in the first semester last year." Artur's voice seemed to lower. "He has, I mean had, wall posters in his room of famous Tajikistan wrestlers and boxers. Might have been one of them. Martial arts is a big deal over there. In my country too, but we're more into bodybuilders, like most former Ottoman Empire countries. Bet you didn't know that?"

You'd lose the bet, thought Vinnie but shook his head no. He made a note about Tariq's fascination with Olympians, then underlined it and added several question marks.

Luck again was with Vinnie as Nuri was in his office and not the library. Before he was halfway through his explanation for the interview he knew it was a waste of his time. Nuri typed on his computer and didn't look up. After a few more questions, Vinnie stopped. He'd been right from the minute he entered the room—a time waster.

Vinnie was out of his depths on the Muslim religion, philosophy, and law. He wondered if Gunter was too embarrassed to say he met Tariq for a romp in the park. But how was it possible for Rita or Ben not to know Gunter was gay? Vinnie smiled. Stupid question. Even his own husband Ben had married his high-school girlfriend, had a son, and didn't accept his homosexuality until their untimely death. Of course Gunter would deny being gay, and the night park walks were a ruse. But that didn't make him a murderer. He had picked the wrong night and wrong person for a tryst. Vinnie knew the cops would see it differently.

Tariq's thesis advisor's secretary informed Vinnie he was unavailable to interview as he was on a half-year sabbatical in California. He would return for the memorial service and she could arrange a meeting then if Vinnie wanted, but implied the timing was not good. Vinnie agreed, mostly because he knew the professor would be the last person Tariq would have confided in about anything personal, especially his sexual proclivity.

Vinnie rode the subway home, confident in his hypothesis that Tariq's late-night visit to Sakura Park was a gay hook-up, but probably not with Gunter. He speculated about the reasons for his murder without reaching a conclusion except he was sure Gunter had nothing to do with it. Eventually the cops would reach the same conclusion.

Eventually.

13

A week after Gunter made his police report, an interview took place in a broom-sized NYPD room at the Stuyvesant Town precinct. Detective Jake Kaplan recognized Sue Finchley's smoker's anxiety, hearing her fingers crinkle the cellophane of a cigarette packet in her handbag.

Kaplan, a tall, thin, brown-eyed detective around forty, placed a Diet Pepsi and a straw on the table. As a former smoker, he knew the carbonated beverage wouldn't satisfy the woman's craving or stem her anxiety but it might distract her. He heard the barely audible thanks behind the taut smile. An older, slightly taller detective with an obvious broken nose sat next to him. Gristle-faced Detective Bob Daven had a full head of dark hair and his paunch pressed against the metal table.

"Just give us your account as best as you can recall," said Detective Kaplan behind a slack, cheery grin, hands clasped and wrists resting on the table's edge.

"I thought you heard this from my roommates?" Sue said, placing the straw to her lips. She paused, sipping the soda.

Detective Daven placed his beefy forearms on the table

and pursed his lips. "Look, Ms. Finchley—"

"Lauder. I go by my stage name," she said, pausing for a sip. "It's a good publicity name. Simple and easy to remember."

With eyes near crossed, Detective Daven's words discharged like an '84 Chevy in need of a lube job. "For the record, we prefer to use your real name, not some fuc... alias. This is not an audition. Your friend was murdered so we would appreciate your cooperation."

The detectives watched Sue withdraw the straw from her lips and turn the can as if examining it for defects.

"Like I told you from the start, we weren't, like, really close."

Kaplan tapped Daven's tense shoulder and he removed his forearms from the table, folding them across his chest.

"But you were with her recently, is that correct?" asked Detective Kaplan.

"Yeah, like sure. At an audition and her party last week."

"Let's begin with the party," Kaplan said with his grin unchanged.

Sue laced her recall with "you know," "like," and "whatever." Guided by Detective Kaplan, she moved her narrative to the detectives' central interest, Katia's guest—Gunter Hoffman. She described him as a humongous gorilla, then sneered about the gorilla leaving after only an hour, pretending "us partygoers, like, offended him or something." Sue fidgeted, before adding, "Like we flexed to show him how stupid it looked. Like a Macy's parade balloon. That's when he got really upset. We were doing the *Name Game*, you know, like that 60s song where you rhyme with the first letter of a word." Sue sang in a low voice, "Shirley Shirley bo burley." She smiled. "The gorilla couldn't take a little joking. Even Katia added a verse to rhyme with balloon and he, like, gets all insulted for, like, no real reason."

Detective Daven interrupted. "By 'partygoers' you mean yourself and your two roommates, Lester Woods and Eric Brinkmann? Anyone else?"

Jake nodded for Bob to continue. The goal was corroboration, not confrontation. So far Sue's account matched Lester's and Eric's with only small, unimportant discrepancies.

"Yeah, that's right—me, Les, and Eric," her face snarled, "and that fucking bodybuilder." She paused. "I, like, told Katia to fucking forget him. That's what I actually said but Katia ran after him anyway when he walked out. She is... I mean was a real softy about feelings. Like, she never would have made it in the theater. You need a tough skin for this business."

Detective Kaplan wrote something in his pad, nodding for Sue to continue. Her story meandered until she mentioned Katia returned to the party upset after chasing Gunter outside.

"That guy probably did something to her. She came back with a real fucking attitude."

"In what way?" asked Detective Kaplan, losing his cheery grin.

"Well, like, her eyes were red. Like she'd been crying. And, you know, she had dirt on her knees, even had a bit of blood, like she'd been pushed over. I don't know. She just seemed like she'd been hit or something?"

Sue's description wandered off down a philosophical path that was less concerned with the factual events. She started to talk about the weed and alcohol consumption, which Detective Kaplan put a stop to. He knew this information diminished credibility should it be raised in court. And the defense would learn this from the CSI evidence, so there was no need to highlight it in Sue's official statement.

She went on to describe Katia's return to the party and Eric and Les, shirtless, imitating the gorilla Gunter's flexing routine. "Real hilarious, like, I mean they had his moves down perfect, you know?" She added that Eric bounced on the couch cushions shaking his legs and arms above his head just like that big goon. "Katia insulted Eric. Said he couldn't lift a paper plate and looked nothing like Gunter. Like, yeah. Who'd want to? He's so gross."

Kaplan scribbled on his pad and pushed it to his partner. *Scrawny thin!!! Couldn't break a matzo.*

Detective Daven nodded, almost cracking a smile.

Sue held her Diet Pepsi, words rolling out between sips.

"And what else?" asked Detective Kaplan, waiting for Sue to take another drink.

She seemed less anxious to Detective Kaplan, as if being center stage gave her confidence.

"Eric's..." sip sip "...good-looking..." sip sip "...and the gorilla's ugly as sin." She finished by pulling the straw from her lips. "I called him Bulldog because of his work but, like, he really looks like one."

The upshot of her story was that Les lay on the floor and Katia rested her foot on his chest.

"She was, like... well, told Les he was an emaciated

little boy. Other stuff too, you know, like his ribcage was no wider than his waist." Sue stopped, the corner of her lips upturned into a smile as she added, "Well, I'll give her that... about him being slim. Makes his clothes fit good. And he's more handsome than Eric, who's no slouch in the good looks department. Well, like, I already told you that."

Kaplan and Daven looked at each other, recognizing their mutual frustration that the interview had gone off-track. Kaplan tried to steer Sue back to Gunter and Katia's emotional state but knew she misunderstood with her next diatribe.

"That's when all hell broke loose. I mean, Katia cleaned while we partied. And she just went on and on complaining about how badly we treated that goon. Said we were the reason he was mad at her. Yeah, right. Like she didn't enjoy his little show."

Sue stopped, clicked her tongue, and a finger twirled her hair.

"She had it bad for him, but he walked away. It, like, really upset her too."

"Gunter and Katia were close?" asked Detective Daven, arms crossed.

"Well, you could tell she had the hots for him," Sue said with a piercing laugh, "and, like, texted him a bunch while we were still partying. Like she really needed the ugly muscle-bound freak."

Detective Kaplan's head tilted.

The two detectives faced each other, communicated with their eyes, and asked Sue if she had used Katia's cell.

"Uh, no, I have my own phone," said Sue, huffing.

"Then how did you know she texted Gunter?" asked Detective Kaplan.

"Well, of course I knew," said Sue, jumping on the question, "I mean, like, I saw her with her cell. Who else was she going to text? Pathetic really." Sue blinked and puffed out her bakery bun cheeks.

CSI had retrieved Katia's cell data. The detectives knew about the texts, confirming Sue's observation. More important, the texts showed Katia's state of mind and her sense of fear.

Kaplan shoved a CSI sheet to his partner, tapping on Katia's last and most incriminating:

11:45 p.m. TEXT: Are you going to hurt me for wh#

The hashtag ending made no sense and was not in her other messages so it wasn't a byline or signoff. It was more likely she had deleted texts and used the hashtag to save her thoughts, explained the CSI tech to the detectives.

Sue continued without prompting. She recalled telling Katia that she could do better than Gunter.

The two men nodded and Sue followed up with, "And I was right, too. Like, look at what it got her."

Detective Kaplan's eyebrow raised to the ceiling, thinking *this is a friend's accusation.* He scribbled on his notepad *plausible?*, then showed it to his partner.

"I think she, like, wanted to fuck a bodybuilder for the experience," said Sue, giggling, "because she might use it in her method acting or whatever. I don't use that stuff. Nobody does anymore."

"Anything else you can tell us, Ms. Finchley?" asked Detective Daven, his hand raking his brow, which Jake recognized as his partner's way to indicate he had had enough.

But Sue didn't know Detective Daven's body language, so whe continued. "Well, like, he was an angry dude," her words rolling, "I mean, we were lucky he didn't do anything to us. We couldn't have stopped him, not even all of us together. The guy's humongous and angry, like an animal in heat. I tell you, we were fucking lucky." She stopped. "Well, I guess not Katia so much."

The rest of her account followed the one given by Les and Eric. They had fallen asleep on Katia's apartment floor from too much booze and weed—and this detail was again omitted from Kaplan's notes.

Sue's next words had the detectives sit bolt upright, as neither of her roommates mentioned it. "She dumped water on us. Drenched us all."

Ah, thought Detective Kaplan, *that's why neither of the men mentioned it. Too embarrassed.*

"She demanded we leave," continued Sue, "and it wasn't even midnight. I tell you, she'd have given Gunter a good screw if he likes it rough." She placed the heel of her hands over her eyebrows. "You know, he stormed out and it looked like he wanted to punch Katia." She looked Detective Kaplan in the eye, her lips pulled together as she asked, "Was she raped?"

Kaplan stared and Sue gasped an apology for asking and said to forget she had done so. She didn't want to know or even think about it.

Detective Kaplan held open the interview room door, thanking Ms. Finchley for her help with the investigation. She turned to the detectives as they escorted her out of the security double doors to the general precinct area, "You know, Katia said if Gunter returned he'd beat the shit out of us. She said he was so angry he was shaking when she caught up with him on the street. Do you think he came back after Katia kicked us out? Like, maybe he didn't find us so took it out on her? I hope you fuck him over for what he did."

After closing the security doors, Detective Kaplan said to his partner, "That's the first time we've heard Sue Finchley or Lauder or whatever the fuck her name is show she cared a wee bit about her friend."

Daven spat into his coffee cup, giving his opinion of Sue Lauder.

Gunter was their next interviewee. They strategized on the interview's purpose—determine if he had an emotional attachment to Katia. Enough to murder her? They needed to decide if he appeared unstable, as seemed likely from all accounts. Would he be physically capable of breaking her neck? If so, then why the knife?

14

The entire downtown cab ride to the Stuyvesant Town 13th police precinct was one long grumble. "I guess officer not-my-case got off his ass," said Vinnie, referring to the duty officer Gunter spoke to the week before. "Finally passed his bullshit notes to real detectives."

The change of precinct seemed odd to Vinnie, but then again most police procedures were Alice adventures to him. He told Rita and Ben that this was probably an internal turf dispute.

He and Gunter arrived just before noon. Sirens penetrated the station walls, adding to the cacophony of the disgruntled mob waiting at only one functioning metal detector.

"A fuckin' zoo. Best to come early before the goons, crooks, and sleazebag lawyers arrive," said Vinnie as they inched forward.

Gunter spoke to a policewoman in a caged reception desk, similar to the uptown precinct if slightly less reinforced. Wives, husbands, girlfriends, boyfriends, children holding their grandmothers' hands, drunks, junkies, and derelicts sat on metal seats attached to the wall. Uniformed police trooped past in Brownian motion. An occasional buzzing unlocked double doors next to the caged desk permitting cops and civilians through. Gunter took a seat that Vinnie held for him.

Vinnie reminded Gunter how to answer possible questions. To stress he didn't listen to TV or radio news. And above all, avoid answering open-ended questions with the "Dunno defense" or "Don't remember" even if it seemed insignificant. No response is better than correcting something later was Vinnie's rule. Be vague was another axiom. Vinnie believed his advice to be pure gold and sure to beat the system. A single, unguarded statement would make Gunter a person of interest. By the time Vinnie finished he noticed Gunter chewing his lips and rubbing his bicep.

"Too much? I'll keep quiet."

"No. It's okay. I'm just thinking about the party I went to last weekend," said Gunter as he released his arm and sat back in his chair.

"Oh?"

"Nothing. Wasn't that good."

Vinnie waited, sure there was more but Gunter wasn't saying. *Keep my nose out, it has nothing to do with me.*

The lobby's humming grew louder. People asked at the front cage for accident report forms or procedural instructions or complained. An elderly man sat down next to Vinnie.

Gunter stopped picking his finger and looked up at Vinnie's outburst. "Fuckin' twenty minutes. We could be another two hours." His voice was angry as he pointed to the station wall clock. "Inconsiderate SOBs. Fuckin' inefficient, incompetent bozos."

The man next to him overheard and spoke loudly, "I come down as a favor and they make me sit and fucking wait."

"Yeah, fuckin' tell me about it," said Vinnie, vigorously nodding in solidarity with the old guy.

Both double doors next to the front desk cage opened wide, exposing the bright fluorescent lights illuminating a long hallway. Two detectives appeared and one called Gunter's name.

Vinnie rose with Gunter but the heavier, older detective blocked him. "Just Mr. Hoffman, unless you're his attorney."

Vinnie patted Gunter's shoulder. "Hey, don't worry, you'll do fine."

The detectives sandwiched Gunter between them as they walked to a small, dingy, sparsely furnished room. "Take a seat at the table, Mr. Hoffman," said the younger, trimmer detective, pointing to a chair recently occupied by Sue Finchley, aka Lauder. "We appreciate your coming down. This won't take long. A few routine questions to help us with our investigations and you'll be on your way."

Gunter thought the man speaking had introduced himself as Detective Kaplan. He couldn't remember the name of the other.

The unnamed detective spoke with a forced, raspy voice. "You're a bodybuilder, right, Mr. Hoffman? Can I call you Gunter?"

Gunter nodded yes.

"Well, Gunter," said the detective, who continued to rasp his words, "it shows. I mean, look at those arms. How big are you?"

"Round three thirty now but I'm three ten for a contest. I don't do many contests."

"Geez, you hear that, Jake?"

"Yeah, Bob, I heard."

The detectives placed business cards on the table. Gunter pushed the top card imprinted with Detective Jacob "Jake" Kaplan's name to the side. He picked up the second and smiled. Detective Robert "Bob" Daven. That was it, Bob Daven, the name he forgot.

"Something funny about your age? I asked, How old are you? Care to answer?" said Detective Daven, his rasping louder.

Gunter looked up. He'd stopped listening. "Twenty-six."

The detective whistled. "Pretty impressive size for your age."

Detective Kaplan leaned forward to take over from his partner.

"How rude of us. Can we get you something to drink? Coffee, tea, a Coke, water?"

"No... uh, thanks."

"Okay, Gunter," said Detective Kaplan, continuing in a soft, flat monotone, "we are investigating a young woman's death. As far as we know, you and three friends were the last to be with her. She goes by the name Katia Tittle, her stage name, but maybe you knew her by her real name, Karen Probinowski."

Gunter stared expressionless, his blood circulation stopped, his brain not comprehending the words he had heard. *Dead? Who?*

Detective Kaplan continued. Gunter did not respond with either words or facial reaction.

A louder voice broke into Gunter's frozen mind. Detective Daven's litany pelleted Gunter, connecting him with Katia. His cell number on her phone. Calls between them. Multiple texts from her to him. Her voice message to him around two in the morning, which was the estimated time of her murder. And Katia's friends identified him as being at her party.

Gunter heard but did not listen. Detective Daven's verbiage seemed inconsequential. He partially heard what the others at the party had reported. They called him an angry person and a big, strong giant.

"I have to say, Gunter," grinned Detective Daven, "they got the part about you being big correct." Daven made a size joke before asking, "So, Gunter, are you an angry person?"

Not missing a beat, Detective Kaplan moved forward as Detective Daven leaned back and asked, "We heard you left the party pretty upset. Can you tell us about it?"

"Dead... Katia? You sure it's her?" Gunter searched the table top for answers.

"I am afraid it's true," said Detective Kaplan and added in a softer voice while tapping a finger on the table, "her parents identified her."

Gunter's eyes goggled on Kaplan's tapping finger.

"And we wanted to know if you were upset at the party? Did Katia upset you, Gunter?" asked Kaplan, no longer waiting for responses.

"Well, were you?" asked Detective Daven, snapping out his question.

Gunter remained silent.

"We'd like an answer sometime before the year ends," cracked Daven.

"Yeah," answered Gunter.

"Yeah what?" asked Daven, his face changing color.

"I didn't feel like staying. It wasn't fun."

Detective Daven pushed a folder across the table to his partner, who opened it as if he'd not seen the contents before. After a pretend read, Kaplan listed mood-altering chemicals bodybuilders use that induce irrational anger. His mixed commentary and heart-to-heart counsel unfolded without a single question. Gunter remained silent, not so much applying Vinnie's advice to volunteer nothing but because he couldn't even if he had wanted to.

Detective Daven tapped his partner's back. "Let me, Jake. This is bullshit," and he leaned forward, resting his forearms on the table. He snapped at Gunter, "Were you born stupid or have drugs rotted you mind? Multiple choice, A or B? Can your simple mind answer that?"

Gunter's index finger swept imaginary dust off the table.

"Listen up, moron, did Katia's rejection make you angry?"

Gunter stayed quiet.

"Could you respond before I retire?" asked Daven, his voice shrill.

"Yes," came Gunter's whisper with a barely visible head nod.

"Where were you in the early morning after the party, between one o'clock and four o'clock?" asked Daven with a piercing voice. After a few seconds he slapped the table and yelled, "Answer the fucking question!"

Gunter froze. The ambush of yelling, table thumping, and blithe accusations had derailed his already fragile thought process. Gunter sensed the specter of Detour Man pointing a sign at him. Detective Daven had walked behind Gunter's chair, leaning to speak into his ear as he bent forward, eyes closed, and hands over his face.

Daven's accusations, threats, and warnings forced Gunter to retreat into himself. He hands tightened over his face. He stopped talking and wanted to stop breathing. He felt small, overwhelmed by the two big cops yelling. He shut down.

* * *

When the double doors opened a slumped Gunter shuffled out. Vinnie rushed over to him.

"What fuckin' happened? You were over an hour and a half for a routine eyewitness report!" said Vinnie, volleying questions while pacing himself to keep up with Gunter who remained silent as he marched out of the precinct.

Gunter arrived home three hours after he had left. He paced the empty apartment, sat on the floor, then recommenced wandering. He wanted to halt time, to erase the detectives' words, to believe he had never heard of Katia's murder. *Don't believe it and it won't be true,* he told himself. He tried this when his father died. He didn't try hard enough or it would have worked. He'd try harder this time.

Gunter brooded, thinking about his decision to forget Katia before the downtown precinct interview changed his mind. He had planned to see her after the interview since he'd be in her neighborhood. She had not answered his calls. Her full voicemail prevented him from leaving a message. He had texted too but received no response after three attempts. He had no choice but to show up unannounced after his interview. If she wasn't home he had resolved to wait on her doorstep; even it meant skipping his training session. He wanted to explain why he had ignored her. Explain how much she had hurt him by exposing his dysmorphia. Sue and her roommates had ignited his fear of bullies. He wanted to explain that calling him a *thing* made it worse.

With head lowered, he stared at his intertwined fingers as swarms of thoughts of innocence and guilt marched past. His brooding became a cheap, stinking melancholy. He had kidded himself, believing a friendship with Katia was possible. She had left messages but so what? She never said she liked him, not really. She just wanted forgiveness for her rude behavior. A friendship probably would not have happened. And her murder made that a certainty.

He thought about the party. A total disaster, not just the outcome but for his mental state. Katia's sweetness and caring voice in his message mailbox. He had a chance with her and blew it. And now she's dead. *I'm a loser.*

He picked his right thumb's fingernail with his left's index finger. Fingernails cut close to the quick for weightlifting. Stupid not to have texted her or returned her calls. If only... she sounded truly sorry. She promised not to humiliate him again. She wasn't like Sue and the men and they were not really her friends.

But I didn't call her back and now she's dead. It's my fault.

He would wish hard for it to be a dream. But he had learned that death has no do-overs.

Gunter sat on his bedroom floor mat, crying for Katia's last moments on her knees begging him. He cried inconsolable tears of sorrow. Anger abated his sorrow, the flow of tears replaced with his knocking his forehead with closed fists.

15

A lion's snarl could not have been more menacing than Blanca's face as she roared at Vinnie. "You left him? Are you loco? You have no idea what he'll do! Get to his house now!" Blanca shoved him out the door.

Vinnie knew she was right. He should have stayed with Gunter but he couldn't bear watching him agonize. He was afraid his own emotions might mix with Gunter's. He had heard the shame and disgrace in the cab ride from the police interview. He also had heard Gunter talk about storming out of the party and Katia's pleas for forgiveness. But he didn't know the half of what triggered Gunter to feel so ashamed that he decided to leave. Or why he felt disgraced.

"It's my fault," began Gunter's explanation to Vinnie, who had arrived less than half an hour after Blanca kicked him out of his own office. "She upset me. And tricked me too. It wasn't a real party. Then everyone made fun of me. But it's my fault."

Vinnie didn't get it. He quizzed Gunter as hard as the cops, too hard, and Gunter shut down. Vinnie took a break then returned, more conciliatory. Gunter seemed calmer, so Vinnie began again. This time he heard about the bodybuilding exhibition, which he found unbelievable. His voice rose with arms swinging, causing Gunter to flinch.

"Why did you do it?" asked Vinnie, taking deep breaths to slow his speech. "Ben never shows off at parties." A pause as Gunter nodded his assent. "Well, sometimes he might among friends, for a little fun and stuff, but otherwise it's just unprofessional."

Gunter walked around the living room shaking his head harder. "She asked me to."

"That's it? She asked. Are you fu—" said Vinnie, his voice loud again. He stopped with Gunter walking out of the room. Vinnie followed. Gunter was perched on the weight bench in his bedroom.

The sting of that night was as if it had just happened. Katia's murder intensified that sting. "You're upset and for good reason," said Vinnie.

Gunter was stuck in time. He couldn't get an apology from a dead person or give one back.

"Those little men teased me," he said, touching his arm, "and made me feel weak." His hand glided over his massive bicep. "I thought I was going to cry in front of everyone."

"You mean Katia, right?"

Gunter fingered his cell phone. "She called and texted. Begged for my forgiveness." He fiddled with a sixty-pound dumbbell, his hunched mass reflected in the mirror. "I ignored her."

He probably wished he had answered Katia's call.

"The detectives told me not to leave the city," said Gunter, putting down the weight. "Why would I?" he asked, which Vinnie thought rhetorical so said nothing. Gunter picked up the weight and drew a deep breath, expanding his chest. His next question came on the exhale. "And why ask to hear Katia's voice messages?"

This wasn't rhetorical and Vinnie's face flushed, yelling, "Never, ever volunteer anything to the cops. Got it!?" Vinnie's fists shook as he finished with, "And never let them hear private recordings. You know how Katia will sound to them? I'll tell you. Like she's frightened of you."

Gunter looked up, his face glowering. "I'm not stupid, you know." He shook the dumbbell like a small stick. "I did like you told me," he said angrily. "I only said she called because they already knew. Anything else you'd like to know?"

Yes, thought Vinnie, *but now's not a good time.* Something changed. Gunter wasn't the sensitive guy anymore. *When pushed too far, does he transform into a Mr. Hyde? Did Katia do this? Had she also agitated, pushed too hard? Did the ridicule at the party fuel his testosterone-laden sinews and set off his rage? Did she sense he'd become violent, prepared to crush everyone at the party? Was her apology only to placate the monster? Did the detectives push him hard, a ploy to release the beast?* Vinnie's mind stormed questions.

"You think I'm a stupid muscle-head, don't you?" Gunter asked, racking the dumbbell and picking up a ninety-pounder without strain.

"Stupid? No, never. I'm worried. You'll be arrested, maybe convicted of something you didn't do. Fuckin' trust me on this."

Gunter set the weight on the floor, stood, and looked at the top of Vinnie's head. "What do I do? You tell me."

"A lawyer, that's what you need."

Gunter nearly dropped onto the bench. "I've never needed a lawyer before. I can't afford one. I've done nothing wrong. You're just like Detour Man, accusing and saying things that aren't true."

The transformation astounded Vinnie. Gunter went back to a scared shitless, cornered animal.

"I'd like to be alone," said Gunter, picking up the dumb-bell again. "Please leave." Gunter's sullenness plastered his entire face.

Vinnie patted Gunter's shoulder. "I'm sorry, I didn't mean to upset you. I'm trying to protect you. I'll call when I'm back at the office. Keep your cell on." He stopped, walked in front of Gunter, waited for him to bend over, and hugged him around his neck. "You going to be okay?"

Gunter remained bent at the waist. He didn't look up. *He's hiding his tears,* thought Vinnie.

"Yeah…" Vinnie heard before closing the front door.

On the sidewalk, Vinnie dialed his cell.

"Hiya, Vinnie. How'd it go?" said Rita when she picked up.

"Invite Gunter to dinner at your place. Tonight."

The conversation lasted the time it took Vinnie to hail a cab, and Vinnie didn't mince words for Rita. Gunter was in breakdown mode and needed the kind of comfort only Rita could provide. By the time the phone call ended, Rita knew exactly what was needed yet she was surprised Vinnie had asked. She was ready, all she needed was for Gunter to show up.

16

Rita held her apartment door open, uncertain Gunter would show. He'd been reluctant over the phone but she had pressed hard, using the excuse it was not about his case but just a chance to relax. And she needed company, which wasn't false but not as much as she implied.

Gunter handed her a neat bouquet but didn't move, as if waiting for a signature on a delivery. "You're not allergic, are you?" he asked.

"Uh, no," said Rita, "and thanks." She fanned the flowers under her nose. "Please, come in." She took two small steps back as if demonstrating the proper way to enter a room.

Rita stood on her toes to peck Gunter's cheek. "They're beautiful flowers. Come in and relax. My place is small, but it's rent controlled. The living room's larger than most Manhattan one-bedrooms."

Gunter lumbered into the living room. She thought him rigid. No conviviality, even unfriendly if she was honest.

She knew Gunter's statistics—body dimensions and weight lift maximums—which were more than anyone she had ever known. She knew his workout schedule. His affability to help others in the X-room. Although rarely heard, his short, bursting laughter was pleasant, or so she'd been told. Yet likes, dislikes, and aspirations were a puzzle to her and Ben. Her job was to uncover Gunter's emotional state the night of Katia's murder. Vinnie put it simply: "Find out what makes Gunter fuckin' tick before the police arrest him."

Vinnie's call shocked her more than his directive. She'd apply her skills, which for Gunter would be less her female guile and more her masters in psychology.

She had once tried to get to know Gunter the other way during her "active days" with men. He was the one person who showed no interest, not venturing beyond gym small talk. She'd feel his muscles and muse about their bulk and he thanked her. She tried overt innuendo. "Want to have a special workout session with me sometime, increase your stamina?"

"Okay, but I'm busy most of the next two weeks helping Ben prepare his preshow demo. Can I get back to you?"

He pushed her away emotionally with the ease of swinging fifty-pound kettles. He never approached her, marking him as different from the other X-room men. Rita's trophies weren't all on a shelf. And she knew Gunter knew. He wasn't immune to uncensored locker-room gossip.

Accepting his disinterest, Rita didn't waste her time. Too many fish to fry. And to be honest, the only thing Gunter had going for him physically was his massiveness. Looks-wise, she'd seen pugs with better faces.

They finished the meal in half the time she took to prepare it.

"That was great. Thanks," said Gunter.

She appreciated his manners, one of Gunter's trademarks at UltraFit. For someone his size, he was easily approached among the X-room builders below ground and the general sandpipers prancing around on the upper floors. Although she failed to seduce him, she heard he'd gone on a few dates in the past with "regular" women, but nothing steady. Why he rejected her she never discovered.

They returned to the living room, and she pointed Gunter to a couch facing a TV screen. Rita retrieved the flowers she'd put in a water jug from the dining table and set them on the coffee table. She remarked about her lack of proper vases, repeating the same comment she'd made at dinner. Gunter returned the same weak smile he made the first time she'd mentioned it.

"What would you like to drink? Neither of us is in competition so beer or wine? I have Johnnie Walker that I keep around for my non-athletic friends."

"Water's fine, or a protein drink if you have it."

With a pat on his shoulder, Rita smiled at a man who made a three-seater couch look like a kiddie's chair.

"How about something alcoholic? Help us relax."

"I'm not much of a drinker."

"Then beer it is." Rita never used drink or drugs to seduce a man. She didn't need to. This was to get Gunter talking. He'd shown no interest in her sexually, and clever dialog wouldn't lead to his talking about himself. She'd hoped he would go for the stronger stuff. Beer was going to take longer to get him talking.

Gunter swigged, then smacked his lips.

"Okay?" said Rita, standing in front of him sipping her

own beer.

"Yeah, it's good." Gunter emptied the bottle in the next swallow.

Rita replenished their stock with four more beers. He finished half of his before she'd managed a single swig of her own.

"I'll get my cardio going to the kitchen," she said with a chuckle. Gunter made no sound but continued swigging.

With a nudge, she signaled Gunter to slide across, giving her a small space next to him. Rita settled, tucking her legs underneath her bottom. She asked typical ice-breaker questions and he treated each as critical life decisions and answered with one word or short sentences at best. He never volunteered more than he was asked—no thoughts, opinions, or beliefs.

He sidetracked her tougher questions about his goals and aspirations, replying, "I'd like to be a personal trainer at UltraFit" and "Maybe I'll own a gym someday." Rita found herself in a monologue recounting events in her own life. She touched on her college years, yoga, and tae kwon do classes, and her experiences as a woman's pro-bodybuilder. She avoided two topics—her bastard ex-fiancé and her various sexual adventures.

For the most part, Gunter alternated between drinking beer and bottle twirling. Rita was exhausted. She stopped, put down her beer, and gave a barking laugh. *What just happened? I've taken the typical man's role in this conversation—reciting my boring self-aggrandizement bio. If I could get that window to open, I'd dive out to the sidewalk five stories below.*

Gunter belched and both of them giggled.

At least let's see if the beer can make him talk, thought Rita as she returned to questioning Gunter. "When did you first join UltraFit?"

She decided to begin again and go easy with something she knew the answer to so she could test his acuity.

"A few years ago."

Correct but not precise, she thought. "Yes, I remember," said Rita, smiling. "Ben said you heard UltraFit was a good place for bodybuilding. Is that how it happened?"

Another question with a known answer and again the reply was not the point. Gunter grabbed another bottle, snapping the cap as he worked on a reply. After a long swig he parceled a few words, stopped, and emptied the bottle's contents down his gullet.

A kitchen trip brought more beers.

"That's it or I have to run out for more," said Rita, handing Gunter an open bottle. "Go on, finish telling me about your entry into bodybuilding."

Gunter drank his sixth beer without chugging. His chest expanded, he was thinking before huffing his words. "I like being in a gym, hearing the guys talk about their gains. Working out at home is isolating and you can learn more watching others train than reading about it in magazines."

He was engaging in a conversation beyond small talk. Rita was proud of her social skills, beer notwithstanding.

She studied him. His head was an Easter Island Moai block atop a twenty-three-inch column neck buttressed by enormous trapezoids. Handsome he was not. Nothing new there. Yet the bass voice surfacing from a cavernous chest lulled her. The resonating tones overshadowed his words.

Rita was sure if Gunter talked more he would attract women. Had the beer unlocked his geniality? Or was it fear?

He talked of loneliness, his search for a companion. With his peeling lament, the physical bulk and fugly face dissolved. An affectionate, tender, and sympathetic man emerged.

Rita slid down into her seat, head sideways so her ear absorbed the melody rising out of Gunter's concert hall chest. He spoke of his preadolescent years scouring bodybuilding magazines to save himself, the threat unspecified. He praised Ben for all his gains, taking no credit for his own dedicated training.

His sudden loud laugh startled Rita.

"What?"

"Big," he said, then exhaled. "I don't feel it... not really." He paused. "Without Ben, I'd be nothing... he saved me—" Another long inhale. "And my mother too. Without them I wouldn't have survived."

Survived what? Rita didn't get it. Had Gunter been threatened? Mistreated as a teenager?

Her finger brushed his quivering lips. She saw Gunter's rapid blinking. He tensed, his shirt expanding.

"Gunter, can I kiss you?"

"What? Why?"

"Well, because I like you. This is the first time we've been together without a barbell between us." Rita thought about her words and realized she meant it. This was not a forced, patronizing affection. She craved someone. She'd been on a man-binge for months since her breakup with her fiancé. She'd been loose with sex. She liked sex. She couldn't stop without the help of her therapist. And even so, she sized men up constantly, trying to work out if they would satisfy her. But not now. She wanted Gunter for... what exactly? She just did.

With her lips touching his she recognized more than desire in his eyes. She didn't expect this, had not planned it. There was no premonition of latent emotions. Had she sublimated her desire for him all these years? Been discouraged by his standoffishness? Had she been shallow like other women, seen only the unappealing face and missed the beauty within?

He tensed. She moved down, saw his drum-tight skin stretch over sinew. Her desire rose. She knew what she wanted. Her body reacted to the sensuality of his. She waited for him to ask, but he didn't.

"Gunter, do you want to..."

He nodded agreement before she finished her sentence.

Too tall for her to massage him, she slid along his body. She wanted this so much. For her. For him.

With a gymnast's hop, Rita straddled Gunter's lap to look into his crystalline green eyes, the kind that mesmerize. This was the secret—Gunter's face required a close-up view to see the beauty.

Her lips brushed his, heads lolling for the correct angle. Rita's long fingers traced his eyebrows. Not pencil thin, but not the typical steroid-fueled bush. Her tongue lunged past his lips. Yearning frenzied her actions. Lust, yes, but something more than that. She recalled Gunter recounting his tormented adolescence, and she sought to console him... more, to let him know she liked him. His fear created a loner with poor self-image. And a monumental body that intimidated everyone. Only one person didn't know how big he was—Gunter himself.

His machinist's vise embrace imprinted her on his chest, and as much as she didn't want him to release, she couldn't take the pressure. "Ugh... a little too tight," she said.

He loosened his manacle clamp and stood, taking Rita with him, her arms locked around his neck.

She hovered over the coffee table, knocking the makeshift vase, flowers, and water onto the floor. Her legs wrapped around his waist, relying on her barroom bronco-riding experience. She massaged his face and steadied his large head between her hands to align their lips.

Any idea of complying with Vinnie's reminder of "Nothing reckless" was long gone. Rita advanced into "G-B-T-F," her invented acronym for Grasp Bird's Tail Fuck, the re-branding of her chi Peking martial arts into sex positions. Of course, not included in her official UltraFit class, but reserved for "special clients" off the books.

Grasp Bird was a good choice for first-timers like Gunter. She decided he wasn't ready for the explanation—that was for another time. And she didn't want to waste one second of enjoyment. She couldn't ignore her own desire and growing attachment. The feeling she'd forgotten, the one crushed by her ex. And Gunter filled that need. For now at least.

Legs and arms shifted. Clothing was shed. Rita examined Gunter's naked body, his sweat seeping along sculpted sinew. He belonged among muscular Greek deities. She'd give him the devotion he deserved. She put her head between his pectorals and twisted his nipples. Her fingers

126

dinged his testicles. She massaged his citadel thighs and her fingers traced chiseled muscle.

"Gunter, it's time."

Rita kissed his upper body. His aftershave aroma infused her nostrils, neither too sweet nor too musk. Rita embraced the man and his virtue.

On her knees, she saw his tiny testicles—the first evidence of his steroid use. *But a small penis?* she thought. An illusion created by gargantuan legs? No drug side effect that she knew of. Yet his underwhelming genitals did not deter her desire and he made no comment as she held all his jewels in her palm. She knew he didn't care. Bulk was the only size that mattered to Gunter. He'd willingly cut off his cock and balls if he thought it would make him bigger. His priority was clear.

"Gunter, when was the last time you had sex?"

"Dunno," he answered, and she stifled a laugh.

She offered him the answer. "A long time, right?"

He nodded.

For her that meant practically a virgin. She wanted him inside her, no waiting around, which meant no condom. No problem given his answer. Yet this sent a wrong message. He'd think her careless, so she asked him to wait, returning with an appropriate-sized rubber from the bathroom. She unrolled and serviced Gunter's member, then guided him into her.

"Are you sure? I mean if you—" Gunter stopped with Rita's finger over his lips. She assured him there was no risk of the moral police kicking down the door and flashlights shinning into the room. "Just touch me, anywhere you like.

I want you to."

He gently explored her Brazilian-waxed pussy, releasing sensations she'd forgotten, so long had it been since a man took his time.

She called out more alphabet letters, legs spreading to near one-eighty degrees, a position few could match. Her hand tucked his penis inside.

He stood on his toes as if doing calf extensions. Her hands tightly clasped behind his neck. Their hard chests scraped together. She whispered, instructing Gunter to move to the couch, which caused him to slip out of her on the way. The couch proved too small for Gunter to lay flat, so Rita suggested the floor.

On his back, Rita called out another slew of letters. Her toes crawled his torso like a spider working its way to its prey. She repositioned, her head between his feet. Gunter's hoist compressed Rita's pelvis. She wanted this. She wanted it all.

They groaned. Sweat ran down Rita's face. Gunter sat semi-upright. With her yoga flexibility, Rita anchored one foot behind his massive back and scratched his scrotum with the toes of the other. He stood, her head resting on his chest. She slipped further underneath, sliding a finger past his perineum but unable to negotiate his tight gluteus maximus ass. A hard squeeze and he'd break her finger.

"Gunter, relax—open up."

He squatted, lifting Rita with a hand positioned under her buttocks, the other holding the couch for support. She breached his anal cavity to massage his prostate. She held on to his girder triceps as he pushed harder. Her legs cramped, jolting her spine as if she'd touched a one-hundred-and-twenty-volt live wire.

But she didn't care. Desire flamed her lust. No stopping, no momentary halt. She rocked back and forth. They howled throughout their joint spasms. The couch shifted along the floor.

His calloused hands scratched at her back. She knew this changed everything for her and him. Their worlds no longer black and white but bursting with color. If she had a drawing of this moment, she'd pin it to the refrigerator door forever.

"Stay the night, will you?"

"Uh-huh," he agreed, their embrace loving and tender.

After a few minutes, Gunter sat up, his back resting on the sofa, stretching over for his pants to retrieve his cell phone.

"Need to make a quick call home," he said, unaware that thinking about his mother was insensitive with Rita folded in his arms.

He left his mother a message. After ending the call, he sank back down and Rita returned to resting her head on his chest.

"She goes to bed by nine but she'll wake and not find me and worry."

Rita left Gunter to shower and held two whiskey-filled shot glasses as he returned wearing only his briefs. He had a new-car-waxed body glisten.

"Here's to us," she said as Gunter swallowed his in one gulp. Rita retrieved the Johnnie Walker bottle, refilling their glasses. Another gulp and Gunter finished his second, holding the glass to his lips with arm tensed.

"Go on, I know you want to."

And he began his on-stage flexing routine to her applause. She knew how to compliment, and praised individual body parts with each pose. It was her trade as much as his.

"You're massively cut even if not in a contest. I've not seen many men to match your lats and biceps, but those legs... well, the striations are incredible." She paused. "Actually, no one is as good as you." Rita knew this had been Gunter's expectation at Katia's party, the reason she had asked him to come prepared to do his show routine.

He strained so hard puffing out his chest she thought he might break his face, which caused her to giggle, but she added another compliment so he wouldn't misinterpret. His earth-digger jaw and fortress-like body could withstand any onslaught but he'd crumble at the slightest humiliation. Rita was certain she was the first woman to praise his physique in a way that mattered, not feigned for a one-time, sex-only praise and abandoned after it was over. Her job was to buttress his emotional state, but she didn't think of it that way, not after this night. Her desire was sincere and not an assignment.

* * *

In the morning she called Vinnie while Gunter was out of earshot, starting with an overview assessment of Gunter's state of mind and the oddity of his calling home before staying the night.

"He's twenty-six. What man calls his mother to say he's

130

staying out for the night?" asked Vinnie. "Did he enjoy himself?"

Rita didn't answer, didn't need to because she knew Vinnie had anticipated she'd do more than have a dinner conversation—the bastard knew her too well, damn it. But he didn't know the details of what she and Gunter did and she wasn't saying. She did say, "His shyness belies his sharp mind. Don't worry about mental acuity."

"I'm not." Vinnie paused. "But given your new... ahem... relations, it might be good for you to talk to Helene."

Rita was surprised Vinnie hadn't chastised her, as he had in the past when she'd become too involved with male clients. "Why?"

"Because as you're, now, *close* to him, then Helene might open up to you."

"Huh? About what?"

"What Gunter told her the night when he saw the murder in the park. And about his recent mental health. Any changes over the last few weeks. That kind of thing."

The conversation ended just as Gunter finished his hot shower and entered the room in only his briefs, his skin a ruddy golden warmed-toast color. He squinted, tilting his head on hearing Rita's request to meet his mother. Even she thought it sounded absurd, but on a par with his call home to say he was staying out all night. She explained it as part of the BIG investigation and not about them.

"Why? She doesn't know anything," he protested.

Another good point, but she didn't want to reveal all, not yet, so she said it was to help get a better picture of their home life. He stood, his eyes vacant.

"Vinnie's thinks it a good idea," she hastily added, and he nodded, picking up his cell.

"She said come about four, which will give her time to get home and prepare." He returned his phone to his pocket. "Her shift finishes at two and she'll want to make sure the house is tidy for guests. That's her. The house is always spotless."

Rita gave a little chuckle. Gunter was so sweet. Would Helene be after she realized her son's sleepover was with her? She'd find out soon enough.

17

Helene was ready when her Gunter and Rita arrived exactly on time. Gunter wanted to get there early but Rita insisted early was as bad as late. "Nothing worse than finding guests arrive and you're not ready yet."

"We're not guests," chuckled Gunter, gently squeezing Rita's hand.

She returned his squeeze, only harder. "Not you, me."

Gunter dropped Rita's hand as the front door opened. Rita saw Helene's nose wrinkle as her eyes roamed over Rita's casual workout outfit.

She and Gunter sat on the living room couch waiting for Helene to bring a tray with iced tea, biscuits, cakes, and protein bars. Gunter went to his mother and helped her place the tray on the coffee table, then returned to his seat next to Rita. His mother sat in a lounge chair, her eyes following Gunter as he handed a drink to Rita, who thought Helene's smile forced.

"Please, help yourself," said Helene, pointing at the food.

"Thanks," said Rita, wary of the formality, "I'm fine. Unlike Gunter, I don't want to put on weight." Rita knew her chuckle sounded nervous, and she felt tense. She'd never met a date's mother, not even her ex-fiancé's. And why would she?

"Well, you look fit, dear," responded Helene, her smile tight, "which is what you do, isn't it? Weren't you in the New York City combined bodybuilding and fitness show last May? Gunter didn't compete but we went to see Ben." She looked at her son. "Isn't that right?"

Of course it's right, thought Rita.

"Yeah, I remember," said Gunter, his words mumbled while biting into a protein bar. "And Rita took first place. Ben was a hit too—" He stopped to swallow. "The crowd went wild. One of the best performances I've seen. And Rita was fantastic."

"Yes, now I remember. You did those flip-flop tumbles and tai chi stick plunges. That's what they were, right, dear?"

With a tap of Gunter's hand, Rita got his attention. "I can't stay long unfortunately. Shall we talk about your police report?"

"Okay, but there's not much to talk about," he replied.

Rita caught his blinking eyes, seemingly empty and unaware of her presence, unlike Helene, whose gaze prickled.

"Yes, dear, we mustn't keep you from your gym," she said with spread lips and a flush of contempt on her high cheekbones.

Rita stopped tapping Gunter's hand and stifled a reply. She focused. Vinnie had set her a goal: gain Helene's trust so she'd reveal details of Gunter's psyche that only a mother could know. Rita braced to push on.

"Before I go, I'd like to ask Gunter to repeat what happened at Katia's party and Sakura Park." Rita held her breath. "And Helene, please feel free to contribute."

"Like what, dear?"

"Anything you feel is an omission or needs clarification."

Gunter delivered his story in drips and spurts. He'd pause to check his mother's nodding head. Helene corrected him once, reminding him that he said two men in Sakura Park had stared for a minute or two. And the knife-waving, too.

Rita recalled Gunter's report. "Why did you leave that out?" asked Rita.

"The cop didn't ask," said Gunter and he finished his iced tea. "But it doesn't really matter, does it? Vinnie said not to volunteer. Besides, they were too far to recognize me." His glass touched his lips and he spoke to the tea. He repeated that he wasn't asked about the men staring at him. Rita thought she'd check this with Vinnie.

"Okay," said Rita, "that means there's nothing to worry about. Let's put the first report aside." She began to ask about Katia and Gunter's eyes closed.

Helene interrupted Rita. "I believe my son. If he tells me something then it's true. My Gunter's honest and not deceptive, which is one reason he doesn't like to compete. Too much falseness in the fitness and bodybuilding profession. More deceit than truth, wouldn't you agree?"

Rita listened to Helene picking apart her profession. She felt herself losing momentum, unable to focus on the assignment. She made an excuse that she needed to get back to teach her fitness class.

"So nice of you to stop by, dear. Don't worry about

Gunter. I'm sure Vinnie knows what to do. I trust him implicitly." Helene stood and extended her hand. "We don't want to keep you, do we?"

Rita left despondent. There was no chance Helene would encourage Gunter to be her boyfriend. By the time she arrived at UltraFit she was fuming. Her hard scowl drew out her words. "She... fucking... hates... me."

"What?" asked Ben and Vinnie simultaneously. Ben added, "Who?"

"Helene, who else? She thinks I'm a phony."

Rita spat out her words about the talk with Helene.

"That's odd," said Vinnie after hearing Rita's repeating Helene's correction to Gunter's story. "I asked him who saw him in Sakura Park at our first interview and again before he filed his police report. He told me no one. I'll check my notes, but I'm pretty sure he said the two men at the limo didn't look at him, but one did wave a knife. He was vague on that point."

"Helene knew."

"And you didn't pursue it?"

"Pursue it?" asked Rita, agitated, giving her account of Helene's personal insults. "Listen to what I'm saying, the woman doesn't like me. Even Gunter noticed."

"Maybe you misunderstood," said Vinnie. "You know, most mothers are protective of their precious sons, and Helene's a Blackhawk among helicopter mothers."

"Misunderstood!" screamed Rita, moving closer to Vinnie. "Her goodbye was like she was wiping shit off her shoes. That women definitely does not like me."

Ben stepped between Rita and Vinnie, touching her

shoulder. She took a step back. "You know, Vinnie's not wrong. Helene has lots of angst about Gunter's PSD from his father's gruesome death. She's had a lot to say to me about his training, and she's not even in the fitness business."

Rita laughed. "Not the same. She had formed an opinion of me before I walked through the door."

"Yeah," added Vinnie, "because she's afraid if Gunter's with the wrong woman he could go off the rails."

Ben turned to Vinnie and told him to keep his mouth shut. He looked back at Rita. "I think Vinnie means—"

"No," said Rita, interrupting Ben, "I know what he means."

"Hey, c'mon, Rita... I didn't mean you... I meant..." Vinnie said.

Rita burned inside but she didn't reveal her confused emotions. She didn't get why she was so upset. It wasn't like she'd never been insulted. Why did she care what Helene thought of her? Was this about protecting Gunter or wanting him? Why? The sex? She'd had sex plenty of times—great sex, exciting sex—and after each man she moved on the next day. This was different, indefinable... Vinnie's words broke through her reverie.

"Huh?" she asked.

"I said I'll handle Helene, you focus on Gunter."

Rita mouthed her words. Suggested maybe she shouldn't be involved in the case to circumvent any conflict. "Besides you or even better Ben would do a great job. He's known Gunter for years." She didn't reveal another reason. If she were off the case she would have more freedom to explore a relationship with Gunter.

Ben laughed. "And after all that time all I know about Gunter is his lifting limits, weight gains, and if he's gone off his diet. Not one thing about his emotional state. In all the years together, he's never said a word about his personal desires except to become bigger. Zip about friends or books or movies or music he likes."

Vinnie pointed to himself. "And you think he'll open up to me? You got more in one night than the two of us did in years."

They're right. I gave him great sex and admired his development. It was real, not prurient or duplicitous. Gunter knew I meant every word. We were intimate in a way he's never known, she thought.

"Okay, I agree," said Rita with a long exhale.

Vinnie moved the discussion to the next topic, suggesting more background checks on the murdered Tariq Mamurov.

"Why?" asked Rita. "The cops don't care. Didn't ask Gunter about him."

"Maybe not, but Gunter can't be ambushed. Let's do this right."

Rita nodded but kept one conclusion to herself. Vinnie had miscalculated in asking her to meet Helene. It had been a disaster. And if it made Gunter angry that might have repercussions for his emotional state. They'd have to wait and see.

18

The wait wasn't long. Gunter's name appeared on Rita's caller ID just after the TV late news program gong sounded. She answered with a cheery voice. "Hi, Gunter." She waited but with no immediate response she continued, "What's up?"

"I just wanted to talk. See if you're okay."

"Why wouldn't I be?" asked Rita, but she knew the answer.

"Uh... you know, about the way she acted toward you."

"Your mother?" Rita asked, wanting him to say it.

"Yeah. She... well, it was rude and—"

Rita interrupted. "No, it's okay, your mother's just worried about you."

"Umm... doesn't matter. I know her. She wanted to make you feel small. She disapproves."

A few seconds of silence passed before Gunter continued. "I told her so too. She said the same, that's she worried. I don't believe her."

"You don't believe she's worried about you?"

"No, I don't like that she disapproves of you."

My thoughts exactly, Rita mused, but she kept it to herself.

"And she doesn't think I should see you. I told her to

butt out. Said I'd see whomever I wanted to. She's not going to tell me who to see and what to do. If I go to a party and want to strip buck naked I'll do it."

Rita suppressed a laugh. She knew what he meant but couldn't imagine Gunter undressing at a party. Yeah, in his posing suit he was nearly nude but that was for competitions or photo shoots or exhibitions. His sport and his job. But the idea of him walking around nude in front of strangers was comical and weird and not Gunter at all.

"I told her she was mean-spirited and she told me to grow up. Then she said things about you... I'm sorry, I shouldn't have said that. You don't need to know the details."

"That's okay. I'm fine. It's not the first time I've been called names. I'm used to it."

"I'm not. I don't like it. People—my mom—shouldn't call anyone names."

Ah, thought Rita, *so she called me a whore, but probably in a polite way. Well, screw her.*

"My mother has no right to judge you. You are good. All the guys at the gym say so too," Gunter said, almost shouting.

Rita hooted and put her hand over her mouth. She knew "good" didn't refer to her inner spirit. She didn't care. She had used the men as much as they had used her. And she went out of circulation after moving in with her boyfriend—someone she cared for deeply and thought he felt the same for her. Until she found him cheating. Her knee-jerk reaction was to resume her activity with the men in the X-room. Gunter must have missed that memo.

"I'm sure you and your mother will get over your tiff,"

Rita said, knowing she wasn't at all sure.

"Not unless she apologizes."

"Don't do anything. Wait until morning."

"She has to."

"Gunter, I don't need it. You'll be humiliating your mother and stressing yourself out."

"Don't care. She can't say those things about you," said Gunter to end the conversation.

Rita called Vinnie immediately.

"Meet tomorrow morning in the X-room after your class," was Vinnie's conclusion.

* * *

"He's very upset, more than Rita implied in her phone call last night," said Ben to Vinnie in a corner of the X-room out of Gunter's hearing.

Vinnie nodded. "What? Did he say something?"

Ben explained the difference between a description and an observation. Gunter's attitude was easily understood by the way he stacked and lifted barbells. This morning, according to Ben, he displayed a lackadaisical indifference. Vinnie snorted, pursing his lips.

"Yeah, go ahead and play down what I say. But I tell you he can usually bench press six hundred fifty and today he stopped at five fifty."

Vinnie's eyes rolled. Gunter's capacity was off the charts for most men, even in the X-room. Vinnie was bored with the weightlifting discussion and thankful for Rita's arrival.

"Tell us more about yesterday's events. Maybe start with the part about Gunter's anger with his mother?" he asked her.

Rita said she'd been thinking about it all night and decided Gunter's upset was more about Helene's treatment of her than him. But on reflection, it might also have been the trigger for Gunter's rebellion. His breaking the mother-son tie to become an adult.

"How?" asked Vinnie.

"She was telling him more or less not to date me. She was controlling, as much as telling him he was incapable of making good choices for himself. I was the perfect example to prove her point."

"Geez, I'm sorry," said Vinnie. "That's harsh, and I mean it."

Rita pecked Vinnie on the cheek. "Nicest thing you've said to me in a long time."

"Yeah, well, like Ben often points out, I can be an asshole sometimes."

"I said wise-ass but asshole works too," said Ben, and he gave Rita a hug. "I'm sure Helene's just worried."

A mother's worry for her son wasn't the issue according to Rita. And Gunter wasn't exempt from teenage rebellion, like everyone, even if it was a little deferred in his case. Rita pointed out that rebellion wasn't rejection, which was the way she saw his current action.

Ben scrunched his nose up at Rita. "In all the years I've known him he's never said one word to me against his mother." He could think of a few times when Gunter had complained about his mother but just the usual stupid issues, nothing important.

Rita looked over toward Gunter on the other side of the room, her voice lowered. "He's never had a serious relationship. I think he's bonding with me and…"

Vinnie knew without Rita saying it. *She's bonding with Gunter.*

"I think," continued Rita, not noticing Vinnie's narrowing eyes, "this relates to Katia. I believe Gunter is so eager for female companionship he'll take any sign as encouragement. That's why he felt betrayed by Katia."

"Anger?" asked Vinnie.

"Yes, but also a loss. Depression mixed with anger, I'd say."

"What's he want now?" asked Ben, who tensed while crossing his arms.

"He wants his mother to apologize to me."

"And that means he can pursue you?" asked Vinnie.

Rita frowned.

"I don't mean it the way it sounds," added Vinnie.

Ben moaned. "It's wrong. I'll talk to him. Get him to understand his mother is concerned about him."

"No, I don't think that's the way to go," Rita said. "Look, Ben, I know you're his training partner and mentor, but this falls outside of your relationship with him."

The truth hung in the room. Everyone knew she was right. She had to talk to him since it was her he wanted. Yet to go from one woman telling him what to do and what to think to another was delicate. Rita knew the risk. The possibility of transference, displacing his anger at his mother and dumping it on her. Guiding someone and telling them what to do changed with a mere wobble in wording.

"This is his battle and we can't lose his trust because he'll need us to get through what happens next."

"What's going to happen?"

Vinnie shrugged. "Fuckin' something. Always does with cops."

Rita walked across the room to Gunter, who was doing deadlifts. "Gotta minute?"

"Yeah, just let me rack these weights." Gunter started to unload a barbell when another lifter came over and told Gunter he'd take care of it.

"Thanks man, I appreciate it," said Gunter to a square block of a man dyed grapefruit orange.

"Did you want to shower first?" asked Rita. "I can wait."

He sniffed his T-shirt. "Nah. If you can manage the stink."

At Ben's suggestion, they went to his UltraFit office for privacy. Gunter sat facing the window and Rita angled her chair to face him.

"Um," Gunter said with a pleasant, soft voice, "I'm sorry I called you so late last night. I, uh—"

Rita interrupted. "Don't worry. You can call me anytime, day or night. Did you talk to your mother? Everything okay between you two?"

Gunter's head shook no. He continued to complain but stopped to stare out the window. "She isn't willing to accept I'm a man. I can make my own decisions on who I date or what I do at parties."

His eyes narrowed, and it seemed his eyebrows moved down his face. A face masking his emotion. This was the first time he'd criticized his mother and the first time he'd examined his relationship with her.

What next?

As if Gunter had read her mind, he said, "I've decided I can't stay with mom anymore."

"What?" Rita's voice was shrill. "Isn't that an overreaction? Where will you go?"

"I'll find somewhere. I'll ask one of the guys to crash at their place until I find my own apartment."

She could not imagine Gunter moving in with another bodybuilder. All the men admired him, everyone. They'd ask his advice. They all jumped at the opportunity to train or spot him. "Fucking best workout I've had in months," was typical. "He's a beast. Pushed me hard but I couldn't match his targets," was another.

But he was considered a loner. He never joined the guys after a workout. He brooded and rushed to get home for supper with his mother. Rita heard through the locker-room grapevine he'd never talked about women, not like the way the guys did. Speculation spread that Gunter was gay, except the gay lifters said he didn't hang out with them either.

"Let's think about this," she said softly, a schoolteacher's trick to lighten the mood.

"Nothing to think about. I've already decided and I told my mother this morning."

"What? No!" cried out Rita. "You'll cause her a lot of pain. She's a good person. She's your mother. Please don't do this. If this is about me, don't... I wasn't offended. She loves you."

Gunter got up and walked out, saying, "I'm doing it."

Rita called Ben, who arrived within minutes. "This is bad," he said.

"Uh-huh," answered Rita.

"Now what?"

Ben walked around in circles. She wanted to join him but there wasn't enough space.

"He'll stay with me and Vinnie."

"Where?"

"Our guest floor, currently unoccupied."

Rita patted Ben's shoulder. She had forgotten he was the beneficiary of a deceased boyfriend's trust fund. *Nice to be wealthy.* She felt mean. Ben was generous, especially to his friends.

"Why not get him a temporary room in an Airbnb? If money's not a problem?"

With a light tap to Rita's cheek, he looked into her eyes. "You know it's not, so don't be coy. There are a few problems. First, Gunter's too proud to accept money. Somehow, he won't consider staying in a rent-free room as taking money, or at least I don't think so—" Rita started to speak but Ben kept on talking. "Second, he isn't ready to be on his own. And last, we'll get to observe him and provide help when he needs it."

"There's another," said Rita.

"What's that?"

"Helene will feel better. I'm worried about her too."

Ben was confused by Rita's support for the very woman casting them in an adversarial role.

"I'm collateral damage," explained Rita.

Ben snorted, "Uh. And?"

In Rita's mind, Helene's intention was not to offend but to protect Gunter. Her actions inadvertently cast doubt on

Rita's sincerity.

"I get why she did it," she concluded.

Ben bounced his fingers together, then took hold of Rita's shoulders. "You really are my best instructor and a truly good person. I'm so glad you're helping Gunter."

Rita pecked Ben's cheeks. She mumbled something about being late for her tae kwon do class, her voice cracking and eyes tearing.

* * *

"This is your room," said Vinnie, pointing at a doorway. He stepped aside for Gunter to peer into a designer-decorated bedroom with a king-size bed.

Ben swiveled on the balls of his feet. "You'll have privacy but remember we're just one flight up. Use the internal staircase," he said, turning to point down the hallway, "and don't be shy. Come up anytime you want to talk."

Gunter said the room was great, maybe too much furniture and too big. He asked about his weights.

"No need," said Ben, pointing to the elevator, "press the down button for UltraFit."

Vinnie mentioned dinner in a few hours, enough time for Gunter to settle in, but he said he wanted to fit in a short workout. "I don't want to be more of a bother than I am."

Gunter's ringing cell stopped their discussion as he stepped away to answer. He returned with a blank stare.

"What?" asked Vinnie.

"Detective Kaplan wants to see me at the precinct tomorrow morning," Gunter replied, his voice barely audible.

"No, that's wrong," Vinnie fumed. "Why?"

"He said to further help with Karen Probinowski's murder enquiry. He means Katia."

Vinnie didn't stifle his anger, barking obscenities at the absurd excuse offered by the police. What else could Gunter add to what he had already told them? Vinnie waved his arms around and banged the headboard. He ended his rant with, "This ain't good!"

Gunter sat on the bed, sliding one palm over the other. "Do you think they'll arrest me?"

Ben stepped forward and took one of Gunter's hands. "Don't jump to conclusions. We don't know what they want."

"Then why ask me back?"

Vinnie tapped his chin, his voice calm, and he stopped waving his arms. He'd forgotten Gunter was easily frightened. He chose his words carefully to reassure him. "Let's take the request at face value. Most likely they'll want you to ID someone," said Vinnie with the confidence of someone trying to convince themselves.

"Who? I only went to the party, I didn't know anyone there."

"No, but you might have seen someone on the street. That sort of thing. Chance encounters. Cops always look for that kind of shit. They'll show you photos of known criminals or even a lineup."

Ben liked the suggestion.

"Or," continued Vinnie, "they want your impression of the two guys and the woman. Could be they found something not right with them."

"I don't like Sue. And Eric and Les are disgusting."

"See," said Ben, "they sound like bad people."

"But why do I need to go the station? I could tell them over the phone or they could come here."

Vinnie repeated the ID or lineup idea. He was still astounded that people like Gunter thought of police investigations like getting a new cable TV service.

Gunter's head moved down and remained on his chest.

"I'll call Rita," said Vinnie and Gunter's head lifted.

19

Rita arrived with a suitcase.

"Guess you're staying," said Vinnie.

She pursed her lips at him, flashing her no-time-to-waste look. She surveyed Vinnie's home study room. "Where's Gunter?"

"Where do you think?" Vinnie pointed to the floor, as if Rita could see through the eighteen stories and into the subterranean X-room.

He reviewed the earlier scenarios he'd given Gunter for the police interview. Rita liked the photo ID best.

"Yeah, but let's not get sloppy, said Vinnie. We'll prepare Gunter for questions about Katia. Let's brainstorm before we talk to him."

Rita agreed, sitting down then standing and pacing.

Vinnie's teeth chomped on imaginary *what-ifs* and *suppose thats*. He moved to block Rita's pacing. "I think we should begin with Katia and Sue. They met at a coffee shop then Katia invites Gunter—a stranger—to a party."

"Something's wrong," interrupted Rita, looking at Vinnie's eclectic collection of male erotica hung on the study walls. "Let's think about it. Two women sit at a coffee shop table and invite a stranger to a party. In general, women don't sit and talk to Gunter and they certainly don't invite him to a party."

"Katia must have been very persuasive," said Vinnie, picking up on Rita's train of thought. "I'm not even sure how she managed to get him to talk, never mind accept her invitation."

Rita agreed, adding, "And why did she want him at her party? Was this a setup? For what?"

Both took refuge in their thoughts. Vinnie spoke first. "Let's suppose I meet someone…" He gave a long-winded story imagining various scenarios in which he would on impulse invite a stranger to a party. Foremost in all cases was a physical attraction.

"A bit shallow, don't you think?" asked Rita. "Plus—"

His dismissive laugh interrupted her. "And you don't?"

Rita's lips strained to show teeth. "Point taken."

"So," Vinnie continued, "if you find a guy gorgeous you might invite him to your place for a party. Right?"

Her laughter pealed. "You have no idea what I would do but extending an invitation to a party wouldn't be high on my list, not if the guy was a gorgeous hunk." Rita pointed to the wall images. "But let's be honest. Gunter's not one of them," her finger again swinging around the wall. "The only billboard featuring his face would be for a horror movie."

Vinnie's jaw dropped.

"Hey, I'm not being mean. It's the truth! Let's be real. And while we're at it, not many women go for the body-builder type—veins and bulges are a turn-off. And all of them are shocked by the steroid-withered balls. Women like

152

airbrushed six-packs, phony biceps, hair styled, and Armani suits. GQ handsome." Her finger aimed at one particular man among Vinnie's poster collection, and Vinnie agreed. His favorite and not even close to a bodybuilder's capital X physique. The guy wasn't even lowercase, but he was drop-dead gorgeous.

Vinnie added that the same held true for most gay men. "I didn't seek out that look. My hooking-up with Ben was purely accidental, literally. Well, you know."

She did.

"I think we can also rule out Gunter's charming conversation," Vinnie said casually as if ticking off items on a grocery list.

"I agree."

With his voice subdued, Vinnie continued, "Did Katia invite him to her party to humiliate him?"

Rita shook her head no, believing that idea too devious and cunning for something spontaneous.

"Uh-huh," agreed Vinnie, "so what then?"

They discussed alternatives and debated various motives. Nothing seemed right yet all seemed plausible. And the bigger unknown was what Gunter thought happened.

"I'm not sure he gave it much thought," said Rita, scowling, "only he realized too late Katia didn't like him. He was in tears telling me. He's fragile."

"Say that again. What do you mean by fragile?... like emotionally? Couldn't handle rejection plus the verbal teasing? Did he imagine he was in a room full of Detour Men and Women?"

Rita understood where this was going. Vinnie was making Gunter out to be mentally unstable and she said as much. He didn't deny it, and his non-verbal agreement upset her more than had he said it. The hypothetical merged into fact as Vinnie barraged her with non-stop analysis of Gunter's mind.

Rita blurted, "This is not your expertise. If anyone should be talking about his emotional stability it's his therapist— not us." Her hand flew to her mouth.

"Gunter still sees a therapist?" Vinnie sat up as if poised to rip the meat off her bones. "I thought he stopped years ago."

"No," Rita sighed. "And he has depression medication, but he says he doesn't always take it."

This changed everything for both Gunter and the discussion. They knew the implications of a roller-coaster intake of powerful psychotropic medication. They also knew it could be even worse when coupled with growth-enhancement injections. Yet Rita protested that for the interview it was irrelevant. Vinnie agreed, but was thinking ahead about if Gunter was arrested. Then the cops would find out and would use it.

Rita was out of her seat. Vinnie tried to block her but she pushed past.

"He's not accused of a crime." Rita stopped moving.

"Not yet. But if he's unstable then it will land him behind bars."

Rita raged, defending Gunter, pointing out neither she nor Ben saw any signs of unstable behavior. "Gunter's sensitive. He'd never hurt anyone. You know he could kick the crap out of a dozen men and not break a sweat, but he wouldn't. He's just too gentle!" Rita ranted, extolling Gunter's timidity. "After the party he went home to bed with his mother."

She doubled over. "Oh fuck! Holy fucking shit!" She swayed and Vinnie's arm prevented her from falling.

"Wait! Are you fuckin' saying Gunter sleeps with his mother?"

"No, just in her bed. And please, Vinnie, swear to me you'll never let Gunter know I told you. I'm an idiot. I have to hear you say it."

"But—"

"No, say it! You'll never let Gunter know I told you."

Rita wanted to puke. Her ashen face suggested she had.

"I promise. But tell me everything. This could be crucial for Gunter's interview. More if he's arrested."

The word "arrest" hung in the room.

Vinnie and Rita repeated their belief in Gunter's innocence and reassured each other that there was no chance of an arrest. The mutual affirmation did not convince either. There was nothing left to discuss.

Rita prepared to walk the fine line of guiding Gunter and not dictating things to him. And could she actually do it given her desire for him? There was more between them. She couldn't explain her sudden affection. Her desire. She'd only had one experience of rapid passion before with an incredibly handsome client. He was quick-witted and self-assured. Not one trait shared with Gunter. And he was fantastic in bed. Gunter matched him on that score.

That affair ended badly and she had been cautious ever since. Gunter didn't fit her usual type of man. Ironically,

Vinnie said the same himself about his repulsion to the he-man type. Yet he fell for Ben and that worked out okay. Did she and Gunter stand a chance? What was the effect of Helene's disapproval?

It didn't matter, not now. Her focus had to be the police interview. What "help" could he give them? What he saw—or was it him they were after?

Rita asked Vinnie one last question before leaving. If Gunter wasn't Katia's murderer—and he wasn't—then who was and why was she murdered the night of the party?

20

Rita and Gunter descended the internal staircase from the penthouse, not exactly joined at the hips but bumping along the way. Gunter sat on the next-to-bottom step, sniffling. His inhales elevated the curve of his hunched back.

Rita rubbed his spine, asking, "What's the matter?"

His breathing slowed and steadied.

"What's upset you?"

"Because…"

She took his hand and he followed her into the guest living room. They sat in matching armchairs. Rita scowled. "I can't guess."

"Do you know how ashamed she'd be of me if I'm arrested for murder? She'll blame you, not me."

Rita knew any attempt to convince him he was wrong was a waste of time. Logic and facts wouldn't overcome his pride, humiliation, and insecurity. She stretched across her chair to hold his hand. He pulled back.

"I didn't help Katia."

Rita screamed, "Stop it! You did not kill Katia! You're not a criminal!"

His face contorted and he turned away. "Yeah, well I'm

having a second interrogation. Means something," he said as he walked to his bedroom.

She followed, her heart pounding. She forced the only words she could think to say, even if she didn't believe them. "It's an interview, not an interrogation. You're helping the police."

"You know what they'll say?" His voice turned into a high-pitch falsetto. *"Oh Gunter, you lift weights. You use drugs. You beat people up because you're strong."* Returning to his natural deep voice he added, "I don't beat people up. I..."

This wasn't the Gunter she knew. His neck swelled. Something changed. The shallow breathing? His eyes? Something was happening, a visible change in his mental state.

"Gunter, sit down." She pointed to a chair flanking a large window and she sat in the one on the other side.

His eyes moistened.

She knew he needed comfort. To feel loved. To know someone cared about him. She had the same need.

Their first sexual encounter had been an unexpected explosion that neither saw coming. Gunter wasn't the typical X-room mammoth seeking quick discharge of a tankerload of injected testosterone pulsing in his veins. He wanted to satisfy her as much as himself. She had experienced it once, with the handsome client—and she'd blown that. She wasn't going to let that happen.

Now passion choked her. She sought intimacy to resuscitate them both from their isolation. She didn't want the thrill of selfish gratification but the joy of sharing. Affection that begets love.

She began to unbutton her blouse then stopped, seeing his blank gaze.

"You do it," she said, standing up.

He rose slowly, his large bumbling fingers unable to undo the tiny plastic buttons. Raising her arms the garment tightened across her breasts. Gunter sucked in air. "Just do it," she said and he tore the fabric. The shredded blouse fell and his hands roamed along her spine. She stifled a squeal. "Slow down."

She enjoyed his calloused fingers sanding her skin. He fumbled, clumsily fingering her sports bra clasp until it unbuckled. He blinked before cupping her breasts. His thumb and index fingers rolled over her nipples. He pulled them gently then touched with the tip of his tongue. She wanted him to swallow the nipple, the entire breast, all of her. She wanted him in every way possible. This was desire, not sex. An ache to merge into him. She craved his all.

She instructed him to make a perfect union. Let each finger tingle every fiber beneath her skin. She wanted him to know this was more than sex. Her body was a love conduit. He pressed down on her as her leg slithered along his massive thighs. She didn't tell him he was suffocating her. She didn't care. Let him overpower her, allow him to use his strength and believe in himself.

She guided his roaming hands until his instinct took over. His natural innate ability surprised her, so good, so much better than most men she'd known.

He released and with her hands behind her neck, tossed her head back as she stretched emphasizing her elongated

Modigliani nudity. He dropped to his knees and she looked down and kissed the top of his shaved head, her arms surrounding his pillar neck. She touched his rigid chest, swollen hard. Desire gave way to lust with each of his breaths fanning her breasts. His strong arms tightened around her buttocks, her excitement unbearable.

One hand held his rounded shoulder to steady herself as the other lifted his chin. She leaned over to push her lips against his slightly opened mouth. She pressed hard, her tongue deep until the frisson made her shiver. She wanted him to consume her.

She whispered for him to stand and proceeded to undress him. With each article of clothing she explored his body. His T-shirt on the floor, her palm stroked his chest muscles along with tracing his deep-channeled veins with her index finger. He discarded his pants and underwear, revealing muscle on muscle. His large naked body could influence the orbit of planets. His gentleness would lull newborns.

Rita wanted him more than anything. Moistening her index finger in her mouth, she painted his lips. She poked her finger into his mouth, then withdrawing to rub her lips, the sweet saltiness of his saliva on her lips. She kissed him so hard he'd have to count his molars.

Her breath misted his shaved chest. Her heart grew bigger than her chest. She labored to inhale.

She held out a tube of lubricant and a condom. He was hard, erect, yet sad eyes stared at her. This was what she wanted. Did he?

She held out the condom. "We don't need this, do we?" she asked and dropped it before he could reply.

160

He took the tube from her and squeezed it into his palm. She scooped a dollop and spread the gel over his hard penis. Her hand ran up and down his hard member as if an extension of herself.

His fingers moved between her legs, caressing to match her rhythm. She touched his eight-pack abs and whispered for him to flex his free arm, kissing the bifurcating peak rising into her face.

"Fuck, it's magnificent." Her hand ran across the bunched sinew. His arms surrounded her like a bath towel. She nudged him back, hands moving between his legs. This closeness consumed her. This was their moment, their reference for eternity.

"Spread," she said and anchored her hands to his ass. She called out, "W-H-M-F" and shifted into her tai chi Peking Wild Horse Mane Fuck but his ensnaring arms immobilized her. His grip was too strong, unbreakable. She didn't care. Let him smother her.

Their tongues darted. She tasted again the sweetness of his saliva. Her face bore into his shoulder, inhaling his musk. Her nose chafed along his sinew. His head buried into her breasts. She wanted him to touch her and never stop.

"Everywhere. Touch me everywhere and do it hard."

"You sure?"

And Gunter's hands explored her body while she rubbed his stiff penis from base to tip. Her eyes closed tight as her fist. She needed this. Him too. Their desires fused. Love seeping out.

He pushed her backward to the bed, placed her down,

and she arched, as if independent and free of him. And then came the contact, his tongue exploring her labia, turning as if a key in a lock, releasing her desire and his.

She shuddered with convulsion to the rhythm, a knot formed in her chest at the sensation of his pressing tongue. The sensation was unbearable but she did not break away. She called out lettered acronyms as she turned over, her breasts imprinted into the mattress.

He was ready and asked her if she felt the same.

"Yes, oh god, yes," she answered.

He poised above her. His voice distant, from another galaxy.

"Yes," she said, repeated as his head neared hers. She whispered letters, her body contorted into a martial arts pose.

His fingers pressed into her breasts, ignoring her words to focus his gyrations to match her position. He lifted her, turned her over, and massaged her as if buttering muffins.

She wanted more, to roll her lips along his, to feel him tighten from his mouth to her nipples as he kissed them.

Her legs moved apart, a gift to him. She'd give him a kingdom of gifts. And he rewarded her with his tongue over every inch of her private area. He stretched and she rubbed his rampart pectorals, expecting his beating heart to burst out. He kissed her and turned to kiss each spinal vertebra. He licked her coccyx between the nook. She jolted and lifted her rear upward. His lips roamed her leg down to her ankle. His tongue swirled around her toes. He kissed her instep and massaged her with his strong fingers. This was everything she wanted. This was the life she wanted.

Rita's breathing increased, "Now, Gunter, do it now," she said, eyes closed, her words inadequate for her desire. She blindly sought his penis, grasped it, and pulled with urgency. The shock brought his foot massage to a halt.

Her legs spread as she rose up on her knees, an invitation. A place for him... in her, beside her. She wanted him.

She heard his sigh, his teeth biting at the sheets as he penetrated her. His movement stopped, and she knew—like her, he wanted their union to remain unbroken and last forever. She didn't want to complete the act. Neither did he. They wanted this moment suspended.

Her sigh became a cry. She knew he misunderstood and lifted her. Did he fear unleashing his desire would crush her? She would have told him do it anyway, she'd risk all to have his full force and weight consume her. She wanted his brute strength to impale her.

He moved rhythmically, his fingers touching her clit with a gentleness she didn't want. She wanted a hard, tough pounding. She squeezed him, urging him to unleash his force and make her happy. He obliged and her youthful mutterings said it all, "Yes, come inside me." His thrusting drove up the heat inside her and sprawled to her skin, hot enough to fry eggs. She sought satisfaction.

And Rita heard in his cry as he spent himself the forging of desire with terror. And she joined him as she herself reached climax. This was no facsimile, no insincere performance. She had been seeking this all her life but had taken too many diversions. And now serendipity had brought her the one she wanted, needed to protect at all costs. Could this last?

Gunter rolled off, looking a bit shocked. She wiped the last of his spurts and put it in her mouth, more as a courtesy than completion of their sex. "Rita, what just happened?"

She smiled. He knew but he didn't have the words. Nor did she. How to explain this? Melding ripped open their inhibition, enabling them to seek a future. Her head rested on his arm. He arched his back by lifting onto the balls of his feet and rolled over to face her.

"I like this," he said, massaging her breasts and shoulders.

Rita's face cooled even as the friction of Gunter's massage warmed her skin. She didn't need to look to see the glow in his face. Her fingers traced his parchment-thin, golden brown skin, tanned under artificial light. The surface veins moving sustenance to his double-down muscles. She stroked his face and stubble. His residual sex sweat filled her nostrils and she inhaled deep and long.

They lay on the bed, their eyes staring at the ceiling, caressing each other's bodies for a long time.

"Did I hurt you?" he asked.

"Shh."

Snuggling closer, Rita pushed his arm and adjusted her head position.

"You okay?" she asked.

"Yeah. That was great."

"No, not the sex, which was great, but…" She turned on her side to look at him. "You know… your mother, you, everything?"

A few minutes of silence until Gunter said, "I liked her. I really did."

"What?" Rita sat up, resting on her elbow, to see Gunter rubbing his eye.

"She's dead because of me."

And with his words happiness vanished, and the stains on the sheets were the only trace it ever existed.

"No—" said Rita but stopped herself from saying more.

Gunter moved his free arm across his forehead. "I didn't want anyone to get hurt because of me. Not Katia... not you... not my mother."

He cried. Big men don't cry. Men that chewed glass and bent steel never cried, even with excruciating injury. He-men never cried for fear or love—and never in front of her.

Her anxiety grew. His contrition made him appear culpable. Guilty. His empathy easily misinterpreted as remorse. She had to tell Vinnie. Gunter wasn't ready for a police interview, not yet. He should have legal counsel before meeting the detectives.

She needed more time to make Gunter understand he was blameless, morally and legally. That he was mixing empathy with culpability. If he didn't believe in himself, then neither would the cops or anyone else.

21

Entering the Stuyvesant Town precinct's double doors, Gunter was escorted to the room of his first interview. He asked about having a lawyer present as Vinnie had suggested. Detective Daven screwed up his face, explaining, "You see, Gunter, you're just helping us with our investigation of Karen Probinowski's murder, the woman you knew as Katia. You're not under arrest. Do you need a lawyer?" Without waiting for Gunter's answer, Daven continued. "Did you know the Columbia University student found murdered in Harlem a few weeks ago?"

Gunter leaned back in his chair. "I thought this was about Katia."

"Tariq Mamurov was a graduate student. Had you ever met or seen him?" asked Detective Daven.

"Uh... no. But what's he got to do with Katia?" Gunter responded, his voice unsteady.

"I'll get to that," said Daven. "So you didn't know him. But you made a police report," he tapped a piece of paper in front of him. "Your statement is about seeing him in Sakura Park."

"Well, uh, yeah, the news requested..." Gunter stammered and tried to recall what he had said in his statement.

Detective Kaplan leaned forward, elbows on the table. "You said you were in Sakura Park, sometime around midnight."

"Yeah, I guess."

Detective Daven interrupted his partner, again tapping the paper. "That's what's written here. Was it or was it not at midnight?"

The detectives' gruff voices disturbed Gunter. They alternated asking questions. Gunter paused before answering. He stammered and prefaced answers with "I think" and "I guess."

"Was he dead when you saw him?" The questions came from Detective Daven, his tongue marching over his teeth.

"Uh... well, I thought so. I... maybe."

Daven's junkyard dog attitude barked out, "Someone is either dead or not. There's no scale of one to ten on death. Was he dead or was he alive?"

"I'm not sure. Maybe not alive."

The two detectives looked at each other, nodding their heads. Kaplan leaned back, letting his partner know to continue. Daven edged forward to rattle rapid-fire questions.

Gunter tried to recollect. He wished the detective would pass him the report they were reading from to remind him of what he had said. Why didn't they show him? Gunter muddled through about the men he saw carrying off the grad student's body. The long distance, too far to recognize them. Nothing stood out about their features.

"That's what you reported. And you said one of them had a knife. Is that right?" asked Daven, continuing as the main interrogator.

"Yes... I saw one waving a knife."

"Only one thing wrong with that, Gunter. You see, Tariq's knife wound is small. Know what that means? A small blade. How could you see a small knife if you were a long way from him in a dark park? Care to explain?" asked Daven.

Gunter shook his head no.

"So your report's inaccurate. There was no knife."

"No. There was. The man waved it at me."

"Threatening you?"

"I guess." Gunter stopped. "I'm sorry. I should have put that in the report."

"Sorry about what? And why would the man threaten you? You said yourself you were a long way from him."

"Well, I was close enough to hear them talking."

Both detectives bolted upright.

"What? Say that again." This time it was Kaplan speaking. "What did you hear?"

"I thought the grad student was moaning. Said something. Uh... maybe... 'Don't do it' or something like that. I'm not sure."

"You're not fucking sure?" said Daven, banging his fist on the table. "That's not in here." He picked up Gunter's report and waved it in the air.

"I didn't remember... no one asked me about... I was confused." Gunter rubbed his face. "It's the truth. I didn't think it important, not at the time. I... well, I thought the men were helping him."

Daven looked up from the report. "I think you were

closer than you said. Your report mentions a limo. Was there a driver?" Daven turned to his partner.

Kaplan nodded. "If there were two men as you say in your report, then one of them was the driver or there was a third person behind the wheel. Was that you?"

"There were just the two of them. I'm not lying." Gunter stopped and stared at the back wall. "I saw them put the man in the town car. One guy waved the knife from the car window... I should have gone over or done something. I don't know." Gunter drank more water. "I didn't."

"Didn't the interview cop ask you about this?"

"Yes, and... well, I told him I didn't see anything." Gunter looked into his empty glass. "I'm not sure what happened."

Daven put the police report into a folder and placed it on his lap. Gunter hoped this meant the interview was over, but then he saw Daven's face come across the table.

"Maybe you were with the men in the limo. Your male admirers. Men who admire bodybuilders."

"What? No, I didn't know them."

"Were they attracted to you, and poor Tariq was looking to be included in any depravity you had in mind? I'm guessing you like men. Isn't your personal trainer, uh... Ben Hausen, a gay man?"

"Yeah? So? And he's married to that man out there waiting for me." Gunter pointed at the wall.

Detective Daven laughed. "That guy out front? A little small, isn't he? Isn't he called a twink? Was Tariq your twink?"

Gunter fumed. "No, he's not."

"Tariq's not a twink or your friend outside?"

"Vinnie's pretty buff if you must know. But what's that go to do with Katia?"

"Lots of big guys at UltraFit. The place is stuffed with muscle-bound bodybuilders. Does Ben like to recruit gay bodybuilders?" Daven's eyebrows furled. "Was Tariq gay? Did he try to get something from you and the men you claimed carried him away are your pimps?"

"I told you I'm not gay. Not that I have a problem with it."

"I bet you don't," laughed Daven, leaning back.

Gunter wished the interview would end but knew his wish wouldn't come true as soon as Detective Kaplan brought the folder back onto the table to splay photos on the surface. Color photos of Katia's mangled body, her head twisted grotesquely.

"See, Gunter, here's the thing. Karen, or Katia if you prefer, well, her neck isn't right. And this…" Kaplan tapped a photo blow-up of Katia's midsection. "This is a knife wound. Small world, eh?"

The photos made Gunter sick. He wanted to leave the room. To run away. He didn't recognize Katia.

"And you know what's odd here? I'll tell you," said Daven, drawing out his words. "The knife wound is exactly the same size as the stab wound found in Tariq. In fact both stab wounds were made by the same knife."

The words meant nothing to Gunter. He couldn't stop looking at Katia.

"Listen up," said Daven, tapping the photo. "The knife didn't kill Katia, a broken neck did. A sick, very strong motherfucker did this to her."

"Gunter, did you feel that Katia had rejected you?" The question came from Kaplan.

Twisting his lip, Gunter shook his head no.

"Then it was the men, Eric and Les. They rejected you. Maybe Tariq did too and that's why he wouldn't pay your pimps."

"You mean the student?"

"Yeah."

"But he wasn't at the party."

"And what did you do at the party? We heard you undressed to only your posers. Skimpy, aren't they? You performed your bodybuilding flexing routine. Was that for Katia or the men?"

"It's what bodybuilders do."

"And that's why Katia asked you to leave. She didn't expect you to display yourself, your perverted exhibition to gain sex. She thought you were trying to seduce Les and Eric. Is that it?"

"I wouldn't do that."

"But you did. You can't control yourself. The 'roids take over. And Katia stood in your way. She prevented you from having the men. You couldn't stand the little woman taking control," said Kaplan as he pulled together the photos of Katia, holding each one up as he did.

Detective Daven barked, "Gunter, admit it, you're a frustrated, oversexed, steroid-stoked, mentally unbalanced gay man."

Gunter walked punch-drunk into the lobby heading for Vinnie, who was staring out the window. Vinnie jolted with the tap on his shoulder. He turned to gaze into a slack face with drooping eyes.

"What fuckin' happened?" asked Vinnie.

Gunter continued to the front door. *This is bad,* thought Vinnie, scurrying behind.

* * *

At the BIG office, Gunter was debriefed in front of Vinnie, Rita, and Blanca. Rita had cancelled her classes to be sure she was available at any time.

Gunter rationed the information, each statement delivered after a prod or clarification request. Vinnie blamed himself for not being tougher in his first talk with Gunter. He'd treated the incident as inconsequential, nothing more than a nuisance. He allowed Gunter to make a careless, inaccurate report. When the news of the Columbia student's murder made headlines, he should have been more vigilant.

Not until Katia's murder did Vinnie understand that everything had changed. The two murders were tabloid headlines. Juicy stories sold papers and increased ratings for radio talk shows and TV news. Social media lit up.

Gunter wiped his eyes describing the photos of Katia's twisted body. Vinnie said this explained the reason Gunter wasn't called back immediately after the first interview. The detectives wanted to give CSI more time to study the evidence to make Gunter a person of interest.

After an hour, Gunter said he didn't want to talk anymore. He was about to leave when Blanca said she had something new, and not good.

"My police contact's gone cold. He says the Katia case, or the Probinowski case as he calls it, is too hot for his further involvement."

"Fuck!" yelled Rita.

"There is one thing," said Blanca, tapping her pad. "I called my guy at Roosevelt Hospital. He says the guy in the park had a broken neck besides the knife wound and he guesses it's the cause of death but he's not a medical examiner so can't be sure. But if true, it means, in his words, 'the murderer is a strong motherfucker.'"

Gunter's gasp made the room turn to face him. "Those were Detective Daven's words."

And we've got a problem, thought Vinnie. *This is not good, not good at all.*

22

The BIG front office door was flung open with Gunter steering his body toward Vinnie's office. Vinnie, Rita, and Blanca turned in unison. His face had a sunflower glow, rain-forest sweat drenched his T-shirt, and his arms and neck were laced with surging veins. Blanca poised her pen over her open notepad.

"Sit down," Vinnie said to Gunter. "Blanca has new information." Vinnie glanced over at her.

"The police entered your home—former home—this morning a little after eight o'clock. They had a search warrant and—"

"They searched my mother's house?! Why?" Gunter stood. "I should call her."

Rita grabbed his hand. "Wait," she said, holding tight, "you can talk to her later."

Gunter pulled, but not too hard. "She'll think—"

"She won't think anything. She's worried and loves you, and—"

Blanca interrupted. "I talked to her and she's okay. Of course she wants to see you, but she understands we have to talk first."

Gunter sat again. Vinnie said they should review the items taken by the New York Police CSI unit. Blanca read them out from the list, which was brief because Gunter didn't own much. They did not remove his weightlifting equipment or wall posters. The main items were clothing. The last item on the list was his footwear, all sneakers.

Vinnie looked at Gunter. "No shoes, just sneakers?"

"Sneakers are shoes," answered Gunter, his lips pouting.

Vinnie let out an exasperated sigh and explained he meant shoes worn for dress-up occasions, "You know, like for a wedding or..." He stopped himself, leaving the word "funeral" stuck on his tongue.

"I have dress sneakers for Christmas and stuff like that. The others are for walking the streets and park, and these." He pointed to his feet. "These are my gym sneakers. The walking sneakers are too dirty for the gym. Not good for the mats."

Vinnie saw Rita's and Blanca's faces change expression as if anticipating his next question.

"And you wore your walking sneakers that night in Sakura Park?" asked Vinnie.

"Uh-huh. Always do."

"Clean them regularly?"

"No, not really. Unless I step in dog shit but the last time that happened was a year ago. I mostly stay on the path and sidewalk, so they're not all that grubby."

"And that night?" asked Vinnie, who saw Gunter's blank stare so clarified the question. "The night you went to Sakura Park, did they get dirt on them?"

Vinnie noticed Gunter's eye movement, his head turning,

a hand rubbing his eyebrow.

"I might have used a shortcut through bushes when I heard the guy calling out."

Vinnie slammed his fist on his desk. "Why didn't you fuckin' tell me this the first time we talked?"

"Why? What does it matter?" Gunter slumped, resting his forearms on his thighs while his fingers dug into the corner of his eye.

Vinnie didn't press and not only because of Rita's scowl. By doing so he would make Gunter feel worse than he already did or look like a moron... or somehow complicit?

Rita stood up to rub Gunter's neck as Blanca patted his back, saying she'd often seen people panic and do irrational things. He wiped his eyes and rationed his story to reveal more about the cut-through from a small path between bushes that ended at the sidewalk.

"Lots of people use it."

"And?" asked Vinnie.

"I think the student must have used it too because I saw blood splotches where the path comes onto the sidewalk."

"Any on the path?" asked Vinnie, who was chewing his finger to prevent an outburst. This was important new information and Gunter had never said a word about it. Something wasn't right.

"Don't know. Too dark for me to see. By the time I reached the sidewalk the two men were carrying the student to the car."

Vinnie's patience ran out. He cursed about blood discovered on Gunter's sneakers.

Rita countered that weeks had passed. "Maybe there

was no blood in the dirt. Did you see blood?" she asked Gunter again.

"No."

"See, no problem," said Rita, but it sounded more like there was a problem.

Vinnie responded with "And pigs fly," while shuffling in his seat. "Let's move on to Karen Probinowski."

"I call her Katia," said Gunter, holding his wrists.

"Fine, Katia. Did you get anything from the coroner's report?" he said, looking at Blanca.

She responded with a negative shake of her head and added, "That leaves us with the hospital nurse's opinion." Blanca looked at her pad. "One more item that seems odd— well, not odd but I didn't expect it. A leather Italian jacket. I've never seen you wear it, Gunter."

"I only wore it once for Katia's party. It was meant to impress her. My mother bought it for me the morning of the party. It's not the kind of thing I usually wear." Gunter closed his eyes. "I wore it one time and someone died. I don't think I'll wear it again."

Vinnie prodded Gunter. "Unless the jacket was involved in the murder, it's irrelevant. No connection to Tariq, and at most some lint or material from Katia's apartment. But Gunter's already acknowledged that he was in the apartment." Vinnie scratched his temple. "Tell us more about Katia; can you do that, Gunter?"

Gunter spoke in a steady, monotone voice. He rubbed an eye with his fist, breathed deeply, wrung his hands, and his arms bunched. He recounted all he remembered about Katia. Her beautiful green eyes, her sweet voice. The words tender, a glimpse into Gunter's psyche. His sobbing was real emotion.

Rita called a time-out. She hovered over Vinnie, her face a foot from his, her eyes narrowed and eyebrows dipped. She waved to Gunter to leave.

"What?" he asked as Gunter shut the door.

"Look at him. He's a wreck. Can't you back off a little?"

"I wouldn't need to if he'd been completely honest from the start," said Vinnie, his eyes piercing Rita's. "I'm concerned about his rapid attachment to Katia. And you too, if I'm honest. It's not normal. And he's crying. A lot. I'm not one to criticize, given my proclivity to shed tears, but it concerns me. I think Gunter could easily be pushed over the edge if he felt used or ridiculed."

Rita loomed over Vinnie, her face closing in on his.

"Come on, don't tell me it hasn't crossed your mind," said Vinnie, pointing at her.

She backed away, arguing that Gunter didn't look like he'd murdered two people, which Vinnie scoffed at. He asked her to tell him what a murderer looked like. She answered that it was someone who didn't look like Gunter.

The words cut across the room. Blanca said she noticed Gunter's hands trembled while talking about Katia's murder and the crime photos.

"I don't know, Rita. Maybe he has a split personality. Or some trigger—" Vinnie stopped with Rita's interruption.

"Dual personality? Really? Out of nowhere?"

The debate became a litany of Gunter's issues that stacked against him, most notably his size and the antipsychotic drugs he took now and then. Vinnie recited his version of the worst interpretation. The point wasn't whether they were true, but that they could be made to seem valid. He built up the case against Gunter, making every action look nefarious and abnormal. Gunter became a monster. Vinnie's vivid rhetoric became real. He'd reinvented Gunter into a humongous, unstable murderer. Someone almost impossible to like.

Rita's finger flicked the side of her eyelid. Blanca patted Rita's arm. "You're upset." She glared at Vinnie but continued to speak to Rita. "Vinnie was just doing his usual worst-case scenario. We know Gunter's a gentle, sweet guy." She stopped to shake her head at Vinnie and continued, "Look at the positive, he's not accused of a crime."

"Not yet," said Vinnie, earning a blast of icy scorn from Blanca. "I'm sorry, but it's true. CSI will find something on his sneakers. They'll also have seen his psychiatric medication. Ipso facto, Gunter's behind bars."

"Ipso facto my ass," said Rita, voice trembling. "And he's not psychotic." She began to cry.

Blanca waved her hand at Vinnie and he walked to the window, his back to the women. A ringing office phone broke the silence. Blanca answered. "Okay, I'll let them know," she said and turned to Vinnie and Rita to say the call was from Ben and he had placed a takeout order so no need to worry about cooking. And the mundane necessity changed the room's atmosphere.

"I'll talk to Gunter before dinner," said Rita. With an upturn to her lips, almost a smile, she added, "Unless you want me and the psycho to move out."

23

Punching his condo door keypad code, Vinnie compared what he knew about Gunter before and what he'd learned over the last few days. First and most obvious was that Gunter was a devoted champion bodybuilder. Second, he had a warped sense of his own body size—the bigorexia complex. With the condo door latch clicking, Vinnie considered his next point, number three. Gunter had a fear of someone he called Detour Man, who was real yet not a threat, at least not anymore given Gunter's size. Vinnie remained in the hallway thinking about the last two points, which made no sense. A twenty-six-year-old man who sleeps in his mother's bed. And then there was the last point to keep in mind: he periodically takes antipsychotic medication.

Did this add up to a killer's profile? In a moment of anger, could Gunter have snapped and done something terrible? Even Rita had said he could easily have beaten the shit out of all of them and not break a sweat. Or did he only focus his rage on Katia? After all, she was the one that invited him to her party, and under false pretenses too. If true, then her death shifts from being involuntary manslaughter to premeditated murder. A whole new ballgame.

A momentary shame came over Vinnie for thinking Gunter might be guilty of murder. But he reminded himself that Gunter was a client and that's what he did for clients. Analyze all angles to protect them. *If I don't, something unexpected will fuckin' happen.* He looked at his hands. Assuming Gunter was charged with murder, what would be the prosecutor's view? Was he looking at Katia's murder as being premeditated? And would he accept Gunter's fragile mental state and lifelong torment with humiliation as sufficient motivation?

Ben startled Vinnie by touching his shoulder from behind. They kissed briefly. Ben pointed to the takeout bags. He placed the food on ceramic plates and shoved them into the oven for reheating. Vinnie moved into the living room.

"When's Rita coming? I thought she'd be here with you?" yelled Ben from the kitchen.

"She's downstairs with Gunter," he answered with a comedian's lilt and gained a rude comment from Ben.

Around forty minutes later Rita entered the kitchen, arms folded. "The police have been to Gunter's mother's house looking for him. She called with the news a few minutes ago. She told the cops he was out but not that he was staying here."

"What! That's fuckin' bullshit," said Vinnie. Neither Rita nor Ben disagreed.

"So now what?" asked Rita.

"A lawyer, that's what," said Vinnie, fuming and kicking kitchen stool over. He knew they'd been too slow to get Gunter a lawyer. They all presumed him innocent, incapable of any criminal act let alone murder. *They were too fuckin'* *complacent. A huge miscalculation.*

"I agree," said Ben, fists balled up, "and we need to do it now." He was dialing his cell.

Vinnie didn't need to ask who Ben was calling but Rita did. Vinnie explained it was Ginny Livorno, who had been a student in one of Rita's martial arts and fitness classes. But everyone at UltraFit knew Ginny Livorno. And if anyone could find a top-notch criminal lawyer in a New York minute it was Ginny.

"She's a Pied Piper of professional men—well, almost all men. I think you can guess why," said Vinnie.

Rita's smile was a little too strained and lasted a little too long. Vinnie had seen the look on many women who came into contact with Ginny. Her striking beauty easily captured the male libido and her intelligence dazzled their minds. Add to that her elegant wardrobe and shoes to die for and envy flowed.

Vinnie ignored Rita's rictus smile to ruminate on what was obvious, at least to him. He waited for Ben to finish the call before revealing his dark thoughts.

"Voicemail. I left a message," said Ben, who sat on the sofa punching his fists into the cushions. "I also called her home line. A babysitter answered. She and Dan are out at a concert so cells are off. She always checks during intermission. The babysitter said she'd relay my message that this is urgent."

To Vinnie Ben sounded despondent and looked worse.

"Stop blaming yourself," said Vinnie, cuddling Ben's arm. "If anyone, blame me. I'm the PI and I'm responsible.

I should have advised Gunter in the first interview to get a lawyer. Especially after the house search."

Hearing Ben's growl and feeling his tightening arm sinew, Vinnie knew Ben's self-recrimination was unaltered.

"So we just wait?" asked Rita, pacing the floor.

Ben nodded and Rita yelled out curses in frustration.

"I'm surprised they didn't arrest him this morning at the precinct interview," said Vinnie, who didn't rise to Rita's outburst but continued in a matter-of-fact tone. "My guess is they had a loose end or were waiting for one more CSI result. Or the DA was on a long lunch break."

Rita turned around and started to walk out.

"Where are you going?" asked Vinnie.

"To spend the night with Gunter. I think he should know that he needs to be prepared. I'll comfort him. Show him I care... *we* care... and that he's not alone."

Vinnie agreed, adding she should do what she could to control his anxiety. "Make sure he doesn't go off the deep end—and no pills."

Rita glared before crossing the room at fighter's speed, her hands outstretched. Ben stepped between them, pointing Rita to the front door, and said to Vinnie, "Sometimes you can be so fucking thoughtless."

Vinnie understood. Ben was right. But Rita was also a hothead. She'd been trouble from the first day she joined the Briggs Investigative Group. Now where was Ginny's return call?

A few minutes before nine Ben shouted for Vinnie, who rushed out of his study.

"Ginny has the perfect lawyer. She called him at home

and he'll squeeze in an appointment on Thursday. He told Ginny that a paralegal would escort Gunter to the police station tomorrow morning. Have him make a voluntary surrender."

"Why not him?" asked Vinnie. *Gunter will be arrested tomorrow,* he thought to himself.

Ben answered with a broad smile. "I asked the same question. To quote Ginny, her lawyer friend said, 'the exigencies of the circumstances do not call for urgent action.' Whatever that means."

"I know," said Vinnie, banging a chair. "The big shot lets a subordinate do the grunt work. He'll say this is a boilerplate arrest, an arraignment. Bail easily arranged. Basic first-year law stuff."

Half an hour later Vinnie called Rita on her cell, not wanting to go unannounced to the lower condo and interrupt something that might get his teeth knocked out. Rita answered on the second ring.

"I'll come up. I've just calmed Gunter with some yoga exercises. He's falling asleep."

Waiting for Rita to come up the stairs, Vinnie thought about the rumors—well, facts since Rita confirmed them when he had asked—that she had modified martial arts positions for sex. But he had the impression this time that yoga meant yoga.

"Why can't this lawyer see Gunter sooner if he's such a good friend to Ginny?" Rita asked with annoyance combined with pleading.

"Because it doesn't work that way. Not even Ginny trumps legal avarice. It'd be different if Gunter was famous.

It's a miracle he can even see the lawyer this week." Vinnie paused, sucking in air. "Don't worry, this is all the initial stage."

Rita walked the room with no apparent destination. She'd go with Gunter and Vinnie to the courthouse. Vinnie wanted to go alone but knew not to try and sideline her this time. He said nothing to discourage her because she'd admitted her limitations. Her strong attachment made her too emotional, too involved. Her self-conceit claimed she could help despite not having the legal knowledge. Weighing these factors did not compare to her being with Gunter, even acknowledging as much for herself as for him. Was it for Gunter or herself that she needed to be in the courthouse?

Vinnie said he'd work on preparing Gunter for the arrest procedures and possible questions during the interview. He would also bring the paralegal up to speed before the courtroom circus began. Rita said she'd contribute her experiences with police arrests, but her body shook and sadness cloaked her green eyes.

"Hey, it'll be fine," said Vinnie, convinced it wasn't. "What's the worst that can happen?"

Rita ran out of the room.

24

A major traffic accident on Route 46 delayed the Karimov cousins an hour before reaching the specialty electronic shop. Dimitri easily found parking in the strip mall's half-empty lot. Like many places the US economic downturn had hit the malls hard, from big box stores to the little mom and pop operations.

As soon as the engine was off, a sullen Dimitri slumped in his seat. A waste of time. He'd cut a class to do this, yet all he heard from Vasi was bitching and moaning. And the fucker was puffing on a cigarette despite being told many times that the smell of smoke lingered inside the limo. Now he'd waste another hour scrubbing and disinfecting to remove the nicotine odor before his father or uncle used the car. *Fuck Vasi. Fuck this waste of time. They shouldn't have killed Tariq. He could have been talked back into the project. Fuck it all.*

"You know what we want, right?" asked Vasily, taking the last draw of his cigarette and discarding the butt out of the window.

"Yeah. I'm not a moron."

A wispy young man stood behind the counter, and could

have been fourteen but then again he might have been twenty-five.

"How can I help you, gentlemen?" he said in a matter-of-fact, flat voice.

"We need a few items. I called ahead and was told you have them in stock," replied Dimitri.

"Okay, shoot," said the sales rep.

Dimitri produced a list and the young man stuck out his hand. A slight hesitation came over Dimitri, but the young clerk's fingers were holding the edge. He released the paper and the kid skimmed it.

"I'm not sure about the second and third items. I think we're out."

"I thought you checked this," said Vasily in stilted English as the young man receded into the stock room's maze of metal shelves.

A few minutes later the clerk placed his cache on the countertop along with Dimitri's list. He withdrew a pen from a plastic protector tucked into his shirt pocket and ticked off the items.

"Like I thought, we're out of the circuit board relay and the delay switch."

"How long before you can get?" asked Dimitri.

"Usually a few days, but the warehouse is doing inventory. Might take until next week."

The growl was followed by cursing in Tajik. The clerk didn't look up from the list, but Dimitri was red.

"I called ahead," he said, facing the young man but the statement was intended for Vasi.

"Fuck you did. We wasted an hour getting here because

of fucking traffic. You're a fucking moron," screamed Vasily, who added a string of Tajik curses.

"And fuck you too," yelled Dimitri.

The clerk's stick body bent across the counter, his voice a whisper. "That kind of language is not allowed in here, sir. We're a family-run business. Please watch your cursing."

Vasily turned to the clerk, moved onto his toes, his arms raised into a fighter's stance. "Fuck off!" he yelled. "You should have things in stock when you say you have them!"

"I'm sorry, but I don't know who gave you that information. It may have been correct at the time you called and we subsequently sold out. It happens."

"I called this morning," said Dimitri, also in a loud voice, "so I don't think someone rushed in ahead and bought the entire stock."

"I'm not sure who—" the clerk's sentence was interrupted by Vasily slamming his fist on the counter.

"You fucking Americans," he screamed, "you lie and make up whatever you want. Fuck you!"

The clerk stood back as Vasily's arms crossed the counter. Dimitri stepped forward. "Leave it. Let's just get what we have and go elsewhere."

"Go elsewhere! Wasted my time. Pay and meet me in the car," said Vasily, staring at the clerk. His arms were drawn up, hands forming fists as he growled unintelligible words at the youth but gave the impression a punch to the face was a real possibility. He turned around with fists remaining clenched as he walked away.

"Not cool, Vasi. That wasn't fucking cool," said Dimitri, resting on the car's hood and puffing hard on a cigarette.

"The guy was fine even after your threats." He held up the brown bag with the purchase. "Suggested substitute components."

Vasily flicked his finger and sent the butt spinning to the ground. He grabbed Dimitri's arm. "I'll tell you what's not cool," he said in Tajik: "your incompetence. I ought to give you a fucking beating right here and let you bleed all over the fucking parking lot." With the last words his left hand jabbed one of Dimitri's kidneys, then the right gave it a second blow.

"Uhh…" gasped Dimitri, stumbling, barely able to stay upright.

"Give me the fucking keys," demanded Vasily. "I'll drive."

Without any traffic accidents, the return drive to their Jersey City home lasted about twenty minutes. Not one word spoken, each cousin content to keep their thoughts private. Dimitri broke his silence as he cursed running up the staircase and banged open the door to his room.

An hour later Vasily entered the room holding two beer cans. He extended one to Dimitri who lay on his bed and ignored the gesture. "We're both upset."

Dimitri looked away, then took the beer from the table-top.

"We were disappointed."

Vasi tipped his beer upward for a long swig. "And maybe I got too angry. Not that the little shit didn't deserve it."

Dimitri turned from Vasi's unfriendly face, which his soft voice and apparent conciliatory attitude didn't hide. He knew his cousin too well.

"We have schedule. Delays are no good. We have too much planning to do."

"Then you shouldn't have killed Tariq," said Dimitri, unable to keep his own advice to not rise to every comment Vasi made. But the nagging was going on too long. "He knew what he was doing. I've never designed a circuit." His hand flew across to the bag of parts. "It's way too complicated, even with Tariq's notes."

"You'll get it to work, I know."

"How? I'm stupid, remember? Or so you keep telling me."

Dimitri flinched and shrank down into the bed as Vasi's hand drew closer. He didn't expect to hear Vasi chuckle. "I didn't mean it. You know I just say things. I know you're smart. I've got too much going on." He tapped his forehead. "Let's just forget what I said."

Dimitri sat up to take a long drink of his beer. "Fuck it, Vasi, it's not easy. It doesn't always work. I can't get my cell to trigger the detonator. Tariq made an app that he matched to exact hardware parts. That's what we need from the store. I'm not sure I can make his app work with substitutes."

"Sure you can. Go online, look on YouTube. I know you know how to find things on the Internet." Vasi's fist moved in an up-and-down motion.

"Again with the porn sites," said Dimitri.

"No. I mean you know how to search. Really. You know about the dark web."

Dimitri looked across to his computer's flashing screen saver with alternating nude female photos. Could he find circuitry similar to Tariq's design and use the available components to activate the detonator? His legs swung to dangle off the bed as he moved into an upright position.

Vasily pulled Dimitri closer, kissing his forehead, saying, "There are girls at the gym always looking at me. The call them gym bunnies or something funny like that. One is always feeling my muscles, rubbing herself against my leg. I think she'd be good for you."

Dimitri pulled back. "You mean it? What's she like?"

"Big tits, good ass too. You'll have fun screwing her."

"Would she? I mean, isn't it you she wants?"

"I'll make her a deal. She fucks you and I'll fuck her after," said Vasily, grinning. "Good idea?"

A few hours surfing the Internet yielded several options but not one with a cell phone app that triggered detonators. None matched Tariq's unique design. Dimitri found a few designs that used a detonator button, and he had all the necessary components. No need to wait for the out-of-stock parts. He told Vasily, who congratulated him on his results.

"Come to the gym tomorrow night. Best fuck of your life, I guarantee it."

Dimitri's anticipation lasted a lot longer than the screw he got from Miss Bunny. And she was not nearly as stacked or pretty as Vasi's description. He didn't seem to understand the meaning of a pretty woman or "a good fuck."

While he was gathering his clothes and still buck naked, Vasily burst into the gym's back room. Miss Bunny walked past Vasi, sliding herself across his chest as she brushed her tits against his arm. "Get the fuck out! You've got all you're going to get from a Karimov. Fucking slut." He pushed her away and she walked out saying, "It's true what they say about you, isn't it?" Vasi slammed the door in her face and turned to Dimitri. "You got what you wanted, now get it done. Your time's up."

25

The petite paralegal walked on Gunter's left, the top of her head below his shoulder by several inches. Rita took the right flank and Vinnie was at the rear. He estimated the paralegal weighed less than one of Gunter's legs. *A stumble and he'll crush her.*

To Gunter's question of why his lawyer wasn't with them, Vinnie explained that the paralegal was a lawyer, only cheaper. "No need to pay a partner's humongous fees." Vinnie doffed an imaginary hat. "You know, anyone who watches *Law and Order* can handle an arrest."

The scowling paralegal looked behind her at Vinnie. "Are you a lawyer, Mr. Briggs?"

"Not with a degree, but I know how cops and DAs think, and that's something not taught in law school," answered Vinnie, pleased he had matched her condescension.

Rita reached back and poked Vinnie.

Gunter's voluntary surrender meant he avoided the customary embarrassing perp duck waddle. No handcuffs. Vinnie scoffed at the thought, suggesting the NYPD didn't have shackles big enough or strong enough to withstand Gunter ripping them apart if he wanted.

The desk officer escorted Gunter and his paralegal through the double doors into a room different from the one he'd been in for the interviews. The paralegal was registered as Gunter's legal counsel. The big man zoned out, engaging his competition mindset. He entered a monk's meditative state, the one he employed before going on stage. Being told where to stand and what to do. Floating between almost naked men, anticipating the next step. Waiting backstage in the checkout queue for handlers with brushes and rollers to spread oil all over his body. The on-stage primping of the glowing, effervescent tanned men with burnt orange skins. The robotic posing.

He stirred, hearing voices outside his head.

"What's the charge?" asked his paralegal.

"Anything you like," said Detective Daven, who looked like he had forgotten to shave.

"That's not good enough," she said.

"Okay. How do you like second-degree homicide? That sounds good, has a nice ring to it."

"I'd like to confer with my client," she said to the detectives.

"We'll be back," said Daven as he picked up his folder.

"It's my fault," said Gunter, rubbing his face.

"Don't say that. You'll have plenty of time to enter a plea. But answer me this. Did you expect a murder charge?"

"I didn't murder Katia, but it's my fault. I should have called her back."

"You'll have time to talk this over with Tom."

"Who's Tom?"

Gunter picked at his fingers as the detectives reentered the room.

"I think my partner," said Kaplan, gesturing to Daven with his head, "misspoke—the charge is double homicide. Karen Probinowski and Tariq Mamurov."

"What!" Gunter stood up and the paralegal's hand partially wrapped Gunter's wrist, tugging him to sit back down.

"Sit, Mr. Hoffman, or we'll have you restrained," said Daven.

* * *

The paralegal entered the waiting area, and Vinnie thought she appeared more diminutive than before. Her eyes were lowered and she held her briefcase against her chest. "How bad?" asked Vinnie.

"Double homicide."

"What? That can't be fuckin' right," Vinnie fumed. Rita joined in with her own curses, then her eyes filled with tears.

"Bail hearing is not until tomorrow," said the paralegal. "I pushed for today but we're too late after they finish processing Gunter into the system."

"What happens next?" asked Rita, rubbing her eyes.

"We'll be back in the morning."

"Will he be okay in jail?" asked Rita. "Safe?"

Vinnie agreed with the paralegal that Gunter would be unharmed in an overnight holding cell. "Unless someone wants to commit suicide by Gunter, no one in their right mind would try to rape or harm him."

* * *

Ben's rear end rested on his desk's edge, his balled-up fists on either side maintaining his balance as he leaned forward, projecting his body halfway across the room. Vinnie and Rita slumped like schoolchildren in front of the principal.

"No bail? What the fuck did the two of you do? And what about the fucking paralegal?"

"That's procedure," explained Vinnie, who sounded a little too know-it-all even to his own ears. "Once you're inside a police station, they have all the fuckin' rules on their side. Forget civil rights and shit like that. I told you, didn't I?"

Rita wiped away her tears. *So much for tai chi control and self-discipline,* Vinnie thought.

The silence extended, with Rita breaking it first. "So what now?"

Vinnie recited what they'd gone over before. He started with the positive. All the evidence was circumstantial. That meant someone had made a point of connecting two murders and linked them specifically to Gunter. Vinnie garbled his next point. Gunter's size made him capable, and this was not helped by his morose demeanor. Vinnie looked away from Ben, spinning the well-known reputation of drug-enhanced bodybuilders and the 'roid rage cliché. It didn't matter if it was exaggerated and not commonplace. "It'll be the DA's first point to a jury," he shrugged.

With extra emphasis, Vinnie made his final point. They couldn't investigate without knowing about the evidence the cops had used to make the double homicide charge. "We need a lawyer not a paralegal. Call Ginny now and tell hotshot legal eagle Galantuomo to get off his ass. Invoke the fuckin' exigency clause."

Rita slipped by Vinnie on her way out of the door. "I'm going to visit Helene."

198

* * *

The clerk read Gunter's name from the docket. Tom Galantuomo was a man of average height but he became pea-sized approaching Gunter at the defense table. Vinnie whispered to Ben that they'd have to do something to make Tom look bigger to distract from Gunter's size. Tom didn't hurry when asked to respond to the question of bail. As a senior partner within the criminal department at New York's prestigious Halborn, McGregor, Galantuomo, and Stern firm, judges gave him leeway in protocol. He stood, exuding confidence as he argued bail release despite the seriousness and notoriety of the two homicides. "At least he's taller than Gunter when standing," said Vinnie, who received an elbow in his side from Ben.

As he watched from the spectators' seats, Vinnie realized the distance enhanced Tom Galantuomo's extraordinary features. He was beyond handsome. His fashionable, hand-tailored Italian suit added an illusion of height, especially as he moved away from away Gunter. The finely crafted suit outlined Tom's well-proportioned body, the broad shoulders and trim waist. His sonorous baritone was another asset. Altogether, Tom cut an impressive figure. Vinnie guessed the ensemble worked even better in front of female jury members.

As expected, the DA wanted bail denied for a double homicide case. Tom pleaded compassion, citing Gunter's widowed mother. He didn't mention that she became a widow some fifteen years earlier or that Gunter had recently moved out of her home. The judge smiled at Tom, setting bail at one million dollars. Ben's quick offer to post the bail bond made it appear he had the cash in his pocket.

The paralegal stayed to help Ben complete Gunter's bail and release papers, and was then told it would take another hour to release Gunter.

"Now comes the unbelievable cost for justice," said Vinnie to no one in particular, scuffing his shoes on the courthouse steps. Tom's rate was twenty-five hundred an hour with a starting retainer of fifty thousand. *He better fuckin' win*, thought Vinnie, knowing that Ben's money also paid the legal fee. Rita moved away, having heard enough of Vinnie's tirade about lawyers and judges.

They found a nearby coffee shop and left Ben with the paralegal. After an hour Vinnie's cell rang. Rita ran to greet Gunter with a hug and kiss. Vinnie waited for Ben on the sidewalk and then they too embraced and kissed. The paralegal kept a lookout for the prearranged cab ordered by Blanca. Ben scowled at Vinnie's suggestion that Tom was on the golf links. The paralegal forced a crooked smile, telling Vinnie Tom was in his office and requested to see Gunter around six that evening.

Vinnie and Rita both saw the cab arrive and called everyone to the curb. Tom had cautioned the group not to talk about the case in public spaces. Vinnie was irritated by the paralegal repeating the message. Besides, the cabbie didn't seem to speak English. Gunter sat next to the driver for the extra legroom. Vinnie squeezed beside Rita in the rear row. The paralegal was shoehorned next to Ben in the middle row.

"We needed a bus," said Vinnie, who didn't think this

broke any client privileges.

Ben was dropped off at UltraFit, as he was not officially on the legal team. The others had a meal together. Vinnie didn't see why Rita had to invite the paralegal, but she told him to be quiet. They arrived at the law firm dispirited by the case and irritated with each other.

Tom spoke with Gunter alone before he asked Vinnie and Rita into his office.

"Gunter," he said, holding his door open, "I'm going to have a quick word with Vinnie and Rita. Please help yourself to refreshments." Gunter remained stuck in place, so Tom signaled his personal assistant to guide Gunter to the front reception area. Then he shut the door.

Tom walked around the two investigators, his back to the huge glass window and its panoramic views over lower Manhattan's financial district. They stood and Tom didn't suggest they take seats. At their request, relayed via Ginny, they'd been assigned "Supplemental Investigator" status, giving them client-lawyer privilege. Tom wanted them to know that did not mean they were involved in the legal strategy. Their involvement was a courtesy to Ginny.

Before Vinnie or Rita objected, Tom held up his hand. "There is something you can do that's, well, let's just say it's unique to this case." His eyes were raised upward before he resumed talking. "I want you to encourage Gunter to seek professional help. While not my area of expertise, I have represented all types of people, enough to tell when someone is in shock or emotionally delicate. Pick whatever term you want, but I believe Gunter needs help that I can't provide."

"Do you mean you'll be going for an insanity plea?" asked Vinnie.

"Like I said, this is not a strategy discussion."

Rita moved in close, her hand stroking Tom's Italian suit fabric. Her one-inch height advantage caused Tom to arch his neck but he didn't step back. "Then what's the reason for psychiatric help, which is what you mean. Am I right?" She paused. "And just so you know, he is on meds already."

"I know. But medication is not the issue. This is psychological."

Vinnie pulled Rita back. "Tom, you brought us into your office. We're on the defense team. Strategy planning or not, give it to us straight. Do you plan on an insanity defense?"

Tom smiled and couldn't stop his chuckle. "Ginny said you were smart and cocky. She knows her men. Okay, Vinnie... and Rita, let me put it this way. First, if I had any worries about Gunter being dangerous I would have a guard in here. I don't think he's a crazed maniac." He paused, his smile broadening and lips parting. "Second, and this breaches no firm secret, we handle..." he paused, slightly shaking his head, "what laymen call an insanity defense internally. In other words, we have our own stable of shrinks. Get my point?"

Rita stepped forward, sticking out her hand as if to shake his, "Yes, Tom, I do. Thank you."

"Me too," said Vinnie. "But now we want something from you. What is the connection between the grad student's murder and Katia? And was Tariq Mamurov gay?"

"I understand your first question but why the second?"

"A hunch. Can you find out?"

"I will during the discovery phase. I'll let you know."

Vinnie had one more question. When would he see the discovery material?

"Soon" was the answer he got.

Vinnie never imagined "soon" meant the next day. He and Rita wasted no time but were unprepared for what they were about to discover.

26

Vinnie stood in front of the building on the 200 block of E17th Street, not far from Stuyvesant Square, his head tilting to a door. "This the place?"

"Should be," said Rita, tapping the piece of paper given to her by Blanca. "This is the address Tom's assistant was given by the DA's preliminary discovery material. They were at Katia's party the night of the murder. The apartments on the second floor."

Neither had expected the DA to give material to Tom the next day. Vinnie remarked that it proved his theory that money counts and the DA acted quickly because Tom Galantuomo was a big-shot lawyer at a prestigious law firm.

They waited outside the eight-story apartment building after pressing the doorbell intercom several times with no indication that it rang. Security was lacking to say the least. Vinnie shrugged his shoulders. "We can come back later."

Before Rita answered, a crackling voice on the intercom said, "Yeah. Don't care. Go away."

"Uh, is this Susan Lauder?"

"Huh? Who's this?"

"My name is Rita Light and I'm here with Vinnie Briggs.

I believe our assistant Blanca Santos called and left a message that we would like to speak with you about the death of your friend Katia Tittle. Is this a convenient time? May we come up? It won't take long."

Ten seconds ticked by on Vinnie's watch until a buzzer unlatched the front door. Rita pushed the door hard and held it open for Vinnie.

Taking the staircase to the second floor, Vinnie counted the doors along the short hallway until reaching the end where an open one invited them into a living area. He estimated the room to be ten by twelve feet—not bad by New York standards. Cigarette butts, marijuana residue, and rolling papers were strewn everywhere. Takeout food and stale beer assaulted his nostrils. The small kitchen seen through the left door of the living area was even dirtier, scattered with empty beer cans and an open bottle of whiskey, a split trash bag spilling garbage all over the floor. Pizza boxes were piled at the hallway entrance on the right-hand side. Vinnie shuddered at the thought of the bedrooms and gagged imagining the bathroom.

Sue sat in a faux leather chair scarred with burn marks, making no invitation for her guests to sit. Vinnie assumed she implied it so gingerly perched himself on the edge of the couch. Rita brushed her hand across the cushion before sitting.

"We want to say how sorry we are about your friend Katia." Rita's voice was soft and monotone but managed to sound sincere. Vinnie's small nod approved Rita's comment.

"Yeah, thanks. We weren't that close, but she was nice enough."

206

The response surprised Vinnie, but he wasn't here to know about the ups and downs of the women's relationship. He wanted to know what happened at the party.

"You were with her the night she was murdered, right?"

"Yeah, me and my two roommates, Eric and Les."

"I see," said Vinnie, "and are they here by any chance?"

A tinkling laugh came from Sue. "Yeah, kinda, but they're pretty wasted from last night."

"Any chance we could talk to them?" Rita took over from Vinnie.

"I doubt it, but you're welcome to try to wake them." Sue laughed as if what she said was funny. "They're down the hall." She pointed, causing Vinnie to shudder.

From a few basic questions, Vinnie and Rita learned Sue was not so much Katia's friend as an acquaintance, their relationship based on being two out-of-work actresses who met at auditions and for an occasional coffee. Their last reading was for a small community theater near Columbia, which explained why they were in Gunter's Broadway deli.

"You were having coffee by chance?" said Vinnie. Sue didn't notice the change in his tone.

The response was a series of derogatory remarks about the theater, its director, the neighborhood, and the deli. Rita twisted and cracked her backbone before stretching her arms.

Sue continued, calling Gunter huge and goofy, and finally, "Ugly as sin to tell the truth."

With those words, Vinnie stood and faced Rita. "You know, I think we might talk to Eric and Les now."

He followed Rita down the hallway. She knocked on

the first closed bedroom door and received no response. With a gentle push, the door partially opened. Clothes were strewn everywhere. Cigarette butts in ashtrays, pot leaves, and used Kleenex tissues were spread across the floor. A fetid odor blanketed the room.

A naked bony body, face down on the bed mattress without sheets or cover, didn't respond to Vinnie's shoulder nudges. Vinnie looked at the man, judged him slightly taller than himself, but with a spaghetti-thin body covered in spots. He had long, black, greasy hair.

Rita was disgusted. "I'll try the other guy," she said and walked out.

Touching the man's face with two fingers, Vinnie received a reaction.

"Fuck off!" yelled the man.

"Hello, are you Eric?"

"Didn't ya hear me? Fuck off!"

"Eric?"

"Next door. Now get out."

"That makes you Les. I'm Vinnie Briggs and I'd like to ask you some questions about Katia."

There was a slight pause. "Who?"

"Katia, you know, Katia Tittle, the woman that was murdered a few weeks ago. Her real name was Karen Probinowski."

Eyelids opened as Les turned his head to look at Vinnie. "Nothing to do with me."

"I know, but you were with her the night she was murdered, right?"

"So what? We partied. A big fucker of a boyfriend was

there, flexing and posing. Looked like he had a washing machine for a head. A real moron."

Vinnie was never so happy that Rita had already gone to find Eric. She would have torn off his balls and rammed them down his throat. Les's eyes closed as he mumbled something about the big fucker.

"Asshole," Vinnie said, walking out to join Rita. He would have thrown something except he didn't want to touch anything.

Several steps along the hallway stood Rita, peering into an open doorway. Vinnie joined her and took a glance. "Eric's not in the same league as Les filth-wise," said Rita.

No clothing littered the floor or any visible detritus. An open laptop rested on a small table. Eric lay in bed under a light cover. Vinnie shook his shoulder and Eric's eyes flew open.

"What! Who the fuck are you?" asked Eric, sitting up.

"Hi, Eric. I'm Vinnie Briggs. My assistant Blanca called ahead to say that my associate, Rita Light," Vinnie turned to point to Rita, "and I would like to talk to you. Sue's in the living room. Would you care to join us?"

"What? Get the fuck out of my room!"

And here we go again, thought Vinnie.

Rita stepped forward. "We are looking for background information on the murder of Katia Tittle, aka Karen Probinowski. Please," said Rita with a sickly sweet singsong voice.

Eric's arm emerged to fling off the bed cover. Unlike Les, he wore sweatpants and a T-shirt. Walking barefoot, he peered down on Vinnie by at least five inches. Skinny too, but not emaciated like Les. He couldn't imagine what Gunter must have looked like to Katia compared to these two screech owls. What did she feel or think?

Eric grunted approval to Sue's statement that the party was just fun until the big goon went ballistic.

"How so?" asked Rita.

Vinnie walked around the room, not finding anything especially interesting or insightful about the three roomies. The stench of liquor, drugs, and used condoms a testament to pigsties, the pad a centerpiece for *Squalid Home Quarterly*.

"First," began Sue, "he, like, takes off all his clothes and then, like, folds them in a pile." She stopped to giggle. "And then does this fuck-ass stupid thing with his leg." She stuck out her leg and shook it.

"Yeah, that's called—" Rita said, but Vinnie stopped her. "Anything else?"

"Oh, remember that thing with him bending over like a crab?" said Eric.

Sue laughed. "Yeah, like so so gross. Ew."

"What happened, why did he leave?" asked Vinnie.

"Too sensitive. Big man can't take a joke," said Eric. "All those muscle freaks are clueless and stupid."

Vinnie lifted his head, pleased that Rita's anger didn't flare. She knew these people were jerks.

"When Gunter, er the bodybuilder left, was Katia really upset?" Vinnie looked to Sue. "Do you think Katia was worried?"

"Could be. But she might have been acting. You know, acting's our profession. To be totally honest, I'm, like, better than her?"

"And what about her murder?" asked Vinnie. "How'd you feel? Were you worried that the big guy... didn't you call him Bulldog? That he might be the killer and come back to hurt you?"

Eric looked at Vinnie. "Shit, man, I feel bad for Katia. I mean we weren't good friends, but damn that was horrible."

"And you, Sue?" The question came from Rita.

Sue wiped her eyes. "Yeah, like, we weren't close, but yeah, I think it's horrible. I hope they get that fucker."

Rita's mouth opened and shut as Sue's words cut into her.

"So you think Gunter killed her? Why? As you actors like to say, what was his motivation?"

Sue looked at her blankly, then said, "He yelled at her when she laughed at him. I think he thought Katia liked him. She even went and touched him."

"And so did you, if I remember right," said Eric.

"Yeah, but she thought touching him was so cool. It was, like, so gross. Disgusting veins and bulges everywhere." Sue shuddered as she said her last words.

"Yeah, really perverted," said Eric.

"Imagine his thing, all veiny and inside you!" said Sue.

This is ridiculous and getting nowhere, thought Vinnie. "Let me ask you something different. Did this guy Gunter appear violent? Did he hit Katia or anyone?"

With a shake of his head, Eric said no and looked at Sue. Nothing was said for a few seconds. Vinnie was about to leave but then Sue spoke up.

"Well, Katia, like, went after him. She, you know, returned with a scraped knee. Like really upset too. She talked about people getting hurt."

"You know, man," said Eric, "we were really wasted. I'm not sure if she fell or if that freak pushed her. But it wasn't good, her knee was bleeding a lot. And he was really angry when he left."

"Yeah," added Sue. "Like Katia took it out on us. She told us to leave. Well, like, that's on her because if we'd stayed she'd be alive."

For the second time, Vinnie saw Sue wipe her eye. "I hope they cut off his balls," said Sue.

Eric nodded in agreement, unaware he was scratching his own genitals. Rita turned to Vinnie, who feigned a disgusted look. Neither Rita nor Vinnie thanked Sue and Eric as they left the apartment.

"Fuckin' idiots. Wrong person got murdered," Vinnie spat and then apologized to Rita for what he said.

She smiled, gave him a hug. "No need, my sentiments exactly."

During the ride back to the office they reviewed the interview. They agreed all three roommates were terrible witnesses. They also agreed that if Gunter had become so upset as to act violently, he would have likely done it at the party and not hours later. Eric's belittling of Gunter belied his own insecurity. Vinnie wondered if Eric wasn't a suppressed homosexual. They also agreed that Eric and Les could be anorexic, even if rare in men. They certainly had appeared to have a body dysmorphia that was the exact opposite to Gunter's.

Vinnie and Rita were also despondent. No action plan

emerged from the interview. They had wasted time learning more about three dreadful, self-centered slobs. Perhaps knowing they were high most of the time would be useful to discredit them as witnesses. But none of them had murdered Katia. No drug-induced rage would give them the strength to snap Katia's neck, not even as a group effort. Vinnie and Rita agreed on one other conclusion: they had to find out what connected Katia and her party friends to Tariq Mamurov.

27

Gunter rode in the front seat, silently protesting the visit to a psychiatrist. His shrink had done little good so why would this be any different? He had too easily succumbed to Rita's bedroom discourse. Now he was taking an hour-and-twenty-minute journey to Stamford, Connecticut. So what that Rita called it a one-shot session with Ginny Livorno's mother? Dr. Anna Swinburne may be a well-respected psychiatrist but it was still a useless waste of time.

Ben leaned forward, touching Gunter's shoulder in the car's front passenger seat with Ginny driving above the speed limit. With a soft voice but not a whisper, he told Gunter that Dr. Swinburne—"Anna," corrected Ginny—didn't mince words. Ginny followed up with a rude comment that made Ben laugh but not Gunter.

"And she's not keen on bodybuilding," Ben added.

This time Ginny howled. "That's an understatement."

"Why?" asked Gunter.

Ben didn't go into Ginny's sthenolagnia—her obsession with muscular men, Anna's diagnosis of her daughter and a major point of contention between them. "Let's call it's a family matter and leave it at that," said Ben, which elicited another rude remark from Ginny.

Vinnie was waiting for them at UltraFit, alerted by Ben's call on the departure from Stamford. Gunter told Vinnie he had a good time with Dr. Swinburne, aka Anna, and was oblivious to the three-hour session passing. Vinnie told Gunter he didn't have to lie. Gunter gave Vinnie a shove that sent him back a few feet.

"No, it's true. Ask Ginny," said Ben, who turned to Gunter. "Forgive Vinnie. He and Anna have... issues."

Gunter waved his hand. "Seems like a lot of people have issues with Anna. I don't." He walked out mumbling they could find him in the X-room if they needed him. He'd let Ben fill Vinnie in on the rest since he'd given Anna permission to reveal all to Ben, who could then share with Vinnie. Dr. Swinburne agreed with the proviso she'd only give an overview analysis, keeping details confidential.

If Vinnie was surprised that Gunter enjoyed his time with Dr. Anna Swinburne, he was dumbfounded by Ben's next report, said with a huge smile—Anna told Gunter she admired his strength and muscular development.

"Now you're just fuckin' with me," said Vinnie.

"Nope, it's true," Ben said, adding it was said in front of him and Ginny. "And there's more," Ben continued, losing his smile. "Gunter's experiencing an identity crisis."

"He's gay?"

"No. I had the same reaction." Ben was nodding as if to assure himself he had his next words right. "It's about him not coming to terms with his father's death, a sort of PTSD. He blames himself."

"We know that."

216

Ben struggled to find the words that captured Gunter's mental state according to Anna Swinburne. His father's gruesome death tormented him because he'd been at the scene, saw the crushed skull and blood on the sidewalk. Over the years, he had confronted what were normal growing-up problems and issues with a skewed mental perspective. For Gunter, everything was stuffed into his personal anguish box compartmentalized into humiliation, injury, and death. His decisions were intended to counter conflict with each of them.

Vinnie's half-smile returned, his head tossing from one shoulder to the other. He asked, "Did she have a solution?" knowing the answer and not liking it. His irrational hope was that posing the question somehow changed the answer. Which he also knew never works, but he waited for Ben's response in anticipation of this time being different.

Ben's eyes narrowed with exasperation. "Really? You think one session and Anna has already come up with a solution?"

Vinnie moved around the room, shaking off the patronizing response.

"But there is something that might help, not exactly a solution but an aid," said Ben. "It's about Rita."

Vinnie's head flew back, ears and eyes on high alert. "Uh-oh."

"No, nothing bad or really a problem. Just a caution."

"Just say it."

Ben tangled his words, burying Anna's caution in generalizations about how people make decisions. "She said experience drives most actions. Except sometimes perception substitutes for experience."

Vinnie rolled his eyes.

"I'm getting to it," said Ben. He explained that Gunter's experiences were filtered into two events: his father's death and Detour Man. Every decision he made was intended to protect, either himself or someone he loved.

"But doesn't everyone?" asked Vinnie.

"Yes. But according to Anna, Gunter's decisions often have no effect on what he is trying to protect."

"Huh?"

Ben regurgitated Anna's conclusion that Gunter had developed an aloof detachment, which he thought protected women from his intense desire for a relationship. That's what Ben gathered from Anna's analysis. "In Gunter's mind, if he's emotionally disconnected then it is a safe path to a relationship."

Vinnie's voice was raised. "That's just fuckin' messed up. Shyness gets him laid. Doesn't seem to be working too well according to Rita."

"Exactly Anna's point," said Ben, brushing his forehead. "It's his perversion of reality and the results are that women run like hell from him." Ben smiled. "And guess her other conclusion, which might impact his case."

Vinnie took a small inhale and held his breath.

"He becomes subservient, that's the word Anna used. It explains why he agreed to Katia's request for the bodybuilding exhibition at her party."

Vinnie shook his head. *This sounded too far-fetched but maybe that's what makes it valid.* "Anything else?" he asked.

"He became a bodybuilder as a result of a bad decision."

Vinnie though this contradictory and said as much. Anna praises Gunter's body and physical development, then says it's a mistake. "Is she playing us?"

Ben disagreed. In his view, Anna told Gunter that he'd achieved his objective, which wasn't the same as achieving his goal. Vinnie called this psychobabble. Ben took some of the blame, not articulating the words as he had heard them from Anna. Vinnie asked for an example, so Ben used Gunter's fear of Detour Man as directly leading to his body dysmorphia—his bigorexia complex. Ben finished with, "In his mind he'll always be weak and puny."

"That's it? More sex for security and go around beating the crap out of people to prove he's strong? Well, he's getting sex from Rita, so that's solved. You don't think he hurt Katia or the Columbia student to conquer his Detour Man fear?"

Ben waved his finger, dismissing Vinnie's simplistic view. The point was to help Gunter learn to achieve his vague goal to protect himself and the people he loved. So far he'd failed, according to Anna Swinburne.

"And what are her views on Rita?" asked Vinnie, brushing aside Ben's rebuke.

"She says Gunter's rapid attachment to Rita—possibly something that also happened with Katia—is his seeking to protect."

"Don't get it. How does going to Katia's party and displaying his body protect her?"

"Yeah, that's tricky. First, remember Gunter said he liked Katia. We know from Rita and Helene that Gunter wants a relationship. Katia fueled that desire and he would agree to anything she asked."

"Yeah, got that."

For a few minutes Ben described Anna's view inside Gunter's mind. His perception that Katia needed protection from Sue's meanness. Agreeing to doing his bodybuilding routine was both to please Katia and to protect her from Sue. "Remember, Gunter said Katia called him the day before to remind him about the show. This confirmed his idea that she needed his help."

Vinnie nodded and Ben continued with generalities linking fragility with fear and injury. The mind warps events into hardened beliefs until broken by a harsher reality. That's how entrenched attitudes change.

From the blank look on Vinnie's face, Ben knew he wasn't doing Anna's theory justice. "Look at it this way. Sue and the two guys mock Gunter, who see this as an assault on Katia, not him."

Before Vinnie could protest, Ben barked, "Just listen! It's illogical but so is a fragile mind. The harsher reality in this case is Katia's mocking Gunter. His mind snaps, recognizing Katia doesn't need protection from Sue. *He's* the one who needs protection. Like bodybuilding failed to make him feel big and powerful, so too he's failed with Katia and abandons her."

Ben stopped and took Vinnie's hand. "According to Anna, Gunter faced the worst possible outcome. He attributes Katia's death as his fault, his failure to protect."

"So he jumps in with Rita?"

"Yes."

"But what does Rita need protection from?"

"Not Rita. Gunter needs Rita to shore him up after his failure to protect Katia. And that explains his sudden love for her."

The whole analysis sounded screwball yet at some level it also made sense to Vinnie. *What causes people to be attracted to anyone? Is it a light-bulb moment or a slow burn?* And he did think Gunter's reaction to his mother's denigrating Rita was extreme.

"Okay, tell me about what Anna said about Rita."

Ben walked around, tapping his chin. "This is even more speculative. Anna said as much since she's never talked to Rita. But she thinks Rita's undergoing a version of Gunter's turmoil. It explains Rita's precipitous attachment to him. I think Anna's right, or at least partially."

Vinnie saw himself in the middle of a psychological broth that was about to boil over.

* * *

Gunter had stopped crying but nothing he said made sense. Vinnie was on a frantic call from Rita. But the crying wasn't her only reason for the call.

"He wants you," she said.

Minutes later Vinnie was in Gunter's room.

"Come on, talk to me, man," Vinnie said, sitting next to Gunter and feeling smaller than he ever had before. "You asked for me to come, so go on."

"Alone."

At first Vinnie didn't get it, then saw Rita's mouth hang open.

"You want me to go? Why?" asked Rita.

"Because I can't if you're here."

Rita kissed Gunter's forehead and left to go for a walk.

For a few minutes Vinnie and Gunter just sat, neither saying anything. *Everyone knows life is fragile, but no one wants to believe it applies to them as well.* The idea shamed Vinnie. Had this blow pushed the big man over the edge? Maybe Gunter was giving up.

They sat in silence. Vinnie listened to Gunter breathing, the gentle brushing of air across his lips.

"It's not what I hoped would happen," said Gunter on an exhale.

"Which is what?" Vinnie wasn't sure what he was asking.

"My mother."

"I guessed that much. What about her?"

"She has to let me choose my own girlfriends. Not stop me from doing what I want."

"This is about Rita?"

"Yes. No, not really."

Vinnie touched Gunter's shoulder. "Which is it? Yes or no?"

"I thought she supported me because she believed in me."

"I'm lost. What are we talking about?"

"I called my mother after my workout. I asked her to apologize to Rita. She refused. Said she had nothing to apologize for."

The discussion lasted an hour, but Vinnie thought he had the point after five minutes. Helene Hoffman blamed herself for insufficient intervention with Gunter's Detour Man fear, which led to her actively supporting his ridiculous bodybuilding.

"Did she use that word, *ridiculous*?"

Gunter wiped his eyes and nodded yes.

She couldn't possibly have said that, thought Vinnie. "And she's refusing to apologize because…"

"Because she doesn't want to passively support my bad decisions anymore. Those were her exact words, *passively support.*"

Vinnie waited until he was back in his study before phoning Rita.

"What did he seem like to you?" she asked.

He shrugged even though Rita couldn't see it and the conversation soon ended. Vinnie became more apprehensive as he thought about his talk with Gunter and Anna Swinburne's theory. Gunter misinterpreted the world, leading him to actions that didn't match his goals. And Helene Hoffman had told Gunter the same thing, only in harsher words.

For Vinnie, the investigation had changed course. The BIG team needed to prove Gunter's innocence, disregarding the fundamental legal tenet of innocent until proven guilty. Showing that he didn't do something was an impossibility which meant finding out who was the murderer. Or, at the very least, pointing fingers at others.

Vinnie didn't think the situation could get worse until Tom Galantuomo's call.

28

From the time Vinnie finished talking to Tom he managed three blinks before he was on the phone to Rita. She arrived at the BIG office ten minutes later.

"Fuckin' prosecutor made a plea offer," he said, still blinking.

"And that's bad because?"

"Two reasons. First, it's bullshit. Second, Tom thinks Gunter should take it, which is also bullshit."

Rita cursed. "What's the offer?"

"Not good. Twenty-five if Gunter pleads guilty on two second-degree murder counts. Tom calls it a fuckin' gift."

Tears filled her eyes.

"Tom wants Gunter in his office in an hour to explain."

* * *

Vinnie and Rita entered Tom's office leaving Gunter in reception. Vinnie's sense of awe returned on entering the impressive five-hundred-square-foot corner room, even though the size hampered friendly chats. Floor-to-wall glass windows provided a panoramic view of lower Manhattan by extra stories that overtopped the girdle of shorter skyscrapers.

Along a windowless wall was an eight-foot table covered in papers, books, and a laptop. A sofa hugged the glass wall perpendicular to the one behind the desk. Three large, outward-facing armchairs flanked the sofa, and a modern ceramic coffee table was in the center. A kitchenette was tucked into a recessed area behind the entry doorway, plus a private bathroom used by Rita moments before.

"I'm going to come straight out and say it," said Vinnie. "We don't think Gunter should accept the DA's offer."

"Why?" asked Tom.

"Because the DA's wrong and he won't win."

With a calm, steady voice, Tom said, "You asked to speak to me first, without my client. I've offered you that courtesy, but as far as I'm aware neither of you have law degrees. I'd say you're overstepping your job description. Maybe you shouldn't be on Gunter's legal team."

"No, Tom, we have not overstepped our bounds. I'd thought Ginny explained this when she talked to you," said Vinnie. He knew she had because Ginny had told him. What Vinnie didn't get at first—not being a lawyer—was that BIG's "Supplemental Investigator" designation granted him and Rita client-lawyer privilege but there would be no billing Halborn, McGregor, Galantuomo, and Stern for services.

Vinnie reminded Tom that his prerogative to use the firm's kennel of sheepdogs did not exclude the BIG team from discussion with Gunter.

Gunter entered the office. He appeared to scrutinize Tom's glass desk, which looked to be suspended in midair— no visible legs supporting the desktop. The surface contained neatly arranged papers, an iMac desktop computer to the side, a Bluetooth keyboard, and no visible electrical cables—a magical array.

Rita signaled for Gunter to move along the couch so she could sit next to him. Vinnie and Tom reclined in the armchairs.

"This is a generous offer," said Tom, picking up his Perrier water glass and raising it to his lips. "With good behavior, Gunter, you'll be eligible for parole in maybe fifteen... twenty at most." He sipped from the glass.

"But he's innocent!" came Rita's high-pitched voice. "Why should he go to prison for any length of time if he's not committed a crime?"

Tom replaced his glass on the ceramic surface, his eyes drooping. Vinnie recognized Tom's move, posturing to pontificate on innocence versus securing a not-guilty verdict. Vinnie knew the litany by heart and was sure Tom had recited it many times.

As predicted, Tom gave the spiel for five minutes and concluded with, "In short, Gunter, you could face double first-degree murder charges with two life sentences and no chance of parole. You tell me which risk sounds better?"

Vinnie snorted.

Rita moved closer to Gunter, rubbing his neck. He looked at his feet.

"This is so fuckin' wrong," mumbled Vinnie, "so fuckin' wrong."

No one spoke. Vinnie recognized Tom's game. Never rush or push, force the client to decide using silence to advocate.

"What do you think, Gunter?" Tom said with an exasperated exhale during the long silence. Vinnie was thinking, *Gunter doesn't understand the game and Tom doesn't know silence is Gunter's companion.*

Tom leaned forward when Gunter didn't answer, shaving off a few inches between him and the big man.

"Tell me, could you manage fifteen years in prison?"

"Dunno. Suppose so, but I didn't do it, I didn't kill anyone."

Sitting back, Tom said he'd heard the same reaction many times. "Everyone's innocent. But crimes are committed and the cops, the DA, the mayor, the public want someone to be guilty, even if they didn't do it." Tom rubbed his chin. "Gunter, it'll be a lot worse if the DA can demonstrate that you lied. If that happens the deal goes away. So far they only have circumstantial evidence, but I know they have teams out there looking into it and making connections."

"They'll not find anything," said Rita, her voice rising.

"I understand, but the evidence against you is strong," Tom said while looking at Gunter. "I reviewed the original arrest sheet with an addendum by the DA's office. There is a new wrinkle, which is why he held up Gunter's arrest. They have a witness statement that IDs Gunter on Broadway near Columbia the night Tariq Mamurov was murdered."

"What fuckin' witness?! Did he see Gunter snapping the student's neck? Or holding a knife? Dragging the kid to the car trunk?" Vinnie stood and was nearly screaming in frustration.

Gunter held onto Rita who called out to Vinnie, "Don't

shout! Gunter's already upset. Shouting doesn't help."

"A grad student returning to his dorm," continued Tom. "That's all I have except his version is he saw a *'big dude'* walking down Broadway. I'll depose him, discredit his recall, and show his identification to be meaningless. But any witness carries significant weight with juries, more so if the witness is a bright Columbia student."

Tom walked to his desk and picked up a sheet of paper. "There's more."

Vinnie returned to his seat, his voice lowered. "More?"

"What more?" groaned Rita.

Gunter leaned away.

"Blood."

Vinnie turned to Tom. "No one mentioned blood."

Tom walked through the preliminary CSI blood analysis of Gunter's sneakers.

"Yeah, we know that. Gunter probably stepped in some blood on the sidewalk."

Tom's lips and nose crinkled like he had just sniffed something putrid. "Except the same blood trace was found at Katia's apartment. An identical match to Tariq Mamurov."

"FUCKIN'..." screamed Vinnie but didn't know how to finish his sentence. He was shaking and saw Rita's face tearing up. Gunter huddled into himself, not making eye contact with anyone.

"I'm not finished. There was more blood from Gunter's leather jacket sleeve. It matched Katia's."

Vinnie nearly leaped across Tom's desk. Rita was cursing.

"And I'm afraid there's more," said Tom. "Neither Katia nor Tariq died from knife wounds—in both cases that injury was inflicted postmortem. Their necks were broken in nearly identical manner. 'Twig snapping' is what the DA will describe it as to a jury to emphasize that only someone strong or skilled could manage to do it so cleanly."

Rita expelled air. Vinnie knew she understood the implication as well as he did. But Tom wasn't talking to them.

"Gunter, do you know how much strength it takes to snap a person's neck?" Tom asked, then answered his own question. "A lot. It takes a very strong person."

Vinnie stood, screamed profanities, repeated "circumstantial" and "anyone with martial arts skills could snap a neck, not only strength but technique."

Rita took hold of Vinnie and moved him to his chair, responding for Tom. "Yes, Vinnie, but it still means knowledge, skill, and practice. A Special Forces kind of training maybe."

"How many people have those skills?" asked Tom, looking away from Gunter to Vinnie.

Rita shook her head and Vinnie didn't answer.

"Do you?" Tom repeated, his voice rising for the first time.

Vinnie looked down. He knew the number was small. Very small.

Tom turned to Gunter. "Let's go back to the blood. Can you think of a reason why Tariq's blood was on your sneakers?"

Looking at his hand, Gunter said he explained to Vinnie before, and gave Tom the overview of the shortcut through the bushes.

"I saw blood on the sidewalk but not much. It was too dark to see if any was on the path, and I wasn't looking for blood anyway. Maybe..." Gunter stopped, sucked air into his lungs and shook his head. "I didn't kill anyone," he repeated.

With waving hands, Vinnie signaled Tom to move on but instead he shook his head, starring at Gunter.

Rita scowled. "Look, Tom, Gunter stepped in the blood on the path, sweated during his posing routine at Katia's place, then fumbled the sneakers with damp palms as he hurried out." She paused, knowing Tom didn't get it. "You probably have no idea how much effort a basic routine requires. It causes profuse sweating, especially for someone Gunter's size. It's like running in Central Park on a humid summer's day."

Vinnie kept quiet, knowing Gunter did not wear the walking sneakers to Katia's party. But the jacket made no sense. He'd ask Gunter to confirm later. Vinnie added to Rita's far-fetched ideas, reading Tom's blank look as disdain. His interjections were vague platitudes: "Interesting." "Unlikely." "I'll think about that." "I wish it were that easy."

Bullshit, thought Vinnie, *this is him regretting he allowed us on the investigative team.*

Turning to Gunter, Tom said, "The decision's yours. The DA wants an answer by Monday, nine o'clock. What do you want to do? My recommendation is you take the plea."

Vinnie sat bolt upright, followed by Rita. Tom flinched at Vinnie's animated cursing, to which Rita added her own.

Tom took his chair behind the floating desk. "Gunter has

to make the decision, not either of you. I understand he's your friend, which means you cannot separate feelings from facts. But it's Gunter I'm obligated to listen to, not you. My advice is strictly legal, not emotional." Tom paused, then looked across to Gunter. "What do you want me to say to the DA? Do you want to risk never leaving prison or coming out when you're fifty?"

"No."

"No what? Please be specific. No, you don't accept, or no, you don't want a lifelong prison sentence?"

"I don't want to stay in prison for life."

"So do I tell the district attorney you accept? Are you sure?"

"I don't know. I didn't kill anyone."

"There!" yelled Vinnie, swinging his arms. "That's the real meaning of his no." He gritted his teeth to the point of cracking. "You tell the fuckin' DA he can go fuck himself. You work on Gunter's defense and we'll find evidence to prove his innocence."

Vinnie's face burned. He hated when DAs applied pressure and the defense lawyers colluded. Offer the innocent a plea applying gambling principles—calculate the odds of winning versus the cost of losing. And Vinnie knew that for people without means or biases against minorities the plea was the best option. Not so for the rich and well connected. Vinnie knew this from his father and brother, who actually deserved their prison time but were never given a chance to defend themselves in court. But Gunter was not a criminal, yet the pressure to accept an injustice and the plea offered to him was hard to refuse. Gunter, given his mental fragility, would find it even harder.

Vinnie's thoughts were interrupted by Tom's voice. "From what I heard, he wants to accept the plea. Is that right Gunter?"

Gunter rose from his chair and followed Vinnie and Rita to the door, saying, "I don't know. You decide."

"Stop!" Tom walked over to Gunter. "You have to decide, it can't be me or Vinnie or Rita doing it for you."

"I can't."

Rita took Gunter's hand and said, "He has until nine Monday morning. Give him the weekend," and she pulled Gunter to the exit. "We'll talk in your room."

"Rita, this has to be his decision." Tom backed away, retreating to his desk.

Her head swung toward Tom. "Give me some credit. I would never make this kind of decision for Gunter or anyone. I get the importance and don't intend to feel guilty or responsible for the rest of Gunter's life or mine. But he deserves time to talk this out. Let the consequences sink in. At least give him that and back off a bit."

Everyone turned, hearing Vinnie mutter, "An innocent man shouldn't have to gamble. I'll find out who did this, I fuckin' swear it. And I'm going to go on record here and say Gunter should not take the fuckin' plea."

Gunter, Rita, and Vinnie walked out of Tom's office, their silence unbroken as the rushing elevator turbulence followed them to the ground floor. Crossing the large marble lobby, Rita turned to Vinnie. "Did we do the right thing? Do you really think Gunter shouldn't take the plea?"

Vinnie didn't answer but walked to the lobby's row of

revolving doors. He waited for an opening, emerging with his cell phone in his palm. "Blanca, call him now. Time's up. Do whatever you need to do but get me in direct contact with your inside guy, Roberto."

"Who the fuck is Roberto?" asked Rita.

"Gunter's last chance." Vinnie walked away to wait for Roberto's call.

29

Vinnie's cell rang early in the morning. "Thanks for the call, Roberto," said Vinnie, reclining in his home office desk chair during the conversation. Ten minutes later he signed off with, "I swear, Roberto, my guy's innocent. And I owe you big time." Vinnie texted Rita as soon as the call ended: Meet at front desk in

Rita arrived rosy-faced. Her skin glistened with sweat, tight leotard leggings swelled around her pumped thighs, and her bosom stretched the Lycra top. Striations marked her pumped biceps as her arms crossed while she waited for Vinnie to explain the reason for the rushed meeting.

"You can't come dressed like that."

"For your information, my class just ended. No way I could finish the class, shower, and change in the time you asked. Besides, tonight's my time with Gunter to talk about his options."

Rita's eyes bored into Vinnie.

"I've spoken to Blanca's inside informant," he said.

"You mean Roberto?"

"Yeah. Not his real name by the way, but he's definitely Latino. His information's reliable but he likes to keep anonymous."

Taking Rita's elbow, Vinnie nudged her to Ben's unoccupied UltraFit office since he was busy training a client.

"We may have something to go on. A long shot but worth a try. A possible witness at Katia's apartment, according to the cop. A neighbor of Katia's. This might be one of the new pieces the DA's dragging out."

"Wait here," said Rita as she rushed out and returned in under fifteen minutes, her hair wet and now dressed in street clothing.

Vinnie rolled his eyes. Rita's jab followed. He rubbed his shoulder, cursing.

"Get over it! You coming or what?" she asked, briskly walking out the door.

* * *

Outside the Stuyvesant Town brownstone, Rita stood behind Vinnie on the stoop. Death had stood here weeks before, the murderer of Karen Probinowski, aka Katia Tittle.

Although the Uber ride had brought them here in quick time, it was not good for discussing an interview strategy following Tom Galantuomo's caution to avoid speaking about the case in front of third parties.

On the doorstep, Rita asked, "Do we introduce ourselves as part of Gunter's defense team or as investigators and let him think we're with the police? Or do we let him guess? Or avoid telling him altogether?" She had a slight tremble in her voice, her lips barely opened.

"Let's see what he's like first. We'll tread slowly with the questioning. I expect he'll not want to cooperate, especially if he thinks we're helping the murderer."

"Alleged murderer," said Rita.

"I know... just saying," whispered Vinnie to calm her.

On any other investigation Rita would not have been so agitated. A college-educated fitness and bodybuilding champion with an uninhibited sexual lifestyle, she exuded self-confidence. She effortlessly transitioned from Vinnie's bodyguard into a co-investigator. Their mismatched styles took the best from their different characters. Today was too personal and Vinnie backed off—the stakes were too high. Vinnie was having second thoughts. Maybe bringing Rita along was a mistake.

The outside video camera light flashed red.

"Who's there?" asked a disembodied voice.

"I'm Vinnie Briggs and this is Rita Light. We'd like to talk to you, Mr. Gormich."

"I'm not interested in buying anything."

"No, we're not selling... look, this is about your poor neighbor, Katia Tittle—" The buzzer sounded before Vinnie finished his sentence.

Inside the main entryway, a door to the right of the staircase opened slightly. A man peered out, the chain still attached to the door.

"Are you with the police?"

Vinnie moved forward. "We are investigating Katia's murder. Can we talk to you please? We won't be long."

The door opened wide to reveal a five-foot six-inch man holding a baseball bat. On seeing Rita he lowered the weapon.

"Mr. Gormich, I'm Rita Light and this is my friend and

colleague Vinnie Briggs. We really just want to follow up on the information you gave the police. We would be appreciative." Rita's flute-like voice and full-on smile contrasted with her nervousness a few minutes earlier. Her professional fitness training kicked in.

"I guess so. Come in."

Vinnie looked around at the hanging lithographs and wall prints. Two themes dominated: one wall devoted to modernism, the other an eclectic selection of portraits of well-known gay photographers. Vinnie pointed to the Mapplethorpe and said, "My partner and I have a similar print." He kept out the part that they had an original. His message got through as Gormich talked about his admiration for the pioneering work of the photographer.

"Yes, they were indeed pioneers, Mr. Gormich." Vinnie smiled, his voice enthusiastic.

"Call me Douglas."

For an hour Vinnie and Rita talked to Douglas. He served cappuccino and biscotti with a commentary on his cat, the neighborhood, and changes to the city. Douglas lamented recent city cutbacks impacting the MTA transit service, for which he had been a senior comptroller before retirement ten years earlier. At least his pension remained robust.

The key moment came when Douglas Gormich confirmed Roberto's inside information. Gormich had seen Gunter and heard the argument with Katia. "A fairytale giant. The Jolly Green Giant, although he was more sunlamp brownish than green. I guess I should call him the Jolly Giant. I wouldn't like to meet him in a dark alley whatever his name, I can tell you that."

A poke from Vinnie on Rita's knee stifled her.

Gormich continued. He had seen two men outside the building the same night as Katia's murder. Vinnie nearly dropped his coffee cup.

"Are you surprised?" asked Douglas with a napkin in hand ready to mop any coffee spilt from Vinnie's cup. "I said this to Detectives Kaplan and Daven. Didn't they find them? I thought they might send a sketch artist. Probably more staff cutbacks."

He continued, ignoring his own diversion. "I know it was dark, but they stood under a streetlamp and I saw their faces. I study men's faces," he said, smiling as he pointed to the wall. "I believe they are related." He gently picked up his cup and seemed to generate thoughts with each sip. Gently placing his cup in its saucer, he said, "They ducked behind a car when the Jolly Giant came out the front door. Isn't that odd?" He smiled broadly as if he'd said something funny.

Vinnie asked him to expand on his thoughts. Douglas's smile marginally lessened as he speculated. His full smile returned as he invented a conspiracy scenario that linked all three men with Katia's murder. "Maybe they hid so Katia wouldn't see them. Or maybe they had a prearrangement with the Jolly Giant."

Vinnie squeezed Rita's arm, knowing she might leap up and crush the diminutive Douglas Gormich if he continued referring to Gunter as the Jolly Giant.

"Did you notice anything else, anything at all?" said Rita with her hands bunched. "Sometimes we don't think we remember but then something related pops up."

"Like what?"

Vinnie stood to look out the front window. "Which car?"

"Oh, it's not there now. Vacant parking spots don't last long round here. Sometimes people take a cab rather than lose their spot."

"Hmm. So you don't think it was their car they went behind?"

"Definitely not. I know the car. Belongs to Joe Veldrano across the street. Nice guy. He and his wife are away this week at their place in Vermont."

"You think these guys took the subway or a cab?" Rita asked her question to Douglas but looked toward the window partially blocked by Vinnie.

"Actually, I do remember something. I watched as the men left and I'm pretty sure they were in one of those black private town cars. I saw them drive by and the side rear door had a name plate."

"License number?"

"No, not visible from here, especially in the dark."

"New York plates?"

"Couldn't tell you."

Vinnie and Rita thanked Douglas Gormich for his help as they walked out the front door. Before they reached the sidewalk, Douglas called out from his doorway. He had just remembered that if the car was from out of state they could check video footage at the tunnels or bridges. Vinnie thanked him again, then Douglas stepped out on to the top step, saying the city budget had shifted to surveillance cameras, another reason for the MTA budget reduction. Then, with near delight, he blurted, "And they even installed cameras on Broadway. The car might have been caught on one even if it wasn't out of state. "

* * *

Blanca wangled camera surveillance tape from another contact at the NYPD. The black town car was clear and similar to the one Gunter described at Sakura Park.

Vinnie called Tom Galantuomo and suggested he postpone deal-making with the DA. Rita's elation plummeted upon learning that Tom called the "new evidence" coincidental at best and at worst it linked Gunter to conspiracy, as Gormich had speculated. Tom did not see a significant shift in Gunter's status and believed the DA's plea offer remained his best option.

"Find something more substantial or Gunter's facing a tough decision."

Dejected, Rita left Vinnie's office to be with Gunter.

Blanca was furious that several hours spent reviewing video footage had been a wasted effort, but Vinnie knew the real fury rose from her disappointment—just like him and Rita. Vinnie heard her pushing papers around her desk. He closed his door, which opened half an hour later with Blanca's head poking in.

"What do I do with the town car owner's address?" She was holding a piece of paper over the wastebasket.

With a hawk's precision, Vinnie swooped to take the paper from Blanca's hand and sprinted out on his mission.

30

Vinnie grumbled crossing the Hudson River as if he'd entered hostile foreign territory. He chose the Holland Tunnel to reach Jersey City. He could have taken the Lincoln Tunnel, but then he would have spent more time driving in Jersey. He was in the middle of rush hour, crawling for miles in bumper-to-bumper traffic.

Vinnie reached his destination after six. The house was in a working neighborhood around McGinley Square amid classic wood-framed, two-story houses built in the 1930s with long stoops leading to wide front doors. There was plenty of on-street parking. Vinnie pulled his Audi A6 Turbo in a few houses from where he would conduct his interview.

Crossing to the sidewalk, he looked at his car, eight inches from the curb, and judged this a reasonable facsimile of good parking. It worked in New York State so why not Jersey City?

Walking to the house, he saw a tall man in a cut-off T-shirt enter the front door, his bare, pumped arms glistening with sweat. Vinnie figured he'd either been working out or doing heavy household chores. The man held open the front door, inviting Vinnie inside. On crossing the threshold

Vinnie ruled out cleaning as the man's physical activity.

"What's this about... er, what's your name?" asked the young man in a clipped New Jersey accent that grated on Vinnie, who much preferred Brooklyn's finer nasal tones.

"I'm Roger... Roger Hammerstein," said Vinnie, hand extended. "Are you... uh..."

"I'm Dimitri," said the man, shaking Vinnie's hand. "So?"

"I had a few questions about a small traffic infraction that may have involved your car. It seems my girlfriend, Jennifer, well, she's not too good at driving and well... anyway, she thinks she scraped a parked car in Manhattan a few weeks ago but she drove away. She'd like to avoid an insurance claim and I'm ready to make restitution for the damages."

Vinnie struggled with his inconsistencies. His explanation was vague on the method he had used to find Dimitri. His rambling mentioned his non-existent girlfriend noted the car plates around Stuyvesant Town. Dimitri seemed distracted, uninterested in the long-winded explanation or incomplete logic of plate numbers to a car owner's address. More important to Vinnie was that Dimitri didn't react to the location.

Dimitri's eyes steeled, lips pursed, and his taut, sinewy forearms folded across his chest. Not the reaction of someone about to be compensated for damage to his vehicle. But not a murderer's response either, although Vinnie was uncertain what that would be. Take out a gun and shoot him on the spot maybe?

Pressing the issue, Vinnie asked Dimitri if he'd been at the location on the specific Saturday of Katia's murder, not saying the last part. Dimitri's eyes drilled into Vinnie, and he spoke with a forced smile. "When I drove away there was not a scratch on it. My car's fine. Your girlfriend must have hit someone else."

Confirmation. Dimitri recognized Katia's neighborhood and the Saturday date, even if not the exact time he drove away. Vinnie had found one of the people seen by Douglas Gormich and his smile broadened. "That's a relief, at least for you. Of course, it means I have another dozen names to check out." This should have concluded their talk, but Vinnie used the oldest ruse in the book to go further.

"Do you mind if I use your bathroom before I go? It's a helluva drive back to the city, especially if I hit traffic."

With a nod, Dimitri walked Vinnie down a central hall, providing him with a good look into the rooms, each with its door open.

Beer cans and fast-food boxes spread over the living room floor. A barbell lay next to the fireplace. Several trophies topped the mantel. Vinnie recognized the figurine poses as boxing trophies. He would ask Blanca to check out matches in Jersey City. Dimitri certainly had a boxer's physique, but something about him didn't scream champion. Vinnie had been around too many high achievers at UltraFit to know their demeanor even if it was different to boxing.

The dining room table was covered with newspapers, dishes, old rags, an oilcan, and pieces of wood. A filthy mess. The last room down the hallway was the kitchen, with pots and dishes strewn around on every counter. It looked like no one had touched them in years.

"Here," said Dimitri, pushing open a door to a utility

bathroom with a filthy toilet and a cracked seat.

Vinnie decided he would pee, risking disease to prove his dedication to his client. The stained toilet didn't seem like it had been cleaned since the house was built. Vinnie touched the water tap with his thumb and middle finger to rinse his hands—no soap. He ignored the dirty tea towel hanging on the corner windowsill, instead drying his hands on his jeans, and overheard an animated conversation outside the bathroom. Coming out, he heard clumping footsteps approaching him.

"Who the fuck are you? Get the fuck out of my house!"

"I'm—"

"I don't fucking care who you are."

"Okay, I was—"

"Fuck off! Now!"

Vinnie recognized the man, not his identity but who he looked like—Dimitri—only shorter, stockier, and older. If Dimitri was in good shape, this guy was seriously fit. He had a thick neck, broad shoulders, and an attitude to match. This was a champion boxer. Vinnie also heard the broken English and thick accent that sounded Russian.

The front door slammed behind Vinnie. He walked down the stoop, pausing on the second step. The closed door didn't muffle the shouting. Vinnie didn't understand a word of the foreign language but knew it was an argument. He listened for a minute, until he heard one English sentence. "Fuck you, Vasi. Stop calling me stupid."

Vinnie inserted his favorite CD into the car's player, then pulled away from the curb singing along as he headed to the Holland Tunnel. Entering the tunnel, he turned up the volume.

"This is good news, isn't it?" Rita paced in front of Vinnie's desk. A few minutes before she had yelled at him for going to an interview without her. She thought together they could have gotten more out of Dimitri, but she was consoled by the information. The cousins had been in Katia's neighborhood, so it was a good outcome.

"Too bad you don't speak Russian or you might have learned more from their argument."

"Next time I'll put a foreign-language CD in the car as I go on a reconnaissance mission. Should I take a culinary class if I'm interviewing a sous-chef?"

Rita shrugged, arms upright, her head tilted toward the ceiling. Vinnie hated her exaggerated posing. He chomped his lips, keeping his mouth shut and taking Blanca's advice that he act like a "mature grown-up."

As Rita dropped her arms, he added, "There's one more thing. As I left, I saw a black limo parked out front that had not been there when I arrived. Same plate number as captured on the CCTV footage." Vinnie was restating facts but thought it important to confirm with Rita.

"Obviously the guy called Vasi arrived while I was in the house. Star Limo Service stenciled on the door along with a telephone number. I took a photo to show Gunter. I'm sure this is the town car he saw the night of the grad student's murder. Let's hope he can confirm."

Rita agreed, adding that it was a long shot. Gunter's mind had blocked out much of what happened the night he saw Tariq.

"Let's call Tom now. This could be the breakthrough we need to get Gunter's case dismissed or at least refuse the plea agreement," Rita said with the lilt of hope in her voice.

"Not yet," said Vinnie, pacing. "We need more."

"And how do we get that?"

"Don't know. Let's wait for Blanca's report on this Vasi guy."

"Wait? We don't have time, remember? We need to do something."

Vinnie shrugged. "We will, don't you worry. As soon as we get the info from Blanca."

He never imagined Blanca's research would yield results so fast or require immediate action.

31

Vinnie stared at the printout handed to him by Blanca, un-covering details about the man who had cursed him—a man called Vasily Karimov. She beamed with self-satisfaction at completing the task by mid-morning.

As Vinnie had guessed, Vasily Karimov was a champion boxer. Blanca learned he had transitioned to mixed martial arts at a local Jersey City gym.

"He has a match tonight. The next is a week later, so act fast," said Blanca.

Vinnie hastily devised a plan that hinged on Dimitri being out of the house at the same time as cousin Vasily. He dialed Rita.

"Pack a bag. You're going to Newark Airport."

While he gave her the details, Blanca was on the phone to a Star Limo Service dispatcher. Vinnie read her scribbled note entering her office—Russian accent. She switched to speaker and signed Vinnie to keep quiet.

The dispatcher balked at Blanca's request for Dimitri, and on such short notice. Blanca explained that Dimitri was recommended by a friend who had used him a week or so ago. Blanca pleaded this was a bungling snafu. The dispatcher offered the town car but with another driver.

Blanca went into a convoluted explanation about the traveler arriving at Newark Airport, a woman with a recent "unpleasant experience with a man. I can't go into details but there will be criminal charges if you get my meaning."

Of course he did and gave words of sympathy. Also thanked her for the compliments about Dimitri, his son.

"A good boy too," continued the father, "and a college student. Has heavy studies so you see is not possible, especially so short a notice."

Blanca's tone stiffened. "My friend's too fragile. Either Dimitri's the chauffeur or I'll have my boyfriend leave work early and do it. And you'll read about this in my social media reviews. And I'm on Twitter, Facebook, Instagram, to name a few."

"I'm sorry, truly, but Dimi only work Saturday and Sunday," he said with contrition. "My other man very reliable. Family man. Also good reputation. Safe driver."

"I'm sure, but no thanks. My friend was told she'd be met by Dimitri. A change would freak her out. She'll arrive exhausted from an overseas trip and will be tired anyway."

Vinnie was impressed with Blanca's fast thinking. He nearly cursed out loud on hearing Blanca offer to double the normal rate and guarantee a large tip for dragging Dimitri from his important studies.

"Done," said Blanca, hanging up the phone.

"Fuckin' double the rate and a big tip? Couldn't you start with one-and-a-half and not mention the tip? What kind of negotiating is that?"

Blanca raised an eyebrow and gave a smug remark that

financial incentives often prove more persuasive than appeals to help a woman.

"You know, you've got to quit that eyebrow shit."

"Stopped you, didn't it?"

* * *

Rita stood curbside at Newark Airport's International Terminal. Despite it being late September, the early evening had a warm breeze. She had three twenty-five-pound weights wrapped in towels inside two pieces of matching luggage and twenty pounds in her carry-on. She looked like a passenger arriving on the American Airlines international flight from Berlin and stood at the baggage claim area. Rita chastised herself for not adding twenty-five pounds to each bag to make a hernia risk more likely when Dimitri lifted the cases into the car trunk. She waited, gauging the time by the passengers from the flight entering cars and cabs. With a dozen gone, she called Dimitri from the airport's taxi and limo waiting area.

Dimitri Karimov appeared taller to Rita than Vinnie's description, and thinner. An illusion created by his tailored chauffeur uniform? Thin appearance aside, Dimitri hoisted each bag with a one-hand lift. *I'd need at least three or four more twenty-five-pounders to make him strain.* Rita didn't see the pug-face Vinnie had described. The slight crook in his obviously broken nose made Dimitri's face slightly asymmetrical yet somehow enhanced his rugged handsomeness.

Rita had seen Blanca's notes on Vasily Karimov, the real boxer of the two cousins. He visited his New Jersey family once each year and stayed the maximum six months stipulated by his US visitor's visa. A few years earlier, the former boxer had changed to the more lucrative mixed martial arts arena. Vasily sought an agent using his online LinkedIn page for MMA gigs on pay-per-view TV.

"Money. I knew it," said Rita.

"Yeah," agreed Blanca, "and he has a built-in fan base. The entire expatriate Tajik community, other former Soviet countries, and Eastern Europeans. Success guaranteed. Yet no agent. There must be something off about the guy that I can't figure out."

Blanca's search revealed that Dimitri, like his cousin, was a boxer, although amateur and nowhere close to Vasily's level. Certainly not good enough for the celebrated national Tajikistan Olympic boxing team. Not even a mediocre amateur. Dimitri was unremarkable. His Facebook bio outlined his career from youth events at a local Y to the Rutgers team, where he once managed third place.

"Reads like a litany of failure," said Rita, "yet mentions his boxing career as if noteworthy. For most people it wouldn't matter, but when your cousin's an international star in the ring... well, you look like a disappointment in comparison."

"Yeah," chimed in Blanca. "I mean, you don't brag about third prize in a science fair when your cousin's Einstein."

Once in the limo, Rita gave Dimitri directions to an up-scale Hoboken restaurant. She engaged him in conversation from the start of the journey without effort as he was of the class of drivers that liked talking with passengers. The Jersey Turnpike stop-and-go traffic prolonged their journey, which suited Rita.

"I'm sorry about the delay. Typical this time of day. Commuters and a single accident can hold things up," he said.

"Not a problem. I'm just glad to be home and I'm very comfortable in the back seat."

Rita noticed Dimitri adjusted his rear-view mirror to have a better view of her. She'd worn a clinging sleeveless blouse to attract his attention and it worked. She saw his eyes linger on her bosom at the airport and knew she'd made a wise choice of apparel. With occasional small chuckles, she smiled at Dimitri as he answered her questions. It was not his reply that amused her, but that he didn't realize she was learning about him and his cousin. She complemented him on his strength.

"I paid the airline baggage penalty for not packing light. I always pack too much and buy more stuff when abroad. I hope it wasn't too much for you."

"No, I'm used to it. I work out at a local gym and box. My cousin is a champion Olympic boxer. You should see how strong he is. Arms like pythons and he can run ten miles in heavy boots with weights on his legs. I bench press two hundred forty pounds."

Rita smiled. She lifted that much as a warm-up. Gunter did that at seventeen.

At the restaurant, Dimitri arranged Rita's luggage on the sidewalk. She paid the double fee and a crisp hundred-dollar tip. He moved closer to accept payment with his arm brushing against her breasts. "You sure you don't want me to carry these inside? Do you need a ride home after your meal? I can wait. No additional charge."

Rita restrained herself from smashing his kneecap and kicking him to make him sing falsetto but smiled at his offer.

"No, it's fine. My boyfriend should be here in about an hour, after his meeting. I'll have the wait staff take this to the back kitchen. They know me and I plan to spend time at the bar. Thanks, though."

* * *

Rita waited at Newark Airport for Dimitri, and in Jersey City Vinnie entered Dimitri's home. He did a quick tour of the filthy downstairs living space before heading to the upstairs bedrooms.

Boxing trophies on the dresser in the master suite were as good a sign as any that Vinnie stood in Vasily's room. A double bed, weights, weight bench, and a large-screen TV completed the room's furnishings. The room was tidy and the bed made. A charging cable suggested a laptop computer, which Vinnie presumed Vasily had with him, although it seemed an odd thing to take to an MMA match. Something to ponder on the way home.

The second bedroom was a pigpen. No deductive reasoning needed to know this belonged to Dimitri, or that he was responsible for the downstairs disarray. Vinnie moved about the room not wanting to touch more surfaces than was necessary. The double, unmade bed had a single light dumbbell beside a desk, and clothes were strewn everywhere. Books lay on the floor next to a desk with a large Mac desktop computer and printer. On the printer table were glossy color photos of naked women. Vinnie shuffled through them and saw pictures of men and women in various positions. He knew these would only be a fraction of those on Dimitri's computer hard drive.

"Okay, let's get to work and find out what this fuckin' bastard does with his time." Vinnie's old habit of talking to himself returned when under pressure and feeling tense.

He answered himself in a higher pitch. "As if you didn't know." A grin came over his face.

To Vinnie's surprise, Dimitri did not use a password to lock his computer. He had come prepared with a USB loaded with decryption software supplied by his former college roommate, now a professional computer programmer. A check of Dimitri's browser history revealed he spent more time on porn sites than anything else—*surprise, surprise*. But Dimitri also cleared his browser history every week, making the information incomplete.

Dimitri's emails proved more useful—messages to Tariq, the dead Columbia University grad student. While nothing specific popped up, nothing obviously nefarious, there were a few meet-up dates. Content was less relevant than the connection between Dimitri and Tariq. Some messages were in a Cyrillic alphabet, probably a Tajikistan dialect in Vinnie's opinion. He was sure Tom's firm had language experts versed in every language if Google Translate couldn't help. There was no time to sort out which information stored on the computer was relevant to Gunter's case, so Vinnie downloaded everything on to a sixty-four gigabyte USB drive.

In the middle of his download he wondered if he really needed all the porno pictures. "Might as well. You can never tell. Maybe Dimitri had a few male/male... now that might be worth a box of tissues."

Before Vinnie could reply to himself, his cell phone rang. He had meant to put it on mute but had forgotten.

"Vinnie, you still there?"

"Yeah. How'd it go?"

Vinnie waited but heard only Rita's breathing.

"That bad, huh?"

"We'll review at the office. In the meantime, you should finish up. He left ten minutes ago. I waited before calling you because I had the feeling he might come back for a second try, if you know what I mean?"

"Mmm."

"Get your ass out of there. Traffic was bad but has probably eased up. I'd give him thirty minutes from now."

After hanging up, Vinnie looked at the computer screen. The download continued with an estimated transfer time on the screen: *26 minutes to completion.* It'd be tight. Vinnie checked his watch. If Dimitri drove like a typical maniacal Jerseyite and hit no traffic, then he'd have five minutes to spare. Otherwise, he had about fifteen.

Vinnie used the time to explore more of the room. A peek into the closet suggested a shopping spree at Barneys. Only it had gone wrong, and most of the wardrobe lay on the floor. He checked the pockets of several items. Nothing of interest jumped out. Returning to the computer, Vinnie saw the clock: *19 minutes to completion.*

Vinnie moved to the third bedroom, about the same size as Dimitri's. This was a dedicated weight room. Nothing like Ben's, yet still impressive. Various preloaded barbells and a dumbbell rack with a combined total of a thousand pounds. One wall had floor-to-ceiling mirrors. In another corner hung a punching bag next to a heavy bag suspended from the ceiling reinforced by a steel bar.

After trying a few weights to get a feel of what they were lifting, Vinnie returned to Dimitri's room. The download was almost finished: *8 minutes to completion.* He paced, poking through draws and under the bed. The computer pinged, and he removed the USB drive. Returning downstairs, he went into the kitchen and saw the basement door ajar. Vinnie estimated he had at least five minutes but probably ten, enough time for a quick check.

The dank cellar had a workbench on one side with a washing machine and dryer opposite. Did Dimitri do laundry?

A soldering iron, electronic components, and pieces of metal lay on a workbench, along with a few glass tubes and wires. Vinnie poked underneath the bench, then heard the front door open followed by loud voices.

"Since when do you take passengers during the week?"

"I do what I want. Besides, people ask for me. I'm polite. The woman liked me. I could tell. I might go back later to check out where she lives. You wouldn't believe her body, Vasi. A set of tits like incredible." He let out a low, appreciative whistle.

Dimitri's voice became louder. "And why are you here? Don't you have a match?"

"Cancelled. Some idiot set a fire in the bathroom. Burnt up the entire wall. The fire department closed down the building until an inspector approves reopening. Monday or Tuesday they say."

Overhead, floorboards creaked with the cousins walking around the kitchen. The refrigerator door opened and shut a few times.

"Listen, Dimi, this mission is important. You need to concentrate, stop thinking about getting laid all the time."

"Fuck off, Vasi. I'll do whatever I want. I know the mission is important. And I'm doing my part. Yes or no?"

Vinnie heard the footsteps of the two men leave the kitchen, their voices growing distant. He waited what he thought was a minute or two but didn't check his watch. He slowly climbed the stairs. As he was about to open the cellar door to the kitchen, he heard a sound.

"Dimitri, is it in the basement?" asked Vasily.

The doorknob slowly turned, but the door did not open. Vinnie froze, worried if he moved the old, creaking wooden steps would give him away. Fear paralyzed him and sweat soaked his brow. He stopped breathing.

Then he heard Vasily say, "What's that? You found it? Okay."

The doorknob released. Vinnie was sure he had peed his pants. He sat on the top step, his breathing labored and irregular.

The cousins returned to the kitchen, again raising Vinnie's heart rate. More sweat ran from his brow to his cheeks.

"Let's go, Dimitri. Better for us to eat at the diner tonight. We don't have much time to finish so we'll be ready for the Americans and their stupid holiday. They pervert their own religion for money—dressing up animals."

"Yes, but they do it for fun too. Right? Don't we do the same?" Dimitri's voice was softer than his cousin's but still audible.

"Don't get sentimental. These people deserve to suffer, just remember that when the fucking bombs go off."

As the cousins left the kitchen, Vinnie's sweat became a near downpour. If he understood what he heard correctly, these men planned to explode a bomb... or bombs... in some public place. Where and when? They mentioned a celebration, something about animals.

Leaving the house, Vinnie chose to make his return journey to his New York condo by driving up Broadway rather than chance the West Side Highway traffic. He cursed the stalled traffic on 34th Street caused by a minor accident. He tuned the radio to a local talk show. The two-commentator format—a man and a woman duo—reminisced about their childhood Halloween costumes. They laughed, revealing their funny outfits. The woman said her worst was a giraffe costume. The long neck and lopsided candy bag put her off balance and twice she keeled over.

As soon as she said it, Vinnie knew what the cousins were planning. A bomb for Halloween, somewhere in a prominent New York location where people would congregate. Overwhelming choices, which meant more investigation. Only four weeks before the end of October.

The first priority was to persuade Gunter to decline the plea offer.

With the Audi parked in the underground garage beneath his condo, Vinnie mulled over whether to tell Tom about the bomb. If he did, Tom would have to inform Homeland Security and end any chance of finding additional information on the cousins and their connection to Gunter and

Katia. He opened his car window, letting the cool air seep into the interior. Vinnie had a basic distrust of authority, especially police detectives, based on his experience. He didn't know about the Feds, but imagined they'd be even bigger assholes then regular cops. Vinnie closed the car window and stepped out.

"Hey, watch where you're walking," yelled a man exiting the garage elevator as Vinnie entered with head bowed.

"Yeah, yeah," answered Vinnie. But he knew he was in the wrong about not watching where he was going. Was it the same for keeping the information from Tom?

Ruminating, he knew that so far he had the cousins involved with Tariq and only a tenuous connection to Katia.

What was Gunter's role? Without the answer, Vinnie knew Tom would argue Gunter looked like a co-conspirator in a terrorist act. That brought the death penalty. He'd seen this before, co-conspirators with tenuous connections to terrorists. *Shit happens.*

He could not make this decision alone.

32

Vinnie rushed from his parked car to the BIG office. He confronted Blanca and Rita, their anxiety-stricken bodies glued to their chairs. He sighed, wiping his eyes. Blanca took out her cell and called her husband, telling him she'd be late and he should feed the kids.

Looking at the floor, Vinnie had no qualms telling everyone he'd been "scared fuckin' shitless" in the Karimov basement. What if he had been discovered?

Something huge was being planned, and soon. Vinnie repeated the conversation he overheard between the cousins, some in Russian or Farsi or whatever it was. "I'm no linguist authority, but one definitely had a foreign accent—Jersey." Vinnie's grin shriveled facing his two glum coworkers.

The room's atmosphere vacillated from anger to gloom to worry as Vinnie revealed with certainty that the cousins were planning to hurt people. Rita expressed hope that it was just macho banter. She placed her index finger against her teeth and chewed.

Vinnie presented cell phone photos of Vasily Karimov's boxing trophies, and the official Tajikistan Olympic Boxing Team portrait taken nine years earlier. Blanca interrupted to point out that doping disqualified not only Vasily but the entire team during the Games. During her research, she had discovered the reason—the USA Olympic Committee filed a complaint. Vasily's gold medal had been rescinded as well as the team's overall gold medal. The *New York Times* called the scandal an outrageous indictment, with particular attention to Vasily's role.

Blanca had scoured sports magazines for more information about Vasily. Even as a teenager he was making news on the boxing circuit. Everyone considered him the most promising boxer, the Tajik version of Muhammad Ali. With the death of both his parents while still in high school, the speculation grew that he might become a US citizen. His uncle, Dimitri's father, became the teenager's legal guardian. Team USA courted him, offering to sponsor his citizenship. Yet it was not to be. Vasily Karimov repeated in interviews that he was a Tajikistan nationalist. A surprising decision but consistent with his pride in his country and his father, a former national boxing coach. In an interview prior to the fateful Olympic games, Vasily cited loyalty as being more important than boxing medals.

Blanca looked at her notepad. "Here's what the *Times* article says, and I quote, 'I am a great boxer. But my best quality is loyalty. I honor my country and my father and mother at the Olympics standing beneath the Tajikistan flag.' He goes on to say he'd never compete for another country."

"Let me get this straight," said Rita, contorting her lips. "The guy cheats with steroids and what? He wants revenge because he was exposed?"

"That's how I see it," said Vinnie, who held back that both Ben and Gunter used muscle-enhancing drugs, and that she probably did as well in her bodybuilding days. He knew they were the reason Ben won his titles and the prized Mr. Olympia trophy. *Now's not a good time to point this out,* he thought, and moved on to discussing Dimitri's hard drive.

"I've not had time to do a full review, but the little I've seen suggests he's got an extensive porn collection. Pretty impressive I'd say and I'll be going through them too."

Blanca and Rita made disparaging noises.

"Yeah, wag your fingers as much as you want. Aside from the fact they'll mostly be women and therefore not of interest, I'm still a professional and the material has to be—"

Vinnie flinched at the women's bursting outcry. "Fuckin' laugh all you want. But I already learned something. Dimitri likes big-breasted women and unusual sexual positions." Vinnie paused to stare at Rita, who showed him her middle finger followed by more raucous laughs from her and Blanca.

"Hey, cut it out. This is fuckin' important."

The women howled louder.

Waiting a few seconds, Vinnie continued his analysis. "He has a few male-male and threesome videos, which are interesting." Vinnie stopped to wait for more derision but none came so he continued. "I think Dimitri's willing to experiment or possibly confused in his sexuality. But overall he goes for big boobs. Does that work as a psychological profile, Rita?"

Rita stood and pushed up her own breasts. "The way he looked at these, I could have told you about his so-called mammary fascination. I saw him adjust his rear-view mirror so it pointed down rather than at my face, and was of no use as a driving aid. A helluva chauffeur—and luckily the traffic kept the speed slow."

"You want to write a TripAdvisor review?" asked Vinnie.

"He even used a clumsy schoolboy move to brush his arm against my breasts while taking payment. I'd say our Dimitri has serious boob issues," said Rita, who pointed at Vinnie as she continued, "and for your description of him being on the thin side, he's one strong son-of-a-bitch. He tossed my seventy-five-pound suitcases with one arm, effortless and no straining."

"Okay," interrupted Blanca, "we have a sex pervert whose cousin is an Olympic boxing medalist even though it was rescinded. And now these two nutcases want to murder innocent people including children." She swallowed hard then added creative Spanish curses ending with, "*Che punto mierde. El diablo.*"

Everyone in the room recognized the delusion of the vanquished, left helpless by their own folly. The worst kind of hate, the vitriol against oneself. The loathing satisfied by brutal violence. Vasily went from noteworthy champion to nobody in under thirty seconds. Dimitri went from nobody to dogsbody. Someone has to pay for the humiliation.

Vinnie knew Blanca was thinking of her sons and toddler daughter out on Halloween in their costumes. He worried over his two godchildren, sure he shared Blanca's chills. Did he have a choice? What was the right thing to do? Should he talk to Tom and alert Homeland Security? Or just take another twenty-four hours to nail these bastards and save

Gunter. And what if Homeland bungled it? Who to blame then? He tossed around thoughts, his mind a mishmash of options. His internal conflict broken by Blanca calling out, her face scrunched for emphasis, "We have to tell the Feds."

Too soon to give up, he thought. A surge of self-righteousness, the challenge to his infallibility gave rise to his Italian-Irish version of *chutzpah*, hardheaded and thick-skulled.

"Let me finish going over the entire hard drive," said Vinnie, fiddling with the USB in his hand. "There's a lot here. Maybe we're overreacting. I might have misheard or misunderstood."

Blanca squinted, moving her tongue around her mouth to push out her checks. She'd act on her own. Vinnie suggested, "I'll give you a copy to check for online accounts and cloud storage. If we need passwords, I'll press Hal and we—"

"Who?" interrupted Rita.

"Hal Greenwood, my former Bennington college room-mate. I've mentioned him before. The professional programmer we subcontract to help in cases of corporate espionage. He gave me the decryption software to break into the Karimovs' computers... not that I needed it."

Rita stifled a yawn, saying she remembered and didn't need to know more.

A small grin turned Vinnie's lips upward. "Bet you didn't know I helped find his missing dog."

Blanca shuffled in her chair. "Not good enough."

"What's not good enough? Finding lost animals?" asked Vinnie.

"Taking time to go through the hard drive, meanwhile

the *mierde* cousins go about their business. What if we don't figure it out? We're not equipped for terrorism. We don't have the resources. There are only three of us."

"What are you suggesting?" asked Rita, her jaw wobbling.

Vinnie knew exactly what Blanca meant and was sure Rita did too. He intervened before Blanca could answer and dig in to her position. "We tell Tom and we call Homeland Security. People's lives... children's lives are at stake."

Rita frowned and crossed her arms. "And what about Gunter? His life's on the line too. He won't survive prison, and forty years from now he'll have nothing."

With a sigh Blanca said, "I know. And I'm sorry but ask yourself how you'll feel, or Gunter for that matter, if dozens, hundreds of innocent children and adults are killed?"

"Are you saying one person must be sacrificed to save hundreds? Is that justice? Is that fair?" Rita's voice broke.

Vinnie stood and crossed over to Blanca. "I promise we won't let that happen, but we need time to get more information that will help Gunter. We have linked the cousins to the murders of both Tariq and Katia. We'll figure out a way to use this to exonerate him."

"I agree," said Rita as she too touched Blanca's shoulder. "We won't let anything happen to anyone. We have time— Halloween is weeks away."

The room's silence a slew-footing of relationships, kicking common ground aside. The moment that would change everything forever. Vinnie was scared of losing all.

After a few seconds, Blanca said, "I don't know the answer. I just know that we have to hand over this information."

Vinnie's face puckered, foreshadowing a friendship to be terminated without severance. He gave one last stab to reassure Blanca as much as himself. No innocent people would get harmed, and they had time to help Gunter. Rita supported Vinnie's view.

Blanca remained adamant. "We have to inform Tom and Homeland. If you don't, I will. I know Gunter would agree with me."

Everyone knew she was right. Gunter would never want children to suffer because of him.

Rita nodded, her tone low. "True, and the consequence would be worse for me. If children get hurt saving him and..." Rita swallowed, "...and he learned I kept it from him, he'd never forgive me. And I believe he'd have a mental breakdown. Why is life so hard and the world so fucked up by evil people?"

Vinnie leaned back, hands behind his head. Blanca had mentioned Tom along with Homeland. Maybe that was the way to work this out.

"How about a compromise? We'll tell Tom and ask his opinion on whether to tell Homeland immediately or take a few days. Is that acceptable?" He looked to Blanca, his hands in a praying gesture.

She nodded once. Vinnie gave a two-fisted victory air punch. He couldn't believe his compromise had worked. And like all compromises, no one was fully satisfied. Vinnie inserted the USB stick into his computer and copied the files onto the BIG cloud server, encrypted with a password: FucktheFuckers*2.

"Really, that's the password?"

"I agree with the sentiment," said Rita with a tiny smile, "but Blanca's right about the crudeness. Whatever happened to random letters and numbers?"

"Go ahead and ridicule, but I'll bet neither of you will need to write it down and you won't forget it either." Vinnie placed the USB stick in the BIG office safe and walked out of the room.

* * *

Late into the night at his home study with a window overlooking Central Park Vinnie stared at the computer monitor. He mulled over Dimitri's porn for an hour, knowing Rita would only skim it and Blanca would avoid it entirely. It was up to him to review in detail. And as he suspected from the start, he didn't discover much new. He confirmed Dimitri's big-boob fixation. But he observed Dimitri's proclivity for videos featuring men dominating women and anal sex, which Vinnie thought supported his theory of latent homosexuality. In fact, he discovered several homosexual videos. He knew a few of them but not many, and all were second-rate in his opinion.

The shock was the recording of Dimitri masturbating during sex chats and bragging about his size, strength, and what he would do to the women on the other end of the chat line. "He's a fuckin' nutcase." Vinnie wasn't smiling.

Dimitri's online calendar was filled with class schedules, advisor meetings, family birthdays, and Star Limo bookings, but not a single dinner, movie, or date going back several months. Except for meetings designated "T," which Vinnie was sure meant Tariq. He cross-checked the dates and emails. Tariq was only spelt out completely on one entry in an early calendar date nine months ago. None of the appointments gave reasons for the meetings, only times and locations. Vinnie thought that most communication was probably done via texts. "Clever bastards," he said out loud. "Fuckin' clever bastards."

His email search included variations in spelling Tariq, then included variations on Tariq's last name, Mamurov. No joy, so he tried a trick Hal taught him, a Boolean search consisting of T AND Columbia that produced three emails between Dimitri and Vasily. The gist was that Tariq would help. Dimitri's reply expressed his and Vasily's appreciation for Tariq's devotion to Islam and his country. Tariq's reply acknowledged the importance of Vasily's father, the late, great Tajikistan boxing coach and superb former minister of Internal Relations. He thanked the entire Mamurov family for their support to rebuild a mosque destroyed by an earth-quake in Tariq's hometown. *Now we're getting somewhere.* Vinnie's memo to himself noted to widen the investigation to include details on Tariq Mamurov's family background.

Around midnight, Vinnie shut his computer down and went to bed. Ben, in a deep sleep, spread across the king-size bed. Vinnie slipped under the covers, his body curled around Ben's naked torso. Although exhausted, Vinnie became excited. He considered activating Ben—too risky. He might arouse more than sex, especially if he had to explain his near-capture by murderers and concealing a terrorist plot.

Better to sleep, thought Vinnie, except he could not stop rehearsing the approach in his mind. The restless night and early rise added to his insecurity. In a few hours he would hear Tom Galantuomo's reaction.

33

Glum barely described Tom Galantuomo's expression as he sat in his home office for the unscheduled Saturday morning meeting with Vinnie and Rita. Working on the weekend wasn't Tom's issue, or the BIG investigators congregating in his private office tucked in the rear of a three-story brownstone house in an upscale Brooklyn neighborhood. His disgruntled attitude was brought on by Vinnie's report.

Vinnie had given a preliminary summary over the phone of his Karimov home surveillance. Tom called it breaking and entering. Vinnie felt the lawyer didn't appreciate innovative methods that would have made Vinnie's father, John Briggs, proud. John was one of New York's finest petty thieves and a burglar extraordinaire, from which, by osmosis and father-son outings, Vinnie had learned tricks of the trade.

"Don't waste my time. You haven't learned enough," said Tom.

"But it shows these guys need to hide any connection to their activity. This explains the reason they killed Tariq and Katia!"

"How do you reach that conclusion?" asked Tom, his

eyes lifting.

"Well... first, Katia's neighbor told me he saw a car like the Karimovs' limo or one like it parked out front on the night of the murder. Second, Gunter saw a car with a logo resembling Star Limo on the side. Third, the police know the Karimov car was in the vicinity of the nightclub where Tariq's body was found."

A small smile stretched over Tom's lips. "Hearsay, speculative, and irrelevant."

"Fuckin' lawyer-speak," said Vinnie, and amended with, "Sorry, Tom. Fudgin' lawyer-speak."

Tom smiled at Vinnie, not a smirk but not pleasant either. "You know I'm right. Your so-called evidence is weak, even if it has potential. Yet I'd say insufficient to rule out a guilty verdict."

Walking around the office, Rita examined a cabinet full of professional baseball memorabilia. She appeared to speak to a photo with a signed personal wish to Tom by a well-known former Yankees ballplayer.

"What do we need? How much time do we have?" asked Rita to the photo.

Tom swiveled in his high-back leather chair. "The question of how long is complicated. First, I'll need to inform the prosecutor of Gunter's plea decision by Monday. That's one marker. The more difficult part is how long to delay telling Homeland Security."

The terrorist threat came up in Vinnie's review. Everyone knew gambling with a delay could be deadly.

"Even worse than declining the DA's offer," continued Tom, "is our withholding the plot from Homeland. Should the Karimov cousins' plot succeed, then I guarantee the FBI will charge Vinnie and your team as co-conspirators."

Tom had just upped the ante by reaching the same conclusion as Blanca.

"I don't think we have a choice but to reveal to Homeland what you know," he said.

"And that means goodbye to Gunter," said Vinnie, his head bent.

They knew Vinnie was right. Homeland would send the Karimov cousins to an undisclosed location, sealed from outside influence and unreachable by Gunter's defense team. No chance to uncover their involvement in the murders of Katia and Tariq. Gunter's hope of winning his case vanished.

"To answer your first question, Rita," said Tom, remaining dispassionate in his analysis, "what is needed? Short of a complete confession by the cousins? I'd say a recording or documentation to prove beyond doubt they set up Gunter with Katia and Tariq. If not a full confession, a concrete statement that puts them at the scene at the time of the murder. Best to have it in their words. But anything tangible to give a jury reasonable doubt over Gunter as the alleged murderer works. Equally important is to offer the cousins as plausible alternative murderers."

"But we have them at the nightclub," said Vinnie, agitated as much by Tom's lawyer-speak as his dismissal of what he had learned at the Karimov house. He had wasted his time, and put himself in danger for nothing. He heard Tom's recitation of the facts. The cousins were not singled out at the nightclub but lumped with all the other people present the night of Tariq's murder. There was nothing to show they'd been in Sakura Park other than Gunter's vague description.

"Then what about the neighbor, Douglas Gormich? He saw them."

"Not really," said Tom, pouting his lips. "Not a good eyewitness."

"What? He's sharp," said Vinnie.

"Too vague. Dark night and his testimony includes seeing Gunter leave dejected from Katia's party."

Tom's litany continued, citing Katia calling after Gunter, Katia asking Gunter not to be mad. Touching ten fingers on his desk as if playing piano, he concluded that Gormich's testimony incriminated Gunter, not the cousins. After a pause with the flatness that proceeds the truth, he added that Gormich had seen the humiliation, enough to merit a motive for Gunter, and premeditated to boot. Tom declared that any prosecutor worth their salt would claim Gunter returned with the intent to kill Katia, her murder not an emotional flashpoint.

Walking over to Tom, Rita sat on the edge of his desk. "Give us two weeks. Halloween's a month away. We'll get what you need. Gunter isn't going to take the plea, I can say that for certain."

"Rita, stop. This has to be Gunter's decision."

Before Rita replied, Vinnie stood up. "We know, and what you also know is that Gunter needs guidance. With his estrangement from his mother, his usual paranoia is heightened. His lack of close friends aside from Ben, Rita, and me means he has no one to talk this over with. It will be his decision. But also understand that Rita and I will give him the bigger picture. And when we finish, we'll let him choose. But I believe he won't accept the plea. And we will find the evidence you ask for, but we need more time."

Rita pulled Vinnie's arm to stop him moving as she pecked his cheek, saying, "You're the best. I mean that with all my heart."

Vinnie flushed and knew if not for the circumstance he would have made a joke to cover his emotion. Instead, with palms pressed prayer-like, he raised them up-down from his wrist, a gesture he'd seen his Italian mother make many times—praying, exasperation, pleading, and resignation. And he knew the Galantuomo family did the same. This was Vinnie asking Tom for solidarity through their shared heritage.

"Okay, you have until next Wednesday, then we go to Homeland. I'll try to delay the prosecutor but I can't guarantee anything."

"Thursday," said Vinnie, watching Tom's hand fly out. He and Rita left smiling.

Outside Tom's home, Vinnie didn't waste time and pulled out his cell to dial Ginny. He didn't want to do this, but he had no choice. She'd already done them two big favors— finding Tom and her mother's analysis of Gunter. This last request would be galactic in comparison.

"Hi, Ginny. I need a favor, and you can't tell Dan or Ben anything about it."

* * *

Ginny returned to New York Sunday afternoon after a fun weekend away with her family. With unpacking completed,

Ginny surprised Dan by telling him she had forgotten about a private training class with Rita at UltraFit. She asked if he minded caring for their children for a few hours. Dan objected, saying he needed the time to prepare for a West Coast client's telephone conference on Monday. Ginny held her gym bag to her chest and the debate ended.

The BIG team formed their usual semicircle around Vinnie's desk with Ginny at the center. Vinnie summarized Gunter's case and Tom's directive. Rita clarified when necessary and Blanca repeated her concerns.

"I'm guessing this is where I come in," said Ginny with a broad smile. She had been silent throughout Vinnie's spiel, her arms folded, until hearing that children might be targeted. Her eyes closed.

"Yes. And you've said nothing to Dan or Ben about coming here, right?"

Ginny nodded at Vinnie. "They'll be furious. I told Dan I was having a private session with Rita." She turned to Rita. "You'll have to cover for me if Dan or Ben asks."

"Let's cross that bridge when we get to it." Vinnie looked away. He hated when he used aphorisms. *I sound like fuckin' Bartlett's.* "We know they would object and stop your participation." He saw Ginny's infamous lioness grin and chuckled, "Okay, not stop but interfere, break your concentration."

"And what exactly do I need to concentrate on that might be interfered with?"

"Dimitri."

"Any chance of a complete sentence? If you want mind-reading I'll call my mother. Is that what you want?"

276

"Playing the Dr. Anna Swinburne card so early, are we?" Vinnie's voice had a slight edge.

And the lioness smile reappeared once again.

"Fine," said Vinnie as he outlined the intricate plan of her meeting Dimitri to extract a confession of sorts on tape.

"We have until next Thursday, is that right?" Ginny's eyes half-closed as she spoke. "So at most I will see Dimitri twice. Too bad. I would have preferred three." She took a breath, then her eyes flew open. "Okay, I should be able to get the macho-sexist Dimitri to reveal enough in two sessions."

Vinnie smiled, thinking Ginny could probably get Dimitri to confess to most of New York's major unsolved crimes over the last year. She had just returned from an exhausting weekend with two kids on a long-distance flight from San Diego, yet looked like a movie star on a red carpet. Perfection in face and form—womanhood's glory on display. Even if Dimitri was a one-eyed, semi-conscious man suffering from erectile dysfunction he would still notice Ginny Livorno.

"I have the perfect setup, too," said Ginny cheerfully. "My colleague and friend lives in Fort Lee and is away on business for two weeks. I'm sure he'll let me use his studio. It's small but tastefully decorated. You'd like him, Vinnie."

"Gay, I'm guessing?" Vinnie stuck out his tongue.

Ginny returned the gesture, then her face froze, her lips stern. "One thing bothers me."

"What's that?" asked Rita. "You're nervous. Don't be. I'll be close by. Dimitri is strong but so am I, and I know moves he doesn't."

"But remember," Vinnie said, his voice a little forced, "he is a boxer."

"Amateur, right?" Rita's face looked tight.

"I'm not worried. I've taken your self-defense class," said Ginny, looking at Rita. "My concern is…" Ginny paused.

Vinnie turned, his eyes meeting Rita's. They knew this was the key moment. Vinnie's head made a nearly imperceptible nod and Rita returned the gesture.

The upshot of Ginny's concern matched Blanca's. Ordinary people and their kids would be harmed while doing nothing more than enjoying Halloween festivities. Ginny's tongue moistened her lips as she imagined the children being harmed were hers and not strangers. She needed to know more, specifically two points.

"Kids being hurt or killed is too horrible," she said, her tongue continuing to wet her lips. "Where do they plan to detonate the bomb?" She waited a few seconds after Vinnie shrugged.

Her second question puzzled Vinnie. "And can you say the exact words you overheard about the bombing?"

Her sullen expression eclipsed her usual perkiness.

"Shit, I don't remember the exact words."

"As close as you can."

"Something about stupid Americans or idiot capitalist Americans and the using of a religious event to dress like animals."

"Are you sure they said 'dress like animals'?"

"Well, I don't fuckin' know, do I? I wasn't taking notes at the time. They said animals, that's for sure."

Ginny's frown crumpled her usually beautiful features.

"Oh no. Fucking hell," she hissed.

Vinnie went white. Ginny rarely cursed, and he could see her shaking.

"What! Tell us!" Rita's voice was screeching along with Blanca.

"It's not Halloween they were talking about. It's the celebration of the Feast of St. Francis at St. John the Divine. The annual parade with the blessing of the animals."

Rita's hand rushed to her mouth. Vinnie stood and slapped his forehead with the palm of his hand screaming, "Fuckin' Fuck... FUCK... FUCK!"

Ginny yelled, "That's next Sunday! The celebration's always the first Sunday in October to coincide with the time of St. Francis's death. The cathedral is famous for this event. Cathedral seating tickets are hard to get but the outdoor campus is free and open to the general public. It'll be packed."

Blanca's sobbing was the only noise in the room. Everything had just changed.

34

With the three weeks no longer an option, everyone despaired.

"We have to tell Tom," said Blanca. "We don't have enough time. Homeland and FBI have much more resources."

"Yes, and do you know how likely it is they'll listen to us?" asked Vinnie.

"I agree with Blanca," said Ginny. "I don't see how we can't tell the authorities."

Rita paced the room. "This is it. You know the Feds won't give a shit about Gunter. But leave that aside, I don't think they'll act quickly."

"Why not?" asked Blanca.

Rita stood up to speak. "Because they've screwed up in the past. Remember, they ignored information before 9/11 and Oklahoma City and the shootings at Stoneman Douglas High School and..." She stopped to wipe her eyes. "They just don't follow up, at least not with the speed we all imagine."

With a bang on the desk, Vinnie turned to Blanca. "And remember last year's case, we told the cops about the serial killer and they didn't do shit? Nearly got a teacher killed. And the guy got away too," said Vinnie.

Blanca and Rita nodded. No one could forget. Even Ginny knew about it.

"And a murderer in San Francisco given the benefit of the doubt because of social standing, instead of listening to what I had to say. And I was the one arrested! So pardon me if I'm a little fuckin' cynical," said Vinnie, shaking.

The room had the tense atmosphere that mixes embarrassment with fear that any contradiction would release latent feelings long buried.

Vinnie took hold of Rita and hugged her. "We can do this. And we'll be sure Homeland and the FBI and any other fuckin' law enforcement agency will have tangible evidence… those are Tom's words. Something irrefutable that can't be ignored. We try, and they'll still have enough time to act."

Blanca was shaking her head, still doubting the wisdom.

"I hate to admit it, but Vinnie has a point," said Ginny, leveling her index finger at Vinnie. "There's too much red tape and Homeland is so focused on illegal immigrants they ignore real threats."

"And one more thing," said Vinnie. "Tom can't know. He's too much a law-and-order man."

Blanca crossed her arms.

The group consensus was that if their strategy didn't seem workable they'd call Tom, the FBI, and Homeland. By the fifth revision the idea was so elaborate no one could repeat it.

"Sounds like we're planning to invade a small country,"

said Blanca.

With only one opportunity for Ginny to snag Dimitri's admission in a way that would satisfy Tom Galantuomo's condition and the FBI, they had to make it simple. A three-week timeframe would have allowed for options, contingencies, and greater complexity.

Vinnie reviewed the ploy Rita used the first time they lured Dimitri. "It worked once, maybe we can do it again, only this time Ginny is at the airport waiting for Dimitri."

Blanca pointed out that this "new ploy" has the same snags as the first—short notice and Dimitri's limited weekend schedule, and no guarantee that he would be the driver and not a substitute.

"There's one more consideration," said Rita. "Star Limo owns two vehicles and a repeat request for Dimitri would raise suspicion, if not with the Star Limo owners then with Dimitri himself."

Vinnie invented a convoluted and unworkable scenario. "This is harder than it should be," he concluded and no one disagreed.

"*Claro*. We're over thinking this," said Blanca, rubbing her chin, "Let's start with the fact that Star Limo has only one full-time chauffeur with Dimitri on call for weekends. His father and uncle alternate driving the second limo. But the father told me last time that neither he nor his brother travel to New York."

Vinnie paced the room, hands behind his back as if on the front line of a battlefield. He stopped, then leaped across the chairs to hug Blanca.

"Reserve both limos. Rita's reservation first to some

Jersey mall or a restaurant where I'll be parked. Ginny will request transportation the same day in... hmm... I don't know that part yet."

"There's a hairdresser in Englewood," said Ginny. "I use him for gigs when we have fashion shows at one of Bloomie's New Jersey malls. He's good, too."

"Yeah, great. Book yourself in for a nail polish," said Vinnie, enjoying himself. "Tell Star Limo the pickup is in Jersey for a New York special event. We'll add a twist to change your location at the last minute, somewhere we can set up ahead of time and with no link to us."

Ginny suggested the imaginary event was her boyfriend—a marriage proposal followed by a special meal after. "I'll work on that part later," she added.

Creative juices flowed. Vinnie suggested, "Wear one of those low-cut designer dresses and the expensive glittery necklaces and earrings you wear at Anthony's soccer games." He laughed at his own wisecrack, earning a disgusted look from Ginny.

"Move on," said Rita, loudly interrupting Vinnie and Ginny. "We only have two days. How do we guarantee Dimitri is Ginny's driver?"

This is classic Rita, thought Vinnie, *taking over.* Rita wiped her brow with the back of her hand.

"Sorry, you're right." Vinnie touched Rita's shoulder. "We can't guarantee anything at this point. But we can bounce ideas around."

Ginny patted Rita's other shoulder, adding that she would do everything she could to make it work, and winked at Vinnie. He wisecracked that the guarantee just became a little stronger, earning a smile from Rita.

During the mini-discussion, Blanca moved out of Vinnie's office to her desk. She returned a few minutes later with a thumbs-up sign. "All set for Rita's pickup," she explained matter-of-factly but clearly pleased with herself. She'd asked for the driver's name, pretending she'd needed to be certain of it. Her ruse was that if the driver's ID didn't match the name she'd been given, she wouldn't take the limo. And with the information she proudly stated, "The driver's definitely not Dimitri."

Vinnie suggest a break of an hour before Ginny called for a town car. He figured Star Limo occasionally received two requests for same-day service at short notice. But two within a few minutes would raise suspicion.

They group engaged in mindless chitchat and Ginny showed them photos of her San Diego trip on her phone. With the hour up, Ginny sat at Vinnie's desk to request a car from Star Limo. With the phone on speaker, everyone listened for clues of a potential problem.

"Sorry, we have no drivers for New York tomorrow, especially on short notice," said a man with a thick accent.

Blanca raised and lowered her head and finger-wagged to confirm this was the same man she'd spoken to earlier.

"I'm so disappointed. You're my third call. My girlfriend recommended you when I told her my bind," said Ginny in a sexy, husky voice imitating Marilyn Monroe.

"Try Uber. They're cheaper too." The thick Tajikistan accent was fading in and out of reception on the phone speaker.

"I'm sorry, I can't fully understand what you said. Is

there anyone else I can talk to?"

"Wait."

The background noise was male laughter with a TV announcer reading boxing match results. An exchange of foreign words grew louder until a strong New Jersey accent bellowed from the speaker.

"Can I help you? I'm Dimitri. My father says you need a driver for tomorrow. I'm afraid we have no one who travels into New York except me and one other driver, but he has a client. I only work weekends. I wish we could help—"

Ginny interrupted Dimitri, seeing Blanca rubbing thumb and index finger together, the universal sign for cash.

"Money is not a problem," said Ginny with a wavering tremolo. "Please," she said, emphasizing the sibilant s in the word. "I want to impress my boyfriend."

Ginny paused, making a long, audible inhale. She spun a tale involving a "special occasion" that she hinted was a marriage proposal. Not getting the response she wanted from Dimitri, she painted a verbal picture laced with strong language to describe tight-fitting, haute couture fashion and a *very* expensive pearl necklace that hung over her low-cut dress to emphasize her assets—her boyfriend had a thing for her breasts, she added with a throaty chuckle. Vinnie choked at her outrageously blunt description.

Ignoring Vinnie's distraction, Ginny explained she needed a ride from her Englewood hairdresser to the Plaza on Central Park, meeting her boyfriend who worked on Wall Street. With an embarrassed giggle came an innuendo of dessert and hot sex in a suite at the Plaza.

"I don't want to Uber." She paused, then started with halting speech, "I... uh... well... uh, I know this is unfair to many good Uber drivers but the few incidences in the news have me worried, especially with my pearls and the way I'll be dressed, if you catch my drift."

The pause on the line told Ginny she had Dimitri's attention. With a deep, loud inhale, she sniffled, "Couldn't you make an exception? It's for eight so traffic will be light."

Vinnie angled his hand, slicing it across his throat as he mouthed, "Cut."

"Have you tried another limo service?"

Ginny feigned a sigh with her "no luck" uttered in a sweet, silky tone. "Like I told your father, my girlfriend gave me your name... and..." She stopped to make a hushing breath sound, "I'll make it worth your while. Please." With a long exhale she continued, "Oh please... what can I offer you? You sound like a good man. I'm sure you know women, and how to make them happy. Just name it. Can I pay you a bonus?"

She held her breath a second, before she released her lungs, the air slipping from the back of her throat through partially opened lips, followed with a soft "Unh, unh, unh... please." The perceptible orgasmic sounds were obvious and didn't go unnoticed by anyone in the room.

Ginny stopped talking and waited.

Dimitri broke the silence, his voice quivering. "I...uh..." he began in a high pitch, then coughed before continuing to say, "this seems very important to you."

"Oh, it is! I swear! Oh I'm so excited. Uh... uh... this is great." Ginny's full throat oozed with sexual overtones.

"Uh... okay. We normally charge one ten an hour, but this is overtime for me so it will be time and a half, say one seventy?"

The call ended and Vinnie said, "Looks like Dimitri isn't too good with math. And... oh... my... god! I nearly shot my load in my pants. Do you talk to Dan like that before you guys do it?"

"*Culo!*" screamed Blanca with a slap to Vinnie's head that nearly cracked his head on his desk. "Say another word and the next noise will be your head splitting open." Her open-palmed hand stretched overhead.

"Take a joke, Blanca. And this is going to cost me too." Vinnie rubbed his head. "Dimitri's a liar. He charged Rita eighty bucks an hour, which means this is more than twice his usual rate."

Rita walked behind Vinnie. He flinched as her hands rested on his shoulders, but relaxed as she gently rubbed. "Sweetie, you and Ben can afford it so stop complaining, unless you want a love tap from me as well. Now let's get started."

* * *

Ginny's first word to her friendly colleague was an apology for waking him, knowing the London time zone difference put him close to midnight. She smiled at her own explanation that her call was about an emergency rendezvous. She repeated it twice, her colleague convinced he misunderstood. She ignored his question, promising all would be explained on his return.

The man told her it was her lucky night, because the

apartment in Fort Lee was vacant, a rarity with so many friends requesting use of his place. "You're not the only one with an emergency affair," he said, laughing. Ginny ignored his attempt to get more out of her. She thanked him and hung up, holding a piece of paper with the apartment codes to the several entrances and the garage.

* * *

The BIG investigators stood behind Ginny in the elevator as she punched the electronic key code for the eighth floor. Once inside, Vinnie opened a long drape over a three-segment sliding door that ran the full width of the living room and opened onto a balcony. The spectacular New York skyline view cost her colleague a monthly rent of three thousand dollars, which he had called extortionate at an office party. Ginny had smirked at his complaint, knowing he could afford twice that amount on his Bloomingdale's salary.

The exploratory visit revealed the apartment's layout and potential locations for surveillance. Beneath the kitchen counter was a well-stocked liquor cabinet. Vinnie removed obvious signs that the owner was male, carefully putting them in a suitcase. Framed posters and photos, although inoffensive in themselves but clearly a man's choice, were taken off the walls and shelves.

"Leave or remove?" asked Rita, pointing to a framed poster over the bed. The print displayed two men on a skyscraper ledge in dueling stance, their weapons shockingly large erections.

"Don't see anything wrong there," said Vinnie, playing

along with Rita's ironic comment. Ginny said she'd return with a landscape canvas to cover the gap.

Finding a location for a recording device proved problematic. The uncluttered, minimalist apartment furniture consisted of glass tables and shelves. Rita suggested under the couch even though the contemporary design of high chrome legs made any device easy to spot. If it was securely fastened underneath it would prevent discovery unless Dimitri crawled on his hands and knees.

"What about sound pickup?" asked Vinnie. "It has to be voice-activated."

Vinnie and Rita tested the activation from across the room in the open-plan kitchen and the bedroom.

"Works fine," said Vinnie. "At least there's one advantage to the small square footage."

Hiding Vinnie and Rita in the apartment was the biggest problem. If Dimitri became violent with Ginny they wanted to be close by. Every space proved too small for a person bigger than a one-year-old. Under the bed was a possibility but best suited a child's hide-and-seek game. Standing on the balcony didn't work either, with the conflicting needs to keep the soundproofing sliding door open and the curtains closed for concealment. The group dismissed the balcony location.

The remaining option was a surveillance transmitter that Vinnie and Rita monitored from their parked car in the visitors' lot. Ginny and Rita accepted this option but Vinnie worried, not that Dimitri would become suspicious but act on his sexual fantasy. Ginny scoffed, "I can handle him." Vinnie noticed Rita didn't object but she didn't rally to support Ginny's defense capability either.

"I'm not happy about this," said Vinnie, "just so everyone hears it."

Ginny looked at Vinnie. "You're right, being in a room with a terrorist frightens me. And I'm only thinking about it. How will I react on the day?"

"We can call this off and take our chance in court if you want."

Rita sobbed, her hand covering her mouth.

"No, we'll do this and I'll soon find out what I'm made of," said Ginny.

Vinnie took one last look around. He picked up the print of the two men on the ledge, covering it with a bed sheet before taking it into the elevator to deposit in the unit's storage box.

35

The Englewood restaurant was suburban posh—pretentious, overrated, half the food prepared from a package, and microscopic servings. Nothing said money-to-burn like a waiter who introduced himself by his first name, smiled with teeth white enough to light up a nighttime ball game, and hinted that he would cut off his right arm to please the patrons.

Vinnie looked over the expensive meal and overpriced wine. He ordered a small salad at the bar, seeing no reason to run up a large tab. He paid the exorbitant check then sat in his parked car waiting for Rita with the radio tuned to the Mets game.

She arrived with the Mets loading the bases. The Uber driver held open the rear door, a man she'd described to Vinnie as "Drove like a drunk skunk and smelled like one too. Otherwise, no complaints."

"How was your meal?" she asked, entering Vinnie's car.

Vinnie puffed his cheeks.

"That good, huh?"

Vinnie drove to be closer to Ginny's hairdresser, Grant's Salon. "Finally, someone that sticks with a simple, unpretentious name."

"Yeah, that's why we're called BIG."

"Smart-ass."

Vinnie parked in a spot in the sightline of the salon but far enough away to be inconspicuous. The plan was to wait for Ginny's signal. Vinnie lowered the radio volume as the Mets took the lead in the game, which he took as a good omen.

* * *

The manicurist finished Ginny's nails. Grant inspected the polish. "Someone is very lucky tonight."

"Yes," she answered, examining her fingers.

"Great shade choice. It's perfect with your outfit," said the manicurist, smiling as Ginny handed her a generous tip.

Ginny came out of the beauty salon door clutching a light shawl, unnecessary for the warm evening but important for her purpose. A pearl necklace adorned her décolletage, and she had as much bosom on show as possible without having her tits exposed. The entire salon stared.

Grant accompanied Ginny outside. He took her elbow as she drifted on the sidewalk searching for the Star Limo town car. Her high anxiety prevented her seeing the limo enter the mall parking lot until a second before it arrived at the curb.

Although Grant walked ahead to the rear door, Ginny didn't move. She waited for Dimitri to come out and reach the sidewalk and she lifted onto her toes, providing a full view of her, squeezed into a tight chiffon pearl-laced dress that accentuated her generous curves and revealed her athletic legs. Grant and Dimitri's mouths hung wide and breaths

294

shortened as Ginny stretched back, thrusting her chest forward.

Vinnie observed Ginny's movement through binoculars. He looked at Rita. "If she doesn't get into the car soon they'll both jump her."

Ginny asked, "Are you Dimitri, my chauffeur?"

"Yes, Ms. Benedict. As requested, I will drive you to the Park Plaza." Dimitri exhaled, as if he'd been inhaling pure oxygen. "Please, let me help you."

Dimitri tapped Grant's shoulder, stopping him from reaching for the car handle. Ginny recognized the move, a fighter signaling to his opponent that he'd break his jaw. Grant backed away, taking Ginny's extended arm as she thanked him for the last-minute appointment. Shaking hands was the prearranged signal to let Vinnie know that Dimitri was the chauffeur and not a substitute. She hoped he saw as she didn't want to seem obvious, scanning the parking lot.

With Grant walking away, Ginny glanced at her ringing cell—Vinnie's caller ID. She moved closer to Dimitri rather than the more usual act of moving away. She wanted to be overheard.

"Say Dan's name," instructed Vinnie.

"Hi, Dan, I'm on my way," answered Ginny, using her husband's name rather than one she might forget in her nervousness.

Vinnie coached Ginny by using sentences that would mimic the words a shmuck boyfriend might say when breaking up by phone, having no balls to do it in person. His script and delivery was too close to the mark, thought Ginny, his delivery too real. She could almost have believed this was a genuine breakup.

After a brief period of pleading, she shut her cell and wiped her eyes. She asked Dimitri for a tissue.

"You okay, miss?" asked Dimitri, taking a packet of tissues from his pocket.

"Yes... uh, no, not really," sniffled Ginny.

"Can I help?"

"I don't think so."

Ginny moved to the open limo door, dipping as she entered the back seat, handing her shawl out to Dimitri, which brought him closer to her. A cold sweat formed in the middle of her back. Her eyes were moist from knowing she was in the presence of evil. As he handed her the shawl she let it drop onto the sidewalk. Dimitri bent on one knee and his head came to within a few inches of her thigh as he picked up the garment. Ginny shivered and was not pretending. Staring at her was undiluted wickedness. She continued to play her assigned role, thrusting her breasts forward to force her nipples out and indent her chiffon dress.

"On to New York and your boyfriend?" he asked.

Ginny gasped, her sniffing stronger, "No, that was him on the phone. He's not coming. Just drive please."

Dimitri closed the passenger door and returned to the driver's seat. "To the Plaza?"

"No. Take me home. I live in Fort Lee." In halting words she recited her colleague's apartment address. "Do you have another tissue?" she asked, sniffling.

While Dimitri twisted and bent to reach the glove compartment, Ginny moistened her face using a wet cloth she had in her purse. Dimitri passed the tissue box through the open glass partition window. Ginny watched, hoping her cheeks were wet enough to convince him she was upset.

She looked at Dimitri's impassive stare and his thin lip curl as he handed her the tissues. She counted out time in her head, giving him as much as he needed to take her in.

On turning back to his driver's position, Dimitri pressed the button to close the glass partition.

"Please don't. Leave it open. I feel a little claustrophobic."

Pulling away from the hair salon, Dimitri never noticed the Toyota Corolla behind him. It was Rita's suggestion to use a cheap, ordinary rental car rather than Vinnie's Audi.

Vinnie and Rita followed Dimitri closely rather than drive ahead and wait at the Fort Lee apartment. This was Vinnie's idea, a safeguard against the possibility that Dimitri might snatch Ginny for his own idea of consolation.

Five minutes into the ride and Ginny whispered, "He left me. Turns out the dinner was not to propose but to break up. He didn't have the balls to tell me to my face, so he did it over the phone," Ginny said, using Vinnie's words that sounded authentic. "He said he needed time alone and cancelled the fuckin' booking. Told me I would understand. Wants to remain friends. What a cliché!"

At first, Ginny thought she was speaking too softly, that Dimitri didn't realize she was addressing him. It was not until he adjusted his rear-view mirror for a better view that Ginny saw she had his full attention.

"I'm sorry to hear that, Ms. Benedict." It was another of Vinnie's suggestions that the booking be made in the name of her colleague, just in case Dimitri noticed the apartment's doorbell nameplate.

"Thanks. I feel so ashamed. Am I not good enough? Is there something wrong with me?"

"How can you say this? You are one of the most gorgeous women I've ever seen."

Yeah, thought Ginny, *you won't find me on your hard drive.*

"That's just not true. Look at me. I'm a wreck."

"No. The man's an idiot. Do you mind if I tell you that you are beautiful? Beyond most men's wildest dreams."

Ginny sniffled. "Apparently not for my boyfriend. My *ex*-boyfriend." She blew her nose.

"He's a fool. I'm sure you'll find someone better than him," Dimitri said.

"But I love him! Or at least I thought I did. How could I be so damn naïve? He hasn't been the same in bed for over a month."

The car swerved.

"I tried everything. I indulged his every juvenile fantasy but he didn't respond. He stopped trying to excite me. He didn't care. I forfeited my desires for him! I want a man to touch and excite every part of my body. Y'know, someone who knows how to treat a woman, not drag her around like a sack of flour. But I pushed aside my needs for his, allowed him to indulge his apparently endless fascination with my tits and ass."

The car decelerated suddenly. Ginny held tight to the passenger strap.

"Sorry, I was concentrating too hard on your story. I'll

drive slower to be safe."

I'll bet you were, thought Ginny. *Well just wait, you fucking terrorist.*

Ginny continued with her rampant innuendo then moved on to explicit details about her breasts and vagina. She described her imaginary boyfriend's ass fetish with lucid detail. She explained an impossible-to-imagine standing sixty-nine, with her inverted, legs around his neck and her rubbing his cock with her mouth and labia, one example of his many perversions. The car swerved, the speed more erratic as Dimitri looked over his shoulder to see Ginny. Her spine jolted every time the car lunged forward.

"You have reached your destination," announced the GPS device.

Parked outside the apartment complex front entrance, two dome lights brightened the car's interior. Before Dimitri was out of his door, Ginny reached over and touched his shoulder.

"I know this is forward of me. Maybe I shouldn't ask…"

"No, please," said Dimitri, twisting to face Ginny through the open partition. "Do you want to go to the Plaza? Is that it?"

"No. I wonder if you would escort me into my apartment? I'm shaking."

Ginny directed Dimitri to drive to the building's rear car park. His hands trembled as he turned off the ignition.

Her door opened and she waited for Dimitri's hand before moving. She wobbled on the sidewalk, not feigned but truly nauseous from touching him. Holding Ginny's arm he steadied her, which increased her shaking.

At the front entrance, Ginny fumbled in her small pearl-studded purse that matched her sequined dress and high-lighted her pearl necklace. She dropped it as she saw Vinnie and Rita's car pull into the driveway. Dimitri bent to retrieve the bag, which Ginny knew was his second exposure to her legs, but this time she revealed a little more of her thighs. She stretched her calves taut, allowing Vinnie time to drive through the front gate unnoticed. Dimitri was transfixed by Ginny's calves and would have missed a tank.

By the time Dimitri stood upright the Toyota was parking in the visitors' lot. Ginny caught sight of his dilemma—his crotch bulged.

Ginny tapped the entry keypad code with her long, glossy fingernails. Dimitri held the door for her, no words spoken. She released his arm inside the mahogany-lined elevator to punch the number eight on the panel. At the apartment, she entered yet another code. Dimitri never looked at the nameplate.

"Would it be too forward if I asked you to sit with me? Would you mind?"

She hardly heard Dimitri's agreement and wondered if he was still breathing.

"Are you sure this isn't too much of an imposition? It's just that I don't want to be alone, not right now. I'll pay you overtime."

"Don't worry. It's not a problem. Please, forget about the fee, Ms. Benedict. It's my pleasure."

Ginny pointed to the large glass window, curtains wide open to ensure Dimitri appreciated the full panoramic New York skyline. She suggested he remove his jacket and she kicked off her high heels, walking barefoot to the kitchen.

"Will you join me in a drink? I need a drink. Is that okay with you?"

"Yeah... that's good," said Dimitri, his voice strained. He followed her into the small kitchen. His audible inhale came as she stretched to retrieve glasses from an overhead cabinet. His eyes were locked on her every move.

Ginny carried two wine glasses into the living room, noticing light sweat droplets beading on Dimitri's forehead. She didn't dare look at his crotch; she didn't need to. She hoped he was in agony, desperate for the release that he'd never have.

So far her performance was perfect but she steeled herself for the second act. It would be more difficult but necessary to reach the goal.

36

The wired microphone under the couch worked as planned, and both Ginny's and Dimitri's voices were audible to Vinnie and Rita inside the Toyota parked in the visitors' lot.

Ginny's opening remarks were loud and clear. "Are you sure this isn't too much of an imposition? It's just that I don't want to be alone, not right now. I'll pay you overtime." Vinnie fanned his face, hearing the seductive voice flowing out of the speakers. Rita rolled her eyes.

Dimitri's apparent kindness about the fare not being a problem had Vinnie shouting, "Damn fuckin' right, pal." Rita's finger on her lips told Vinnie to keep quiet.

"Will you join me in a drink? I need a drink. Is that okay with you?"

Dimitri said it was good. Vinnie shouted at the speaker, "Everything's *good* for you, isn't it, you fuckin' pervert." Rita slapped Vinnie's arm and told him to shut the fuck up. Both sat upright listening to the exchange, straining to pick up on any non-verbal noise. Vinnie regretted not installing a surveillance camera. Ginny was going into full action.

"Would you like a vodka tonic?" asked Ginny.

"She better not say Russian," said Vinnie. Rita sighed,

shaking her head.

"Yeah, I would," answered Dimitri.

Ginny poured two drinks, adding Rohypnol to Dimitri's—the date-rape inhibition drug, but if she added too much she'd have him sleeping for hours. She motioned for him to move next to her on the couch as she talked about her boyfriend—now ex—reviewing their two years together. With intermittent sobs, she contrived a story about the man of her dreams who broke her heart.

Edging toward Dimitri, she reclined to rest her head on the back of the couch. She asked him to remove her necklace, and he looked over her shoulder and down her cleavage. She leant back, which opened up her neckline further. Her eyes closed, and Dimitri stared at her sublime breasts.

"I'll bet you'd never do this to a girlfriend, would you? I mean, string her along. I did everything for Dan, anything he wanted." She briefly flicked open her eyes to glance at Dimitri's crotch. He was excited. *Have I moved too soon? I need to slow down.*

"Tell me about yourself. I don't want to talk about Dan anymore. Do you like driving a limo? When did you start your business? It must be successful, given the attention you provide clients."

Dimitri provided vague or false answers. He showed no enthusiasm for the job or the thriving business.

Vinnie pounded the steering wheel. "He sounds like he would have as much fun getting the hair on his balls removed with duct tape, the fuckin' liar."

"Shut it, Vinnie. I'm trying to concentrate," said Rita.

"I'm sweating with nerves." She cracked open her passenger window but shut it after a minute to prevent anyone passing hearing the speaker.

Ginny refilled their drinks but turned to see Dimitri pulling out a white powder and snorting. She knew this wasn't good.

"This is good stuff. Makes you feel better."

This was not the time to act shy, so Ginny snorted a little but most she surreptitiously swept into her palm. Dimitri took no notice. She had to hurry. His crack would counter her roofies.

"Did you hear this?" she asked, trying not to alert Dimitri.

"Yeah, that's fine," he answered without considering her question.

In the car, Vinnie shrugged his shoulders at Rita. "What's that about?"

"Don't know," said Rita but wished she could see what was happening.

"Can I tell you something?" asked Ginny, pushing to get to Dimitri's knowledge of Gunter. "I get off on bodybuilders. I mean bulging muscles are so sexy. Is that crazy or what?"

Ginny hated telling this story because it was her life. Muscular men fascinated her, and her sthenolagnia syndrome had nearly ended her marriage.

Vinnie looked at Rita. "Please tell me she's not going to give her full psychological profile."

"Shut it," said Rita, leaning closer to the speaker.

"Dimitri, do you know any bodybuilders?" asked Ginny. "You look strong yourself." Ginny's hand touched Dimitri's bicep and she cooed. He flexed and she increased her cooing admiration even though his bicep was nothing compared to Gunter's or any of the X-room bodybuilders.

"I box. I'm on the Rutgers team and pretty good."

Ginny saw the twist to his face and his eyes squinting. She touched his nose. "I can tell. Any bodybuilders at your gym?"

"No, not really."

"Too bad. I would have enjoyed visiting, have you introduce me." Her fingers moved under Dimitri's chin, then rubbed his chest.

"My cousin's an Olympic boxing champion and MMA semi-pro. You should see him," said Dimitri, a little off in his voice. "He's very strong. Benches three ten."

"If you'd stood next to a bodybuilder, you'd know what I'm talking about. Have you?"

Dimitri stammered. "Well, I met one." His voice rose a half octave.

"Really? Where?" Ginny sipped her glass and pointed to Dimitri's. He took a large swallow.

"At a park near Columbia. He was, like, gigantic," Dimitri slurred. "It was night and I swear he looked like a big ape. Name's Gunter if you can believe it." A burp followed and he continued, "A fucking German, like Arnold Schwarzenegger only bigger."

Ginny grinned. "I think Arnold's Austrian."

"Whatever. Ugly bastard. Stupid too."

"That fucking bastard. I'll break his neck." Rita was pounding the dashboard.

Vinnie smiled, and although he couldn't see it he knew

Ginny was smiled along with him. Dimitri had just connected himself to Gunter with the bonus of a location.

"Were you afraid? I mean at night, meeting someone like him? Did this guy... Gunter you said... did he approach you?"

Dimitri grinned. "Ha. He was a lug. I could have flattened him. Scared of his own shadow."

She pointed to his drink, smiled at him, and raised her glass to Dimitri, a real, virile man unlike the lunkhead Gunter. Dimitri gulped a large amount, then swiped his lips with the back of his hand. His smile was lopsided.

"I saw him crying too. A big fucking baby."

Ginny leaned forward, touching Dimitri's arm. "Really? In the park?"

"No, outside a girl's apartment. She must have said no to sex because I heard her scream for him to go away. Ha! He'd have crushed her too. Small tits but she had a nice figure. I'll give her that. He's a freak. Who'd have sex with him?"

Vinnie looked at Rita. "Did you hear?" asked Vinnie, fist clenched. "He used the past tense. He's talking about Katia. And there's no way he could know her body size and shape if..."

Ginny saw Dimitri's crooked grin, followed by a weird giggle. The sex talk clearly excited him. Vinnie's personality description of him was one hundred percent accurate. She examined his slightly dilated pupils. *Not enough Rohypnol in his bloodstream to counter the crack.* She lifted Dimitri's glass and handed it to him. He swallowed a mouthful.

"Girl? What girl?" asked Ginny, ignoring Dimitri's fingers twirling her dress.

"Someone in the East Village," Dimitri answered, slurring his words.

Finally, thought Ginny, although his red-flashed eyes were a sign he had absorbed more crack than roofies.

"Not hot like you." Dimitri wiped spittle off his lips. "I mean you are a fucking hot bitch. I could cream all over you and never stop."

His jittery words did not sound like drunkenness to Ginny. Sex talk was Dimitri's drug.

Vinnie's hands banged the dashboard and Rita's balled up.

Dimitri sought adjectives to talk about Ginny's breasts. She nibbled her lips to disguise her disgust. She didn't expect his lunge and his hands grabbing her breasts.

"These are unbelievable. So fucking firm." Dimitri's head went down to nuzzle in Ginny's bosom. With a speed she didn't think possible, he straddled her to restrict her movement. His chest rested on her face. He stumbled with the clasp to unfasten her dress. "Fucking clasp," he mumbled into Ginny's bosom, undetected by the microphone. He tore open her dress, both breasts bared.

"Yes, look at them. Fucking great."

His hand covered Ginny's mouth, stifling her yell, her words unintelligible. She wriggled to free herself, but his weight on her legs limited her movement. She bit his hand. With a swiftness she didn't think possible, his boxer's jab landed on her chin.

She awoke from her semi-conscious state with a handkerchief stuffed in her mouth and Dimitri holding one wrist and with his knee compressing her lungs. The cloth stifled her voice. Her flailing provoked Dimitri. He twisted her arm. She winced as her shoulder socket strained. She leaned forward to reduce the pressure and pain, but afforded Dimitri leverage to pull her free arm behind her. He bound her wrists then jabbed her chin, not as hard as his first but enough to curtail Ginny's feverish thrashing. A dull ache spread across her bruised jaw.

Dimitri's buttocks rested on her thighs, his full weight immobilizing their movement. Her panic rose, tears no longer possible.

He discarded his pants and underwear, and Ginny felt Dimitri's engorged penis rubbing her breasts. She felt him further tear at her dress so that her upper body was exposed. He moved his penis tip across her nipples while his hand massaged her clitoris through her panties. With a yank he ripped them off and she was completely exposed. She felt his dry, desert breath as his tongue licked her body.

Ginny twisted with no effect. Dimitri's demonic eyes penetrated hers. He sat upright on her body, rubbing himself with one hand as the other played with her nipples. He appeared to be in a trance, unaware of himself. He stopped then removed his belt and looped it around Ginny's neck in a makeshift noose. The free end was wrapped around her wrists. Ginny felt the pressure when she moved. If she struggled she'd choke. Maybe not enough to suffocate but enough to cause excruciating pain.

The long silence was inexplicable to Vinnie and Rita. They heard sounds, but not words. Had the microphone failed? Some sort of radio signal interference?

"We'll wait a few more minutes. Ginny may get the information we need even if we can't hear it," said Vinnie.

"Not too long," Rita replied, cracking her knuckles. "I don't trust chance events."

They heard unfamiliar noises and they inched close to the speaker. Neither spoke but Vinnie looked at Rita and she confirmed his alarm. Any doubt vanished upon hearing Dimitri's voice say, "You are better than the Internet whores. Look at those breasts. I'm going to fuck you and it will be your privilege when you see the size of my cock. I'll fuck your tits and ass and cunt and mouth all night long, and you're gonna love it."

Rita was running to the elevator. Vinnie's car door hit a parking garage column, bounced, and smacked him—he cursed himself for parking in such a confined spot.

Ginny moved her arms despite the shooting pain. She jerked forward, causing the belt to tighten around her throat as intended. Yet a drug and alcohol-impaired Dimitri had not secured the belt binding. With each small move Ginny made the belt's grip loosen.

Dimitri lowered his head to lick her nipples again. Ginny levered herself to head-butt him, but the range was too small. She received a retaliation punch that knocked her into semi-consciousness. She awoke after a few seconds to heavy breathing on her face and felt Dimitri's fingers inside her. Her tears blurred her vision.

Rita sprinted to the elevator and punched in the building code. Vinnie reached the elevator seconds after the door closed. He frantically pounded the up-button, watching as the floor numerals reached eight. Each passing second seemed like minutes; each minute felt like hours. Anxiety fanned impatience, and Vinnie ran to the stairwell at the opposite side of the elevator shaft. More seconds wasted. He keyed in the building entry code. More time wasted. *Fuckin' security!*

Dimitri's probing fingers scratched Ginny. Her breasts ached with his crushing squeeze. She felt the poking of his raging hard penis at her clitoris. His pork-rind sucking smacked her nipples until his bite brought excruciating pain. The room seemed a thousand degrees. He swayed. Not from the alcohol or Rohypnol. The crack took charge. He cursed, his delirium fueled by rage rather than desire. He struggled to find purchase and enter Ginny, his raging dick and balls flailing against her. He sniffed at Ginny's ripped panties. He attempted once more to angle an entry and penetrate her. Impatient, he thrust two fingers into her vagina then pulled out. He clawed at her breasts then fell backward, disoriented. Lifting himself, he moved forward, tilting his pelvis to bring his genitals to Ginny's throat. With a slide down her torso, he tried again to force entry, pushing hard.

Ginny anticipated the pain, the violation, the humiliation, but suddenly he stopped. The front door burst open.

37

Rita charged into the room, screaming profanities. Hitting the dining room table, she stumbled and fell underneath it, taking a chair with her. Her door bursting and screaming increased Dimitri's adrenaline blood level, already flooded by sexual arousal. He jumped off Ginny to reach Rita as she pushed aside the overturned chair.

He flung himself forward, deflecting Rita's jujitsu leg thrust to his groin with his rapid reflexes honed by ring training. His short right uppercut punch hit Rita's chin, followed by two rapid left-hand face punches. She fell back, hitting her head on a table's edge. The blow slowed Rita, allowing Dimitri time to pound five rapid blows to her head and render her unconscious.

Ginny's moan caused Dimitri to stop bashing Rita's skull. He ignored Rita when he saw Ginny's struggle to stand up. He grabbed the decorative long cloth runner on the dining room table and tied Ginny's legs. His soft penis stiffened, and he thought about continuing to fuck this gorgeous babe. He touched himself to re-engorge his cock but stopped as Ginny's moaning increased. The spell was broken. He'd wait to complete the fantasy in his bedroom.

Bending over Ginny, he said, "You'll never know what you missed." He looked at Ginny's near-naked body. *Me too. Would have been the best fuck of my life.* He touched his stiff penis. Was there time to jerk off over her? No, he'd have to rush and that wouldn't be the same. Instead, he spat on Ginny and got dressed. Returning to her prone body he licked her earlobe and whispered, "In a few days you'll learn who you've been dealing with."

Reaching into his jacket pocket, Dimitri pulled out a knife. Standing above the unconscious Rita, he spoke as if she heard him. "I know you. You're that fucking bitch I picked up at Newark Airport." He kicked her in the ribs. "Unlike your friend, you'll never know what glory me and my cousin have planned."

While Dimitri finished getting dressed Vinnie climbed the stairs two steps at a time, his heart pumping gallons of blood into his legs and making him feel light-headed. He concentrated on his aim: reach the eighth floor and save Ginny. On the sixth flight he stumbled, banging his knee on the steel tread. Quick reflexes brought his hands forward to avoid landing on his chin, dislodging a front tooth, and knocking himself out. His hands stung and his knees ached but sucking air and cursing he limped up the last two flights.

The stairwell door on the eighth floor did not budge as he pulled. "Locked. Fuckin' stupid goddam security door. Fuckin' fuckin' fuck!"

He should have known the fire safety doors required keys to open, with access limited to exterior hallway entrances. His cursing reverberated within the stairwell as he hobbled back to the lobby. He repeatedly pressed the elevator call button. It took its sweet time.

Adjusting the knife in his hand, Dimitri dragged Rita by her arm to prop her upright for a better angle to slit her throat. Bending over to pull her straight, he had a view under the glass coffee table of Ginny's wide-open eyes; she looked like a Byzantine icon portrayal of a suffering mother. The handkerchief muffled her words but Dimitri knew what she was saying.

"Take a good look. Your bitch friend deserves to fucking die for interfering." Dimitri didn't see the tears filling Ginny's eyes, nor hear Vinnie enter.

Vinnie first saw Ginny across the room. He missed Dimitri, bent over Rita underneath the dining table. He froze, sure the pool of blood meant she was dead. He ran across the room when peripheral vision caught sight of Dimitri. He wanted to beat the shit out of him, but a glinting knife reminded Vinnie that this man knew how to slice and dice.

Dimitri moved across the room, slashing his knife in the air and revealing Rita on the floor. Believing she was dead, Vinnie was so overcome by grief he dropped to his knees to double over. The sudden, unexpected move deflected Dimitri's knife to graze Vinnie's shoulder rather than enter his chest cavity.

Missing his target, Dimitri tripped and fell to his knees. The delay gave Vinnie time to stand and kick Dimitri's tailbone, which released the knife. Vinnie's strength was a result of weight training with Ben. His power did not match Ben's or Gunter's, yet it was still something to be reckoned with.

Lifting Dimitri, Vinnie flung him onto the coffee table,

a feat normally impossible if not for the adrenaline coursing through his veins and boosting his strength. The tempered glass top splintered with a thunderous noise. The energy expended increased Vinnie's exhaustion. His back to Dimitri, he doubled over for deep breaths to recuperate. In the delay, Dimitri stood to kick Vinnie's groin from behind and the searing pain made Vinnie cry out. Dimitri applied his boxer training, mounting to his toes to dance around and strike Vinnie's head. The temple blow knocked Vinnie into a wall before he slumped to the floor.

Vinnie wobbled to rise. He was no match against a semi-pro boxer. His only chance was the element of surprise but rage kept him going. His new goal was to cause delay, not chase victory. Before he was fully upright, he saw Dimitri walk out of the front door.

Dimitri turned in the direction opposite the elevator. He descended the emergency staircase, the same one used by Vinnie ten minutes earlier. Skipping down the steps, Dimitri reached the ground floor in under a minute.

He hesitated at the exit. His disheveled appearance and bloodstained jacket would create an easily remembered impression for any witnesses. He pushed the door ajar and peered into the lobby entrance. No one was waiting at the elevators. He turned behind to stare up the stairwell. Fuck, he almost had sex with the most beautiful woman he'd ever seen. And her tits! He'd actually rubbed his cock between them. He decided he would jerk off and shower as soon as he was back home.

* * *

Vinnie looked to Rita. No movement. He went to Ginny, splayed out on the floor behind the couch, her legs tied and mouth gagged. She was fixed in her position. A noise caused panic, a quick swivel. Had Dimitri returned? He saw Rita struggling to raise herself and she shouted, "Did you get him?"

"No."

Reaching around Ginny's neck he released the noose, then slipped off the gag. He bowed, his ear rested on her lips. "Ginny, you okay? I'm so sorry. Please be alive." Vinnie quivered. He felt a puff of breath.

He held Ginny's hand, his eyes closed. Rita moved Vinnie aside to cover Ginny's naked body with a bathrobe. Vinnie cried. She was alive but hurt. How badly he couldn't tell. He didn't dare ask what Vasily had done to her.

"You can stop crying. I'm okay," said Ginny, touching Vinnie's arm. "I'll probably have a black eye that's going to be difficult to explain. I don't think Dan or Ben will buy walking into a door, do you?"

Vinnie's mouth gaped. He blubbered, "...oh Ginny!... oh..." He sucked in air, tears running down his cheeks.

Rita untied Ginny's legs. With Vinnie's help they lifted her onto the couch.

"Looks like you'll have a shiner too," said Rita. Vinnie winced as she touched his cheek. "I remember Ben's exact words when you hired me. 'You'll protect him, I know you will.' He said you were strong but lacked fighting skill, which is my specialty. Well, looks like Ben was wrong on both counts. You did pretty good against a trained boxer."

Vinnie shrugged.

Ginny spoke up. "I sure hope we caught enough on the recording to satisfy Tom."

"We did, I'm positive," said Vinnie while dialing his cell phone.

Rita hugged Ginny, saying, "You'll be okay. Don't think about that fucker now, just that we got him."

"Hi, Tom, we have a situation—hold on... give me a fuckin' chance to explain. You know what, forget the explanation. Call Homeland. NOW!" Vinnie stopped. "Oh and Tom, meet us at the hospital."

38

"Of all the stupid fu—" Dan stopped before he cursed. He very rarely swore and never at his wife. He had not intended to scold but his fury was uncontainable. He sat on one side of Ginny's hospital bed with Ben on the other.

Vinnie hunched at Ginny's bed's end as if praying. Ben walked over to him and put his hand on his back. Whispering, yet loud enough for everyone to hear, he said, "We'll talk at home."

Vinnie moved to Rita's bed, parallel to Ginny's in the double room, with no effort to hide his response to Ben. "Fuckin' lecture me is what he means."

"Let him, Vinnie," said Rita. "We deserve it. He needs to vent his anger and concern. Our idea was stupid. What were we thinking? And for all my martial arts training I had the crap beaten out of me."

Ben and Dan spoke their thoughts, fueling their anger: Stupid act—reckless—thoughtless—dangerous. Their anger ebbed as Ginny's doctor entered the room requesting everyone to leave, except for Rita in the bed, but he drew the curtain.

"No need, Doc. This is my family. Say what you have to say."

To everyone's relief, Ginny's examination and fluid test showed she had not been raped while unconscious. Everyone exhaled a collective sense of relief. Yet they also knew Ginny would bear the emotional scar as if she had.

She refused overnight observation. "Dan will take better care of me and I need to see my children."

"If she goes, I'm leaving too," said Rita.

Vinnie did not require medical attention for his slight shoulder injury and his head wounds were treated as an outpatient procedure.

"Did you tell Gunter?" Rita asked Ben.

"Thought I'd wait until I knew your condition. You know, everything," Ben answered.

She felt her bruises. "He'll be upset, but I'll help him to get over it."

Vinnie snickered, "I bet you will."

"Screw you," said Rita in a flat monotone.

Vinnie's ringing cell broke the forced lightheartedness. He answered with a sullen voice.

"Uh-huh. Yeah. Thanks, I'll tell them."

Vinnie stood as if making a public announcement. "Tom's called Homeland and the FBI. They're on their way."

* * *

Six investigators paired up to interview Vinnie, Ginny, and Rita in separate spaces. Vinnie went to a doctor's consultation room. His interview was the longest because throughout it he interrupted, complained, and cursed. An hour into the interview, one agent said to the other, "Let's just arrest him and get this fucking over with." Vinnie's debriefing finished after an additional thirty minutes.

Rita and Ginny were discharged as Vinnie came out of his interview. The women linked arms, laughing at Vinnie's non-stop cursing. "Bunch of fuckin' bozos. Paint dries faster in a damp tropical hut. And more interesting. They're clueless. More concerned with what we were doing, not the fuckin' terrorists. Threats too, about our indirect involvement. Fuckin' bozos!"

Homeland Security, FBI, and local police found the Karimovs' Jersey City home vacant, but CSI discovered enough proof that explosive material had been stored in the basement. There were no notes or hard drives providing details of a time, location, and delivery method. The agents confiscated the two Star Limo Service cars parked a couple of streets from the house. The presumption was the cousins had walked to Journal Square Transportation Center, boarded a PATH subway, and had passed through New York's Penn Station—destination unknown.

Homeland and FBI had no choice but to rely on the amateur BIG team's intel and speculation. They too were under advisement that the most likely target was the Cathedral of St. John the Divine during the celebration of St. Francis. The BIG cooperation, along with legal representation from Halborn, McGregor, Galantuomo, and Stern, managed to stop the FBI from charging Vinnie, Rita, and Ginny with concealing evidence of a terrorist act. Tom Galantuomo and his prestigious law firm had too much political capital—the potential flak from Washington on all agencies would be too much. Months later the FBI and Homeland Security final reports cited "beneficial cooperation of the Briggs Investigative Group" for not pressing co-conspiracy and obstruction charges.

At the hospital exit, the friends had a collective group hug. All believed the Karimov cousins' terrorist plot had been foiled. Everyone except for Vinnie.

"Mark my words," he angrily prophesied, "those government bozos won't stop the bombing. Dimitri and Vasily are laughing their asses off with an image of FBI and Homeland agents crammed into their Bozo clown car."

Their combined moan expressed universal weariness with Vinnie's relentless cynicism. They would be less unkind in a few days upon learning that Vasily had made contingency plans for screwups by his cousin.

39

The moment Vasily saw blood on Dimitri's clothing he cursed without waiting to learn the reason. On hearing the explanation he screamed insults, gave several body punches, and spat in Dimitri's face. Battered from Vinnie's assault, Dimitri was unfit to defend himself either physically or verbally.

"You stupid dumb fuck," said Vasily, his barrage of invective starting anew after hastily packing their bags and closing the front door of their Jersey City home for the last time.

Vasily adjusted his backpack, slung over one shoulder, and the other supported Dimitri's arm as they trudged toward uptown Manhattan.

"A woman flashes her tits and you become like a dog in heat."

Dimitri wanted to protest, tell Vasily that the woman wasn't ordinary. She had more than big tits. Way beyond the Internet's standard offering of bulging implants and bloated, botoxed lips. His Fort Lee woman was a goddess. "Enough bitching," said Dimitri. "You agreed it was a setup with the same Newark airport passenger, and the guy seeking to compensate me for non-existent scratches to my car."

"Doesn't matter," answered Vasily. "If you had stuck to your chauffeur duties, dropped her off, and then come home, then nothing would have happened."

A few blocks from the PATH Journal Square station, Vasily stopped complaining. Dimitri continued to ruminate in private. He fixated on Ginny's well-sculpted body and how if he had only five minutes more he would have fucked her hard... maybe twice.

"Hey Dimi, you there?"

"What?"

Dimitri dragged himself along, limping. The darkness and lack of people out late meant no one would notice his arm and face, bruised by the smashed glass coffee table.

"Walk faster," growled Vasily. "We want to catch the late train to Manhattan."

They arrived at 33rd Street before midnight. Vasily pulled and dragged his cousin along Broadway. They entered an Airbnb studio loft near Herald Square that had been booked a month earlier. Vasily had insisted they start their rental the previous week for contingencies.

Dimitri had protested about staying at an Airbnb. He didn't sleep well in a stranger's bedroom. He was okay with hotels because they weren't private residences. Vasily called him stupid, his patronizing explanation being that an Airbnb provided seclusion. They could remain indoors unseen for days. The FBI would close all airports, train stations, and bridges, and monitor all movement in the city. Sequestered in a private residence they'd be unobserved. And with the apartment available the week before the St. Francis celebration, they could stock the refrigerator. And, more important, store the bomb material days before the attack. That plan now seemed even more prescient.

Vasily had requested the booking for three weeks. The landlord had handed Dimitri the apartment key seven days ago. He didn't notice the discrepancy between Dimitri's NJ driver's license and the PayPal payment name, which was from an account of Vasi's Tajikistan sparring partner. Anything the great Olympian asked of the Tajikistan community he received—no explanation needed or given.

They stayed in the apartment the entire Friday. Dimitri cursed. He had no Internet, was bored with the TV, and still felt sore from his injuries. Added to his discomfort was the fact Vasi's took the double bed and wouldn't share. "I'm no gay fag," had been his reason, but Dimitri knew the wrestling team often shared beds during boot camp training. "C'mon Vasi, what harm would a little walk do? Get some fresh air."

"No. It's your fault," said Vasi, piling dirty dishes in the sink. "We have to stay out of public view. We'll wait and we'll walk uptown on Sunday morning."

"Fuck, Vasi, that's at least five miles."

"They'll be looking for us, thanks to you and your whore."

"I told you not to call her that."

Sunday morning both men rose early. Neither had a good night's sleep. Dimitri yawned non-stop, his slow pace adding twenty-five minutes to the uptown walk. He was still sore from the fight, and two nights on the couch didn't help.

"Why do we have to get to the cathedral so early? I'm

fucking tired and in pain," complained Dimitri. He knew the answer. In addition to making the bomb and detonator, Tariq's other task had been to scout the cathedral grounds for places to plant two bombs, and where to hide when he detonated both with a single switch. He had told his cousin about several possible locations but underscored that the final decision would not be made until the actual day.

"Safety barriers, emergency vehicles, and other temporary obstacles can interfere with the transmitter signal," Tariq had explained. "I'll go the day before to check signal quality once the barriers are in place." He promised to arrive a few hours before the event for any final alterations. His death annulled that part of the plan.

"You know this was Tariq's job. He knew how to evaluate the distances," said Dimitri. "For fuck's sake, Vasi, I don't have Tariq's knowledge. I haven't a fucking clue what barriers might prevent the thing from going off."

Vasily spat. "Let him suffer for eternity in the afterlife. You'll do good, I know it."

* * *

St. John's Cathedral never failed to impress Vasily. The imposing edifice, the world's fourth largest cathedral, mixed Romanesque-Byzantine and neo-Gothic architecture. On this day Vasily believed the mighty structure paid homage to him and the noble act he was about to put in motion. He'd made the right choice of venue and event. The building's grandeur suited the scale of his grievance.

Barricades cordoned the Close and the Pulpit Green had limited access. Vasily cursed. If they had not been forced to hide, he and Dimitri could have toured yesterday without any concern they'd be recognized. He strained to avoid venting his anger against Dimitri. *Focus,* he reminded himself. *Find the best location to hide the knapsacks stuffed with explosives and shrapnel.* He and Dimitri reviewed Tariq's preselected areas. They need to look for high barricades and large trucks. They'd check distances to pathways against the detonator specs.

But an unanticipated problem came into play. Although Dimitri had purchased advance tickets, using the same sparring partner's PayPal account he'd used to pay for the Airbnb, the entry remained closed to the public for another two hours. They'd have to wait—making them visible for too long. And while Vasily and Dimitri debated their options, a van pulled up nearby and the rear door opened as several men hopped out.

Vasily saw the work pinnies. Steering Dimitri to walk behind him, Vasily snatched two of the high-vis jackets. Placed over their hooded jackets they looked just like the other members of the work crew. Spotting a group at the site entrance nearest the cathedral, Vasily gave his backpack to Dimitri before talking to a woman holding a clipboard. She didn't look at the men entering, each holding flags and gardening tools. He called to her, "Hi. Me and my coworker are part of the inside crew, but we're a bit early. We were told you could use some extra help. What can we do?"

"We're almost finished with the landscape work, but plenty of flag markers need placing on the far side. Grab a handful." She showed Vasily a map. "I like them in pairs along the path, but not opposite, and spaced a foot or so apart. Do you understand?"

Vasily guessed it was his accent that made the woman doubt he understood English, which was typical of the racist Americans. He nodded as if he cared. "We'll get started right away."

"Great. Then we can finish this section sooner."

"Is there a locker for our backpacks? We brought our own gear for inside the cathedral."

The woman was back to checking her clipboard and she spoke without looking up. "Take them with you. Why come all the way back here? Save time."

Vasily walked over to a pile of flags and signaled Dimitri to join him. He pointed to a large oak. "Leave the backpacks behind that tree. We'll get them after we've done some work to avoid suspicion."

The cousins moved to the designated pathway and methodically placed flags in the ground. Dimitri noticed someone on a divergent path heading toward the entry gate. *He looks like the man I fought in the apartment. No, can't be. I'm tired after that five-mile hike. Better not tell Vasily or he'll just start his cursing again. I'll check myself.*

Dimitri waited fifteen minutes. "I need to pee." He grimaced with another jiggle. "Too much coffee. Won't be long."

"Hurry up," said Vasi. "Nothing can stop us now."

"Yeah, okay," answered Dimitri. But he didn't articulate his real thoughts.

Something's not right.

40

Repeating his hospital refrain, "Bunch of fuckin' bozos," Vinnie faced his kitchen refrigerator at five in the morning. He had a sleepless night, disturbed by not knowing if Homeland Security and the FBI could act in time, and if they couldn't how many people would be dead or injured by the end of the day as a result.

Around six Ben found Vinnie sitting at the kitchen table in front of a glass of juice and a bowl of soggy cereal.

"How can three seemingly smart people make such a poor decision?" asked Ben, repeating his hospital comments. "I'll never understand. One person with bad judgment, fine, it happens, but not two and definitely not three. And Ginny of all people!"

"Enough," said Vinnie. "I know it's bad and I said I'm sorry."

Ben walked out, saying he was going to UltraFit to take his mind off recent events. "Maybe a heavy workout will distract me." Before leaving, he touched Vinnie's shoulder. "Will we know if the Feds find them?"

"Only if they don't."

A few minutes after Ben had gone, Vinnie talked to

himself. "Two hours wasted having me repeat the same fuckin' story over and over." He thought of calling Rita but decided waking her wouldn't help his anxiety. And what if she was with Gunter? Then he would agitate two people. After chewing one spoonful of mushy cereal he emptied the rest into the sink disposal.

Walking to the living room window, he imagined seeing the cathedral's spires two-and-a-half miles north, closer to the Hudson River, close to Gunter's former home. He did not leave Ben a note since that was evidence that he'd broken his promise to remain home and recuperate. Wearing a light jacket, Vinnie ignored the cheerful condo concierge's greeting. "Air might be a bit crisp now, but it won't stay that way for long. Forecast is warm sunshine."

Descending the Columbus Circle subway steps, Vinnie waited five minutes for the 1/C train. He surfaced at 116th Street and marched double-time to Amsterdam Avenue. He arrived around six-thirty in the morning, in time to observe a work gang at the cathedral complex preparing the grounds for the ten o'clock animal procession. He anticipated that the barricades to corral people had been set in place one or two days ahead of time, so this was last-minute final additions.

Most online tickets sold out a month in advance, but day-of-event tickets were always available. The box office opened at nine o'clock, giving Vinnie a jump on others. He knew most parents couldn't organize children and pets at sunrise, adding to his first-in-line status. He was relieved to see the cathedral doors closed. If he couldn't enter, neither could the Karimov cousins. His relief was short-lived when he couldn't spot one FBI, Homeland, or NYC policeman. Not a single uniform visible.

"Fuckin' typical," Vinnie mumbled to himself. "I wasted my time telling them the plan. Ignore my information and advice. Good thing I came early to do their job for them."

With no one else in the line, he abandoned his prime post and walked the cathedral perimeter, noting surveillance camera locations and their absence—blind spots. If he noticed, so would Dimitri and Vasily.

By the time he had circled the cathedral, a handful of people had formed at the ticket entrance. He had learned nothing to prevent the bombing. Vinnie stomped his feet. He needed access inside the cathedral grounds, and now. He was sure he could identify obvious bomb locations, unless this was a suicide mission. But he didn't peg either Karimov cousin as willing to self-sacrifice. Their mission was personal not religious. He dialed Rita's cell.

"Vinnie, do you know what time it is?" Rita was not so much agitated as bewildered.

"Nearly seven?"

"Time is not my point. I mean why are you calling?"

"I'm at the cathedral."

After a short delay, Rita said, "I'll take a cab. Be there in fifteen."

"Meet me at the small coffee shop a block down from the cathedral. I need caffeine and a pee."

Eighteen minutes after the call, Rita entered the coffee shop, Gunter at her side. His jacket fastened to his neck suggested a hibernating bear after an L.L. Bean shopping excursion. Vinnie's head tilted toward Gunter without speaking.

"He saw me walking out and insisted on coming," said Rita, shrugging her shoulders. "He makes his own decisions in case you didn't know."

"Fuck you," said Gunter.

"I offered," smiled Rita.

"I repeat, fuck you."

"Enough," said Vinnie, "we've got to get going."

The trio grabbed their takeout coffee and marched to the cathedral.

"What's the plan?" Rita asked, an arm draped through Gunter's elbow with no objection from him.

"I thought we would enter inconspicuously into the cathedral grounds." Vinnie's head tilted toward Gunter, the same gesture he made at the coffee shop. "But that ship's sailed."

"Like I said," grumbled Rita, "he insisted on tagging along. Brought up our fiasco as proof we needed him."

"Fuck-up is what I called it," interrupted Gunter. "And I'm standing next to you. I can hear everything you say. And my leaving the condo doesn't mean I don't care. I...uh..."

"What! You're moving out? Since when?" asked Vinnie, who stopped walking.

"Not the time, Vinnie," said Rita. "I'll tell you later." Rita pulled her hand from Gunter's elbow to face him. "I know you care. And you're upset, as are we. We made a mistake that we need to resolve. I'm sorry... for everything. We'll talk later." Rita's voice sounded contrite.

Vinnie touched Gunter's arm. "I'm sorry, too," he said, his tone subdued. "We were stupid. What can I say? Now let's focus." He resumed walking.

"What are we looking for?" asked Rita as she tossed her empty cup into the nearest refuse receptacle provide by New York City Transportation, which was near capacity. She stopped walking.

"What?" said Vinnie in an irritated voice. "Keep moving, we don't have time to waste."

"Look. These things haven't been emptied for weeks."

"You want to file a complaint with the Sanitation Department?"

"No, Vinnie. What I am pointing out is that it would be a perfect place to hide a bomb and be near lots of people."

Gunter backed away, looking at the refuse can as if it were radioactive. Vinnie slapped his forehead.

"That's our plan. Let's check all the garbage cans inside the grounds. For that matter, any kind of receptacle."

In contrast to the forty-five minutes before, a line had formed at the main gate, lengthy but not as long as it would get. The open gate allowed entry onto the cathedral campus. No tickets required for anyone only going into the garden area and not into the cathedral for the blessing. A standard security check slowed people and pets but it was still too early to create much of a delay.

Inside the grounds, Vinnie suggested to Rita and Gunter that effectively covering eleven acres meant separating. "The cathedral doors are shut. We'll enter together. I'm not sure how we'll get in without tickets but we'll cross that bridge when we come to it."

Entering the Close, adults, parents with children, and pets of every kind abounded: dogs, cats, rabbits, hamsters, fish in plastic bowls, and… "What the fu—" A nudge from

Rita stopped Vinnie.

"Watch your language, there are children here."

"Is that kid holding a monkey?"

"I think it's a chimpanzee or a closely related species. Definitely in the Pan genus," said Gunter in a flat tone.

Vinnie and Rita gawked at Gunter, who laughed. "National Geographic channel. I've lifted in front of my TV since high school. You'd be surprised how much there is to know about the animal kingdom."

Vinnie rolled his tongue around his cheek, "Yeah, yeah."

Rita smiled for a brief second. "Okay, concentrate. Let's decide on the search plan."

"I'll head to the Pulpit Green while you and Gunter go to the Tranquility Fountain. Keep your cell phones on."

Gunter stopped Vinnie, asking why he should stay with Rita. He knew what to do and didn't need an escort.

With a smile, Vinnie walked up to Gunter, patted his chest, and said, "Because if you are on your own, someone will think one of the large animals got loose."

"Fuck you, Vinnie!" said Rita, her voice raised ten decibels.

"Language, Rita, there are children present."

Gunter stepped forward. "He's right. People stare at me. And Vinnie? Fuck you."

"I'm sorry. Rita's right. I'm nervous, upset... I don't know, anxious maybe. You know I live with Ben so I'm used to what you big guys put up with, y'know, the goofy stares and all."

Vinnie stuck his hand out and shook Gunter's. He grimaced on the release and walked away cursing under his breath as he rubbed his hand.

Rita punched Gunter's arm. "You didn't hurt him, did you?"

"Nah, he's used to it. He lives with Ben."

Vinnie checked every waste bin along the path toward the forty-foot Gothic spire pulpit. Self-conscious about poking in the trash, he'd look around each time before rolling up his sleeves. No one watched him—it was as if poking through bins was an ordinary activity. He spotted four FBI agents in their windbreakers with large, gold letters. The jackets he understood. Only four agents he did not. None noticed him.

A few people stared at Gunter. One child excitedly called to his father, asking if the big man in blue was going to tame the wild animals. Rita whispered to Gunter, "Just me, isn't that right?" Rita took hold of his arm. For fun she squeezed and he responded with a flex.

"Do you think you can handle my training tonight?" asked Gunter with a wide smile, bigger than Rita had seen since returning home from the hospital. He removed his jacket as the sun rose high and temperatures climbed. "Uh, I need to go to the bathroom."

"We passed the porta-potties at the entrance near the first-aid tent. You go and I'll keep looking here. Meet me on the other side of the Archangel Michael statue. Do you know where I mean?"

Rita sat at the statue for fifteen minutes, imagining Gunter's bladder to be the size of a set of bagpipes. As more time passed she became anxious and was soon on the verge of panicking. *Where has he gone?*

41

Gunter entered the last of five men's portable toilet cubicles placed against the iron gate along the avenue. Coming out, his eye caught sight of a person in a dark, hooded jacket on the sidewalk outside the grounds. The man held a sign with block letters: ANIMAL DETOUR. Beneath the words an arrow pointed at Gunter.

Is it possible? Did Detour Man follow me? Gunter thought.

His shoulders slumped as he sat on a bench across from the toilets. In his mind he heard Detour Man's clipped incantations of years before: "You small. You puny. Puny punk. You *nothing*."

Words that had frightened him ever since he was a schoolboy. Words inconsistent with his chiseled physique, the same dimension as the statues guarding the Gothic cathedral.

Gunter shivered. Had this vision returned because of Rita's attack? Was Detour Man warning him? Warning that he could not save Rita? Gunter closed his eyes.

His shrink gave him mental exercises that he had stopped using; didn't need them anymore. He told him to think about his size, imagine a barbell. Recall his heaviest gym load.

Flex. Feel his strong thighs and arms. Think about the people that loved him. Friends and people at the gym. Remember their words admiring his size and strength. Control and dominate his thoughts. *Rebuke the Detour Man.*

The exercises worked in the shrink's office but were ineffective when he was alone. The psychiatrist meant well, but he didn't understand. His methods didn't always work. Not under extreme stress and never in direct confrontation with Detour Man. Gunter had his remedy: get bigger, get stronger. Go to the gym, eat more, stick more needles in his arm, and swallow boxes of supplement pills. Do not deviate from his regimen—eat, lift, sleep—and nothing else.

A breeze evaporated his sweat, creating a chill even in the warm sunshine. He donned and zippered his fleece jacket up to his chin, raising the collar to cover his neck. He'd seen Detour Man on the sidewalk. He was real. He recognized the hulking specter in the hooded jacket with his sign. To save himself, did that mean leaving Rita? He would not let Detour Man take her from him. No one would— not his mother and not the terrorists. He would fight, he'd ignore Detour Man.

Gunter hunched, tensed his body, and his jacket tightened around his chest. He felt his arms, and stretched his legs to see the swelling of his thighs that contrasted to the twigs trotting in and out of the toilets in front of him. He looked to the avenue. No Detour Man. His throat was dry and his face hot. He needed to splash water on himself to cool down, so left the bench to return to the facilities. The cubicle he had used was occupied, so he entered the center porta-potty cabin. Shaking water from his hands, he held the door open for another person, then returned to the bench, slumping as he sat. He thought of ways to confront Detour Man, but the last cabin door banged open, breaking his trance. A child came out, while a hooded man stood outside waiting to enter. He didn't have a sign and wore an official workman's pinny. He wasn't Detour Man, yet Gunter was sure he'd seen him before.

People flowed past the main gate on to the Close. Dogs barked, caged birds squawked, and a general animal/human cacophony echoed throughout the cloistered area.

Gunter didn't hear his cell phone buzzing until the fifth ring.

"Where are you? Are you filling the fountain?" asked Rita.

Gunter's response was a muted, "Uh… uh."

"You okay?"

Another delay. No response. Rita panicked. "Where are you?"

"Uh… uh… a bench outside the toilet. You better come."

Rita tried to run but the oncoming flow of people and animals made even a brisk walk difficult.

"Stay on the line. Talk to me."

Her arms pumped, her face sternly accusing anyone who didn't promptly move aside. A few times she stopped rather than force baby strollers off the path. A small child tethered to an animal delayed her passing. Two dog leashes wrapped around her ankles, the owners apologizing profusely as they struggled to untangle their frenetic dogs. She calculated she'd need another five minutes to reach the porta-potties.

"Gunter! You still there? Talk to me."

"He's back."

"Who?"

"Detour Man."

"Gunter, he's not real."

"I saw him."

"You mean the hooded man?"

"Yes... no... there are two."

A family of five spread across the path with a menagerie of pets, making passage impossible. Rita left the pathway to negotiate the grass areas and moved behind a tree to better hear Gunter.

"Who did you see? Detour Man? Was someone with him?"

"Yeah, Detour Man on the sidewalk, but the other went into the toilet. It's him."

"Who? Him who? Be specific. Is he still in the toilet?"

For a few seconds Gunter said nothing. He watched a toilet door swing open and out stepped a boy of twelve in a hooded sweatshirt. "Not sure?"

Then the last door opened and the man with the hood walked out, no longer wearing the pinny.

"There's an emblem on his jacket but I can't see what it is. Sweatpants too. He's walking away."

"Wait for me. I'm almost there."

"I... he's getting away. I have to go."

"Gunter... Gunter? Hello? Hello? Gunter?!" Rita stared at her phone. The connection was lost.

The pathway filled. People and pets resembled salmon swimming upstream. Like Rita, some thought the grass provided unimpeded movement. That advantage vanished with increased congestion. Rita's momentum slowed.

She went around a knoll to bypass exotic tree species and shrubbery. Her advance improved but remained slow. Her orientation lost, she dialed Gunter.

"He has a hooded black sweatshirt and sweatpants," said Gunter, raising his voice to be heard. "His sweatshirt has boxing gloves on it." He instinctively tapped his breast pocket.

"Is he my height or shorter?"

"Yours. Crooked nose."

"That's Dimitri. Wait for me," she said but the dial tone sounded. The connection dropped.

Rita changed direction to cut across to the Biblical Garden while dialing Vinnie, who answered on the first ring.

"Rita? Speak up. The background noise is loud," Vinnie shouted. "I can't hear you!"

Rita yelled, "Gunter's seen Dimitri." She described the man. After a brief pause, she added, "Gunter's upset. He believes Detour Man is outside the entrance or something. I'm worried. He's following Dimitri and freaking out. I'm freaking out too. I don't know where he is or what he'll do. Call the FBI and meet me at the Tranquility Fountain, which is my best guess for the bomb's location. I'll be there in five."

* * *

Gunter followed the hooded man, losing sight a few times. Under normal circumstances Gunter's three hundred forty pounds moved at tugboat speed. He'd have no chance of keeping up with the agile boxer. But the crowd democratized their pace.

341

For a few seconds Gunter lost Dimitri, then saw him on the grass darting between bushes. Gunter saw a shortcut and pumped his girder legs to move his massive body across the grass to reach Dimitri, waiting by an oak tree.

Far from being paralyzed, as Rita thought, Gunter felt invigorated by a new sense of purpose. His motive was no longer to protect himself but Rita, children, and animals. He recognized the hooded man's gait. The one Rita had identified as Dimitri. The man he saw carrying Tariq. The murderer, which meant Katia's killer as well. This man intended to harm innocent people. Dimitri had tried to harm Rita, Ginny, and Vinnie, and very nearly succeeded.

Gunter's rage, dammed up over the years, burst, sinew uncoiled unlike anything he'd ever known before. He'd never experienced hatred. He had never thought about violence—the act of physically hurting someone. He didn't harbor wrath. He'd become a bodybuilder to help himself, protect him from others, not do harm.

The horror of Rita's hurt and Ginny's rape in all but deed. His therapist had not provided an exercise to quell this particular fury. No gym session could satisfy this rage. He had no answer, only a goal. He was close but falling behind. Dimitri was getting away.

42

Vasily waited for Dimitri, cursing him for taking so long. He placed their backpacks filled with Semtex in a crevice behind a one-hundred-fifty-year-old oak. The location was not hidden but would not easily be spotted by patrolling security officers. It was near enough to quickly retrieve when ready to put into the optimal place for maximum damage. But where was Dimitri?

Nothing infuriated Vasily more than waiting for his cousin and his bullshit excuses. Thinking over their conversation during the five-mile hike to the cathedral, certain phrases by Dimitri suggested hesitation. His enthusiasm had vacillated during the months of planning and waned after Tariq's death. Dimitri became more focused on the women he'd look at on the Internet. Vasily fumed. *I don't give a fuck about his porn or any of his perversions as long as he remains dedicated to this cause. Has he changed his mind? Is he getting careless? Might his need to pee be a coward's excuse? Is he jeopardizing the plan?*

Vasily fumed. His thoughts darkened as he paced the ground.

It was me and not Dimitri who was denied an Olympic gold

medal. I was humiliated. If it had happened to him then he'd have my commitment. Doping didn't make me a champion, it just accelerated the time to reach my full potential. I was always going to win with my intense training, rigorous routine, and sacrifice. Dimi could never understand the shame hearing the words "cheater."

Bitterness overtook Vasily. He kicked the ground and mouthed Tajik curses with gesticulating arms. He paced around the tree, searching along the converging paths for Dimitri. The crowd grew larger. He saw hypocrisy on every happy American face, their kids' teeth white and perfect. He remembered every word of the American affidavit that had disqualified him and the Tajikistan boxing team. And he knew they used enhancement drugs but had not been caught. The pretense by the whole goddam world that every athlete on a podium is drug-free. The superstars that never doped in their entire careers. Then a collective shock when a few are exposed. The unlucky few caught because they stopped a day too late for clean blood. Or were chosen by random selection for the test. Or Americans taking the gold medals by affidavit when they could not win them in the ring.

Vasily stomped the ground, his kicking creating divots in the soil. *Look at the self-righteous Americans blessing their fucking animals. They'll soon find out how much their blessings matter.*

More people passed and still no Dimitri.

He had to take a pee. Couldn't wait. He should have pissed in his pants. No one would notice among all the smelly pets. *Animals belong in barns or the wild, not on leashes in a big city.*

Vasily walked away from the hidden backpacks. They should have had the location decided weeks before, but that was Tariq's assignment. He should suffer in hell for his treachery. *And Dimitri foolishly lured by sex into a trap that prevented our reconnaissance ahead but confined us to stay inside an Airbnb.* Vasily's hands balled into fists and made short jabs in the air.

He remembered that Tariq had identified three locations to examine, among them the Tranquility Fountain, less than two hundred feet away. The area was overrun with people and animals and highly exposed with no barriers. Why wait for Dimitri? He could retrieve the bags and place them behind a bush next to the pathway. Better to wait and not chance discovery by security or a member of the public.

But what about the two of them? Where would they hide to detonate the bomb and not be hurt by the blast? Stand on the other side of the fountain? A food van was parked there with a long line of hungry people purchasing refreshments. Would the van or the people block the signal? Where was Dimitri to make the calculation?

Vasily's fists tightened. He walked back to the oak tree. The grass glistened, even as the morning dew evaporated.

The crowd grew larger than Vasily had imagined, even after reading the Cathedral promotional material. He hadn't appreciated the popularity cited in the brochure, the three thousand celebrants in attendance. Standing among the mob, the abstract number—the magnitude—sunk in. He felt good. The injuries and dead would surpass his expectation.

He squatted behind the large tree, cursing Dimitri's delay. The plan called for the maximum crowd to achieve the maximum damage. They should have been ready fifteen minutes before the cathedral's scheduled ten o'clock opening and now it was almost nine forty-five. Many were moving toward the cathedral. He and Vasily had to be in a safe area yet close enough to detonate. Dimitri's delay made this tight. Couldn't he wait to pee? What a fuck-up.

* * *

Dimitri moved toward the Biblical Garden then took a side path to the Tranquility Fountain. Gunter increased his pace to keep up with him. Moving his massive body at speed took more exertion than pushing a half-ton off his chest. His lungs became oxygen-deprived. He was falling behind. He broke into a trot but stopped when aches cramped his side. If he continued, he might pass out. And then Gunter saw that Dimitri had slowed, the overcrowded path preventing his movement. He stepped off onto a small hillock, his head twisting as if surveying an alternate route.

Dimitri stopped moving to check his watch, which provided Gunter time to move behind him. He gripped Dimitri's shoulder to turn him around.

"What the…" Dimitri blinked, squinted, and laughed. "Oh, it's you. The dumb fuck muscleman. What are you doing here?"

"I know you. You're Dimitri."

"Yeah, so what? Fuck off."

"No. You are going to do something bad. Stop."

Dimitri turned to walk away but Gunter held him back. "Stop. You can't do it."

346

"Let go! Didn't you hear me the first time? Fuck off!"

Gunter released him. Dimitri stood on his toes, crouched, elbows at ninety degrees. His right fist slammed into Gunter's steel-plated abdomen. Dimitri rubbed his fist and wrist. He stepped sideways but slipped, causing his second jab to go low and land on Gunter's chest. The jolt traveled from Dimitri's wrist to forearm as he cursed.

Dimitri cocked his arm. Gunter tensed his torso and waited for the third punch, this time to his rib cage. Again no damage.

Cursing, Dimitri shook off the sting as if drying a towel. He adjusted his balance, higher on his toes and shifted slightly right. His arm shot forward at the moment a child's loud wail caused Gunter to quickly turn. Dimitri's blow went off-center from Gunter's nose to glance off his temple. The slam pushed Gunter back.

Dimitri hunkered down, threw several jabs, each aimed at Gunter's head. With no fighting experience, Gunter remained flat-footed as he threw wild punches to empty air and never landed a single one on the agile Dimitri.

As Gunter regained his stance, Dimitri's hooking right arm stunned Gunter, who bent to one knee. Dimitri moved forward, again slipped, providing Gunter the seconds needed to stand up.

But his stance was unstable and it prevented his first punch from landing on the dancing Dimitri. Gunter's instinct brought him forward, a wrong move inside the ring as it allowed the opponent to pummel with repeated blows. Gunter deflected Dimitri's punches, each less effective as the distance between them closed. The disadvantage shifted to Dimitri. Gunter's steeled chest and abdomen withstood the rapid jabs. Gunter's only punch that landed cracked Dimitri's rib cage.

Dimitri doubled over as Gunter stepped back, not trained to press his advantage. The space allowed Dimitri another swing, but it went wild and hit Gunter's shoulder. Dimitri grimaced as if he had punched a cement wall.

Gunter moved forward, his arm outstretched. He snatched Dimitri's hooded jacket, pulling him so their chests touched. In the huddle, Dimitri was unable to swing. Gunter twisted the jacket's cloth, his grip secured. With his one hand he lifted Dimitri overhead and shook him like a baby's rattle.

"Fuck you and your fucking girlfriend!" screamed Dimitri, cocking his fist to punch Gunter's head.

No one took notice of the fray. The din of people and animals was too loud to hear the cursing. People concentrated on shepherding their families and pets to the opening ceremony. Even without cathedral seats, the grand parade into the cathedral's main portico was a spectacle to behold. One man stopped to observe Gunter and Dimitri slugging away at each other. He continued to march by after the momentary pause. The carnival fracas was not his concern and he obeyed the New Yorker rule, "Never stick your nose in other people's business."

Gunter twirled like a discus thrower to fling Dimitri several feet into a large oak. He didn't see Dimitri's mouth open. No words were spoken. Nor did he notice Dimitri's hands moving to cover his ears.

Gunter would later learn that Dimitri had heard two

small crunches—the first his pelvis cracking, the second the detonator's thin case crunching. The metal casing contacted wires curled to screws on the circuit board. An electrical arc discharged in the microsecond contact. The week before Dimitri had proudly announced to Vasily his detonator design success. The signal confirmed his bragging, as the ear-piercing boom echoed across the cathedral's meadow. People screamed. A symphony of animal screeches resounded across the campus.

The blast wave reached Vinnie as he was halfway to the Tranquility Fountain. He fell to his knees and prayed for the second time in as many days. He lifted himself up and ran like a sprinter seeing the finish line, his arms swinging. He gained enough speed to shake the tears from his face.

43

People screamed or fell to the ground. Security guards ran in all directions. Dimitri tried to raise himself but was immobilized by his fractured pelvis. He cried out in pain. Gunter again lifted Dimitri with a single arm as if waving a trophy. He cocked his arm, broadened his stand, and took a pitcher's aim.

Vinnie yelled out, "No, Gunter! No! Don't do it!"

Gunter stopped.

"Put him down!"

"Why? Why the fuck should I? I should snap his neck like he did Katia's."

"Because that makes you the murderer you say you're not." Vinnie had reached Gunter's side. "Can he walk?"

"Probably not."

Dimitri was crying out, the pain unbearable as Gunter held him aloft.

"Then he's not going anywhere. I'll call the FBI and Homeland. Let's find Rita."

Gunter let go and Dimitri dropped to the ground, his loud howl masked by the louder emergency vehicle sirens.

Vinnie pulled Gunter's wrist. He dialed the FBI contact,

giving Dimitri's location. Gunter's call to Rita went to voice-mail. Vinnie ran ahead and Gunter varied between jogging and walking.

Arriving at the Tranquility Fountain area, Vinnie saw a body on the ground. He jumped a temporary barricade, racing ahead. He reached the body. Despite the bloodied face, he recognized Rita.

"Rita, can you hear me?!"

Gunter arrived, yelling, "Rita! Rita!" He knelt next to Vinnie.

"Is she...?" Gunter didn't finish his sentence, seeing Vinnie's streaming tears.

Gunter's anguish was too big to escape his throat. He opened his mouth wide but not one sound came out. The men knelt side by side, each holding one of Rita's hands. Vinnie saw her eyes staring into the abyss.

A breeze carried the pungent residual odor of burnt cordite. Vinnie swiped his nose. He moved aside, providing Gunter space to cradle Rita's body and wipe her bloody face with his sleeve.

Gunter had her body draped across his lap, her legs dangling over his, her head nestled into the crook of his arm. He leaned forward to kiss her lips, forehead, and cheek. He released his cry, the sound crossed Rita's body, the river, and distant lands. He choked, his words hushed. "It's my fault," he repeated over and over as if Rita had not heard him the first time.

"What's your fault?" asked Vinnie, but not really caring about the answer. He sat next to Gunter, who was lifting her hand to his lips. He bellowed, not his usual curses but the lament of consciousness, the awareness that this could not be reversed. Death was unalterable, there was no do-over. Vinnie wept.

Gunter's tears flowed, the kind that would not stop until death claimed him.

A two-man medical emergency team stopped to ask if Rita needed assistance. They looked at her and confirmed what was already known.

"We'll send a stretcher to take her to the first-aid tent."

"No," said Gunter with an anger that stopped his crying. "I'll take her."

"You sure?" asked one man. "Do you want us to bring a blanket to cover the body?"

Gunter's chest filled the entire hillock. "Rita, not *the body*."

The other medical attendant pulled his partner away, understanding the unintentional error and that no apology would undo it.

Gunter carried Rita to the first-aid tent that had been set up for the festivities to treat minor bruises or heat exhaustion or lost children, not mass injuries or casualties. He entered the tent, buzzing with adults wiping their eyes and holding crying children. Doctors, nurses, and orderlies barked out triage instructions. A lineup of ambulances waited for turns to take the seriously injured to hospitals. In a neighboring tent, a team of veterinarians corralled animals into cages arranged by species.

One of the medical staff directed Gunter to a secluded area and pointed to a gurney. Vinnie touched Gunter's arm.

"It's okay. She'll be better on the bed."

The doctor asked a medical aid to place a sheet over the corpse, but Gunter pulled it away, nearly tossing the man into the tent wall.

"Leave it," said Vinnie to the aid, "we'll do it. We just need a few minutes."

The medical aid stepped back, handing the sheet to Vinnie. "I'm sorry for your loss," said the man as he closed the curtain. Vinnie knew that Gunter would hear those words many times over the coming weeks and not one would console him.

* * *

Footage of the bombing replayed on the twenty-four-hour news cycle around the world. The video went viral on YouTube and social media. A parent had recorded on his cell phone the moments before the explosion. Stooping behind a barrier, he had pretended to be the family dog making the recording. He saw Rita's erratic running pattern and focused on her, believing she was part of the festival's entertainment.

Vinnie watched the recording many times. Blanca, Ben, Ginny, and Dan only once. Gunter never.

Rita was caught jumping the barricade, running toward a man crouched behind an ancient oak tree. He was later identified by newscasters as Vasily Karimov. Rita's wild jumps and flapping hands would have been comical if not for what happened seconds later. The wind carried a few words as she leaped the barrier. "Stop... No... NO!" For no discernible reason, Rita veered toward a group of children entering the knoll and waved them away. Her scarecrow antics had children laughing at her performance, reinforcing the idea this was a fun activity. Then adults running to the children soured the cheery scene.

"Run! Bomb! Run! Run!" The words became clear as Rita moved back toward the man making the video. She turned in circles, yelling to people on an adjacent pathway. Her screaming became louder, the man recording focused on Rita as she ran toward people. She veered away again and advanced toward Vasily when the bomb exploded. The video stopped, and the parent later explained in TV interviews that he dropped his cell phone with the explosive shockwave released by the bomb. "If not for the cement barricade and my foolish antics to play with my dog, I would have been seriously injured or killed. Rocks flew all around me."

Vasily had removed his backpack out of the hole and placed it on the ground in front of him. He knelt over to pull out Dimitri's backpack at the moment the detonator went off. The hole limited Dimitri's backpack force. Vasily's hunched body and the tree contained the deadly shrapnel. His body absorbed most of the high-pressure wave and heat blast spreading to the area behind him. The tree took the forward brunt. Anyone over fifty feet away on either side was spared—Rita was not.

The medical examiner's report detailed how high-pressure blast waves moved faster than the speed of sound. They jettisoned debris and small rocks, which concussed Rita. A negative pressure after the initial blast wind pulled Rita back, ripping her aorta from her heart.

"Call her. She'll have seen it on every news channel," said Vinnie. Gunter promised he would.

Helene felt the general public's distraught reaction to senseless violence against ordinary people living their lives. But the amateur video gave a clear shot of the woman running across the field. Helene recognized Rita. Her frantic calls to Gunter went straight to his voicemail. Her texts went unanswered.

"Call her now."

He tried but couldn't speak. Each time his mouth opened he cried. Vinnie and Ben rubbed his shoulders as he managed to say two words, "Rita's dead." He dropped his phone. Saying her name was enough to vanquish his stoicism. Gunter's bleak desolation resisted solace and kindness, seeking companionship in unabated sorrow.

* * *

Vinnie, with the zen of denial that this was his idea and not Ben's, went with Gunter to visit Helene. His answered questions, the ones Gunter could not or wished to avoid.

To Vinnie's surprise, he underestimated Helene's sensitivity. She avoided headline-seeking questions and did not want to know the reasons for Gunter and Rita's presence at the cathedral festival. With a sincerity that only an honest person can offer, she said, "I'm sorry about Rita, I truly am. And I'm sorry for you too."

Gunter cried hearing Helene's "I'm sorry," dispelling Vinnie's cynical opinion of the power in words. The torrent of tears comforted. Grief blanketed by unconstrained embrace.

Helene used her nurse's training and hospital experience to evaluate Gunter. She concluded that her son was physically unharmed. She could not say the same about his mental state.

She agreed without argument that Gunter should remain with Ben and Vinnie. She packed any belongings he had not already taken. Vinnie made plans to have the boxes picked up by courier the next day.

* * *

Sitting in Vinnie and Ben's condo guest bedroom, Gunter gazed out the open door across the hall to Rita's room, as he called it, although she only used it the night before his arrest.

"Stay as long as you want," said Vinnie.

"There's no rush," added Ben. "We don't use this floor except to host visiting contestants. Nothing going on for six months so you'll be left alone."

That isn't true, thought Vinnie. *Gunter knows the schedules. His nodding confirms the lie.*

During periodic checks through the week, Vinnie found Gunter looking out the window or gazing at the living room walls. He never turned the TV on.

His mind wandered when Vinnie tried to start a conversation. No two sentences linked up. "I hate the sunshine," said Gunter, then added, "Do you know I can still smell her on the bed sheets?"

On one visit, Vinnie found Gunter in the massage room

installed for visiting bodybuilders. Three bottles of oil were lined up on the massage table.

"They were her favorites," said Gunter as he unscrewed the cap of one and sniffed it.

After supper, Vinnie and Ben broached their stifled concern.

"Gunter, we know you're grieving but we feel there's more to it. Do you want to talk about what happened? It might help," said Ben.

Vinnie recalled the day of horror. He didn't need to shut his eyes to remember. He was sure the same held for Gunter.

Gunter sat upright, one leg crossed over the other. "I can't. I want to but it isn't right. I..."

"What?"

"Many people died or were injured because of me."

"That's not true," said Vinnie, who only counted two deaths but was sure Gunter included Katia's. The official St. John's bombing tally was twenty-nine injured, one critical with a severed foot, and, against all odds, only two human fatalities: Rita Light and Vasily Karimov. And one miniature terrier that had slipped its leash.

Headlines labeled the event the St. Francis's miracle. Gunter called it the St. Francis Day slaughter because the only person who mattered died.

Ben sat beside Gunter and leaned over him. He hugged him tight. Not a contest victory hug or pretend man-hug, but an embrace that swallows a friend. Ben released to sit upright.

"There's something else," said Ben, resting his eyes on

Gunter. "Vinnie heard that the coroner's autopsy report will be released in a few days. They moved Rita ahead of others. They'll release her body in about a week."

Gunter shook and Ben rubbed his back.

"Rita has no family, only distant cousins," said Vinnie. "We'll have to plan the funeral or the state will take her away. What do you want to do?"

"I can't," said Gunter.

Ben looked at Vinnie, who nodded.

"Shall we start organizing it and you can modify or add ideas?" asked Ben.

"Yes," Gunter cried, his soul shivering and alone.

44

Autopsies for Vasily Karimov and Rita Light came out on the same day exactly a week after the tragedy. Added to the analysis were eyewitness accounts and amateur video. The coroner released preliminary findings to the public. Vinnie, Blanca, and Ben didn't need the report to predict the result. The detonator's signal reached the bombs at the moment Vasily pulled out his backpack. Dimitri's backpack remained buried in the hole. The large oak tree, the rows of ornate shrubs, and the temporary cement barriers prevented mass casualties. Rita's frantic yelling alarmed people, and they ran from her, increasing their distance from the blast. Ironically, Vasily's body also shielded people, minimizing the number injured or reducing the severity of their wounds. The only fatalities, already noted in the news, were Vasily and Rita.

Tom Galantuomo requested Vasily's full autopsy report, which he shared with Vinnie. Gunter declined to see it. The medical examiner detailed the extent of Vasily's injuries, enormous trauma to his lower intestines, ripped aorta, and esophagus filling with fluids. His body parts had been strewn across the cathedral lawn, making analysis incomplete. His charred skull was found twenty feet from the tree. Muscles ripped from bone made him a skeleton even before he lay on the ME's examination slab. Gruesome color photos reinforced the written account.

On the day the preliminary report was released, a six-foot six-inch guard escorted Dimitri like a small dog into the court docket. Vinnie, Ben, and Gunter sat in gallery seats next to Tom Galantuomo. New York State prosecuted Dimitri rather than a Federal court—a turf battle. The move allowed Dimitri to plead guilty to the New York terrorist act and the murders of Tariq and Katia.

Dimitri answered District Attorney's questions with short sentences or yes and no answers. His confession wasn't necessary to clear Gunter Hoffman of all charges but permitted a public explanation and restored Gunter's reputation.

In his testimony, Dimitri explained Vasily's reason for framing Gunter. The usually dispassionate judge scoffed at the incredulous stupidity. Vinnie hyperventilated, his throat constricted. Katia's murder was an absurdity—Gunter never remembered the limo insignia. Dimitri's voice warbled into a chuckle. He explained Gunter was an easy target and easily fooled. He ranted, talking about Gunter as a muscle-headed dumb fuck and inferior to Vasily, an Olympic champion.

The judge's gavel ended the rant. No one in the courtroom showed sympathy to the perceived injustice done to Vasily or the boxing team. The Tajikistan government had been quick to denounce the Karimov cousins, joined in the condemnation by the Tajikistan National Olympic Team.

Social media blogs and tweets clung to the view that the Karimov cousins were religious fanatics despite the court testimony. They ignored an official denouncement by the Muslim imams that not one mosque in Jersey City recalled seeing Vasily Karimov. Vinnie complained for weeks to whoever would listen. "Goes to show people don't like facts to interfere with their opinions."

Tom Galantuomo sat at the defense table beside Gunter as soon as Vasily left the courtroom in handcuffs. The short proceeding allowed the District Attorney to formally drop all charges against Gunter, but he made no apology. Vinnie accepted the dropped charges as being as good as one. The mayor acknowledged that Gunter's action prevented a major tragedy, which Vinnie also thought came close to an official apology. Neither Homeland nor FBI nor NYPD felt the same, expressing lingering anger over the delay by the Briggs Investigative Group to inform them of a bomb plot. Under different circumstances, they would have arrested the entire BIG team and held them indefinitely behind bars. But the circumstances were such that the public accepted the city's official spin, making Rita, Gunter, and Vinnie heroes at a time when heroes were needed.

With court adjourned, Detective Daven stood at the exit and nodded to Gunter. Detective Kaplan approached Vinnie and whispered, "Bob believes everyone guilty of a crime *if not the one they're arrested for.* Tell Gunter he just received a Daven one-time not-guilty pass." Kaplan patted Vinnie's shoulder, which Vinnie interpreted as a Jake Kaplan gold star apology. Gold star and back patting aside, there was no celebration at the BIG office or UltraFit.

For the week after the bombing, newspapers, magazines, TV, and the Internet bombarded people with Gunter's bodybuilding pictures. With his exoneration and newfound status as a hero came phone calls and emails requesting him to pose at private functions. Calls by fitness magazines to Ben begging him to persuade Gunter to consider their offers, something he had already refused. Promises were made of lucrative payments for interviews and guaranteed cover photo. Supplement producers dumped samples at UltraFit's front desk.

Helene sent her invitations a week after the trial, and unrelated. She requested assistance from Gunter, Ben, and Vinnie at her apartment, with the details unspecified. Entering the apartment revealed the motive as the men navigated a jungle of packing boxes in every room. Thirty years of accumulated debris littered the apartment.

As was typical of Helene, she gave no fanfare or preamble but simply announced she was moving to the suburbs. She had purchased a two-bedroom house north of the city yet only a twenty-minute commute to her nursing job. She had paid cash, dipping into her savings and the wise investment of her husband's life insurance and accident settlement compensation.

"And I'm frugal," she said proudly. "I've never gone for expensive, big-ticket items or luxury vacations." She stopped, a small smile on her lips, before continuing to explain her finances. "No college tuition debt for Gunter although his grocery bill amounted to nearly as much." Her smile diminished.

Gunter nodded.

After a small lunch, Helene gave each man a bag filled with tags. "Green go with me, red to discard, yellow for donation, and white for Gunter."

"I really don't need much," he said.

With a survey of the rooms, Vinnie thought the apartment resembled a discount warehouse sale.

Helene pulled Ben and Vinnie into the kitchen, asking Gunter to consolidate the red and yellow tags into his old bedroom.

"I never listen to gossip and yet I did about Rita. The very moment Gunter needed support—mine and Rita's—I made a bad situation worse and maligned her..." Helene's voice cracked, but she waved Ben's arm away as he tried to comfort her. "She was a good and kind person..." her voice trailed off. "I'm sorry, more than I can possibly express. Will you tell him for me? I'm too ashamed." She stopped talking as Gunter entered the room, his arms folded as if waiting for the next assignment. She told him about some boxes in her bedroom and he walked out.

Ben brushed Helene's hand and leaned in to say, "I will. You were worried for Gunter, your only son. Others have taken advantage of him and—"

Helene stopped Ben. "That's doesn't excuse me, nor will I hide behind that old hobby horse of protecting my son. I was wrong. I should have talked to Rita, learned more about her, not allowed gossip to shape my opinion." Gunter entered the room. Helene saw it in his eyes. "Gunter, I'm so sorry. Can you forgive me?"

With a few steps forward but not touching her, Gunter said, "Yes, mom, I do."

He walked out and returned a few minutes later carrying a box with his name on it. School memorabilia with a red tag stuck on top.

Helene stared, then said, "I should have done this years ago... the move, I mean." She stopped shaking. "After Gunter's dad's death... well, the memories were too much I suppose. But if I had done it right away, maybe Gunter would not have needed to become a..."

And there it is, thought Vinnie, turning to see Gunter's reaction.

"I'm not bullied anymore." Gunter lifted up his sleeve to flex. "Not with these." His mother laughed and Gunter smiled for the first time in weeks.

What happened? thought Vinnie. Neither he nor Ben was laughing. *Did Gunter misunderstand or is this what psychologists label deflection?*

"And your sense of humor is pretty big too. You're like your father," said Helene, eyes shining.

"Yeah, Dad had a great sense of humor, didn't he? He'd chase me around that table on all fours," said Gunter, pointing to a cherry dining room table with a green tag, "and pretend to be a dog growling but sounded more like a stray cat. Remember? And that Christmas he came in dressed like Santa but the fake beard over his nose gave him a sneezing fit."

Vinnie heard their genuine laughter and he realized that this was the first time he had heard Gunter's father talked about as a person and a loved one, not just an event marker.

Helene's eyes glistened at seeing Gunter wipe his. She hugged him. He bent and lifted her off the floor and she kissed his cheeks.

On the weekend, Gunter arrived at the apartment with a Bulldog moving van loaned at no charge. Ben and Vinnie joined him.

"Helene's happy," Vinnie said to Ben. "Is Gunter?"

Gunter was lifting three boxes stacked with books that for most men would be a strain if not impossible.

"No, I don't think so," answered Ben. "He has one more hurdle to cross."

45

Rita Light had been baptized at birth but listed no religious preference in her medical documents at UltraFit. She never attended church services as far as anyone knew. Her one religious connection was to St. John the Divine, where she died trying to save lives. That was good enough for the dean to grant special permission to have her funeral service at the cathedral.

More than seven hundred people filled the pews, a number usually seen for politicians or celebrities. Gunter, Ben, Vinnie, and Helene took the first row. Blanca sat with her husband and children in the second. The ushers were walking fortresses, four men and one woman who were all X-room champions. The other X-room members and UltraFit staff sat on the opposite aisle. Anyone directly behind and not tall enough might have thought they were sitting behind the cathedral's pillars.

Distant cousins came, many UltraFit clients, and everyone of Rita's martial arts students. The entire Bulldog crew took seats further back.

No politicians or figureheads were invited, and any asking to attend were politely refused. TV and media were kept off the campus grounds, but allowed to park on the avenue as the event was too public to invalidate freedom of the press and First Amendment rights.

"You know she would have hated this," said Gunter.

Vinnie looked around. "Yeah, she fuckin' would have."

Ben knew funerals were not for the dead, so sat quietly bracing himself for an emotional onslaught.

Choosing music proved hard, more than Gunter, Ben, or Vinnie had thought possible as they planned the service. They were able to make their own selection to reflect their feelings of painful loss. The harder part was no one knew what Rita would have wanted since she hadn't prepared to die.

"Everyone in their thirties believes they're the exception and will outlast the human race," said Vinnie, culling Rita's download lists at UltraFit. "These are too upbeat, meant for her fitness contests and classes." Vinnie had discovered a small vinyl collection in Rita's apartment while choosing her funeral outfit. "Who has records?" he said out loud, which was a dig at Ben with his collection of "dust collectors" in their condo. Vinnie settled on "Stand by Me," as he believed Rita would have wanted this for Gunter to hear.

The dean of the cathedral delivered the first eulogy, his focus on Rita's heroism. He read letters from survivors that praised her courage. Ben and Vinnie delivered the next two eulogies. Gunter and Blanca declined to speak.

Ben's usual sonorous, rock-solid voice was less resonant, less commanding as he began:

> *Stop all the clocks, cut off the telephone,*
> *Prevent the dog from barking with a juicy bone...*

370

He stopped mid-sentence, his eyes drenched as if he'd been caught in a summer shower. The words on the page disappeared. After the poem, Ben looked to the pews, his eyes blood red, and spoke with his throat constricted with grief. He whispered his love for Rita. He went off script, telling everyone what they already knew. She changed lives, saved lives, and inspired. He had nothing else to say, returning to take his pew seat as if punch-drunk.

He later asked Vinnie if he had finished reading the Auden poem, because he couldn't remember doing it.

"You did, Ben," but he omitted to say the eulogy was truncated, different to the one he had read the night before.

Vinnie's tribute took twenty minutes, not for length but by interludes of crying and staring at the casket, lost for words. Gunter's forehead rested on the prayer banister throughout the eulogies.

Six pallbearers carried her casket: Ben, Gunter, Vinnie, a young neophyte from the X-room that Gunter mentored, and two women, both fitness champions. Other than Vinnie, any of the men could have carried the casket single-handed. After the service the body returned to the funeral home to await probate.

* * *

The next day, Vinnie, Ben, and Gunter were in Rita's apartment. They crept around as if she might be hiding behind a door. Ben knew their entry was illegal until after probate. Vinnie cited the spare key Rita had given him for emergencies during a BIG investigation when she was indisposed but had vital work documents in her apartment. Vinnie had laughed at her euphemism, saying it was more likely he'd be indisposed than her. He wished now that was true.

Vinnie claimed this constituted permission, and pointed out that they had already used the key to collect Rita's funeral garb. Ben called the latter a special circumstance. He also knew her death voided the tacit permission of Vinnie having her key. But he didn't care about legalities and went along with Vinnie's logic.

Inside Rita's sparse, neat apartment, Vinnie, Ben, and Gunter rummaged through her belongings. Holding one of Rita's trophies up, Vinnie looked to Ben. "I think this belongs at UltraFit, don't you? I mean, it's not like it costs a lot."

Ben acknowledged that the fitness trophy's value was the esteem, not the scrap metal market price. Even a melted-down Oscar didn't amount to more than six hundred and fifty bucks. In comparison, Rita's memorabilia's net worth was the equivalent of a Cracker Jack prize.

"You want her record collection?" Vinnie asked Gunter.

He didn't, but said, "I'll take the framed photo of her receiving the first-place IFBB Fitness trophy. She was proud of that achievement."

"It's yours. Now, shall I hack her computer and transfer assets to you?"

"No!" shouted Ben and Gunter together.

"But she died intestate. The court will rob her estate. Probate judges are state-appointed thieves. They'll name an unknown executor, and some cretin in her bank's legal department will charge for doing nothing. Then withdraw funds from her account, and any meager residual gets handed to distant relatives. We all know Rita would have wanted her money to go to Gunter."

Vinnie was proved wrong. The probate court appointed Ben as the executor as an adjunct to Halborn, McGregor, Galantuomo, and Stern's estate and tax planning division. It was unusual yet Ben figured the law firm owed him that much as he had paid all of Gunter's legal fees. Tom Galantuomo guaranteed the firm's costs would only apply to filing fees and a legal assistant's hourly rate. Rita's bank account was not enormous but not insignificant. Ben awarded all her money to Gunter, who refused it. Ben explained in terms Gunter understood—he either took the money or he was barred from the X-room.

A few days after being appointed Rita's executor, Ben consulted Gunter, who was surprised to be asked about what he wanted for Rita's remains. He didn't know and Ben suggested cremation as there was no family cemetery plot. A few days later Ben handed Gunter an urn with Rita's ashes, which seemed too heavy for him to carry.

"Can you keep it safe until I figure out what Rita would have wanted?" asked Gunter, kissing the urn and handing it back to Ben.

* * *

A month after the final probate settlement and six since Rita's death, Gunter called Vinnie.

"Can we meet?" he asked.

"Of course. I'm at the BIG office, come anytime," answered Vinnie.

"Can you meet me at the coffee shop near my mother's old apartment?"

"Uh… Gunter, what's wrong?"

"Just do it, please. I'll explain when I see you."

Vinnie spotted Gunter in the back booth, his usual place. He sat looking at him, nursing a coffee and a bagel. A man heading to the toilet stared at Gunter. With a smile, Gunter flexed his bicep. The man lowered his eyes and turned his head.

"Stop that, you'll frighten him," Vinnie said.

"He's already pissing, so no worries there. I'm going to miss doing that."

"You never did that."

"Okay, I'll miss not being able to start doing it."

As quickly as Vinnie's laughing started it stopped.

"Wait. Why can't you start? Not that I'm encouraging intimidation or anything like that."

Resting his meaty forearms on table, Gunter pursed his lips. He stopped smiling. "I've been thinking about the cathedral bombing, Detour Man… and Rita."

"Yeah, we all do. Not a day passes when I don't think about her."

The way Gunter looked around the room, Vinnie thought he was expecting her to walk in through the door.

"Why are we meeting here?"

"Because this is where it began. Where it should have."

"You mean Katia, the party?"

"Yes, but this is where all my big decisions or events took place. It's where Rita asked me to marry her."

"What!? I never knew."

"Yeah, well that's because I told her I wanted to wait. No one knew. I guess I waited too long."

He and Vinnie sat without saying a word. The man came out of the toilet and passed by, his head lowered. Gunter didn't raise his arm.

After a few sips of coffee, Gunter said, "I'm going to stop training." The casual remark was no more important than chitchat about the weather.

"Have you told Ben?" asked Vinnie.

"No, but I will. I wanted to talk to you first. Here."

The door was held open as a man in a wheelchair negotiated the entrance. A cold March wind blew in and the entire room fixed on the man and the open door.

"Something has changed," began Gunter. "I don't feel the panic if people gawk at me." His head motioned to the space the pissing man had stood moments before. "I even passed a big, hooded person that could have been Detour Man but wasn't. He brushed up against me, took hold of my hand begging for spare change. You know what I did?"

Vinnie shook his head no.

"I told him to fuck off and shoved him into the wall." Gunter closed his eyes. He suddenly stood then just as quickly sat and rubbed his thighs. Vinnie recognized Gunter's shame but realized there was more to it, a panic but unlike the kind he used to have.

"Take deep breaths," said Vinnie, who demonstrated by inhaling as if Gunter didn't understand the words.

"I… I don't know how to explain how…" Gunter slumped, his chin buried into his chest. After a few seconds Gunter sighed, "Until Rita, it's like I never really lived."

Vinnie got it. Rita challenged Vinnie to the point of arguing, wounding each other with harsh words. Because of her pushing he reinvented himself as an investigator. She forced him to evaluate his motivation for starting the Briggs Investigative Group. She had made his life more vibrant. And if she did this for him, he couldn't imagine what it was like for Gunter, who she truly loved.

"I've obsessed about myself, certain I knew the answers to everything," said Gunter, his eyes penetrating Vinnie. "I never considered I might be wrong." He rubbed his forearm. "Strength and size didn't protect me or Rita. I used bodybuilding to avoid my demons and responsibilities. I didn't help anyone, least of all myself. Rita paid the price for that."

That is the price for becoming subhuman, a caricature, thought Vinnie. Gunter's life was an achromatic gray. Rita's life was full of color, enough for both of them.

* * *

That night at the condo kitchen table, Vinnie and Gunter cleared the supper dishes. Ben started for the living room but Vinnie asked him to stay. They had to talk, or rather Gunter had to talk.

The prelude began with Gunter saying how much he loved the X-room, the camaraderie of being among an exclusive group. He called UltraFit Health Club—the Gym—his salvation, the reverence for weightlifting, his praying to get big.

"Yeah, I know," said Ben, "and I sense a '*But.*'"

Gunter gave a half-smile. "But... it is superficial. My mother knew. She saw the terror in me. I believed the entire world threatened me. A single thought dominated my existence. My bigorexia was an outgrowth of monomania."

376

Gunter paused. "Yeah, that's the word Anna used during therapy. I had to look it up too—it means an unhealthy obsession with something. Lifting weights in my case. So I'm quitting."

"I understand. Don't you think I haven't felt the same? It's what we bodybuilders do. We live for the adrenaline high that creates the so-called *bodybuilding disease*. But why quit? You're not telling me everything."

Gunter's voice lowered. "I've thought about this a lot. I've been so afraid of dying and now I'm afraid I won't."

"Huh? I don't get it," said Vinnie.

"It means I don't know what I'm fighting for. No, that's not right. I mean, is there a battle to fight?"

"So, you've decided to what? Quit? And do what?" asked Ben.

With a finger to his lips, Gunter said nothing. He asked Ben for Rita's urn, packed his bags, and left the next morning.

* * *

Gunter's handwritten postcard invitation sent by US postal mail arrived early September. Ben and Vinnie puzzled over the formal invite the weekend of the Feast of St. Francis. They understood the date and guessed Gunter wanted company on the anniversary. Ben phoned to accept, telling Gunter they looked forward to seeing him after so long. Vinnie took over the conversation, saying he'd email their flight details. They didn't ask him why he didn't come to New York for a memorial held at St. John's. Gunter didn't volunteer any additional information. They'd have to wait until their arrival to learn his reason.

46

The person who came to meet Vinnie and Ben at Bangor International Airport resembled the man they called Gunter. Yet something was different.

During the ride in Gunter's 4x4 the conversation was little more than small talk and banter. The flight. Delays. Other passengers. Air travel shortcomings. The longest exchange centered on Ben's difficulty settling into the fourteen-passenger aircraft's narrow seat.

"A bitch, aren't they?" said Gunter.

The Appalachian Greenville lodge's warm central heating seemed to Vinnie like a hot towel had been thrown against his face after the freezing outdoor wind buffeted him. He and Ben took off their light jackets, which suited the warmer New York climate they had left behind a few hours before. Gunter wisecracked about it being their own fault for ignoring his advice about packing heavy winter coats. He hung his winter parka on a moose antler peg.

Vinnie yelled, starring at Gunter. "What have you done? Do you fuckin' graze at McDonald's?"

Gunter laughed like neither man remembered as he patted his stomach.

"I went wild in the first weeks after I arrived. Breakfast was a five-stack smothered in Maine maple syrup, side orders of blueberry muffins, and home fries. I binged. There wasn't a fatty product I passed up. I ate more high-cholesterol foods in a day than I had during a year of training."

Gunter's wide smile suited him. "You can't imagine how good it feels to be off the diet." He looked at Ben. "Sorry, but it's true."

"I know," said Ben. "I do the same after every competition just like you did. Remember? I still do in the off-season or when not preparing for photo shoots. But I always go back. That's me. But I'm happy you've broken the cycle."

"Yeah. I eventually stopped the junk food addiction. I lost thirty pounds of muscle too. Maybe more, but I've started light training again. See?"

Gunter rolled up his sleeve and flexed. The bicep would have impressed anyone except those that had seen his twenty-five-inch mound a year before. This was maybe eighteen at best.

"You know what?" asked Ben. "Leaving iron is not easy. The routine, discipline, and the feeling of the bar suspended over your head lingers."

Gunter bunched his arm. "So true. I've had urges at times, missing it more than I can say. But I've learned that muscles are not my friend."

Like many others, Gunter had come to realize his body was a pasture needing constant tending. He was nothing more than a migrant worker, never the landowner. He never had control of his body or himself.

"Well, you're lucky," said Ben. "Did you know recidivism

among bodybuilders that quit is higher than high school dropouts retaking GEDs?"

Gunter and Ben continued to compare previous and current recipes. Gunter recalled how Rita watched him stray from his regimented diet and commanded, "Pick up your weight belt and get thee to a gym."

Ben recalled another of Rita's gems on fitness, diet, and training. Gunter asked about his former colleagues, their competitions, training routines, and who won their pro cards.

Vinnie's patience ran out. He didn't come to Maine to hear chitchat about bodybuilding, which he could have done with a short walk to the X-room. He wanted to know the reason for travelling to Penobscot County. He walked to the lodge's bay window to see a fresh snowfall covering the lawn. The glistening crystals broadcast the winter bleakness. Undeniably beautiful, yet Vinnie preferred New York's grit.

Gunter interrupted Vinnie's thoughts. "I miss her." He held out his palms in front of him. "We weren't together long, but it seemed like I knew her forever."

"Yeah, me too," said Vinnie, "and our relationship was rocky to say the least."

The men laughed, a trace of solace excavated from memory shards, but none that abated their collective grief.

"I can still feel her turn over in her sleep. I see her smile. Her silly alphabet sex... did you know about that?"

"Yeah. Everyone did," said Vinnie.

Gunter laughed. "I'm not surprised. Rita was out there, if you know what I mean."

Ben and Vinnie nodded, big grins across their faces.

"She wanted children. Did you know that too?"

This time neither Vinnie nor Ben answered.

"She also liked solitude. We fantasized about the place we'd live in after we finished with the trial." Gunter stopped to take several deep breaths. "She said she'd like to live in Maine. I didn't have much travel experience, so I agreed but I never believed we'd move here."

Vinnie sighed. "I guess you didn't."

Standing up, Gunter said, "Actually, she's here now." He walked to a cabinet, returning with Rita's urn in his hands, which he kissed. Vinnie crossed the room. Gunter held out the urn and Vinnie softly kissed the metal enclosure.

"You know," said Gunter, placing the urn on the fireplace mantel, "Rita said we were all optimists about time. Everyone believes there will always be time to tell someone you love them, to tell someone how much they mean to you." He wiped his eyes.

By nightfall Gunter had explained he chose Maine for no reason other than to follow Rita's dream. He had no plans, just took a flight to Bangor and headed into a local café in town for a meal. As luck would have it, he saw an employment notice posted for a full-time lodge manager. The application was done online, but he had no computer so he took a cab and showed up at the lodge to apply in person.

The two staff members had never heard of someone showing up, but neither knew of any protocol that didn't allow it. They went ahead with the interview.

Gunter laughed, recalling he did not meet the minimum requirements that included a bachelor's degree in forestry or environmental studies. Nor did he have wildlife experience or a certificate in outdoor survival. However, he did excel in one area. The interviewers showed animal photos that he easily identified by common name and their Latin genus and species nomenclature. He smirked, admitting the flora threw him off, but he managed to identify the beech, birch, and maple that grew all over Maine.

"They said I outperformed most undergraduates. I told them I learned it by watching TV."

Vinnie and Ben smiled and gave pretend high-five slaps to Gunter.

"Wait," said Gunter, who was laughing before he finished his next sentence. "They asked me the name of the show. I told them *The Simpsons*."

Vinnie was on the floor laughing and Ben was doubled over.

"Gunter, I never doubted your intelligence," said Ben, holding his side, "but your humor has really improved."

"Knowledge isn't the only job requirement." Gunter pointed to the window. "An important part is keeping the paths cleared. You can't imagine their faces when I picked up three large logs and carried them across the road. Wasn't that much, maybe weighed two-fifty or two-seventy."

Vinnie lips spread, exposing his teeth. "Bet they got hernias just watching."

"Plows don't reach this place for a week after a big storm. One guy thought my strength could be a big advantage. The other said I was stronger than two other candidates put together."

* * *

Ben and Vinnie rose early on the morning of the feast of St. Francis, only to learn that Gunter had been up since dawn. He asked them to follow him outside and gave each of them one of his sweaters. Ben's was long in the sleeve. Vinnie looked like a small child wearing a hand-me-down.

A crisp wind buffeted their faces but the air was not as cold as the day before. Gunter had cleared newly fallen snow before Ben and Vinnie had dressed. The private pathway led to an area fifty feet behind the lodge. "I'll put down stones in the spring and a flower bed on each side," he said as if an explanation was required. He cradled Rita's urn.

Gunter's foot rested on the spade's blade embedded in the ground frozen to three inches deep. His thighs were no longer of a size comparable to the surrounding ancient forest trees, but formidable nonetheless. A year before he easily pushed six hundred pounds of metal for a dozen repetitions. Today he concentrated on the spade. Without strain, he created fissures in the soil. He continued sinking the blade until a hole appeared, twelve inches wide by eighteen inches deep.

"I only want to spread a little," he said as he handed Ben a small trowel.

Ben carefully scooped a single spoonful and handed the utensil to Vinnie, who cried. His tears mixed with Rita's ashes.

"Sorry," said Vinnie, sobbing.

"Don't be," said Gunter. "Rita used to say you cried better than anyone. I think she'd be pleased to have your tears with her."

Vinnie's howl choked him. Ben's arm reached out, preventing Vinnie from toppling into the hole.

Gunter added ashes. He pulled two first-place medals from his jacket, one his and one Rita's, and lowered them into the hole. He refilled the hole with soil. A five-foot iron bar painted with Rita's trademark fitness colors rested on a nearby tree, which he hammered into the newly replaced soil.

"Let's get you inside," said Gunter.

At first Vinnie thought he meant Ben and him, until he saw Gunter hold up the urn, kiss it, and turn to the lodge.

This wasn't the Gunter Hoffman that had come into his office a year before, a man devoted to pumping iron out of fear. He had discovered courage on a grassy hill outside a Gothic cathedral. Love was what vanquished fear. This new Gunter Hoffman would live the life he wanted, not one dictated by a man with a detour sign.

Author's Note

A huge thank you to everyone who has taken the time to read *Detour Man*. Readers help writers improve and sustain them, so I am grateful for your encouragement.

If you enjoyed *Detour Man*, then please remember to leave a review. I listen to comments and use them to understand what works best for readers. I can't do much on the characters base personalities, but they mature, develop, and seek new interests.

You can learn more about the series and find more content by joining my mailing list. Be the first to learn of new releases in the Vinnie Briggs Mystery series by visiting the official website:

http://www.charlespuccia.com/

My experiences inspire my stories although the characters are fictional. Tell me your thoughts. What captures your interest in a mystery or romance novel? Describe a memorable event: outrageous, moral dilemma, unusual, or funny. If something similar has happened to me, then this may be Vinnie's next case.

Share your opinions with others on Vinnie and his crew. Learn what others think. And, please, if you enjoyed reading Detour Man, leave a rating or review.